PRAISE FO

"With *The Floating City*, Craig
    The Book Plank

"What I did not expect when I first read the synopsis for this novel was Cormick's dark sense of humor. This is a story filled with assassins, murders, kidnappings, and both graphic and unsettling visuals. But even in some of the darkest parts of the book I found myself laughing out loud. I guess if I would have to make up a genre for *The Shadow Master* it would be called acid grimdark."
    Avid Fantasy Reviews

"I recommend you to read *The Shadow Master*, a story that takes an adventure where love is the key for everything; happiness, justice, revenge, and always does what is better for the everyone. Read of a land lost to diseases and a battle for power where there is more than just two adversaries but much more hidden in the shadows."
    Open Book Society

"I really enjoyed my time spent with *The Shadow Master*. The dynamic between the two families was interesting and I loved the rivalry – that wasn't really one – between Leonardo and Galileo. There were also some fun nods to some of their real historic works and inventions. I especially loved the way Cormick incorporated The Vitruvian Man in the story. The idea that magic is as much artifice as it is alchemical was intriguing, especially considering that one doesn't need to have any nebulous aptitude, but just have a rigorous mind. Additionally, here is magic that isn't without cost. It'll be interesting to see if this magic system will be transferred to the next book or if Cormick creates a different one".
    A Fantastical Librarian

FICTION
The Shadow Master
Shackleton's Drift
Of One Blood: The Last Histories of Van Diemen's Land
The Boy's Own Guide to Wedding Planning
Kormak's Saga (novella)

FOR CHILDREN
Time Vandals
The Monster Under the Bed
Pimplemania

COLLECTIONS
The Prince of Frogs
The Princess of Cups
The Queen of Aegea
The Kind of Patagonia
Futures Trading
A Funny Thing Happened at 27,000 Feet
Unwritten Histories
When Angels Call (with Hal Judge & Steve Harrison)
A Meeting of Muses (editor)

POETRY
The Condensed Kalevala

NON FICTION
Kurikka's Dreaming
Cruising with Captain Cook Amongst Cannibals
Shipwrecks of the Southern Seas
In Bed with Douglas Mawson
The Last Supper
Words of Grace

CRAIG CORMICK

The Floating City

ANGRY
ROBOT

ANGRY ROBOT
An imprint of Watkins Media Ltd

Lace Market House,
54-56 High Pavement,
Nottingham,
NG1 1HW
UK

angryrobotbooks.com
twitter.com/angryrobotbooks
The Othman cometh

An Angry Robot paperback original 2015
1

Copyright © Craig Cormick 2015

Craig Cormick asserts the moral right to be
identified as the author of this work.

A catalogue record for this book is available
from the British Library.

ISBN 978 0 85766 423 5
EBook ISB 978 0 85766 425 9

Set in Meridien by Epub Services.
Printed in the UK by 4edge Ltd.

To Sharon and Caelan, who always float my city!

I

The story starts with a murder.

It is a warm autumn night in the Floating City, and the waterways are still between the turning of the tides, and a little fetid. A dark gondola moves across the Grand Canal with a tall man and woman seated together in the boat. They wear ornate masks of birds, beset with tawny orange feathers and jewellery, and hold hands gently. Were there not such a large blood moon this evening it would be possible to see a soft glow emanating from where they touch.

The gondolier also wears a mask – but his is a plain white face, as if all the features have been erased from it, except an enigmatic smile. Ahead of them is a large golden palace that seems to float on top of the water. It is ablaze with light as if there were a party for a hundred guests going on inside. But in fact it is empty except for servants. The master and mistress of the house are on their way back from a troubling meeting of the city's Seers.

They will need to discuss it with each other until late into the night, but for now they sit in silence, the only sound the soft splash, splash, splash of the gondolier's oar, moving them forward.

They are close to the palace now and the gondolier slows as he negotiates some debris in the water. It is not unknown to find barrels and logs and sometimes even a corpse floating in the canals. These are troubled times, after all. His master and mistress pay no attention as he turns the gondola a little to the side to negotiate a dark shape in the water. The reflection of the lights of the palace on the water is broken by its outline and he tries to see what it is. It is large. Perhaps a horse?

He turns the gondola a little further away, not wanting to come too close to a putrid bloated corpse of any animal. He has seen rats sitting on such before and knows their hunger for survival would send them leaping towards the gondola. His master and mistress would surely chide him if he allowed a rat to climb into their vessel. It would be a waste of their powers to have to kill it, he knows.

His mistress, he sees, lays her head on his master's shoulder. She has always liked the pleasure of a gondola ride at midnight and is perhaps remembering other rides they have taken on similar warm nights. He knows that in the darkness, when their bodies touch, the unearthly blue glow it sends out makes the hairs all over his body stand up, so he would know what they were doing even if they were not half hidden under a cloak. But he has rowed their gondola for many years and his featureless mask is a mark of his discretion.

He sees his mistress now turn her head to his master. Perhaps she is going to whisper something to him, or perhaps she is going to seek a kiss. The gondolier turns his head sideways and looks off towards the bright lights of the palace before them, and so he misses seeing the dark object in the water suddenly rise up in a hiss of foam.

All three of them turn at once and they barely have time to make out the shape of the great beast there as it thrusts a taloned claw into the boat and rips open the throat of the Seer closest to it. It is the gondolier's master and he gurgles something as life starts gushing out of him. The beast then reaches out to the lady, but she has one hand up to ward it away and a hot light crackles from her fingers.

The beast gives a low roar and pulls back. Then it sinks back into the dark waters. The lady has one hand around the master's as the light fades from her fingers. Then the soft glow is gone from where she holds his hand. His head lolls forward heavily and his now lifeless body tips to the edge of the boat and then falls into the water also.

The gondolier, his masked face showing nothing, watches in horror as his mistress calls out after her husband and tries to stop him sinking into the waters. But he is gone. Then she sinks back into her seat in the gondola and turns her head to the palace. She knows what is going to happen. The gondolier stops the boat and tries desperately to turn it around.

First the lights start flickering and then begin fading, but before the last window has turned black the palace crumbles apart and sinks heavily into the waters. A wave rushes at the side-on gondola and swamps it quickly. The gondolier tries to reach his mistress as she calls out and shrieks as the water bubbles around her. Then she, too, is gone.

He alone survives to tell the story of what has happened this evening and let the city know that the stories of invading monsters living in the waterways are true. The Othmen have at their command mighty enchantment and are determined to use it to conquer their city.

Every citizen needs to know they must be vigilant to the danger, and be willing to put their lives into the hands of the three remaining pairs of Seers. Only they have the power to defeat the Othmen and return their city to its position of power and splendour once more.

Vincenzo the scribe lays down his quill and reads over what he has written. He is not happy with that last paragraph and will have to rethink it. He knows he is meant to be working on his current commission – a history of the Montecchi family. Signor Montecchi who sat on the city's Council of Ten and had three beautiful adopted daughters, Disdemona, Giulietta and Isabella – yet the manuscript of his family history has sat on a shelf above his desk, untouched for several days. For how could he work on that story when he has to tell the story of what is happening to his city? It is vital to capture the truth of it, he thinks. How could the petty trials and daily lives of three young women compare to the deaths of the city's Autumn Seers?

Signor Montecchi might not agree now, but surely years from this moment historians would look over this text to gain some understanding of what had transpired in his city in these dark days.

And yet it was more than that too. Vincenzo was filled with a feeling that the world was all at odds with itself and could only realign when he was writing its story. And that was a feeling that often threatened to overwhelm the urge to eat or drink or sleep at times. A feeling that he was the only person preventing the world slipping into chaos.

But how did you explain that urgency to a patron in a way that did not lead to you losing the commission that paid for your food and drink and gave you a roof to sleep under?

II
THE STORY OF DISDEMONA

"You should obey and fear your husband," Otello the Moor said to Disdemona, standing up from the table near the window where he had been studying his maps. "I said you must let me be."

"I would consider obeying my husband, but I'm unlikely to ever fear him," she said, meeting his glare. "Yet I must ask, who is this angry tyrant I find seated at the table moping like a school child? He looks like my husband, it is true, but it can hardly be him."

"Do not mock me," Otello said, trying to hide the pleasure he derived from her strong will. "I deserve your respect."

"You shall have it," said Disdemona. "But come to bed and earn it." She reached out for his hand. Otello took it and then pulled her to him and sat back down beside his maps, with her on his lap. She wore a silver silk nightdress that moved lightly against her skin as she sat there, and he felt the smoothness of her body beneath it.

"I am not in the mood to come to bed just now," he told her.

"Not in the mood?" she asked with mock astonishment, leaning in closer to him. "Does my love have a fever?" She placed a hand upon his forehead. "No. Does he have some sickness in his stomach?" She poked a finger into his hard stomach muscles. "No. Perhaps he loves his maps more than he loves me?"

"Of course not," he said. "It is just that I am heavy with troubles and they weigh upon me too much to let me come to bed."

She pulled a face. The palazzo that the city had granted her husband was old and decrepit in places, but she had told him that when they were in bed together they were kings and queens. Then she said, "Ah, troubles." And she laid her head on his large dark shoulder, her light hair seeming golden in contrast. Then she felt some of the anger flowing out of him. She could always find the truth of what was worrying him, even when he did not know it himself.

"Is it the Othmen?" she asked him.

"Yes, it is the Othmen," he said. "And the Council of Ten. And the Seers. And the future of the Floating City itself. So many troubles circling around my head like angry bees."

"Tell me," she said.

"I am sworn to secrecy."

"You are sworn to me," she said. "My general."

He sat silently for a moment until she reached a hand into his shirt and took hold of his large dark nipple and gave it a twist. He said nothing and so she twisted harder. "I surrender," he said suddenly, grabbing her hand and pulling it out of his shirt. "You should come and work for me as a torturer."

"I asked to come with you to the East."

He shook his head. "No. It was far too dangerous. We barely escaped the Othmen with our lives. Those men of ours that they captured they sawed in half while they were still alive."

She shuddered a little. "They are inhuman."

"They are very human," he said, "but they possess inhuman abilities."

"What do they look like?" she asked. "They say the Othmen have horns on their heads and their bodies are covered in dark hair like a wolf."

He laughed. "The horns are a single spike worn on their helmets and they favour sharp pointed beards."

"They sound like men."

"They look like men."

"Then how did they slay the Autumn Seers?" she asked.

Otello stared at her. "How did you hear about that?"

"The whole city is talking about it," she said. "Some Othmen beast rose out of the water and devoured them. Is it true?"

He nodded his head. Just a little.

"The whole city is in fear of them," she said.

"So they should be," he replied. "They have destroyed our eastern colonies and now send ships and spies and monsters to destroy us."

"But they will not be able to defeat us here," she said. "Surely."

"If we can protect the other Seers," he said. "If we can form a defensive strategy against their vessels. If we can root out their spies. If we can counter their enchantments. A hundred ifs."

"And that's what you have been charged with, by the Council of Ten," she said. "Isn't it?"

He nodded his head again.

"I think perhaps you have as much reason to be troubled then as the city has to be afraid."

They sat there together in silence for some moments. "The Othmen are enigmatic. Cruel and yet brilliant. Their jewellery is exquisite. Their textiles divine." He reached across to a small leather pouch on the far corner of the table and said, "I have something to show you. I was saving this up, but perhaps now is as good a time as any."

"What is it?" she asked.

"The Othmen call it the skin of the virgin."

"Is it skin?" she asked in horror.

"The Othmen love their metaphors."

She watched him open the pouch and pull out a small parcel wrapped in light paper. He placed it in her hand.

"It feels empty," she said, giving the parcel a small squeeze.

"Because what is inside it is as light as air," he said.

She knitted her eyebrows in curiosity, her eyes shining with delight as she carefully unwrapped the parcel. Inside was a silk kerchief. Or perhaps it was not silk. It felt like nothing in her fingers, like it really had been woven from air. She opened it up, wondering at the detail on it. It was embroidered with small green leaves and bright red strawberries. Such detail in each that it looked as if she could pick them off and eat them.

"It is beautiful," she said.

"As are you," he replied. "So it is a fitting gift."

She held it to her face to catch what felt like a tear of happiness forming there. Then she reached down and hugged him. Gave him a deep kiss. "Ah," she said. "I think I have found my husband again. You pretend to be so angry and gruff, but it is all your armour. Inside you are loving and soft."

"That is a greater secret than any other held within this city of secrets," he told her. "And I fear if anybody else should learn of it."

She kissed him again. "My lips are sealed. Tell me, what do the Othmen fear?"

He thought on that for a moment and then spun her on his lap to face him. "They fear me," he said. "They tell stories that I am twice the height of a man and my skin is black like the coals of a fire and to touch me is to be burned by me. They say that I am able to bite a man's head off in my mouth and that I can rip a man's arms from his torso without effort."

"And what else do they say?" she asked him, wrapping her arms about his neck.

"They say that I am afraid of nothing!"

"Then they don't know how much you have to fear if you don't come to bed now. And anyway, you'll deal better with your troubles after a good night's sleep."

"Are you planning to let me sleep?" he asked.

"No. Not at once."

"And you'll be wanting me to obey you?"

"Of course." Disdemona knew the bedchamber was the one place she was certain he would obey her. As she knew there was only one thing he truly feared. Failure in any challenge set him.

III

ELSEWHERE IN THE FLOATING CITY

The room smelled of mildew and rats' droppings and sweat. And menace.

Half a dozen men were gathered in the dark basement of an old building in one of the more dangerous parts of the city. The basement leaked, and the men shuffled their feet amongst the puddles, trying to find drier spots in which to stand. None was entirely successful. There was a single lantern in the basement room, sending flickering shadows of the men along the wet walls. Some glanced quickly at those around then, noting scars and thick fingers and the way they stood. Clearly at home in this part of the city.

The dancing light also showed that the men wore masks. All the same mask. White with black lines showing narrow eyes, arched eyebrows and a thin-line moustache, framing a mocking close-mouthed grin. And although grinning, the mask had a certain look of menace about it.

The only sounds in the room were those of an incessant dripping and the coarse breathing of the men. They were also clearly used to waiting, eyes flicking about them like animals of prey. Then the sudden sound of a single furtive rodent making its way along the wall's edge, its claws clicking softly as it scurried towards what it obviously thought to be safety. A hurtled piece of stone struck the wall just in front of its nose, startling it to change direction.

It ran through a puddle, narrowly dodging a foot that kicked at it, and changed direction again. This time a cudgel struck the ground close to it, and it squealed and changed direction once more, making for the darkest shadows. But even the darkness was not enough to protect it from these men. It suddenly stopped, as if it had hit the wall, squealing again as the bones in its head and shoulders snapped, crunching into its brain in sharp shards.

The man, less interested in toying with the creature than the others, lifted his foot off the dead rat and resumed his position. The men around him said nothing.

And they waited.

At the first sound of a door above them opening, all the men turned. Some moved hands into jerkins and grasped hold of knife handles or cudgels. Some just shifted their weight a little onto the balls of their feet. Two men came down the stairs. Both were hooded and wore dark cloaks. The one in front was thick-set and carried a lantern in one hand. In the other he carried a short sword. At the bottom of the steps the man behind him, a thin man, looked around the room and then put a hand on the other man's arm, stepping in front of him. The two newcomers threw back their hoods to reveal the same white masks. In their black cloaks they seemed to float there in the darkness.

The thin man stepped into the centre of the room, disregarding the puddles at his feet and said in a low voice, "I smell death here about."

Nobody moved. They could also smell the smoke of Othmen spices, or perhaps drugs.

The thin man turned around slowly, regarding each of the men. "You are my brothers, assassins, and we shall fill the city with the smell of it."

IV

THE STORY OF ISABELLA

Isabella Montecchi sat at her large ornate desk high up in her tower room, looking out over the oceans beyond the Floating City. She loved this view. Fine tapestries and frescoes were lit by the soft light from outside, giving the room a golden hue. But she found the view out the window even more majestic. The first time her late husband had brought her into the room and showed her how she could look out beyond the cluster of the city's floating islands, and the mouth of the lagoon, right out to the eastern sea, she knew it was a view of the world that she would always want to have.

And now, she had the view every day, but she no longer had her husband. He had died six months ago aboard one of his many merchant ships lost to the Othmen pirates. He had been a good man, if not a little more obsessed with commerce than with romance. Other women she knew had lost men at sea and lived in vain hope that they'd somehow be miraculously found, living on a small island with wild men and strange beasts for company. Or perhaps their men had lost their memories and would come into port one day on board a strange ship and be recognized. But they were fanciful dreams, she knew. Her husband had certainly died slowly at the hands of the Othmen, who were now advancing upon their empire, cutting it off small piece by small piece. The same way they dealt with those they captured.

She shook the thought from her head, and folded a lock of her dark hair back behind her ear as she turned back from the window to the table before her. There were documents and debt notes spread out on it. Her husband had left her a wealthy woman and she had discovered she had a strong head for business, probably acquired from her father. She knew there were those who said that only a fool could lose her husband's fortune, but, truth be told, any fool could make his or her fortune during times of plenty. It took a particularly wise person to make their fortune during the lean and hard times. And she had no illusions that they were now living in such times.

The Othmen had all kinds of nefarious enchantment at their control which they used to attack vessels of the Floating City. Some survivors talked of sea monsters that arose from the sea and wrapped themselves around ships. Others told of giant multi-armed beasts that snatched sailors off the decks and devoured them. And others told of temptress creatures, like semi-clad women, that wooed ships onto the rocks where they sang from before climbing over the sides of the ships to reveal fangs in their mouths as they attacked the crew.

And now the Othmen were threatening to invade their city. They had slain the youngest of the Seers within the city itself, leaving only three aged pairs to protect them. And who knew how many foul monsters swam in the canals already? And who even knew what dark powers the Othmen might possess to turn against them? Most of the citizens were in fear of their lives every time they stepped into a boat these days.

And yet the Othmen still enjoyed the hospitality of the city, meeting with the Council of Ten like there were no hostilities. No threats to city shipping. No threats to the lives of the citizens. She had heard the lies of the envoy of the Othmen herself. There were no such things as monsters. Ships were lost to inclement weather, not Othmen attacks. The conquering of the Floating

City's territories to the east was simply legitimate reclaiming of land that was once their own.

The envoy of the Othmen was a Graecian nobleman who had once been the envoy of the Floating City to the Othmen. Clearly they offered him more wealth, since he now spread their lies as easily as he had once spread them for the city, telling everyone they had nothing to fear from the Othmen. They just wanted better trade terms than they had previously enjoyed. The worm! And to add insult to injury, he was now laying suit to her! She could see the lust in his toad-like eyes when they met, though never quite knowing if it was lust for her body or for her wealth. Either way it made her skin crawl.

She picked up the small card on the table before her and cast it aside. He had come calling again. She had left him downstairs waiting at least half a candle's length already, but she knew she could not put it off for much longer. She would have to admit him to the room and listen to his lies and accept whatever gifts he pressed upon her. Probably stolen from the ships of her fellow citizens.

It was like he was laying siege, she thought, coming with an army of flattering words and gifts in an attempt to breach her defences and rob her of her independence. She would rather set an army of soldiers upon him and drive him not just from her house but from the city. But who knew what vengeance that would provoke from the Othmen? It would give her satisfaction, but would imperil the city.

She gritted her teeth and considered her options. There were not many. What would she do if she were on a ship at sea and a slimy man-like creature rose up before her? She'd fight, of course. With every weapon available.

She turned again and looked out the window. The horizon seemed further away than usual. Made her stretch her gaze to look beyond it. Perhaps there was an answer. Her best weapon was her guile, she mused, and she could surely outmanoeuvre a man whose brain was filled with lust. She thought on it a moment longer until a plan began to form in her mind. Then she called to her handmaiden, Nerissa. "Show the envoy in," she said. "Tell him I am quite ready for him."

V

ELSEWHERE IN THE FLOATING CITY

The shadows seemed to move on the dark canal water. It rippled in a way that was strange enough for the lone figure in the boat to stop and turn to regard it. He scanned the water carefully as the ripple disappeared, and waited to see if it returned. It did not. He pulled on the single oar at the rear of the vessel and it moved forward. Very slowly.

He watched the water on all sides of the boat, noting every movement on its moonlit surface, observing those that looked like currents or wind and those that did not. That was one lone swirl in front of him and ahead to the right. A counter-clockwise movement of the water as something was moving beneath it, or perhaps sinking lower there. Then it stopped.

He pushed the oar, moving the boat forward a little more. Eyes still on the water. One stroke. Then another. Now the water's surface moved a little to the left and behind him. A good position to attack from, he thought. He pushed the oar again, less carefully, almost as if a challenge. The water calmed. Then it bubbled, much closer to him.

He took a hand from the oar and reached into the long dark cloak he wore, resting it on the handle of an ornate weapon. "It is not yet the time to face each other," he whispered and the bubbling stopped. He let his boat drift a little and then reached up

21

and took hold of the oar again. He pushed it once. Then pulled it back towards him. Then pushed it again.

He had the feeling that he was being watched. Stalked. But he refused to adopt the stance of prey. When the movement on the water appeared again, he steered the boat directly towards it. As a hunter would. The movement ceased more quickly this time. He rowed to where it had last been and brought the boat to a halt. He stayed there a moment and then turned the boat around again, pointing it back towards the mist-shrouded lights ahead of him.

He only turned his head once, to see the swirling of the water following him from a distance as he rowed his boat right into the canals of the Floating City. He tied it up to a striped pole that jutted up out of the water and leaped across to land lightly on one of the stone paths of the city. He looked back and saw two red eyes regarding him from the dark water and reached into his cloak and drew out his weapon, pointing it at the creature. But the eyes submerged into the water again – and did not return.

The figure returned his weapon to the darkness inside his cloak, knowing he would see the creature again before too long. If it had followed him all the way from the mainland to the Floating City it would as likely follow him whenever he crossed one of the many canals of the city as well. And then a thought came to him, that perhaps the creature had not been following him, but was shepherding him into the city.

VI

THE STORY OF GIULIETTA

Giulietta was having one of her tantrums. "I don't want to have a ball anymore," she said. "I want you to cancel it. I want to stay up here in my room and I never want to talk to you again. I hate you. I hate you. I hate you!"

Her father, Signor Montecchi, sighed heavily, as his daughter thrust her head under her silken pillow. He was one of the most powerful men in the Floating City, a member of the Council of Ten, a wealthy merchant and had dozens of servants to do his every bidding, but his three daughters were beyond his ability to control. On days like this he wished they were young girls again. They had been so easy then. Or perhaps he just liked to think so. They had been adopted when he and his wife discovered they could not have children of their own, but they had always been raised as if they were their own. And they certainly had their own strong wills.

First it was Disdemona insisting she marry that Moorish soldier. Then Isabella insisting she marry that aloof merchant Bassanio – who died at sea soon after, leaving her a widow, albeit a very rich one. And now Giulietta, behaving like she was still a child, although she was about to celebrate her coming of age. At least she wasn't making demands of whom she was going to marry. He and his wife might have some success in matchmaking for at least one of his children, he hoped.

23

"Giulietta," he said sternly. "Enough of this. The ball is going to happen. Hundreds of guests are going to attend and if you do not attend I will put a mask onto your handmaiden and tell everyone it is you!"

Giulietta lifted the pillow from her head and stared at her father in outrage. "You cannot!" she said. And then she hissed, "Maria has fat ankles! You cannot tell people she is me."

"Then if you do not agree to attend the ball everyone in the Floating City will believe that you have fat ankles," he said.

She moaned as if he had driven a spike into her chest and fell back to the bed in a faint at the thought of having fat ankles. "I will go, but only on one condition," she said at last.

"Of course," he said.

"Promise me?"

"Yes, I promise you."

"I want a new dress for the ball. Something special."

"Oh," he said. "I see." The one thing his wife had expressly forbidden him to agree to was if Giulietta asked him for another expensive dress, as she had a whole wardrobe full of them that had hardly been worn. She sensed his hesitation and threw her pillow over her face. "If I can't have a new dress I'm going to lay here and suffocate myself, and then what kind of a ball will you have? It will be a funeral and everyone will have to leave their fancy masks and gowns behind and come in plain black."

"I don't believe it's actually possible to suffocate yourself," her father said. "Like trying to hold your breath until you pass out. You just can't do it."

"I'll be the first," she said with a determination that unsettled him.

"You know these are not good times to be having new dresses made," he said, hoping at least to be able to tell his wife that he had made some attempt to talk her out of it. "The Othmen and their pirates are attacking merchant ships so that they come back empty."

"One small dress won't make any difference," she said.

Her father narrowed his eyes. How small? he wondered.

"Just one dress isn't too much to ask for, is it?" she asked, peeping out from her pillow, and giving him her sad eyes.

He shook his head a little. The Council of Ten should put his daughter in charge of the city's defences. She was a genius with tactics and probing for weaknesses to get what she wanted.

"I'll be the best behaved daughter ever and do whatever you want of me."

"Whatever I want?" he asked.

"Yes," she said. "All evening at the ball, whatever you ask me to do, I will do it."

Her father tried to keep the smile off his face. This might just turn out better than he had expected. He would be able to go back to his wife and report that he had conceded ground in order to gain a major victory.

"I will have to think about it," he said. "And I should discuss it with your mother too, you know."

She sat up again quickly. "No," she said. "You don't need to discuss it with mother. You're the lord of the house, aren't you? And you're a councillor. Whatever you say becomes law, doesn't it?"

"Well, it's not quite as simple as that," he said.

"But you have the power to say yes to a dress though, don't you?"

"Well…" He was starting to enjoy this, he found. Baiting his own daughter into a trap she didn't know she was creating for herself. "Perhaps if your mother agrees."

"But she doesn't understand me like you do," she said.

He really should start grooming her for a life in politics of some kind, he thought. Well, as much as a woman was ever allowed to be involved in politics in this city. "On one condition then," he said, trying to sound doubtful.

"Don't worry," she said. "I will do whatever it is you ask of me. I promise."

He turned his head this way and that, as if considering a very weighty topic, and said, "All right then. But let's not let your mother know straight away."

"Oh, I love you, I love you, I love you," she said, springing from the bed and wrapping her arms around his neck. He smiled and patted her on the back, each thinking they had outmanoeuvred the other.

"It will be a very memorable ball," he said. "Did I mention that the Seers will be coming?"

VII

ELSEWHERE IN THE FLOATING CITY

The ship had been blown off course during the night and, come first light, the navigator was desperately trying to take their bearings from the sun, but it was still as cloudy as it had been during the night and he could make no accurate readings. If they had drifted too far to the east they would be in very dangerous waters, they all knew, and all eyes scanned the horizon sharply for any sign of friend or foe.

But it was not a ship they first sighted. It was an island. And as they came closer they saw a man on the beach, waving to them like he was possessed. As the shore was very rocky, the ship could not risk coming too close, but the man saw this and, grabbing a piece of wood, threw himself into the water and using it as a float, swam out to their ship.

Everyone on board was surprised to find that he was one of their countrymen, and when asked to tell them what had happened to him, he had an amazing tale to share. He told them first though that they should turn their ship around at once before the evil necromancer who lived on the island could call up a storm to drive them onto the rocks.

He told them that the old man had control of an Othmen Djinn to do his bidding. An evil and base creature – more animal than not – that ate his comrades one by one in the night. The necromancer also had a beautiful daughter, he said, who could turn to mist. Everything on the island was put there to torment men.

"Did you see any Othmen?" they asked him.

"No," he said. "Yours is the first ship that I have seen. I have been living on olives and roots and drinking water from muddy puddles, afraid to sleep at night for fear of the evil Djinn."

The captain and ship's crew followed his advice and turned the ship around at once and sailed far from the island of Othmen enchantment. But the poor man expired from his ordeal before the ship could return to the Floating City.

Vincenzo the scribe laid his quill down and stretched his cramped fingers, then rolled his neck to and fro. "No sea monsters?" asked a voice behind him.

Vincenzo spun around in his chair to see a hooded stranger standing behind him, wrapped in a long dark cloak. "Who are you?" he asked at once.

The stranger sighed. "It's always who are you? Not how did you do that? Or how did you get in here?"

"How did you get in here?" asked Vincenzo.

"Too late," the stranger said. "Only one question." Then he stepped across and picked up the document that the scribe had been working on. "I thought you had been commissioned to write a history of the Montecchi family?" he said.

Vincenzo scowled. "You've been sent by Signor Montecchi?"

"No," said the stranger.

"Then how do you know about the family history?"

"How do you know about the island of Othmen enchantment?"

"I was told it," Vincenzo said.

"Hmm," said the hooded stranger. "So you've no reason to doubt it, then?"

"Why would I doubt it?"

"Why indeed?" asked the stranger. "It's a pity that the man who told it was half mad with thirst and torment and died before you could hear it from his lips though."

Vincenzo looked around his small room. The door, next to an overflowing bookcase, was still barred, though his small window was open. He felt like asking once more, "How did you get in here?" but instead he asked, "What are you implying? Are you suggesting that it's not all the truth?"

"The truth can be many things," said the stranger.

Vincenzo scowled again. "The truth is the truth," he said. "There is only one truth."

"Ah, only one truth? That's an interesting idea."

Vincenzo didn't quite know what to make of this man, but had decided that if he had come to harm him he probably would have done so already. "If you are not sent from Signor Montecchi, then why are you here?"

"I've come to bring you a gift," he said.

"Well, give it and be gone. I'm a busy man."

The hooded stranger stepped closer and drew a curved knife from his belt. It looked to Vincenzo like those that he had heard the Othmen carried. Had he been wrong in thinking he had not come to harm him?

"What is this?" the stranger asked him.

Vincenzo's stare moved between the blade and the stranger's face, trying to find his eyes. "It is a knife," he said. Then he added respectfully, "Signor."

"Is it?" the stranger asked. "Just because it looks like a knife, is it therefore a knife?"

"You are talking in riddles," Vincenzo said.

"What does it feel like?" the stranger asked and, almost faster than the scribe could follow, the blade was pressed against Vincenzo's bare neck. He gulped and felt the sharp edge cutting into his flesh.

"Please, signor," he protested. "I am but a humble scribe."

"No false modesty please," the stranger said. "I asked you a question. What does it feel like?"

"It feels like a knife," said Vincenzo. His hands moved around shakily, grasping at nothing in the air, as if no longer under his control.

"And what looks like a knife and feels like a knife must surely act like a knife, correct?" the stranger asked.

Vincenzo could not answer.

"Correct?" the stranger asked again.

Vincenzo closed his eyes tightly and shook his head just a little. "I don't know."

"And how does a knife act?" the stranger asked, very slowly.

Vincenzo was trying to stop his throat from gulping, certain the blade had already drawn some blood. It was sharper than a razor. He wanted to ask the man why he was doing this to him. Was trying to think why anybody would want to kill him. Knew it could only be because he was writing about the Othmen. He was searching to find some words that might make the stranger remove the knife from his throat, when the man suddenly said. "A knife acts like this!" And he drew the blade across Vincenzo's throat.

It cut deeply and Vincenzo tried to cry out that he was being murdered, but his voice would not come. He threw his hands up to his throat as he fell forward onto the desk, gasping for air and trying to stop his life blood draining all over his work.

"Or does it?" asked the stranger.

Vincenzo looked down at his hands. There was no blood. He looked at the table and his papers. Nothing there either. He sat back up and felt his throat. There was perhaps a mark there, but he had not been cut open. He looked up at the stranger who was holding his quill pen in his hand instead of a knife.

Vincenzo rubbed his hands across his throat again, and now saw ink on his hands. "But how? But why? But…" Vincenzo began.

The stranger tossed the quill pen to the table and said, "Are you as certain now that the truth is the truth, and there is only one truth?"

Vincenzo said nothing for some moments.

"Can you imagine that there are many and multiple possibilities for any event, and that it is possible, in the right hands, to steer a course through them, ensuring only one possibility eventuates?" the stranger continued.

"Another riddle," said Vincenzo.

"Not at all. Imagine that you had the power that whatever you wrote became the one truth that you talk of. Imagine that you could not just chart the history of your city, but steer it as well."

Vincenzo took a deep breath. That was something that he had indeed imagined at times. The power to recreate events. To write them to turn out differently. To save his city from the perils that beset it. "Is such a thing possible?" he asked in a low voice, as if they were talking sedition.

"And why should it not be?"

"Because it is just a dream."

"Like the knife was a dream?" asked the stranger.

Vincenzo chewed his lip, the feeling of the blade on his neck still strong in his mind.

"What is the weather outside today?" asked the stranger.

"It is overcast."

"Then take up your pen. Write that it is sunny."

Vincenzo hesitated. Then the temptation overcame him. He picked up his pen and wrote on a blank page of his manuscript, *The sun shone over the Floating City.* Then he turned and looked out the window.

"It is still overcast," he said.

"Patience," said the stranger. "The sun will return soon enough."

Vincenzo looked at him and glared. "You are mocking me!"

"No," said the stranger. "I am not." And behind him a ray of light shone down on the street outside the window. Vincenzo scowled. It was probably just a coincidence. "I was not sent by Signor Montecchi," the stranger said. "But I have an interest in seeing that you complete the history of his family."

"I would but I have another more urgent task to record," said Vincenzo in a huff.

"The recording of the terrible events that mark the decline of your city?" asked the hooded stranger.

Vincenzo blinked, then said, "Yes. It is important that they are recorded accurately."

"I believe you will find that both histories are intertwined," the stranger said. "The fate of the Montecchi daughters mirrors the fate of your beloved city."

"I don't understand," said Vincenzo.

"You don't need to understand yet," said the stranger. "That will come with time. All I need of you for now is to accompany me and to write some events anew."

"Now?" asked Vincenzo.

"Yes. Now," said the stranger and walked over to the door and unbolted it. "This is the gift. We will be shadows in the night. We will be strangers in the crowds. We will observe everything and be unobserved. We shall watch the story of your city unfolding around us. And you will record it all and amend it when it is vital that it be amended."

Vincenzo blinked again.

"The idea compels you, doesn't it," said the stranger.

And Vincenzo could not deny that it did. Could not deny that it truly was a gift. "What will we observe?" he asked hesitantly, but rising to his feet.

"The truth," said the stranger.

VIII

THE STORY OF DISDEMONA

"I am going to leave my trusted ensign Ipato to watch over you," said Otello, as he dressed in preparation to meet the Council of Ten. "There may be no danger, but I will not risk it, cherub of my heart."

"I worry more for you," she said. "If there is any danger afoot, you are the one who will be confronting it, not I."

He turned to her and took his face in his large dark hands. "I would rather stay here by your side and see you safe from any perils, but my duty splits me in two. Half of me I rather leave behind to be with you and half I would send off to ensure the city is safe."

"So the city is your mistress then," she asked him, "who I must share your heart with?"

"Nobody has my heart but you," he said. "If I could I would cut it out and press it inside your bosom so that it always beat beside that sweet heart of yours."

"Do not even jest about spilling any of your blood," she said. "Instead I will wear that strawberry kerchief that you gave me next to my heart, knowing it was a gift from your own heart."

"Then let me place it there," he said. She reached into her sleeve and pulled it out from where it had been tucked and pressed it into his hand. Leaning forward he loosened Disdemona's bodice and slipped his fingers in against her breasts. "I think it feels most happy just here," he said. She smacked at his fingers playfully. "I would have it stay nestled there forever," he said.

"Then it shall." She took his head in her hands and standing up on her toes, kissed him on his large full lips. "And something to sustain you in your absence," she said.

"A drink from your lips is more sustaining than the sweetest of wines."

"As are your sweet words. Now go," she said. "Your mistress the city is calling for you.

He took her hands and squeezed them to his own large chest and then turned and left the chamber. Disdemona sat down at her bureau and began brushing her hair. She had never been so happy, she thought. Her Moor was back from the wars and she didn't care if the Othmen were invading them if every day could be as happy as this one.

She was interrupted by a sudden cough from the doorway. She turned to see the ensign, Ipato, standing there. "Yes?" she asked.

He stared at her pointedly and then said, "The general said I should make sure you were safe."

"I am quite safe," she said. Then she noticed his gaze was fixed on her still-undone bodice. She turned back to her bureau and began re-lacing it, only realizing too late that he had watched it all in her mirror. She scowled and turned back to him. He was a thin man with lank dark hair and a thin moustache that she thought looked too much like a worm over his lips.

"So tell me, what danger are you protecting me from exactly?" she asked him.

"These are dangerous times," he said, stepping closer into the room, as if invited. She did not like the man overly, though his manners were always good and his demeanour never insulting. She much preferred the company of her husband's captain, Casio, a kind and humorous fellow who always made her feel at ease. Next time she would ask her husband to appoint him to watch over her.

"What dangers do you see around you now?" she asked him. "Does my chamber contain great threats to my safety? Does the ceiling threaten to fall upon my head?"

The ensign took another step closer to her and said, "One can never be too certain where dangers lurk. As one never knows where faith and love might be hiding."

"I know where faith and love are," she said. "They dwell in this room."

He nodded his head. "Then you see it?"

"Of course I see it," she said. "I see it every evening when I go to bed with my husband and I see it every morning when I waken beside him."

The ensign cast his eyes down at the floor a moment as if she had stung him with her words in some way. "What troubles you?" she finally asked. "Is there a danger lurking by that you are afraid to tell me of?"

"Not a danger as such," he said. "But something I would much like to share with you but I fear the consequences would be dire."

"You are a brave man, are you not?" she asked. "My husband has often admired your bravery and told me you are amongst his most able of men."

He lifted his head up and looked to her. "He says that?"

"Often," she said, knowing that he had perhaps said it once or twice. The ensign seemed very pleased to know this, she thought, and seemed to grow more courage at hearing it.

"Then perhaps I should tell you where danger lies," he said.

"Please do."

He walked across and sat on the edge of her bed. "They say," he said softly, "that affairs of the heart that run hot soon cool."

She regarded him warily now.

"They say," he continued, "that the allure of novelty wears off and one's heart then has a great longing for things of one's homeland."

She lowered her eyebrows into a frown.

"They say that true love is often the quietest that makes no proclamations or poetry."

"Do they?" she asked him. "Who exactly says that?"

"Well. Wise men and women," he said.

"Which wise men and women exactly? Give me their names?"

She watched him squirm a little. "Well, not specific wise men and women as much as the wise men and women of the ancients," he said, trying vainly to make his answer seem authoritative.

"I've never heard that said," she replied at last. "I have heard however that true love is never tainted. And also that while true love does not always love wisely, it can love well."

"I know enough of love that does not love wisely," he said.

"Be a fool for love and you will not regret it," Disdemona said. "Trust me on this. If there is somebody you love, then tell her." She turned back to the mirror, adjusting her earrings and wishing for the conversation to be ended. She'd had enough of this weary fellow. "Better to show your heart than hide it," she said.

"Do you advise me so?" he asked.

"I do."

"Then lend me your kerchief," he said, "and I will make it into a gift for you in thanks for your advice."

"There is a kerchief on the mantle," she said, indicating a pile of folded cloths.

"I would rather the one you have tucked into your bosom there," he replied.

"No," she said firmly. "That is not for lending and must remain where it is."

"Then this will have to do," he said, rising and going over to the mantle, and taking up the small cloth, he began folding it.

"But would you not hold it against me if I was to tell you who I loved?" he asked, now walking across to her. "Would you harm my heart if I exposed it to you?"

"I would not," she said distractedly, paying more attention to her hair than to him.

"Do you promise?"

"I promise," she replied.

"I will hold you to that," he said, and with a flourish he snapped the cloth and it was folded into the shape of a flower, which he held out for her. She was amazed at the trick and let him place it in her lap. "But I would hold you first," he said and placed one hand upon her breast, holding it firmly, right above where her husband's kerchief sat.

Disdemona was too shocked to respond at first and then said, "Sir, I think you forget yourself!"

"I remember that I am in your bedchamber, my lady, and I remember what use bedchambers are best put to."

She was speechless for a moment and then pushed him away from her. "If my Moor had heard you say that he would rip your heart out and eat it," she said angrily.

"But you have vowed to protect it," he said.

"Do not toy with me," she snapped.

"As you toy with my feelings?"

"I have done nothing to encourage your feelings."

"Nothing but to ignore them, and then tell me to express them."

She looked at the man and saw the desperation in his eyes. And lust. "I will ignore this incident," she said. "But only this once. I think it is time you left, for I would rather face the dangers of the Othmen beasts than be left in your protection any longer."

The ensign stood there a long moment and Disdemona could have sworn she witnessed the exact moment that his lust turned to hate for her before he turned and stomped out of the room, recalling his words that you could never tell where danger lurked.

IX

ELSEWHERE IN THE FLOATING CITY

The city guards were walking along the edge of the canal cautiously peering into the waters which were dark and ill-smelling in this part of the city. "Watch your footing," said the lieutenant of the guard. "It's slippery along here." The men were making their way along one of the narrower passages where the buildings pressed close to the water's edge. It was dark and the stones covered in slime. He didn't need to add that if any of them slipped and fell into the water it wouldn't be the dunking and jeering he had to most fear.

There were only a few citizens out on the streets, mostly keeping to higher paths, on the bridges or the built-up areas, keeping away from the waters. To their surprise an occasional gondolier had rowed past them with a nervous or ignorant-looking merchant sitting in the boat, glad to not have to jostle for space on the narrow canals for once. "Clearly more money than sense," one of the guardsmen said.

"They'll all be back out in a day or two," said the lieutenant. "It will just take a few days for everyone to realize that the canals are not full of Othmen monsters and life will go back to usual."

"You sound certain," said one of his men.

"Think about it," said the lieutenant. "If the Othmen could invade our city with monsters, they would send a legion of them.

But if there was but the one they would have it attack only the most valuable targets."

"So you're saying you don't think they will attack the common people?"

"If I was an Othmen I'd be saving my enchantment for where it most counted."

"But what if the beast needs to eat while it's waiting for its targets?"

"There are plenty of dogs and rats that hang around the waters," said the lieutenant. "Why risk going up against a man who might fight back?"

"What if they cannot be harmed by mortal weapons?"

"What if their purpose is to sow fear into the city?" another asked.

"Well they've done that sure enough," said the lieutenant. "But as I say, people will be back out as usual in a few days when there have been no more attacks."

"What if there is another attack?"

"Then we'll cross that bridge when we come to it, as the architect said to his mistress."

Nobody in the troop laughed. The men made their careful way along the narrow alleyway and the man at the back of the line, who was quite new to the guard, heard what sounded like a splash far behind them. "What was that?" he asked quickly.

"Rubbish going into the water," said the lieutenant of the guard without turning his head. They went on a little further and there was a second soft splash, on the far side of the canal.

"What was that?" asked the last man again.

"Rat," said the lieutenant, again without turning his head.

The next splash was much louder and closer and it even made the lieutenant turn his head in alarm. He saw the furious splashing in the water and then saw the flailing hands of one of his men there. He had drawn his sword before he understood that the last man in the squad had slipped and fallen into the canal rather than be taken by some beast.

"Quick. Fish him out!" he ordered his men, and two of them dipped their pikes into the water, snared his clothes and dragged him across to the canal's edge where he started scrabbling out. "Something touched my leg," he said fearfully. "Something soft touched me."

"A turd most likely," said the lieutenant. "Now get in line and watch your feet!" He turned back to lead the men to the end of the dim alleyway, when they heard a man's scream ahead of them. "Forward on the double," he called. The men rounded the corner expecting to see a beast of some kind, but instead all they saw was men. One was on the ground and the other was standing over him with a blade of some kind in his hand.

"You there!" called the lieutenant of the guard. The standing figure turned and the guardsmen could see that he was masked. A strange pale mask with a wide closed-mouth grin framed by an angular dark moustache and thin strip of beard from the lips to the base of the chin. The raised cheeks had no colour in them, the dark eyebrows arched in mockery and the eyes were thin enough to appear empty.

"Stand away!" the lieutenant of the guard ordered him. The masked man raised his hands, and the lieutenant could see the weapon was a small trident, like the gladiators of old used. "Drop that!" the lieutenant said, drawing his own sword and advancing on him. But suddenly the masked man threw something to the ground in front of him with his other hand and a cloud of acrid red smoke rose up about them all.

The guards jostled each other, coughing for breath, and could not move for fear of accidentally impaling their comrades, until the smoke had cleared a little. And by that time they could see only one man was still there. And he was lying on the ground with the trident thrust deeply into his neck.

The lieutenant looked at him and then looked at the men gathered all about, staring like imbecilic children at a circus show. "Do you know him?" asked one of the men.

"It's Signor Flavius," said the lieutenant. "He's one of the Council of Ten."

"It was sorcery," said another man.

"It was an Othmen beast disguised as a man," said a third.

"I was frozen to the ground by his spell," said a fourth.

"I was blinded and made deaf," said another.

"Save your stories," the lieutenant said. "None of them is going to appease the Moor's anger about this."

X
THE STORY OF ISABELLA

Isabella Montecchi strode slowly around her chamber as if actually considering the Othmen envoy's offer. She was wearing a white dress, woven through with multiple golden threads, and puffed sleeves, and suspected that to him she probably looked a prize gift-wrapped in gold. She had, on previous occasions, refused his entreaties rather unceremoniously and asked him to leave her house. But she knew it was a slow path to ruination. The envoy, she was certain, controlled the Othmen spies in the city and was spreading news to the Othmen pirates as to what ships were leaving the city at what times and where they were headed. He was a dangerous man for a businesswoman to enter into conflict with.

"Do you find my offer a tempting one?" the envoy asked.

Isabella turned and looked at him. He was neither fat nor balding, but she could tell that in just a few years he would be both. He was the wrong end of his best years for courting a woman, that was certain, and certainly past his dancing days. But that was only the beginning of the catalogue of things about him that she found distasteful. His small stubby fingers that always felt sticky; his leering eyes and the way he licked his lips when he talked to her, like he was tasting sweets; the list went on.

"Most tempting indeed," she said. "But I fear that if I married you I would not be able to stay in this city that I love so much and would be forced one day to relocate to the land of the Graecians, or worse, the Othmen, where I would know no joy or comfort!"

The envoy licked his lips and said, "That is something you should not fear. The lands of the Graecians are those of the ancients and they are a wonder to behold and filled with every comfort a noble lady could imagine." She cocked one eyebrow. She had heard they were barren lands, over-tilled, where rich nobles lived in luxury while slaves did all the work and lived in squalor. "And the lands of the Othmen make them pale by comparison," he added.

"Have you been to the lands of the Othmen?" she asked.

"None are allowed to travel there and return again," he said. "But I have seen pictures of them and I have read the poetry they write. They are a very cultured people."

"Indeed?" she asked. "Then tell me what you know about the lands of the Othmen."

"Ah," he said. "Where to begin? They are lands of milk and honey. There are palaces of gold and jewels and cushions of silk and ermine. The weather is never too hot nor too cold, nor the days too long nor too short. There are deer that are as tame as a house cat and will feed from your hands. There are fountains of water that are as clear as crystal and cool to the throat. It is a land that anyone would wish to live in one day."

"And you have been promised this?" she asked. "To be allowed to live in the land of the Othmen one day?"

"Indeed I have," he said, emphasizing the word *I*.

"I have heard that the lands of the Othmen are deserts," she said. "And the people wage wars over the few water ponds and forests that exist. I have heard that sand devils live beneath the ground and can rise up and take an unsuspecting passer-by. And I have heard that the noblemen have fifty wives, and treat them as little more than servants."

The envoy waved his hand in the air, like he was shooing away a pesky insect. "These are malicious lies spread by those who most fear the Othmen and wish others to hate them. How can you trust the word of anyone who has never been to their lands?"

"Indeed?" she asked again.

The envoy then changed tack. "We are entering the times of the Othmen," he said. "They will soon spread across the land and rule all countries. Those who oppose them will find it was a poor decision, and those who work for them will find themselves richly rewarded."

Isabella had to turn and look out the window towards the far-off sea so that he would not see the sudden rage on her face. These same Othmen had killed her husband and sacked their ships and murdered the crews, and not because they had ever opposed the Othmen. Merely because they were traders from the Floating City whose wealth the Othmen longed to possess, as their envoy longed to possess her and her wealth.

"Here is my offer back to you," she said, picking up the jewelled ring he had laid on a silver tray for her as part of his bridal price. She turned it to the light and saw the way it sparkled. It was not of Graecian nor Othmen make. It was probably crafted by a jeweller in the Floating City and stolen by Othmen pirates and given to the envoy in payment for his work for them. "I am a widow as you say, and in need of a husband who can look after my interests. But I am also a businesswoman and so I am going to set a task for you as a suitor. Indeed the task will be set to all suitors and he who can complete it will win my hand in marriage."

The envoy looked at her cautiously. He did not like the idea of having to compete with other men. He considered a moment and decided that there would be ways of tipping any competition in his favour. "Tell me what you propose."

"Well," she said. "As you yourself have intimated, a woman who has known the passions of a husband finds it hard to sleep alone at nights and by all rights needs to find a husband to fulfil her desires."

The envoy's face reddened a little at such blunt talk, but she could also see lust descending over his face like a veil. She turned and stepped close to him and reached out one hand and touched him gently on the sleeve. He licked his lips rapidly.

"I propose that he who wishes to win my hand must sleep with me." She saw the envoy nearly choke on just the idea of it. "And if you can enjoy me, and also please me, then I will become your wife. But if you cannot enjoy me, then you forfeit a large sea vessel filled with your most precious cargo."

The envoy stood as if turned to stone for a long while and then his tongue darted out and licked his lips again. She saw his eyes were almost completely misted over. "And when should one attempt this challenge?" he asked in a strained voice.

"This evening," she said coolly. "Bring a vessel filled with precious cargo and have it docked down below the window here. I will be waiting with a fine meal."

The envoy's eyes narrowed a little, his mind trying vainly to find the trap or trick to the offer. But whatever small part of him was protesting to be cautious, it clearly could not be heard above the roar of his own blood filling his ears. "It will be laden with the most precious cargo I possess," he said. "And I'm sure it will please you as much as I please you myself."

"I look forward to this evening," she said.

The envoy bowed and nearly tripped on his own puffed-up shadow as he gleefully departed.

XI

ELSEWHERE IN THE FLOATING CITY

Romeo Cappalletti turned to look over his shoulder and made sure that no one was following him, before knocking on the old wooden door. Once. Then twice. Then once again. He turned and looked back down the narrow alley that he had walked along as he waited, just to be certain nobody was lurking in the shadows. Each alleyway in the city was like no other in its shadows and shapes and smells, and even the sounds of the water lapping against stone walls nearby, and Romeo knew the sight and smell of this alley well.

A small window in the door slid open and a hooded figure stared out at him from the darkness.

"It's me," said Romeo.

"I can see it's you," the figure said.

"Let me in."

"Why should I?"

"I have some good news."

"For me or for you?"

"I have something you desire," said Romeo.

The hooded figure looked at him for a moment and then asked, "Or something you desire?"

Romeo tossed a lock of light hair over his forehead, as he did often, and pouted. His youthful attitude was lost on the figure behind the small window though. "I can pay," he said.

"That *is* news," said the hooded figure.

There was a sudden splashing in the canal nearby and Romeo turned quickly, all composure suddenly lost. "Be quick," he hissed. "They say there are monsters in the canals."

The figure drew the bolts back and opened the door enough for Romeo to squeeze in. "In my experience the worst monsters are those in men's hearts," the figure inside said as he rebolted the door.

"You should write a book of your lyrical thoughts one day, Friar," Romeo told the older man, as he turned and lowered his hood. Friar Lorenzo da San Francesco was a thin man of middle age and average height, with sallow pale skin and possessed of such sunken eyes that he always looked sickly.

"Are you well?" asked Romeo, as he often asked of the friar.

"Well enough," the friar said. "Now what business brings you to visit me today and disturb my work?"

"It is your work that I wish to talk to you about."

"You have need of spiritual guidance?" asked the friar in mock surprise.

"I have need of your other work," said Romeo. "That which you deny you are conducting."

"Should I now feign ignorance of what you speak?" the friar asked him.

"You would do well to feign ignorance," said Romeo. "For if the Council of Ten ever found you were experimenting with the spells and potions of the Othmen I'm sure they'd be more than displeased by it. They might even think you were in some way in league with the Othmen devils and hand you over to their inquisitors, who boast they can make a man curse the day he was born."

"Rather I curse the day that you found out about my secret works," said the friar.

"But who else could procure the things you need?" asked Romeo.

"One must barter with imps to sup with the devil," the friar muttered.

"Enough word play," said Romeo. "To business. I have need of a love potion."

The friar sighed, turned and sat down at a table where there were vials and potions laid out. "I have advised you already that your obsession with the Lady Rosaline is a misguided one," he said.

"Only because you lacked the necessary ingredients to manufacture a love potion," said Romeo.

"That's correct enough," said the friar. "You know well that I require a water lily of the Nile, and that only grows in the far-off heathen lands where neither you nor I are ever likely to go."

"But where traders might venture?" asked Romeo, reaching into his shirt and bringing forth a small pouch.

The friar's whole face changed. "Show me," he said excitedly. "Where did you get this from?"

"From a certain merchant who got it from a certain merchant who got it from a certain merchant," said Romeo.

"Or from a certain charlatan looking for a spoiled rich boy to fool out of his gold?"

"I am assured it is genuine," said Romeo.

The friar took the small pouch and opened it delicately. Inside was a dried white leaf. He considered it carefully, turning it this way and that. "It may be," he said at last. "It just may be."

Romeo smiled. "So, for the potion, I need something that I can administer to the Lady Rosaline at the masked ball of the Montecchis this week," he said.

The friar looked at him in alarm. "The Montecchis? Are you mad? There is a blood feud between your Houses. If you're caught at their ball they will cut you open."

"They wouldn't risk breaking the Council's Peace," said Romeo. "Any who do will be banished. And anyway, I will be masked."

The friar looked pained. "Is there not a simpler way? Could you not contrive to visit her at her home and give her the potion there?"

"She would be too suspicious of my motives," Romeo said. "I have tried to charm her in her own chambers before and it went badly."

The friar laughed. "That must have been a slap in the face for you. Beautiful and handsome Romeo who all the young girls of the city dote on, and the one woman he is interested in spurns him."

Romeo's face turned a little red. "Do not mock me," he said. "Others have done so and regretted it."

"Yes, yes," said the friar. "Do not take offence. I can remember the impetuousness of youth that always demands immediate satisfaction, whether it be in love or in war."

Romeo stared at him in surprise.

"I was not always a friar you know," the old man told him.

"I had always imagined you emerging from your mother's womb wearing a friar's robes," Romeo said.

"Yes, yes," said the friar. "And I can remember the incessant dull wit of youth too. Now leave me to my work, and leave me with two gòld coins, and I will have the potion ready on the morrow, and then you can test whether this is indeed a water lily of the Nile or not."

XII

THE STORY OF GIULIETTA

"Giulietta!!" Signora Montecchi called upstairs to her daughter. But there was no response. "That girl needs a good talking to," she said to her husband.

"Of course," he said, worried that he would be the one volunteered to do the talking. Then he turned to a maid and said, "Run upstairs and see what is taking her so long, would you?"

The maid bowed and set off up the stairs. "I think we both know what is keeping her," said Signora Montecchi. "She is staring at herself in the mirror and has a head full of silly ideas about being the most important person at the ball."

"It will be in her honour," her husband reminded her.

"It will be to find a husband for her," his wife said in a hushed voice. "But she will be too busy thinking about how pretty her dress will look and what type of hair-do she will wear and what type of mask to wear to even suspect it."

"Well, we were young once too, you know," said her husband. His wife smiled and put her hand on his arm. It was true, she could remember her own masked ball and the feeling of excitement of knowing everyone would be looking for her, and she'd be hiding behind a mask for most of the evening until the unmasking. She was able to spark up conversations about herself and see what other people had to say – or didn't. She even asked people if they could point her out, and they usually pointed to some poor girl with a pretty mask and said, "I believe that's her."

"I wish we were living in such times still that we could indulge her so," she said. "But you know this is about securing her future."

Her husband nodded his head sadly. They had already decided that they were going to try and find a suitor who had estates far from the Floating City, and so could take her far away. Somewhere much safer. But the thought of losing her, their youngest daughter, filled them with anguish.

"It will be the best for her," Signor Montecchi said. "It is far too dangerous for her to stay here. Just imagine what might become of her if the Othmen managed to invade the city? She is so fair and so young."

Signora Montecchi had imagined it far too many times already. Much better she was in a dull marriage far away than here and in such danger. "Do you really think such a threat is possible?" she asked him, although she knew her husband was a cautious man not prone to flights of fancy.

"The council believes we are all in terrible peril," he said. "If the Othmen manage to assassinate any more Seers, our defences will fall."

"But there are still three pairs," she said. "They could not hope to kill them all, could they?"

He shrugged. "We never imagined they could manage to kill a single pair." His wife shivered a little.

"Shouldn't the council send one pair away then? Somewhere safe?"

"What good would that do?" he asked. "They could not use their power to keep the city afloat and could not hold back the powers of the Othmen if they were not in the city. No. We need them here. Our only hope is that the city's defences hold. The council is trusting the military defence to the Moor. He is our most capable warrior."

"But he's not one of our city," his wife said. "Not really."

"Our daughter Disdemona might beg to disagree on that," he said. "Once wedded to a citizen of the city, he is wedded to the city."

"Yes," said his wife glumly. She still had a strong feeling that the marriage would end badly.

"And the Seers have begun a search for younger Seers with potential that can be paired."

"Oh dear," said his wife. "There hasn't been a pair found for over forty years has there?"

Her husband shook his head. "No. But the Seers say they feel the presence of them. They are young but if they can be found and brought under the tutelage of the older Seers they might be able to bolster our city's defences."

"I imagine you were sworn to strict secrecy over that," she said.

"Of course," he replied. "Upon pain of expulsion from the council."

"Thank you," she said, letting him know how much it meant to her that he shared such matters with her, and she placed a hand on his arm again.

"Have you been looking over potential husbands?" Signor Montecchi asked her.

She laughed. "Yes. I have met with several of their mothers already and I think there are at least two very good candidates."

"That's promising. Who are they?"

His wife looked horrified. "I can't tell you that. I'm sworn to strict secrecy!" He laughed. And then they both turned their heads to see Giulietta and the maid coming down the stairs.

"I'm definitely going to need new dancing shoes," Giulietta complained loudly. "All the ones that I have are either worn out or completely out of fashion. I simply must go shoe shopping this afternoon."

Signor Montecchi looked at his wife. "New shoes would be a good idea," he said. And then much softer, "Walking shoes."

"Shh," she said, and gave him a small playful slap. "We will talk about it," she proclaimed as her daughter continued down the stairs. Giulietta looked at them and wondered why they both seemed to be just a little sad, especially when she had her hair done up in such a pretty style today.

XIII
ELSEWHERE IN THE FLOATING CITY

The first pair of Seers, known as the Summer Seers, sat in their high chairs, with their eyes closed. They were very old. Way beyond one hundred summers. They were also so thin it looked as if their parchment-aged skin was wrapped tightly around their bones, holding them together. They were dressed in ornate green and yellow robes with arcane symbols embroidered into the fine cloth, and they wore stylized masks with gold leaf and feathers, symbolizing their season. And they each held the other's hand.

In the dimness of the chamber it was possible to see the faint glow emanating from where they touched. They sat completely still, as if rehearsing for a time when they would leave their aged bodies, and only stirred when the door to the chamber opened. They looked up with piercing bright eyes, alive with an intensity that glittered in the dimness.

The second and third pair of Seers came in to the chamber. They were the Spring and Winter Seers, and each couple's gowns and masks depicted their season. They were also aged, although younger than the Summer Seers. Each couple walked like a dignified old man and his wife might walk around the piazzas of the city, supporting each other, also holding each other's hand. Also revealing that soft glow where they touched.

They made their slow way across the chamber and sat in a pair of high chairs to the left, and directly opposite the Summer Seers. Each pair then turned their eyes to the two empty chairs. The question of which couple's chairs would be next to be left empty hung unasked in the air between them.

Finally the female Summer Seer spoke. "We feel the weight of the city has grown heavier."

The Winter Seers both nodded. "The Othmen are determined that our time has reached its end," the male said.

"Then they will find there is still fight in us yet," said the male Spring Seer. His wife squeezed his hand in support. "They have sent beasts against us before," she said, "and we have vanquished them."

"But there were four of us then," said the female Summer Seer, speaking in the plural. "Now we are but three."

"It is harder to hold the city afloat," said the male Summer Seer, his voice thin and soft. "Do you not feel it starting to crumble in places?"

"We feel it," said the male Spring Seer, "but we cannot contain it and combat the Othmen at the same time. We must, I fear, sacrifice some of the city to save the whole."

The female Summer Seer nodded her head. "The Othmen are growing stronger and will press home their attacks on us. We must be ever vigilant." Then she said, "Come. We must look to our defences."

Together the two Summer Seers rose and slowly stepped into the centre of the chamber. There was a dark wooden table there with four glass balls upon it. One was filled with water. One with fire. One with earth. And one appeared to be empty. The other couples joined them. They reached out and all six joined hands around the table. As soon as the connection was made the fire began to leap and dance inside its glass ball, the water churned and swirled, the earth churned and the last glass ball glowed with an arcane light.

"Water. Fire. Earth. And life," the female Summer Seer said.

"The Othmen shall take none of them from us." Then she closed her eyes. As did the others.

"Can you feel some of the city's buildings subsiding into the waters?" the male Winter Seer said.

"Our power weakens," said his consort.

"No," said the female Spring Seer. "It is just that our number has diminished."

"I fear it is more than that," the female Winter Seer said. "I feel we have seen the peak of our powers and now they contract."

"It is just fear you feel," said the female Spring Seer. "Put it from you. It is fear that weakens your powers."

"And that weakens the city," said her consort.

"We must sustain it," said the female Summer Seer. "To let parts of the city sink would send fear and panic into the people."

"No," said the female Winter Seer. "Let them go. We must search the waters for the beast of the Othmen. It sends more terror into the people than any buildings in the city sinking a little." Her voice betrayed her as she spoke, though, letting the others know that it was her that the beast of the Othmen sent more terror into than any part of the city sinking.

"There is time for that," said the male Spring Seer calmly. "We should concentrate our efforts on finding new seers. We can renew our power by finding a young couple and uniting them. I can feel them in the city, but they are too young and immature to find easily."

"But they have great potential," said his consort. "Have you felt that too?"

"They may grow to be stronger than any of us if nurtured and taught well," he said. "But they prove elusive. They are not even aware of each other yet."

"We do not have the time," the female Winter Seer said. "Our priority must be on defending our own lives."

"They will come to an end eventually," said the female Spring Seer. "And then what of the future of the city?"

"They will not come to an end prematurely though," said the female Winter Seer, her white and frost-jewelled mask looking around at the others in turn. "Not if we devote our energies to protecting ourselves from the Othmen. It is the only way. We are not strong enough to fight them on all fronts."

"Our lives should matter less than the lives of the citizens of the city," said the male Summer Seer.

"We *are* the city," said the female Winter Seer harshly. "Their lives are our lives."

The female Spring Seer said nothing and her consort squeezed her hand to tell her to let the matter go. She gave him a small squeeze of acknowledgment and the male Summer Seer asked of the Winter Seers, "Have you had a vision?"

"We were seeking the younger seers," the male Winter Seer said, his voice rasping a little in his throat. "But all we saw was death at the hands of a Djinn. We must prevent it!"

There was quiet in the chamber and then the female Winter Seer spoke again. "We must probe the waters of the canals and try and find this beast that has been sent to defeat us. And when we find it, we shall destroy it. Then we shall turn our energies to sustaining the city."

"Are we agreed?" her consort asked.

Nobody disagreed.

The male Summer Seer said, "All right then. We shall turn our attention to the beast first, but we shall not ignore any chance to locate the young ones nor to allay panic in the city if we are able."

"Or beasts," said the female Spring Seer as they broke the circle and the light went out of the glass globes.

XIV

THE STORY OF DISDEMONA

Otello stepped out onto the city streets to find his captain, Casio, waiting for him. "Well met," he said, holding out one arm to clap his captain around the shoulders, but Casio stepped back and said, "It would not be proper. We are no longer equal brothers in arms. You are my general."

"Then we will walk together and recall the times when we were both equals," Otello said.

"That would please me greatly," said Casio with a smile, falling into step beside the taller man. "I remember well when you first came to us as an unknown mercenary."

"I think there was much fear and suspicion of me when I first stood in your ranks," said Otello.

Casio shrugged. "We are not used to seeing one of such dark skin and fierce countenance within our ranks. But we only had to see you in battle against the Othmen one time to see what mettle you were forged from."

"Well spoken," said Otello, and he did reach out and clap Casio on the shoulders. "We have stood shoulder to shoulder many times, my friend."

"We have fought many battles and survived them."

"I remember you boasting that one day you would be my commanding officer," Otello teased him.

Casio nodded his head. "I did honestly believe that," he said.

"Does it not cause you ire that I have risen to such an office above you? Or that I have wed one so lovely while you have no sweetheart in the city even?"

"Who said I have no sweetheart in the city?" Casio laughed. "Although it might be true to say that I do not have a single sweetheart."

Otello laughed too. "Ah, Casio, there is such joy from having a woman that you know is yours alone. It is a feeling that anchors a man and gives him strength. No matter what trials I face, knowing Disdemona will provide me succour allows me to continue on. Her embrace is the mortar that strengthens my soul and allows me to believe I can hold up the world." He smiled. "I cannot describe to you the pleasures of lying abed with my sweet Disdemona."

"But I'm sure you're going to try nevertheless," Casio said.

The Moor stopped and his face grew serious. "No," he said. "Do not make fun of me where my lady is concerned. You can make barrack-room jibes about my quick temper and my undue haste to seek vengeance, but never think to lessen or make light of my feelings for her."

Casio put up both hands quickly. "Your temper is quick indeed, but I would no more make fun of your feelings for your lady than I would ask for details of how she looks beneath the bed covers at night."

The Moor's face grew darker still. "It is more improper of you to speak so of your general than it is to let him embrace you!"

"Now I was too quick to apologize and am tripping over my words," said Casio. "I mean no offence in any way and have only the greatest respect and love for you both. You know well that I knew her as a child and have a sense of familiarity with her because of it."

"I know that, but now she is my wife, and your lady, you should pledge your respect to her as you do to me."

"Then that is what I pledge," Casio said. Then when he saw

Otello had calmed down and turned to continue on, he added, "In truth, being a friend with you can be much more dangerous than being an enemy of the Othmen, though I think her company takes the bite off your temper and softens you. Have I not seen you playing with a stray kitten in the streets that once you would have kicked away from you?"

Otello gave him a glance.

"Though I would never tell anyone!" Casio said quickly, "lest they think your bite any less fearful."

This time Otello smiled. "My bite seems worse than it actually is. Unless you are an Othmen."

"And I have seen the way you dispatch the Othmen with sword, dagger and bare hands," said Casio, "and I think it altogether more preferable not to risk your anger."

"Then we will speak no more of my lady and instead will speak of the dangers to our city. The Othmen will be sending spies here to learn what they can. They will be trying to buy the favours of unscrupulous merchants. We need to hunt them down and turn them to our advantage."

"I shall put men onto it at once. We will treat every stranger in the city with suspicion and treat them as a foe until proven otherwise."

"And we must be vigilant for their assassins above all," Otello said. "Before they send their ships against us they will try and weaken us from within. They have already slain two Seers and one of the Council of Ten – for this is more than a war of property and territory, but a war over beliefs. And we must ensure we protect the others from their reach."

"I will put our best men onto the task of being their bodyguards," Casio said. "They will not be able to piss or place a hand upon their wives' privates without being observed."

"That might prove a little close guarding for the comfort of the council," said Otello with a wide smile. "But I will convey the intent of that to them, if not your actual words."

"Ah, and I had always thought you a brave man," said Casio. "And now you prove not willing to discuss the council's wives' privates with them."

"The only privates you need to concern yourself with are those in your rank and file who must obey my commands," said Otello.

"The day that my privates obey any man's commands but my own will be a rare day," said Casio.

"They will obey mine if I order it," said Otello. "So don't make me put it to the test."

"Then I will make sure I have two privates posted outside your bedchamber. Just in case you find you have need of them in the night."

"I warned you, Casio," said Otello in a low growl.

"I apologize again for the jest and for the next ones I may make while not thinking," Casio said. "I know our city is at war, and that is a dreadfully heavy thought, only made lighter by light banter."

"I think I should advise you to put away your light banter and rather concentrate on the heavy thoughts for the time being, and rather than practise your quick wit, concentrate on practising your quick sword strokes. For I'm sure the Othmen will be even less appreciative of your humour than I am."

The two men walked in silence for some time, and then Casio asked, "How are the council reacting to the crisis?"

"Like old women," said Otello. "They are scared and divided. And as such are driven to make poor decisions. Like having me report to them at every hour of the day, and then quiz me as to why I am not spending more time on the streets keeping the city safe."

"Rather you than me," said Casio.

"Yes. I fear your mouth would get you into trouble," Otello said.

"Which is odd," said Casio, "as my father once advised me that a mouth would get a man into much less trouble than any other caves of delight he might seek."

Otello laughed heartily and clapped Casio on the back again. "I suppose I could no more ask you to hold your tongue than one of your many wenches could."

"Well spoken, my general," said Casio. "And so you will have to watch your own words in front of the council."

XV

ELSEWHERE IN THE FLOATING CITY

The climb to the top of the city bell tower was a slow and arduous one and Vincenzo the scribe lost count of the number of steps somewhere after three hundred. As he had long lost the stranger who had led him up the tower. When he finally got to the top he was panting and sweating and just wanted to sit down and rest.

The masked stranger had already led Vincenzo along many narrow alleys and over the smaller bridges of the Floating City, keeping away from the larger thoroughfares and remaining in the shadows wherever possible.

"Where are we going?" Vincenzo had asked.

"To see your fair city," the stranger told him.

"Wait," said Vincenzo, puffing a little. "You go too fast for me. I am not a man of action. I am a scribe."

"You will become a scribe of action over the next few days," the stranger had said, pausing to turn back to him. "Were you not a keen sportsman in your youth?"

"How do you know these things about me?" Vincenzo asked. "I do not even know your name."

The stranger stopped and turned to him. "I have been called the Shadow Master."

"I think it a fitting name," said Vincenzo. "As would be the Peril Master or the Mystery Master."

The stranger tilted his head a little and thought about those. "No," he said. "They don't have the same ring to them. Normally I'd say, don't give up your day job, but in your case we'll let it slide."

"Slide?" asked Vincenzo. "I don't understand many of your words. You talk like a native of the city by your tongue, but the words you use often seem foreign to me."

"Don't worry about it," said the Shadow Master. "You'll get used to it."

Vincenzo shook his head a little. "Please," he said. "Tell me a little more of our endeavour."

"First we are going to climb the tallest tower in the city," said the Shadow Master.

"The bell tower?" protested Vincenzo. "It is a very tall tower. There are many hundreds of steps. Could I not use this power you have promised me to write it to be much smaller?"

The Shadow Master laughed. "You should not squander a gift so easily. Come, it will make you feel more alive." Vincenzo groaned and fell into step behind the Shadow Master as he set off again.

Finally they reached the top of the tower, and Vincenzo sat down on a large stone and gasped for breath like a fish pulled out of one of the canals.

"Have this," said the Shadow Master, who had clearly been waiting at the top for some time, holding out a small bottle to him.

"What is it?" asked Vincenzo.

"You will find it refreshing."

Vincenzo took the bottle. He sniffed at its open mouth, but it had no scent. Then he took a small sip. It had a sweet taste and fizzed in his mouth. He felt it travel down to his stomach, and then smiled. "It is very refreshing," he said. Then he drank the rest of the bottle. He was surprised to find his energies returning to him and he stood up and wiped his sweating brow with the sleeve of his shirt and let the cool breeze blow over him.

"How do you feel now?" the Shadow Master asked him.

"Surprisingly well," Vincenzo said. "You must tell me where you obtain this drink."

"All in good time," said the Shadow Master. "Come over this side and look out over the city." Vincenzo came and stood beside him. It had been many years since he had climbed the bell tower, and he had quite forgotten how beautiful his city looked from above. It was the view the birds and the angels of the ancients would have had of her. He could see the many red-tiled roofs and the curved domes of the larger buildings and the white flat roofs of others. He could see the canals snaking their way between the floating islands and the large S-shape of the central canal, and the many bridges linking the islands, binding them together. It was more than a city, he felt, it was like so many disparate floating pieces all held together by the buildings and bridges and the very life and history of the place.

"How does it look today?" the Shadow Master asked.

"It looks at repose," he said. "Like a beautiful maiden at rest, waiting for the night to come and perhaps a suitor to visit her."

"Yes. Not too shabby, is it?" said the Shadow Master.

"I'm not sure what that means," said Vincenzo, "but I probably agree with your sentiment."

"It means I like this place and could willingly waste my time in it."

Vincenzo nodded.

"But looks are deceiving and danger lies ahead for your reposing lady, and we are here to prevent it. So enough wistful sightseeing and time for work," said the Shadow Master. "First I want you to observe that rather grand white building by the water's edge." He pointed to a white flat-roofed building with battlements running across it. "Do you know it?"

"Yes," said Vincenzo. "That is the palazzo of the widow Isabella Bassanio, who goes by her maiden name Montecchi after her husband died. She is one of the three daughters of Signor Montecchi, whose history you seem so keen that I continue writing."

"Good man," said the Shadow Master. Then he turned to the east and pointed out another building. A much older one, showing its age. This one had a red-tiled roof and thin windows. "And who lives there?" he asked him.

"That is the house of the Moor who is the new general of our army, and now protector of the Floating City. And of course his wife Disdemona, the second of Signor Montecchi's daughters."

"Full points," said the Shadow Master. "And do you know what I'm going to ask you next?"

"I believe you would ask me to identify the Montecchi residence, where the youngest daughter, Giulietta abides," he said.

"You are as sharp as a cut-throat's blade," said the Shadow Master. "It's a privilege to be working with someone of your intellect."

Vincenzo suspected the Shadow Master was mocking him, but could not be certain. "Why is it important that you point dwellings out to me that I already know?" he asked.

"This is just to remind you that there is a big picture involved and not to get too lost in the small detail of things. Do you notice anything about their locations?" Vincenzo turned from one building to the other.

"Nothing," he said. "They are not even close to each other."

"But what do you notice about their distance from each other?"

Vincenzo looked at them again and considered. "They seem to be equally far apart from each other."

"Exactly," said the Shadow Master. "On a map you might even notice a pattern to them. But they are the three main corners of the story you are going to write. Three different stories with all the other stories contained between them."

"Won't that be too complex to try and tell?" Vincenzo asked.

"Perhaps," said the Shadow Master. "But if you remember that the larger story is bound by those three stories it might make it more manageable."

Vincenzo didn't look convinced. Then the Shadow Master said,

"Now, can you point out to me where the palazzo of the Seers was, before it sank into the waters."

Vincenzo turned to the west and pointed at a spot on the water's edge where the palazzo had previously been. He felt an awkward discomfort inside, to look at that empty water where once such a great palace had stood, like one gets when observing a dead animal.

"What else do you see there?" the Shadow Master asked him.

Vincenzo stared at the spot for a long time and then said, "Nothing."

"Drop your head down to the level of the brickwork of the tower here and then look at it anew," he said.

Vincenzo did as he was bid and lowered his head and looked across the city to see it framed by the straight line of the brickwork. He blinked and looked again. "It cannot be," he said.

"To see or not to see," said the Shadow Master, "That is the question."

"I see the palazzo of the nobleman Signor Flavius and those around it, on the island closest to where the Seers' palazzo was. They do not sit straight like the buildings on the nearby islands. They seem to be sinking into the water."

"Very observant," said the Shadow Master. "Now, here before you we have your scene, your characters and your plot problem. All that is left to do is to observe and work out how to write what you see."

"I should write that they are not sinking and repair this problem?" asked Vincenzo.

"Stay your quill hand for the moment," said the Shadow Master. "First we observe and try and understand what is happening."

"And what is happening?" asked Vincenzo. "You seem to possess knowledge that you have not yet shared with me."

"Indeed," said the Shadow Master. "This is a city of masks. Consider the buildings as just masks hiding what lies behind those walls. Look deep enough and you see it all."

"You talk in too many riddles," protested Vincenzo. "Your puzzles would befuddle a philosopher. But I am only a humble scribe."

"Only a scribe!" laughed the hooded stranger and clapped his hands. "Yes, and I am only a humble Shadow Master!"

XVI

THE STORY OF ISABELLA

The Othmen envoy had arrived early, panting like a too-eager puppy, Isabella thought. She had to fight off a temptation to throw a bone into the corner and tell him to fetch it. Again he had brought gifts with him. Othmen silks and also Venetian jewels that could have once belonged to any of her family and friends. She smiled and took them from him graciously, admiring the softness of the cloth and the quality of workmanship in the jewels.

The Othmen envoy puffed up like a peacock strutting up and down a garden path, as if he had created them with his own hands. Indeed he was dressed something like a peacock and appeared to have spent the entire day preening himself, having his hair and nails groomed and scents applied to his body. She pitied the poor servants who had the task of washing him and dressing him so that he almost looked handsome. But they could do nothing about the lust in his eyes that made her skin tingle like she had swallowed something bitter.

"Come and sit beside me," she said, indicating some cushions on the floor. They were going to sit Othmen style, he could see and he frowned before lowering himself most ungraciously to the ground. Clearly he had never mastered this, despite having to adopt it in the presence of his masters.

"Would you like a drink?" she asked. "I have some sweet wine."

"Just a little," he said, never taking his eyes off the curve of her body, in particular her fulsome bosom, which she had chosen to leave a little exposed to divert his attention. He licked his lips repeatedly, staring at it, like it was a sweet dessert on offer for him.

"Certainly," she said and called on one of her maids to pour them both a cup of wine. As she had been instructed she poured quite a large cup each. Isabella took the smallest sip from hers and then placed it beside her. "I trust you have the vessel of riches ready below?" she asked.

"And I trust you have your vessel of riches ready for me?" he replied.

He was really most distasteful, she thought as she forced a weak smile to her lips. "I would like to examine her if I may," she said and stood to her feet, rising slowly and exaggerating her hips just a bit as she walked to the window. Down below, tied up to the small dock outside her house, was a truly magnificent ship. It was Graecian, she could see, with two rows of oars for slaves to propel her along. The sail was tied up closely and she could see several boxes of cargo on the deck.

"The greatest treasures always lie deep within," he said.

She made as if to not understand the allusion and asked him what cargo he had placed on board her.

"There are crates of gold and silver plates and cups. There is fine furnishing. Rugs and paintings. And books. Many books. In Italian of course."

She smiled. It sounded like they were all goods stolen from the ships of the Floating City that he was bargaining with.

"And may I be allowed to examine your vessel in turn?" he asked.

She suppressed a shudder and said, "All in good time."

He opened his hands as if to demonstrate that he was a patient man, despite no other part of his body indicating it. Indeed he was no longer making any attempt to hide his excitement.

"First we dine together," she said, coming back and sitting on the cushions next to him. "If I am going to wed, I want to make sure my husband has a healthy appetite."

"I have a healthy appetite in all things," he said with a leer.

"I am pleased to see it," she said and asked her maid to bring in some food. They supped on cold meats and small birds and other treats and he ate with his hands and sucked at his fingers noisily, never taking his eyes off her.

She in turn smiled and tried to make small talk with him.

"Enough," he said, finally. "I am sated."

"Won't you have some sweets?" she asked him, but he shook his head and waved the maid away.

"Perhaps later," he said. "When I have worked up some more appetite."

She reached out and laid a hand gently on his lap. "Let me explain how this will work then," she said. "You will retire to my bedchamber and disrobe and wait for me. I will go into the small chamber beside the bedroom and prepare myself. Then I will come into the room and disrobe too. You will need to be patient with me of course. You cannot rush a woman in such a situation as this."

He nodded eagerly.

"And then, as per our agreement, if you have managed to enjoy me before the morning comes, I will agree to be your wife. And if not, then I will take possession of the fine ship you have brought with you."

She saw a faint warning bell seemed to be sounding in the back of his mind, just loud enough for him to ask, "I will not find you – uh – unassailable, will I?"

She put on a look of puzzlement. "I'm not sure what you mean?"

"With such a device as husbands sometimes have their wives wear when they are away to ensure they cannot be enjoyed by other men."

"Oh," she said and gave a little laugh. "What a preposterous idea. I assure you that when I come to bed I shall be entirely without clothing and will remain that way the entire night."

She could see the thought of that drowning out the peal of any warning bells, and his nostrils flared widely and his eyes almost rolled back in his head. "If I am unassailable, as you put it, it will be through no fault of mine," she assured him.

Then, before he could ask any more questions, she clapped her hands. "Well then. There's no time like the present. My handmaiden Nerissa will lead you to the bedroom," she said. "And I will join you presently."

He struggled to his feet and Isabella said, "Shall we have one more toast to the evening ahead?" She lifted her cup and raised it to her lips. He took the cup off the tray being offered to him by the maid and drank it greedily, wiping the remains on his sleeve, staining the fine fabric.

"I will see you momentarily," she said.

"Oh yes. I will most certainly *see* you," he said hoarsely, licking his lips rapidly. She smiled and watched him leave the room.

XVII

ELSEWHERE IN THE FLOATING CITY

The Council of Ten – now nine – sat a little further forward in their ornate seats as the Head Councillor, the Duca, said to Otello the Moor, "We have all read the reports, but tell us of the fall of Cyprus. We would hear it in your own words what the Othmen are like when they attack a city."

The Moor looked about the room and knew he had not just every man's attention, but also their respect. He, a Moor, a heathen to these men, had become their greatest general. And he loved their city for it, even if he did not love the nine old men around him. They had not sailed to the east to face the Othmen threat. They had not spilled any blood to keep their trade routes and empire safe. They had not seen the horrors of the fall of Cyprus.

"As you well know, my lords," he said. "The fortified city of Famagusta was our last stand on the island and we had been besieged by the Othmen and their mighty cannons for a year, forever looking to the western horizon for relief."

The Council of Nine did not respond to the baiting. Monumental efforts had been enacted to raise a rescue fleet, but it proved too slow for the defenders.

"We held out for a year, but we were without food and ammunition and eventually we knew our only hope was with a dignified surrender, and so we sued for peace."

The Duca, an old man with a pointed white beard who wore his chain of office like it was a very heavy weight around his fur-lined neck, waved a hand at Otello to continue. They knew all this. General Bragadin had led the peace delegation into the tents of the Othmen generals and faced the Pasha himself, who had promised to allow all citizens of the Floating City to leave unmolested and had even put his ships at their disposal. "Tell us about their betrayal," he said.

Otello looked around the room slowly. That was the point of so much conjecture and debate. Particularly from those who had not been there in attendance. But in truth, he was the only man of rank to walk away from that alive – perhaps because of his dark skin, the Othmen decided he was not an officer but a slave of the Venetians, so whatever version of events he told would be uncontested.

"And?" asked the Duca.

Otello shrugged. "The Pasha demanded that we leave some noblemen behind as ransom for the safety of his ships. General Bragadin said he could not order any freeman to stay behind as it was not the way of the Floating City to command free men to do anything."

The council nodded. They too would have made such a statement as a preliminary point of bargaining. That was the trick with the Othmen, they had been told. Everything had to be a matter of bargaining.

"And the Pasha flew into a rage," said Otello. "He had guards bind all those who had come to surrender. He had those assembled outside as part of the retinue cut down where they stood and he sent his army into the city. They revelled in death and destruction for three days. Men were beheaded where they stood begging for mercy. Children were put into the chains of slavery and women were raped in their homes. Even holy women were raped on their sacred altars."

Several of the members of the council looked down at their

feet, or wrung their hands as if noticing sudden stains on them. Perhaps the stains of the blood of their people who had waited for the relief ships that had been so slow in organizing, Otello thought.

"But the general stood defiant of the Pasha and refused to beg for mercy," he continued. "So the Pasha, rather than killing him there and then, cut off his ears and nose." He stared around the circle of nine, but none would now meet his eyes. "And then, after having much sport with him, they finally tied him to a pole in the city square and slowly flayed his skin from his body. They had drawn it all the way down to his stomach before he finally cried out in agony, and then soon after died."

He waited a few moments before adding, "They stuffed his skin with straw and made an effigy of the man and hung it from the city gates."

Finally, after a long silence, the Duca looked up at him and said, "You alone escaped to bring us this news. You alone were spared."

Was that an accusation? Otello thought, and glared at him. "Several dozen escaped," he said.

"And we are grateful for it," the Duca said, and he smiled. A kindly smile, Otello thought, as if the old man could see what he was feeling. "And we are grateful that you were one of them, and grateful that you now lead our city's defences." Otello relaxed a little. "For you have seen the enemy and know his strengths, but also know his weaknesses," the Duca said.

Otello nodded. "The Othmen are but men and can be slain like any other man."

"No," said one of the councillors. "No man could engage in such savagery. He is a beast disguised as a man."

"And he has control of beasts through his enchantment," said another.

"He is a serpent gliding into our homes, seeking out our children," said another.

"He is beyond description," said a third.

"He is all of those things," said the Duca, reining in the growing hysteria. "But he is our enemy and he has his eyes on our city and we charge you, General Otello, with its protection from our foe. What we want to know of you is, are you equal to the task?"

And Otello now smiled broadly, showing his large white teeth. He held up his strong hands and said, "I have slain Othmen soldiers too many to count with these hands and I will likewise slay their spies in the city, their necromancers and any beasts they may conjure. For anyone who threatens this city also threatens the woman that I have wed, and I have vowed to defend my love with my life."

XVIII

THE STORY OF GIULIETTA

Romeo had no eyes for the danger he was in. As he had no eyes for the high-arched ceiling above him with its painted images of cherubs and knights. He had no eyes for the fine tapestries hanging from the white marble walls, nor the intricately laid tiles that most guests coming to the palazzo of the Montecchi family for the first time stopped to admire. He only had eyes for the Lady Rosaline.

Romeo wore the feathered mask of a hawk and he stalked her around the ball room as his prey. It had taken him but a moment to recognize her amongst all the fine ladies of the Floating City. No one was as tall and graceful as her. And no one had the exact same curling red hair that she had. No one had a body shaped like hers.

He circled around the room watching her dance with various men who would invariably become captivated by the lightness of her step and the gracefulness of her limbs, or perhaps even the soft curves of her half-hidden bosom, but she would bow and flick her fan and abandon them at the end of each dance to watch after her wistfully. He had been left like that many times himself.

But not tonight.

At one point she broke off from the boorish oaf who was trying to charm her, and walked across to the long table where the refreshments were laid on a sparkling white cloth. She had barely glanced at the array of wines and cordials when he was there at her side. "Good evening, mysterious lady," he said, bowing low, his arms spreading out wide, as if he was swooping down from on high. "I have been admiring your movements. You remind me of a lady I once knew, but are much more gracious than she, and surely more beautiful as well."

Rosaline wore an ornate silver mask inlaid with jewels that covered all her face but her lips. He had hoped to see them smile, but they turned down instead. "Romeo, Romeo," she said, "Whyfore art thou here? Is it not past your bedtime already?"

"I am here but to enjoy the dance," he said. He had long become immune to her snipes about their age difference.

"If anyone discovers your presence you will think it lucky if you are only hurled into the canal. You may even go home with a thin sliver of steel pressed between your ribs."

Romeo waved a hand in the air. "The animosity between our two houses is not so extreme that it would lead to violence during a party."

"I believe the animosity between your houses is such that it would be considered a terrible insult that you have attended this party uninvited. It is, after all, being held in the honour of young Giulietta Montecchi. Your presence would be seen as an insult to her."

"I have no interest in insulting her or praising her," he said. Then added, "Mystery lady."

She sighed and snapped open her fan and looked away as if suddenly bored. "Allow me to offer you a refreshment," he said, and pressed a fine silver goblet of wine to her. The same goblet he had been carrying around for much of the evening, laced with the Othmen love potion.

"You are forever pressing gifts upon me that are unwanted," she said.

"Surely you are in need of refreshment," he said. "Consider it a token of peace that I will trouble you no more." She turned and looked at him. "Unless of course you request it," he said.

"And when have I ever requested your attentions?" she asked.

He gave no answer but held out the wine goblet to her. "To peace between us," he said.

She took it reluctantly and said, "I fear we are not living in times meant for peace."

Romeo bowed low again. She considered him a moment and then placed the goblet onto the tray of a passing waiter, turned and walked off across the room.

Romeo watched her go and felt she had been right. Somebody had just pressed a thin blade between his ribs and into his heart. And it had been her. He watched Rosaline make her way back onto the dance floor and accept the hand of a tall man dressed like a harlequin. Then he turned his head quickly to follow the waiter with the goblet. But he had already been stopped by an elderly woman who took the goblet off the tray and started sipping from it.

Romeo closed his eyes and muttered a curse. He watched the elderly woman slowly finish the drink and then turn to the old man behind her, obviously her husband. He was in for a surprise this evening, he thought. But the elderly lady only passed him the empty goblet and turned to a younger man beside them and laid one hand on his forearm and started whispering into his ear. That young man was in for an even bigger surprise, he thought.

Romeo frowned and folded his arms. There was some old saying about the best-laid plans of men being nothing but clouds being torn apart by the wind, but he'd never paid enough attention to learn it properly. There was a sudden bitter taste in his mouth and he looked around for a glass of wine to wash it away. And then another.

Finishing the second cup and finding it had not washed away the bitterness, he was considering leaving the ball, when a matron who stood nearby leaned close to him and asked, "Do you know which one the young Giulietta is?" Romeo turned his head towards her without answering, glad only that it was not the elderly lady who had drunk his love potion. That would have been the final mockery for the evening. "They say she is the fairest of all the Montecchi daughters," the woman said.

Romeo nodded his head, still without answering.

"They say that there are many suitors here this evening hoping to win her hand. I expect you might be one of them, yes?"

"No," he said bluntly. "I find women little but trouble."

"Oh?" she asked. "But surely some things are worth a little trouble."

"And some things not," he said sullenly.

She shrugged. "Since you are not a suitor," she said, "I can confide in you that I have an eligible son, and I am hoping to represent his case to her."

"Ah," said Romeo, "I see. Well, I believe that lady there with the red hair is Giulietta." He pointed to the Lady Rosaline across the dance floor, fanning herself gently during a pause between dances. "I think it would be to your advantage to introduce your son to her and I'm sure she would be most pleased to meet him." The lady gave a small bow, and scuttled off across the dance floor.

"I hope he has some contagion or fleas of the nether region that he passes to her," Romeo mumbled. Then, as the music restarted and the dancers took their places for the next dance, he set the empty wine cup down and stepped out onto the dance floor. He would at least enjoy a dance or two before going home, he determined.

The musical introduction told him this would be a dance in lines, so he took his place on the floor in the appropriate position. As he waited he saw several of the servants walk around dousing candles until the hall was much dimmer and then others came out carrying flaming goblets. Ah, the fire dance, he thought. Splendid! Each goblet was filled with a small amount of oil that had been lit so a ghostly blue flame danced out of it. The servants walked down the centre of the hall and each maiden took a goblet and held it in her right hand. Then they were ready to begin and the orchestra moved into the dance proper.

Romeo was feeling a little better already. This was a most excellent dance and he was a most excellent dancer. Each woman had to hold onto her partner's left hand, while her right hand with the flaming goblet was held out from her side, as they danced. At the end of each set, as they changed partners, she would press the goblet into her new partner's hand who would then pass it back to her as they danced.

His first partner moved well and he smiled to her as he moved around her, playing up his hawk's mask and leaning in and then out again. He could see he was charming her. Of course. Who wouldn't be charmed by him?

He danced with two more partners before it happened. He had been smiling wickedly at his former partner, who had clung to his fingers as if reluctant to let go of him, when he turned to take the flaming goblet from his next partner. He only had time to register her mask was also that of a bird, a dove, he thought, before their fingers touched around the goblet. The flames within suddenly erupted and burst upwards towards the ceiling, exploding like a firework and illuminating the whole room.

Everybody stopped and stared in awe and then clapped their hands in appreciation at the clever entertainment their hosts had provided. Everybody except the three pairs of Seers who had been seated at the top of the room, masked heads bowed deeply in conversation with each other, dancing around the politics of the city as much as those on the floor danced. The moment they saw the bluish flame climb to the ceiling they knew what it meant. "Where did it come from?" the female Spring Seer hissed to her consort. "Did you see which couple it came from?"

"No," he said, standing to his feet. "They are here though. We must find them."

But the music had not paused and the dancers had moved on to the next partner to catch up to the dance. The music continued for one more set and then stopped at the sudden chiming of a bell, indicating that it was time for everyone to unmask. Romeo frowned again. He had hoped to be gone by this time in the evening. He looked across for the strange dove-woman who had performed the enchantment trick with her flame cup. He was curious to see what she looked like. The brief touch of her hand had left his fingers tingling. Though perhaps it was the effect of the dancing fire.

The man opposite Giulietta whipped his mask off quickly and she saw it was Marcuccio Guercio, one of the men that her mother had ambitions to marry her to. He would take this as something of an omen of destiny when he saw who she was. He was handsome enough, but rather dull and boring. So instead of unmasking to him she turned her head to look for the strange hawk-masked man who had performed the fire trick. When he had touched her fingers she had felt some tremble run through her entire body, and wondered how he had done it.

Romeo, and Giulietta, turned their heads and lowered their masks together and the moment their eyes locked it was as if they were suddenly alone in the hall. They each felt the echo of the tingle and the tremble within them. Felt the need to step out of line past all the ladies and gentlemen gently applauding as the whole hall took off their masks, and generally pretended to be surprised at who they were standing next to. Felt the need to walk across to each other and touch again.

She could not take her eyes off his face, as if it was familiar to her in some way, but she was sure she had never seen him before. She was close to touching him now, reaching out her hand to take his, when her mother was at her side, threading her arm through hers. "Giulietta," she said. "There is a young man I want you to talk to."

"Yes, there is," she said, not taking her eyes off the young man in front of her.

"He is the son of Signora Guercio," she said, referring to the partner she had just walked away from.

"What is your name?" Giulietta called to the young man who

had worn the hawk mask, staring at her, with his arm out to touch her.

"Romeo," he said. "Romeo Cappalletti. And what is your name?"

But before she could answer her mother spun her head suddenly and stared at him. "A Cappalletti!" she snapped. "In our house? Are you mad?" She turned her head and looked around her. "Leave quickly before any of my cousins recognize you. I will not have blood shed on this evening. Come Giulietta, away." And she pulled her daughter across the floor, though she kept turning her head to watch him. And he could see the look of sudden sadness on her face.

"Giulietta?" he said softly. It was impossible. Montecchi's youngest daughter. They were sworn enemies.

XIX

ELSEWHERE IN THE FLOATING CITY

Vincenzo the scribe sat up in bed violently, and then put out a hand to steady himself. He looked around in the darkness, certain a flash of light had illuminated his room. His heart was beating and he thought he could hear the faint echoing ring of a small child crying. But there was nothing. Just the fading images of the dream that clung to him.

He closed his eyes and laid his head back onto his pillow. And the memory of it filled him again. He had been flying. Travelling across to the city that was floating not on the waters of the lagoon, but up in the clouds. Somebody was carrying him. A tall dark figure. A strong man who held him in a protective grip and as they reached the city he lowered him to the stones of the streets. And the moment his feet touched, the city began sinking through the clouds. Falling softly out of the sky and down to the waters of the lagoon.

There was a small boy standing on the very edge of the city, holding a hand up for the dark man to take him up again. Calling out to him in fear. But the dark man just hovered there, watching him.

The city was bobbing on the waters now, not steadily, but rocking like a boat might rock in a storm, a boat of many buildings and pathways and landings and dark alleys and fine palazzos, all floating upon the waters, held up by the enchantments of the Seers. But then it started sinking below the waters. The small boy cried out in terror now and held up his hands for the dark man to save him, but he was just a distant dark figure, like a grey speck in the corner of your eye that forever danced out of sight when you tried to follow and focus on it. Then he was gone. Then there was the bright flash of light and he was awake.

Vincenzo felt that child's terror and knew that it had been him. Knew that the dark figure had been the Shadow Master. As he knew he would follow his strange quest around the city, to find out what the vision meant, even if all memory of the dream disappeared with the morning's light.

XX

ELSEWHERE IN THE FLOATING CITY

"This is a power that I fear will destroy us," said the female Winter Seer. The six Seers had locked themselves together in a small room of the Montecchi's household, despite entreaties from Signor Montecchi that they should come out and bless his daughter. He had knocked at the door and told them how vital it was that they attend to her, but they had ignored his pleas until he had left them, mumbling about ingratitude and lack of civic duty.

They paid him no heed, as something much more vital demanded their attention. They had a metal chalice on the table before them that was still humming slightly. Each had held it in their hands in turn and felt the residue of power still within it.

"It speaks of a pair who will be very powerful," the female Summer Seer said, her husband's hand held in hers, as ever.

"But so young and untempered," the female Winter Seer said. She had held the cup in her hands and tried hard to see the faces of those who had held it, but it was if they were hidden from her. It was frustrating that they had been right there in the same room with them, but they could not identify them. "I can feel it," she said. "Our destruction is written here."

"I feel no such thing," said the female Spring Seer. "They will strengthen us."

"No," said the female Winter Seer. "They are dangerous to us."

"Whichever they are, they must be found quickly," said the male Summer Seer. "Power such as this needs to be tamed to be beneficial to us." He picked up the cup again and turned it over in his hands. "And they probably have no notion of their abilities."

"They may not even have manifest until this evening when they came into close contact with each other," his consort said.

"They are a danger to us," said the female Winter Seer again. "I can feel it."

"Are you sure it is their future you are reading?" the female Summer Seer asked. Both Winter Seers hesitated to answer.

"Their future can only be written by themselves," the male Summer Seer said adamantly.

"No. Their future will be written by us," the male Spring Seer said. "We cannot allow them to remain unknown and uncontrolled. We must bring them under our wings and train them."

"They would need to be kept in isolation from each other," the female Spring Seer said. "Their power is too raw to enable them to be together until they can control it."

"But they will be naturally drawn to each other," her consort said, giving her hand a squeeze, as if reminding her of some secret between them. She looked back at him and smiled. "And that might be how we shall find them," she said. "We wait for them to be reunited and we look for more signs."

"We cannot afford to wait," said the female Summer Seer. "We must start searching for them now."

The Winter Seers had withdrawn from the conversation, looking at each other closely, as if trying to console the other of a fear they both shared.

"We should begin our search this evening," the female Spring Seer said to the Summer Seers. They knew what that look between the Winter Seers meant. "You will look for the young man and we will look for the young woman. We will test them by water or fire or life, but we will find them. Agreed?"

"Agreed," said the Summer Seers.

"And what of Signor Montecchi's daughter?" asked the male Winter Seer. "Should we not attend to her and give her our blessings?"

"That is hardly a priority," the female Spring Seer said. "We have much more at stake than the blessing of a silly girl looking for a husband."

XXI

THE STORY OF DISDEMONA

The night was as black as the feathers of a crow's wing. Otello walked along the dark city streets with his ensign, Ipato, close by his side. The city light seemed ghostly this evening, with a thin mist about. The harsh clomp of their boot steps echoing about them marked their authority as they walked. "There seem to be a lot of boats on the canals tonight," the Moor said, watching a gondola row past, a lantern on its prow lighting the way and throwing a dappled path across the water. "I had thought people were still too fearful to venture out."

"The Montecchi ball," said the ensign. "Can you not taste the excitement in the air? Risking a possible Othmen beast in the waters is one thing, but risking not being seen in high society is quite another."

Otello smiled. His ensign had an occasional quiet wit that he appreciated. "Indeed," he said. "Disdemona had asked me to accompany her there to celebrate her sister, but I told her I was needed on duty. It had slipped my mind."

"And how is your fair wife?" the ensign asked. "She seemed a little out of sorts when I last saw her."

"How so?" asked Otello, turning to the man. The ensign immediately held up his hands as if to protest what he had said. "Perhaps I overstate things," he said. "It was just a feeling I took away with me."

The Moor considered him for a moment and then frowned and turned back to the path before them. They were walking along a street with a canal on one side and tall houses stretching overhead on the other, so that their voices echoed eerily when they spoke.

"Anyway," the ensign said, "perhaps it is just that I think she likes me not."

"Why do you say so?" asked Otello. "Has she ever given you reason not to like you as much as I do?"

"Perhaps it is just that I notice that she does not enjoy my company as much as she enjoys that of Captain Casio." He noted how the Moor slowed his steps just a little as he said it. He knew she had asked her husband already that Casio be appointed her guard in preference to him and had given no credible reason for the request. "She is forever cheerful in his company, but never so with me," he said.

"I am sure you imagine it," said Otello.

"I had thought so too, but she is never as familiar with me as with him."

"How do you mean familiar?" Otello asked, slowing his pace just a little more.

"It is nothing, it is nothing," the ensign said quickly.

"No, tell me," said Otello.

"Well, I am reluctant to say anything about a superior officer that might be taken amiss."

"Then I am ordering you to tell me."

The ensign squirmed as if in acute discomfort, and then said, again, "I would rather not say anything against him. He is a most excellent officer and I would fear to say anything that might jeopardize his position."

"You jeopardize your own if you do not," Otello said, a tone of impatience in his voice.

"Then only because you order it," said the ensign. "I must confess then that it causes me some disquiet to overhear the bawdy nature of their jests and conversations."

"Bawdy?" asked Othello in a grim voice. "What do you mean by bawdy?"

"Well," said the ensign, putting on an aggrieved face. "We all know our Captain Casio is quick to make a bawdy jest in the company of his fellow guardsmen, but it is not the type of jest that I would have thought appropriate to make with a lady. It has a taste of a certain familiarity about it that I would hesitate to even imply."

"And yet you do imply it."

"No, no," said the ensign, holding up his hands once more. "I only do as I am commanded by you. I would rather seal my lips than say any more."

"And I would rather I do not have to cut your lips open for you to tell me what you know," Otello said darkly.

"The word *know* is too strong in this instance," said the ensign. "I think the word *feel* might be more appropriate."

"Then tell me what you feel? And tell me plainly."

The ensign looked around him as if the night moths might be enchanted flapping ears, flitting about in the shadows to overhear him. "I feel that there is a certain familiarity between the pair that favours bawdy humour between them."

"I think you should tell me more plainly still."

The ensign looked at his feet. "Is it not true that Captain Casio and Disdemona were quite close in their youth? And is it not true that she is somewhat headstrong in giving rein to her desires? And is it not true that a man never fully leaves his past."

Otello stood completely still for some long moments and the ensign could hear his breathing. "I think you should now put name to your feelings even plainer still."

"That is all I am willing to say," the ensign said. "I would not wish to be the cause of slander when there is no rightful case for it to exist." He made to turn away, but Otello commanded him, "Stay. You will not walk another step until I have heard everything that you have to say."

"I would rather you cut me down with your sword than I be forced to say anything ill of your wife," he protested.

Otello tapped his sword hilt and said, "Then say nothing ill of her when you tell me what it is you have to say."

"Let me then ask but one question," Ipato said. "Would not a child who has grown up in the light and found the thrill of the dark an adventure, then long for the familiarity of the light again?"

He watched the Moor's hand tighten around his sword hilt, and wondered for a moment if he had gone too far. Otello followed his gaze and saw his hand was sitting on the hilt of his sword, ready to draw it.

"What do you say, my lord?" the ensign asked in a clearly frightened voice. "Have I been disloyal to obey your commands of me?"

Otello took his hand from his sword and lifted it up before his face. He looked at the dark skin and said, almost in a growl, "I thank you for your words. Only a true friend would have the courage to tell me this."

The ensign nodded his head and smiled. For he looked at the Moor closely and could see the seeds he had planted were taking root behind his very eyeballs, filling them with tendrils of doubt and anger.

XXII

ELSEWHERE IN THE FLOATING CITY

The Shadow Master led Vincenzo the scribe along the quieter streets of the Floating City, weaving their way over bridges and down streets, along the stone paths less worn by the everyday tread of feet, where mosses and lichens grew undisturbed. Eventually Vincenzo asked what had been preying on his mind for some time, "We have known each other before, have we not?"

The Shadow Master paused and turned around. "Is that something you wrote so that it would happen?"

"No," said Vincenzo. "It is something I feel."

"If you wrote this scene now, between us, standing here, would you write that I would answer you or walk on?"

"I would write that you would tell me," said Vincenzo.

The Shadow Master nodded and walked on. Vincenzo glowered and chased after him, calling, "Do you even know where we are going?"

"We are going to see Disdemona," he said.

"Then are you sure you know the way?"

The Shadow Master said nothing. Vincenzo suspected that he was lost in the maze of stone pathways and pillared corridors and turnings and small bridges and brickwork buildings. The city was a puzzle to those who did not know it. Some of them even claimed it moved and re-arranged itself so that one path could never be found again. But they simply did not know its ways and byways.

"Would you like me to lead the way?" Vincenzo offered.

"In a moment," he replied. "We have somewhere we need to be on the way."

"Why didn't you say so?" Vincenzo asked.

"You would ask me for details," he said.

"And what's the problem with that?"

"I don't think you'd like the details."

"I would also write that you stop talking in riddles," said Vincenzo.

"Think of them as philosophical challenges."

They walked into a small square and the Shadow Master held up a hand for the scribe to stop.

"What is it?" he asked.

"The details!" He scanned the buildings around them carefully and then called out, "Come out, come out wherever you are!"

Vincenzo watched him turn around on the spot, looking carefully at the doors and windows of each of the buildings. "Hmmm," he said. "I could have sworn this was the right place. Too many of the dark nooks in this city look the same." He turned to Vincenzo and said, "Let's keep looking."

"For what exactly?"

But the Shadow Master didn't answer. He heard the sharp metal-on-metal hiss of a sword being drawn from its scabbard and smiled widely. "Oh, splendid!" he said. He turned and saw a man stepping out from a darkened doorway, with a short sword in his hand and a grinning white mask with arched eyebrows over his face.

Vincenzo took a few steps back, but the Shadow Master didn't move. In fact he clapped his hands and then beckoned the man to come closer to him. "Come on, we haven't got all day," he said. The assailant didn't take the goading well and suddenly rushed at the Shadow Master, with his sword flashing through the air.

Vincenzo waited expectantly for the blow to strike the Shadow

Master, but he moved so quickly he barely saw it, stepping out of the way of the sword and lashing out with his bare hand. The attacker fell to the ground as if struck by a cannonball.

The Shadow Master looked down at him briefly and then looked up at the buildings around them again. "And the rest of you. You might as well come out too." Nothing happened for a moment. But then three more men with the same grinning white mask stepped slowly out of the doorways with swords drawn, and slowly began circling the Shadow Master. Vincenzo observed they were keeping a little out of his reach but incessantly closing their circle about him. Vincenzo knew he would never survive this attack and drew in a deep breath. But then the Shadow Master struck. Vincenzo didn't even see him draw his swords but they were flashing left and right like a striking snake and before he could even finish the breath he was taking it was over. The three men were dead on the ground.

"How... how did you do that?" he asked.

"That's the right question at last," he said. But before Vincenzo could say anything in reply, the Shadow Master put a finger to his lips and turned his head a little to the side, listening. Then he spun on the spot and his sword flashed and something fell to the ground at Vincenzo's feet with a clunk. It took him a moment to understand it. Someone had fired a crossbow bolt at them and the stranger had cut it out of the air with his sword. Unbelievable.

Then the stranger was rushing at the doorway beneath the window from where the bolt had been fired. He kicked at the door heavily and there was a deep hollow thud. Vincenzo saw him step back cursing and limping a little on one foot. "Oh mother of mercy," he said, followed by an even stranger curse that Vincenzo had never heard before. The Shadow Master gave him a quick look and said, "That wasn't meant to happen." He stepped back to the door, walking carefully and then slid one of his swords into the gap of the door jamb, then prised up whatever beam had been secured in place there. He then took a step back and kicked it with his other foot and this time it burst open and he limped into the darkness.

He was gone a short while before returning, shaking his head. "I lost him," he told Vincenzo. "A pity, he was probably the leader." He walked across to the men on the ground and kicked the first one he had felled. "No matter," he said. "This one here is still alive."

But Vincenzo the scribe looked at the way the man's head was twisted on his neck and stepped across and knelt down beside him. "I don't think he is," he said.

The Shadow Master looked down and kicked him again. "That wasn't meant to happen either," he said again. He shrugged and said, "Oh well, it can't be helped. We'll tell it better in the written version, eh?"

Then he bent down and took the mask off one of the men. "Do you recognize him?" he asked Vincenzo.

"No," he said. "And I don't recognize the mask either. It's not one I've seen before in the Floating City."

"They are probably mercenaries from one of the other city states," the Shadow Master said.

"What will we do with their bodies?" Vincenzo asked.

"We'll hide them," he said. "But not so well that the city guard won't find them. But long after we've gone, hmmm." Then he dragged the four bodies into a doorway and closed it on them, just as a small party of men walked into the square. There were also four of them, but they were dressed richly and Vincenzo recognized them all at once. He bowed while the Shadow Master nodded, and said, "Good day."

Two of the men didn't even pause in their conversations with each other, but the third regarded him and nodded back.

Vincenzo watched them depart and said to the Shadow Master, "Do you know who that was?"

"Tell me," he said.

"It was Signor Tradonico, one of the Council of Ten."

"Council of Nine, I believe," the Shadow Master said. "But we just prevented it from becoming the Council of Eight. Well done." And he clapped Vincenzo on the back.

"I don't think I did very much," Vincenzo said.

"Such a modest fellow," the Shadow Master said. "Now I believe we were on our way to visit Disdemona? Yes? Perhaps you could lead the way now and I'll just follow and enjoy the scenery."

"And I'd write that you tell me what is going to happen before it happens!"

XXIII

THE STORY OF ISABELLA

The Othmen envoy woke up slowly. He had been dreaming something about being a school child again, and discovering he was standing in the classroom with no pants on and all the children were laughing at him. It was most unsettling. He had not had that dream for many years.

He tossed and pushed his head deeper into the soft pillow, wishing to shake the dream from him fully before opening his eyes, as if it might somehow follow him into the waking world. When he did finally open his eyes it took him a moment to realize that he was not in his own bed. And then he remembered where he was. He sat up a little too quickly and felt his head protest. He put one hand to his forehead and winced. The sunlight was shining in with an intensity that hurt his brain as if it was boring through his eyes.

He shielded his gaze a little before realizing it was the light of late morning sunshine. He had slept very long. He turned his head a little to the side and winced. Too much wine again.

Then he looked at the space on the bed next to him. It was empty but bore the indent of where a woman had been sleeping, and still smelled of her scent. Then he looked down and saw that he was naked. And then he saw the old hag of a maid kneeling at the foot of the bed, trying most unsuccessfully to hide a smirk from her face.

He gathered the silken sheets about himself and glared at her. "What are you doing here? What do you want?" he demanded of her. And then, "And where is your lady?"

"My lady asked me tell you," the old woman said, looking down at her hands, "that when you awake you are to be escorted discreetly out the back door of the house."

The envoy glared at her harder and struggled out of bed, unsuccessfully trying to keep a grip on the smooth sheets. "I came in my ship," he croaked a little hoarsely.

"I am also to remind you that it is now my lady's ship, as is all the cargo on board." She tried, unsuccessfully, to keep her eyes low as she talked. He looked down again. His member had never looked so small and shrivelled. He had gone to bed with a proud stallion there between his legs waiting to impress the widow Montecchi with its magnificence, and now he found this old maid smirking at this aged donkey he now possessed. He grabbed hold of the sheets to cover himself again.

"Where is your mistress?" he demanded.

"She told me also to tell you that she had a most unenjoyable night and hoped never to be reminded of it again."

He felt himself reddening. "Who does she think I am?" he spluttered.

"Why the envoy of the Othmen," she said. "Everybody knows who you are."

The insolence of the old hag! If he had not been so speechless he would have struck her. But she rose to her feet, bowed a little and quickly left the room, saying, "I will wait outside. While you dress."

He fell back onto the bed and his head felt the worse for it. He suddenly understood what the message from the widow meant. If he wished to raise this with her, or accuse her of trickery, she would tell everyone in the city that he had failed to bed her. That he had fallen asleep naked in her bed and would not even wake up when she came to bed – most likely naked herself.

He felt tears of anger welling in his eyes. The woman was a witch, curse her. She didn't dare mock him in public. Did she? And then he thought, if she did, the Othmen spies would hear of it for sure. The thought of that made his member shrink even more. If they were to learn how he lost the ship, with so many treasures on board! He had loaded it up to impress her of his wealth. Now all gone. It would take months to rebuild such a fortune. The Othmen were generous, but did not suffer fools gladly. He had seen the way they both rewarded and punished.

He licked his dry lips and then picked up the pillow next to him and slapped it. As if it was the old hag. Or the widow. But that was all the violence he would be capable of for the moment. No, he thought, climbing out of bed and searching around for his clothes, it would be altogether better if word of this matter was never shared with anyone.

He went to the window and looked down in dismay, watching workers busily unloading his favourite ship. He ground his teeth and spat out the window. She had been too clever for him, but he would find a way to exact some vengeance in good time. Working for the Othmen had taught him a thousand ways to be cruel.

XXIV

THE STORY OF GIULIETTA

Romeo Cappalletti was in high spirits. The highest his close friend Marcuccio had seen him in for a few weeks. And that meant only one thing – a new love in his life. And that meant he was fair game for his torments.

The two men sat in one of the illegal dens where Othmen pipes were available for smoking that dark oily substance known as Othmen Dreams. The room had a low ceiling and the windows were darkened, the light being provided by a few stubs of candles on the tables. A low blanket of smoke hung throughout the room adding to the gloom.

The two young men shared a tankard of cheap wine, served by women with low-cut tops and wide hips. Marcuccio watched them carefully as they walked close to him, but Romeo paid them no heed. Clear confirmation that there was a new love in his life.

"So," said Marcuccio, "I've arranged a special banquet this evening in a private chamber, just for you and the Lady Rosaline and me and a woman of my choice."

Romeo looked at him and frowned. "You shouldn't have done so without consulting me."

"When does a friend need to consult to do a favour? It will give you and the Lady Rosaline a chance to spend some precious time alone. That's what you've been complaining about a lack of for the past month, isn't it?"

Romeo looked a little pained and took another puff on the pipe on the table. It was a tall brass device, like a large vase, with four snaking red tubes coming out of it, like some sea creature. Each of the tubes was for inhaling the simmering Othmen oil through the water in the base of the pipe. It bubbled softly as Romeo took a long breath in and slowly exhaled.

"Things are – complicated now," he told Marcuccio.

"Complicated? Marcuccio asked. "I don't understand. You are a man and she is a woman and let me see if I can recall how that works?" He made a circle of the index finger and thumb on one hand and raised his pointer finger on the other hand. He stared at them as if not understanding how they might fit together and waved his fingers around as if unable to connect them. "Am I doing something wrong here?"

Romeo rolled his eyes and took another puff on the pipe, the soft bubble sound his only response.

"Aha!" said Marcuccio, sticking his index finger into the circle made by his other fingers. "That's it! Now I remember. Do you remember too?"

"It's not that I don't appreciate your efforts," said Romeo, "but I am not in the mood for such an intimate dinner this evening."

"Not – in – the – mood?" asked Marcuccio. "Lay down and rest, I will fetch an apothecary. You are clearly very ill."

Romeo looked more pained and then said, in a soft voice, "I have met someone else."

"Aha!" said Marcuccio and slapped the table hard. "I knew it at once."

Romeo frowned. "So there is no meal organized for this evening with Rosaline?"

"No, no. I just wanted to hear you say it," said Marcuccio, laughing. "Oh dear, poor Romeo has another wench to try and win."

Romeo didn't share his mirth. "You don't understand. This time it's different."

"Yes, yes," said Marcuccio. "It's the same song every time. They are the fairest wench and the one your heart most desires until you bed them and then you lose interest."

"Not this time," said Romeo.

"How so?" asked Marcuccio. "No don't tell me, let me guess. Her bosoms are fairer than any other maiden you have seen. Wait, that was Lady Rosaline. It is her hair, it is soft and like a web of silk that you desire to get entrapped in. No, that was Lady Valeria. It is her smile and her lips. They desire to be kissed and you cannot wait to drink from them. Or was that the Lady Rosaline too?"

Romeo punched him hard on the arm. "You are a villain," he said, "to make so light of a friend's love so easily."

Marcuccio looked at his arm and said, "I think a gnat just bit me." Then he asked, "Who is she? Anyone I know, or perhaps anyone I've *known*!"

Romeo punched him on the arm again. Harder. This time Marcuccio pretended to fall to the floor as if he had been knocked unconscious, but he could not stop laughing, and picked himself up and dusted himself down. "The insects in here are something to be contended with," he said.

"You are the worst villain ever," Romeo said. "And to think I was foolish enough to ever consider you a friend!"

"A friend indeed," said Marcuccio. "Who else but a friend could advise you of the folly of your ways and expect to be thanked only with a beating?"

Romeo took another deep breath through the pipe. "We will be wed," he said.

Marcuccio's smile broadened even wider. "Wed? That is a statement you should be saving to try and convince her of your intents, not me."

"We will be wed," Romeo said again. "There is enchantment between us."

"Yes, Othmen enchantment," said Marcuccio.

Romeo shook his head. "I have it all planned out. We will

disguise ourselves as two lesser gentlemen, and make our way out
of the city, convincing the city guard we are merchants or some
such, and run away to live in some distant city such as Verona."

"As two gentlemen?" Marcuccio asked.

"We only need to disguise ourselves to get out of the city."

"I take it her parents don't approve of the match. Indeed, I
suspect her parents don't have the slightest idea of the match."

"No. I don't think they'd approve."

"Then who is she? My curiosity is aroused as much as your
appetites for a woman are clearly aroused."

But Romeo shook his head.

"Would I not know her?" Marcuccio asked, and then added, "In
the most gentlemanly of ways, of course."

"You know her," said Romeo and looked around the
room carefully.

"Then why not tell me her name?"

"It will do you no favours to know it," said Romeo.

Now Marcuccio finally stopped jesting. "She's married, then?"

"No."

"Betrothed to another?"

Romeo shrugged.

Marcuccio rubbed his chin and thought hard and then his jaw
dropped. "Oh no," he said. "What is her first name? Just tell me
the first name?"

"Giulietta," said Romeo softly.

Marcuccio took hold of a pipe and drew in deeply, causing the
water to bubble like a cauldron. "Dio mio!" he exclaimed finally,
sending a puff of thick smoke out of his lips into the air between
them. "You have a death wish. You will start a war between your
houses. You will bring ruin to the city's peace. You are mad."

"We will be wed," was all Romeo said.

XXV

ELSEWHERE IN THE FLOATING CITY

"I think you will be pleasantly surprised by our Rosa," Signora Polani said once more.

The two Seers, the younger of the remaining three pairs, sat as impassive as if their faces were masks. Yet despite the lack of response from them, Signora Polani kept fiddling with the locket round her neck and asking them repeated questions.

"Can you tell if a child has the gift just by looking at them? Oh, I asked that already, didn't I? It's just that we knew Rosa was special from a very early age." She leaned a bit closer as if to share a strict secret with them. "My husband was slow to acknowledge it, but as she got older it was more and more evident."

The male Seer looked at the locket in her fingers and noticed it contained a tiny portrait of a girl who was undoubtedly Rosa. He also hoped she had at least some of the gifts that her mother professed she might have. The last three families they had visited had proven singularly disappointing and one of the little girls was lucky to have survived. He suspected Signora Polani would not take it well if her daughter's test went the same way.

Finally Signor Polani arrived, leading a young girl. She seemed too young to be a possibility, as they knew the first signs of a person's gifts wouldn't begin appearing until a child entered maturity.

"How old is she?" the female Seer asked, looking at the child, but clearly not addressing her.

"Thirteen," said her mother.

"She appears younger."

"It is just that she is small. But she is very strong and resilient."

We shall see, thought the male Seer.

He stood up and went across to the girl. She had quite large eyes and dark hair tied back behind her head. She wore a very fine dark blue dress, woven through with white lace. And she did not step back nor flinch when he placed a hand on her head. He felt the tell-tale tingle beneath his fingers. She had the gift, undoubtedly. But to what extent was the question?

"What is your name?" he asked her.

"Rosa Polani," she said.

"Do you know why we're here?" he asked her.

She nodded her head.

"Are you afraid of us?" he asked.

She shook her head.

He almost smiled. Almost.

"Well, then," he said. "Come and sit over here, Rosa and we shall see just how strong your gift is."

She followed him obediently and sat on the chair that had been placed between the two Seers.

"You have the power over water, yes?" the male Seer asked her.

She nodded.

"Good," he said. "Now we need you to sit very still. All right?"

She nodded again.

The female Seer with a basket at her feet, lifted out a canvas bag. Without saying anything she placed it over the child's head, tying it tightly around her neck.

Signora Polani's fingers went frantic, fiddling with the locket. "What are you doing?" she asked. "This won't hurt her will it?"

"We are doing what we need to do," the male Seer said. "If you think it might distress you to watch, then I advise you to leave us to do our work. We will call you when it is done."

She chewed her lip and shook her head a little. She was determined to be at least a little bit as brave as her daughter. "I will stay," she said in a thin voice.

The female Seer nodded and lifted the bag open at the top, showing its shape. It was more a tube than a bag, Rosa's parents could see, with a small opening at one end to be placed over the child's head and a larger opening at the top.

"Now the water," the male Seer said.

Signor Polani clapped his hands and two servants who had been standing outside the door came in with large pitchers of water on their shoulders. The female Seer indicated the top of the bag and the servant hesitated. He looked to Signor Polani, who nodded his head. The servant started pouring the water into the bag while the male Seer held it open at the top.

"Don't be afraid, dear," Signora Polani said to her daughter, although it was probably more spoken to herself. He daughter didn't respond. She clearly wasn't afraid. The male Seer looked down into her eyes and she met his gaze. Could she be the one they were searching for?

He softened a little and said, "This will get uncomfortable for you, but we sometimes need to do that to trigger your gifts more."

"She can do wonderful tricks with a cup of water," her mother said. "She can make whirlpools appear in them even."

Both Seers ignored her, they had seen many children who could do party tricks, but were looking for something more. They watched the water fill up close to her mouth and then cover it. Rosa breathed through her nose, never taking her eyes off the male Seer. Yes, perhaps she was going to pleasantly surprise them as her mother had said, he thought.

The female Seer then indicated to the second servant to start adding his water into the bag and he stepped forward and poured it in. The water splashed noisily and quickly filled up the bag over her head.

Rosa began struggling now. And Signora Polani tried to step

forward and help her, but the female Seer held out one hand to warn her back. This was the moment. The point of urgency. The water might dissipate outside the bag. Might suddenly stand off from her head inside the bag, leaving her room to breathe. Might even just disappear entirely. Well, never entirely. It would reappear somewhere else. In the canal. In the kitchen. In the courtyard.

The male Seer willed her powers to do something miraculous, but Rosa lifted her hands to her neck scrabbling frantically with the cords there. Just a moment longer, thought the male Seer. She would astound them all. But Rosa tried to stand, held down by the weight of the water and started scrabbling in panic. He could have sworn he could even hear her shrieking, even though her head was submerged under water. Perhaps just a moment longer though. It might still be possible.

But with one deft move, the female Seer reached out and pulled a cord, opening the bag around Rosa's neck, spilling all the water over her fine gown. She gasped loudly for breath, panting, wet hair hanging down around her face, like a half-drowned cat.

The male Seer looked at her in regret, as if she had personally let him down, and then turned to her mother and father. "I'm sorry," was all he said. Then he began gathering up their things. There would still be time to visit one or two more children before the day ended.

XXVI

THE STORY OF DISDEMONA

Otello felt that his wife was so close he could reach out one hand and close it around her slim white neck. She sat in the garden below and he stood silently on the balcony above, half hidden by vines that wove their way thickly around a stone pillar.

Disdemona was talking with Captain Casio and was clearly enjoying herself. Greatly. She even blushed once or twice and pulled the strawberry-embroidered kerchief out of her bosom and hid her face behind it. Otello felt himself reddening in the face likewise, but not with embarrassment – with rage.

He wished he could fly down close to them, as small as a wasp, and overhear what it was they talked of. Surely it was something bawdy to evoke such emotion from her. But then he felt rather he should be a hawk and settle on the branches nearby so that he could then swoop down and pluck both their tongues out if it was confirmed they were engaged in love banter.

She laughed again, throwing her head back and letting the silver pearls of her voice spread over the garden. Otello clenched his fist tightly by his side. That was a laugh he had observed many times when he first used to watch her with her friends and had become enraptured in her. But it was not a laugh that she had ever shared with him as her husband.

Was that all it took to win a woman over? The ability to make her laugh? Would a woman really be more willing to share her bed with a clown than a great warrior? He would crush them both for this.

Then he watched his wife stand and turn to take up a white flower and smell it. Her hands were so gentle with it. The captain watched her for a moment and then turned to gaze up to the sky, leaving her with the pleasure of the flower. And at that moment Otello was filled with doubt. It was the way she was with him. Gentle and attentive.

What was he really witnessing here? Love play or just friendly banter? He knew the captain had a quick wit, as did his wife. They enjoyed making word games with each other. He'd long known that. Was that enough to prove she was being unfaithful to him?

But the captain was also a bawdy devil and loved to make improper suggestions. Had he been making them now to her? And was she encouraging him in it? He watched as she now plucked the flower from its stem and began to remove the petals one by one, as if needing help to make a difficult decision.

Otello found he was holding his breath, as much as if he might be watching the tide of a battle, knowing it could turn either way, for him or against him. What would Disdemona decide at the last petal? Could he know it from her face?

Then he heard a servant's footsteps approaching and turned his head, placing a finger to his lips. The servant stopped at once. Otello beckoned him closer and the man stepped carefully, as if there might be a deadly serpent underfoot.

"What is it?" the Moor hissed.

"My lord, there are two men at the door asking to see your lady."

The Moor's eyes narrowed. "Are there indeed?"

"Yes," said the servant. "Two."

Otello looked back to the garden, but saw he had missed Disdemona reaching the last petal. Instead he saw her turn and throw the empty stalk at the captain, who made as if it was a deadly spear entering his heart, and then they both laughed heartily.

"I will rather see these two men," Otello said and pushed the servant on ahead of him.

He made his way to the ground floor and first took a long look through the spy hole in the wall before suddenly throwing open the door. The foppish scribe stood there, surprised, with an awkward smile on his face.

"I was told there were two gentlemen at the door," said the Moor, glaring at the scribe.

"Yes," said Vincenzo, and turned to look to the Shadow Master, who had been standing behind him as the door had started to open – but was now nowhere to be seen.

"Then why do I see only one?" asked the Moor gruffly.

"Well, it's just that... I mean..." Vincenzo looked around blankly and then back at the Moor's steely gaze. It pinned him like nails to a cross, and he started stuttering, as he always did when the Moor confronted him over anything, staring at him as if he was guilty of some crime that he did not even realize he was guilty of until the Moor glared at him. "He was just... right here..."

The Moor let his eyes half close, in a way that made Vincenzo feel more uncertain and vulnerable than when they were wide open. "I suppose you have come to interview the Lady Disdemona yet again for that never-ending history her father commissioned," Otello stated.

"Well, yes, if it's not too inconvenient, I mean..." Vincenzo began.

"It is most inconvenient," Otello said. "My lady is greatly preoccupied. As am I. We have no time for your history today."

"Ah, I see," said Vincenzo. "Then perhaps another time, if we could set an appointment–"

"Yes. Another time," said Otello, and closed the door before Vincenzo had even finished speaking. He blinked and looked around himself once more before stepping back from the house and then turned to return to his own quarters. The Shadow Master seemed to detach himself from a wall and fall in beside him.

"That didn't go quite as expected," he said. "You could have been a little more assertive I think."

"Where did you go?" Vincenzo asked. "You were there one minute and then gone."

The Shadow Master waved a hand in the air. "It would not do for the Moor to meet me yet," he said. "That time will come."

"But it was fine for me to be humiliated in front of the Moor?" Vincenzo asked.

The Shadow Master waved a hand in the air again.

"You dismiss me. You drag me around the city. You promise me I will have control over how things turn out, but I do not even have control over where I am and what I am doing? Perhaps my time would be better spent sitting at my desk and writing. I could write something to save Disdemona from peril, yes?"

"No. We have to let this play out. It is vital."

"Then how will we warn Lady Disdemona of these dangers that surround her?" Vincenzo asked.

"What would you suggest if you were writing this scene?"

"We could wait for the Moor to leave the house and then try knocking on the door again," the scribe said.

"A splendid plan," said the Shadow Master, clapping him heavily on the back. "We'll make something of you yet. Now where do you suggest we wait?"

"Perhaps down the street a bit," Vincenzo said. "In one of the taverns there. We could keep an eye on the door without being seen."

"Brilliant," said the Shadow Master and clapped him on the back again. "Why didn't I think of that? Lead on." The two men walked down the slick cobbled street and the Shadow Master looked briefly back over his shoulder as a spy hole in the wall of Otello's house snicked closed.

"And the game is in play," he said with a smile, as Vincenzo led him into the tavern.

XXVII

THE STORY OF ISABELLA

Isabella Montecchi was feeling very pleased with herself. She had been looking over the ledgers that her accountants had made up for her, detailing the profits she had gained from the Othmen envoy's ship and cargo. The challenge for her now was whether she would make an offer to sell it back to him so that when his Othmen masters demanded to know if it was true that he had been tricked by a woman, he could deny it.

She would dearly like to see him on the receiving end of some Othmen cruelty, but suspected that they would pay him with exceedingly brutal wages. His humiliation might be payment enough for now. She lifted out a single sheet of paper and began writing a note to him, inviting him to come to her house to negotiate the purchase of a ship with cargo that had come into her possession.

She was trying hard to keep a sarcastic tone out of her finely formed letters when her handmaiden knocked lightly on the door. "Yes?" she asked, looking up.

"There is a man come to see you," the handmaiden reported.

"Who is he?" she asked.

"A sea captain," she said.

"What does he want?"

"He said he has a business offer for you."

"Where is he from?"

"He is a native of the Floating City and says any other sea captain will vouch for his name, and is considered a lucky man." Then she added, as it was needed to be said, "He is aged."

Isabella knew that a sea captain's life was such that any who was old enough to be considered aged was a lucky man.

She sighed. "All right. Show him in then."

She turned back to the letter and added a line, describing how fine the ship was and that she had hardly had the opportunity to use it, when there was a tap at the door again. The handmaiden stood there and indicated to the sea captain that he could enter her rooms.

He came in slowly, and the handmaiden followed and stood just inside the doorway behind him. She watched the way he stopped and admired her mistress, clearly impressed with her beauty. She had seen that reaction on many men's faces who had come expecting to find a widow confused by business matters and instead found a lady of considerable bearing and beauty who had a sharp eye and sharper mind.

"Can I offer you refreshment?" she asked the man and the handmaiden couldn't help smirking a little as the captain became a little tongue-tied.

He recovered a little and said, "Captain Domenico Selvo at your service." And he bowed formally.

"Please have a seat," Isabella said and watched as the man sat down. He had grey streaks in his dark beard and hair, and could be considered a little short and stout, but seemed to have an honest face.

She could see he was ill at ease and said, "Perhaps we should get right to the point?"

"Yes," he said, fidgeting with a gold chain he had tied to his jacket. "I have a ship."

She waited for him to go on, but he did not. "Are you in need of employment?" she asked. "Are you seeking a contract?"

"Ah, yes. A contract," he said.

"Tell me about your ship."

"She's a fine vessel. *The Windchaser*. Do you know her?"

"I'm sorry, I do not, though undoubtedly my late husband would have known her."

"Yes," the captain said. "He would have known her. And me."

Mention of her husband seemed to make him feel awkward and he fiddled with the chain again for a moment.

"Where have you sailed?" Isabella asked him, to put him a little more at ease.

"Ah – where haven't I sailed?" he said. "I've travelled all the shores of the inland seas and have crossed to the desert lands and all the Graecian islands.

"And the lands of the Othmen?" she asked him.

"Once," he said. "Many, many years ago. And I've no strong desire to return there, I don't mind saying."

She nodded her head. So he was brave but clearly not foolhardy, and did not rely overly on his luck. He could be a useful man to employ. And it would please her other captains to think they might be able to share some of his luck.

"Do you have a proposal for me, or are you waiting for an offer from me?" she asked.

Now he looked even more awkward. "Perhaps…" he said, then trailed off.

"Yes?" she asked.

"I think I should make the proposal," he said.

"Then go ahead," she stated, spreading her hands wide.

He cleared his throat and said once more, "I have a ship."

She nodded her head once and then suddenly understood what he meant.

"What have you heard?" she asked him.

"Your offer," he said, looking down at his feet.

She closed her eyes. "Tell me what you have heard," she said softly.

"That – um – that a man might win your hand if he puts up a ship of cargo as bounty and can – um – spend a night with you and – um…"

She held up her hand and then opened her eyes. "You don't need to go on," she said. "And who has said this of me?"

"The Othmen envoy. He has said you are keen to be wed again, and miss the company of a husband. He is telling all the sea captains around the city."

Isabella wanted to put her head into her hands, but kept her head straight, looking coldly at the aged captain.

"My hand and my fortune for a night of pleasure, yes?"

He fiddled with the gold chain again. "Yes." He looked up with a hopeful smile.

"And your ship will be forfeit if not?"

"Yes," he said, with a tone in his voice that suggested he knew that would never happen. She reached out one hand and scrunched the letter she had been writing up into a small ball as hard as the sudden chill stone in her heart. She smiled to the captain and said to her handmaiden, "Captain Selvo will be staying the night. Please bring us some wine."

XXVIII

ELSEWHERE IN THE FLOATING CITY

The Shadow Master had insisted they sit at the back of the tavern, in the darkened corners, which Vincenzo said made no sense. How would they see Otello leaving his house if they could not see its door?

"But neither can its door see us," the Shadow Master said enigmatically and asked his companion to sit beside him and order them two cups of cheap wine.

"Wouldn't you prefer a more enjoyable wine?" Vincenzo asked.

"This is better," he said. "We won't be tempted to drink it and no one will think anything of it when we leave the two cups untouched.

"Why should we leave them untouched?" asked Vincenzo.

"Just a sip then," said the Shadow Master as a waitress came by and Vincenzo ordered the wine. She brought it back in two battered metal cups. Vincenzo looked to the Shadow Master, but he made no effort to pay the girl, and so he reached into his pouch and grudgingly gave her two copper coins.

"Cheers," said the Shadow Master and lifted his cup to his lips. He took a sip and pulled a face. "Splendid," he said. "It tastes like goat's piss."

Vincenzo took a sip of his own cup and didn't seem as bothered by it. "So that implies you know what goat's piss tastes like," he told his new companion. The Shadow Master rewarded him with a rare smile. "Yes. I do. It tastes just like this." He set his cup on the table and looked at Vincenzo carefully. "Tell me about yourself," he said.

"What is there to tell?" Vincenzo said.

"Everybody has a story worth telling," said the Shadow Master. "And often an untold story that nobody has ever heard. What's yours?"

"I still contend that there's not much to tell," Vincenzo protested.

"Where were you born?" the Shadow Master asked him.

"Padua," he said. "On the mainland."

The Shadow Master nodded. "Tell me about it."

"I can't remember it. I was orphaned when I was young. Plague."

"Let me guess," said the Shadow Master. "Orphanage. Religious education. Turned out at twelve when you elected not to take vows. Itinerant scribe. Got an apprenticeship somewhere and finally citizenship on the floating island."

Vincenzo paused for a moment. Remembering this, but also remembering the vision of having been brought to the city by a hooded stranger as a very young boy. He closed his eyes briefly until the memory of the vision had passed. "Mostly," he said. "But I did take the vows. Or attempted it. I found it wasn't for me though."

"A lack of belief or not convinced of the dogma?" the Shadow Master asked.

Vincenzo looked pained, as if his companion were opening wounds he'd rather not have exposed. "More a feeling, or a belief, that there was something bigger in the world."

"Bigger than religion?" the Shadow Master asked.

"Yes," said Vincenzo eventually. Then, "But you make me sound like a heretic. It's not that I reject religion, it's just that I have this undeniable feeling that there is a lot more to the world around us."

The Shadow Master raised his cup again. "I'll drink to that," he said. "Even this goat's piss." He took a small sip and grimaced again.

"And what about your story?" Vincenzo asked, feeling a little bolder, having shared his story and consumed half the cup of wine.

"Another time," said the Shadow Master. "It's time to go. And quietly."

Vincenzo turned his head to look to where the Shadow Master was watching. Six men had just stepped into the tavern. All Otello's men. And they were clearly looking for somebody.

"Come," he said, taking Vincenzo by the arm. "We will slip away into the darkness like belief itself slips away."

But Vincenzo was clumsy getting up from the table and knocked over his chair. Then he stopped to pick it up. One of the guardsmen looked up at the movement and spotted him. "Uh-oh," said Vincenzo.

"Quickly," said the Shadow Master and half led, half pushed him out the back door of the tavern, past rows of hanging fowls and the putrid over-filled privy. The path led to a canal's edge though, and without a boat there was nowhere to go.

"Uh-oh," said Vincenzo again.

The Shadow Master looked left and right and then grabbed Vincenzo tightly around the neck and spun him into the lower corner of the stone wall beside them, crouching low and drawing his cloak around them. Vincenzo tried to protest that the guardsmen would see them, but the Shadow Master now had his palm tightly over the scribe's mouth and hissed into his ear, "Not a sound and not a movement or you will likely be run through with a sword. Close your eyes and think you are stone. Believe you are stone!"

Vincenzo tried to protest again, but the Shadow Master hissed again, "Your life depends on it."

Vincenzo did as he was bidden and closed his eyes tight and tried to imagine that he was stone. The cloak was incredibly dark, and he could almost imagine they were safe in the darkness except for the sound of approaching feet.

Two guardsmen stepped out onto the worn stone pavers right

beside them and one said, "You sure you saw someone?"

"I'm certain," he said. "Two men, just as they were described to us. They fled out the back this way."

"Hmmm," said the other. "They must have had a boat waiting here and made a very quick getaway."

The other stepped right to the edge of the canal. "No boat is that quick."

"Then where are they?"

"Well perhaps... No. I don't know."

"Well I know one thing. The Moor won't be happy that you let them escape."

"You know," said the other guard. "Perhaps I was mistaken after all."

"So you didn't see anyone?"

"Well perhaps I only saw them because I wanted to see them."

The other fellow sniffed in a big noisy gob and spat into the canal's water. "Well I didn't see them. And I only believe in what I can see."

"I'll join you in a minute," said the first guardsman and Vincenzo heard him shuffling his feet and then start pissing into the canal.

Then the Shadow Master slowly unwound his cloak and just briefly Vincenzo could have sworn that its material was made of small ceramic bricks like the wall beside them, but then it was suddenly a black cloak again. He blinked his eyes and reached out one hand to touch it, but the Shadow Master stepped away and soundlessly struck the guardsman from behind. He barely seemed to touch him and the man slumped to the ground. The Shadow Master reached into his own garments and pulled out one of the white masks of the men who had attacked them earlier. He laid it on the ground beside the unconscious man and trod on it so that it split.

"What are you doing?" Vincenzo asked.

"Creating a belief," the Shadow Master said. "Come. We still have much to do."

"And much explaining I am still owed," Vincenzo said.

XXIX

THE STORY OF GIULIETTA

Romeo may have passed for a smuggler, dressed in black, with a black cloak and black hood, if not for the expensive black ornate mask he wore. He stood at the prow of a small black-painted gondola – the type that were commonly used by smugglers – and guided it stealthily along the dark sides of the canal. His own secret cargo was his lust and desire for Giulietta Cappalletti, which would only be apparent if any customs man or guardsman chose to search inside his trousers.

He was pleased to find the canals near deserted of other craft, and mocked the masses for their ignorance and superstitions. As far as he was concerned, monsters in the canals were about as likely as the stories that he had heard about the Mongol princess who could piss diamonds or the elixir of youth that could reverse a man's ageing.

He would have added the story of the talking Moorish cat – but you could never tell with cats.

He made his way, not a little awkwardly and with more splashing than he'd prefer, along the canal, and now that he could see the Cappalletti palazzo he slowed down and brought the gondola closer to the canal's edge. He was starting to find a grudging admiration for the smugglers he often dealt with, and the way they made their small boats move so silently and rapidly.

He approached the palazzo close in the shadows where the moonlight did not fall and brought his boat to a stop under one of the balconies. Now, he thought, as young men with wealth have always thought, good fortune would reward him for being – well – just for being himself. He sat down and waited a full five minutes before becoming impatient and wondering if he should risk climbing up and looking through one of the windows to find Giulietta's chamber.

And then, as improbable as it might seem to anybody not young and wealthy, a balcony door opened above him and he heard a person step out onto the balcony and look up at the moon. He grasped the slippery stone walls and pushed the gondola back a little way, bumping on the stones.

The person above leaned over the balcony to see what the sound was and he was surprised to see it was Giulietta's mother, her face illuminated by the light behind her. She peered into the blackness, but obviously saw nothing as she soon disappeared. Then he heard her call to her daughter, "Giulietta, come and see the moon."

"Why should I care for the moon?" he heard her reply from inside the building.

"It is beautiful," her mother said.

"More beautiful than me?"

"Of course not. It is different."

"I'm busy," Giulietta protested. "I've seen the moon before and I've no doubt I'll see it again."

"Then just come and talk to me," her mother said.

"What is there to talk about?"

"So much."

"We can talk tomorrow."

He heard her mother sigh wearily and then step in from the balcony. Giulietta and her mother continued talking, but now that their voices were not raised he could not make out the words so clearly. He pondered a moment and decided to risk it and, tying the gondola to a vine on the stonework, he lifted another rope out of the vessel and threw it up onto the balcony's edge. The anchor struck the ironwork there with a clang, but nobody seemed to notice. He waited a moment longer and then drew himself up the rope.

It was harder work than he imagined, getting over the balcony's edge, and he scraped the skin on his leg and swore softly, hoping it was not bleeding. He found the glass-paned balcony doors had been closed and inside the room beyond them he could see Giulietta and her mother. It was a sitting room or some such and his love had her arms crossed and was stomping her foot, clearly in disagreement with her mother over something. It made him smile to watch her.

Now was the moment he knew that her mother would leave the chamber and then he could knock on the glass to attract Giulietta. But, surprisingly, Signora Cappalletti did not. She remained seated while Giulietta stormed out of the room.

Romeo stood there, locked out on the balcony, waiting for Giulietta to come back. But, inexplicably, she did not. Finally her mother rose and blew out the candles and left, closing the door to the room.

Romeo was perplexed. This wasn't how it should have happened. He was just readying himself to descend back down the rope, without grazing his other leg on the ironwork of the balcony, when he heard the door on the next balcony along opening. He knelt down quickly, peeping between the metal bars of the railings to see who it was. This was it, he knew. It would be Giulietta. That would be her chamber and now she was coming out for some fresh air.

He lifted his head a little but pulled it back down when he saw an elderly maid in her nightdress standing there. He watched in fascination as she clasped a hand tightly to her breast and seemed to be praying to the moon. It took him a moment to understand, she was probably praying for love. And he remembered a story he had been told about a young nobleman who had been taken captive by an old maid and chained up in her attic bedchamber, where she had pleasured herself with him three or four times a day until the young man was nothing but a wasted shell.

He lay down lower on the balcony stones and did not move until she, too, had returned inside the building and closed the door. He climbed to his feet and exhaled. The night was certainly not going as he had planned.

He turned his head as a cloud moved across the face of the moon and he smelled rain coming. That was all he needed. He climbed back over the balcony, only skinning himself a little this time and had both hands on the rope, when he heard the balcony door behind him open.

"Merde," he muttered. He hoped it wasn't her father this time, for he was hanging there defencelessly. He leaned in close to the wall hoping his black clothes would shield him, but his foot suddenly slipped on the stonework. He scrabbled frantically before regaining his footing.

"Who is that?" an alarmed voice behind him asked.

He turned his head around awkwardly to see who it was and heard Giulietta ask, "Romeo? Is that you?"

He smiled. "Giulietta," he said, trying to swivel around without falling from the rope.

"What are you doing here?" she asked.

He caught a glimpse of her in her nightgown. A green silk dress with a red ribbon at the neck that would surely come undone with the most gentle of tugs. His feet slipped again and he scrabbled once more for a footing.

"I had to see you," he said. "I need to talk to you."

"I've been thinking of you ever since the ball," she said.

He felt the pressure in his pants increasing. "And I of you."

"But it is dangerous to come here. If my father or his men catch you they will seek to kill you."

"It was worth the risk," he said. "I have come to ask you a question."

"And my answer is yes, whatever the question is," she said.

"Anything?" he asked.

"Yes, anything," she answered in a cheeky voice. "Ask me to kiss you and I will. Ask me to open my bodice to you and I will. Ask me to touch you in intimate places and I will."

Romeo scrabbled madly at the slippery stones again, coming very close to falling into the dark water below. "I will ask you all that and more," he said, "but first I will ask if you will run away with me."

Giulietta was quiet a moment, as if weighing up the question. "To marry me?" she asked.

"Yes," he said. "I want to live with you as man and wife somewhere where nobody knows us as Montecchi or Cappalletti."

"Then yes," she said unhesitatingly.

"We shall have only ourselves as company," he said.

"Except for the servants and retainers we hire," she said.

"We shall not be wealthy," he said.

"Except for what jewels I steal away with," she said.

"But we shall be happy."

"No one will have ever known such happiness," she replied.

Romeo turned his body around on the rope and saw Giulietta leaning over the balcony towards him, her nightdress surely a little more opened than it had been a moment before.

"I will make the plans and send a secret message to you," he said.

"What will it say?"

"I will use the word *moonlight* in it," he said.

"And I will wait for it and think of you in the moonlight…" She reached out one hand to him and he took one hand off the rope and reached out to her. "…whenever I touch myself," she said.

Romeo's feet slipped again and his single hand was not enough to stop him from falling. But as he fell she called his name and leaned out over the balcony. His hand caught hers and for a moment they were both falling. But then it was as if the moonlight solidified around them to hold them in the air, and the waters of the canal beneath them rose up, lifting the gondola to catch Romeo. Then their hands parted and Giulietta was standing on the balcony, breathing heavily and her knees trembling, and Romeo was lying in the boat breathless, drifting away on the current of the resettling waters.

XXX

ELSEWHERE IN THE FLOATING CITY

"It's a catastrophe!" said Signor Orseolo, throwing his hands into the air. "There must be something you can do to save me."

The two Seers known as the Winter Seers had come at his summoning, for as one of the richest merchants in the city he was a benefactor of anyone who lived off the city's purse. They arrived, hand in hand, to find him standing ankle-deep in water in the ground floor of his Palazzo. The two Seers looked at each other uneasily. They had heard that some of the poorer parts of the city were experiencing flooding, such as the tradesmen's ghetto and the immigrant islands – but there had not been any sign that the richer parts of the city were being affected.

"You must have a spell to hold back the waters," Signor Orseolo said, pleading with them. There were thick carpets underfoot that squelched like seaweed when they stepped on them. They would be smelly ruins when they were retrieved.

"Of course, of course," said the female Seer, placing her free hand on Signor Orseolo's shoulder. "We shall do what we can."

"Is it an Othmen attack?" Signor Orseolo asked, worriedly.

"No, no," said the male Seer. "There has been an unseasonably high tide that is affecting parts of the city." He looked to his wife to confirm the lie. She nodded her head. "We can of course turn back the waters here. It is a minor thing."

Signor Orseolo seemed pleased to hear that. The female Seer smiled. But her husband could see it was strained. They could not be doing this for long. The city was starting to sink and they were too few to sustain the energies needed to keep it afloat. But they could at least hold back the fear.

"Come," said the female Seer, taking Signor Orseolo by the arm. "Return to the upper floors and leave us to our work. We shall not take long."

He looked back at them with a look on his face that clearly showed he wanted to stay and watch, but the male Seer shook his head just a little. Signor Orseolo then bowed to them both and squelched his way across the room to the marble staircase.

After he had gone the male Seer led his wife across to a large candlestick standing on the floor and reaching head height, and brought it across to the centre of the room. "Fire," he said.

"Water," said his wife, pointing at their feet. He smiled and reached into his garment pockets with his free hand. He brought out a handful of dirt and sprinkled it at their feet. "Earth," he said.

"And air," said his wife, blowing hard on the candles. Instead of extinguishing, they glowed brighter, and then she took the candlestick holder and plunged it into the water at their feet. It entered the water with a slight hiss, but the candles kept burning.

She looked up into her husband's eyes. He was ready. But before they even began the incantation the waters started draining out of the room. The Seers looked at each other in confusion, then she was pulling her husband to the doorway. They hurried out, watching the water run up the few stairs there, across the piazza and into the canal.

They both turned their heads, this way and that, looking into the darkness. "There," she said. Her husband spun to look. He could see the fading glow of silver light, over the rooftops, like concentrated moonlight, barely half a league away.

"It is them," she said. "It has to be."

"We must find them," said her husband. "They are more

powerful than we dared hope."

"Hurry," she said, but he was already leading her across to the canal edge where their boat remained. They stepped in quickly and told their oarsman to make haste in the direction of the fading glow. He pushed the gondola off at once, the waters swirling around them, still running out from the palazzo, drawing them along a little. It was as if the waters were heading in the direction of the glow as well.

The male Seer was the first to lower his gaze and note the strange behaviour of the water. Thus he was the first one to see the large eyes rise from the dark water beside them, followed by the upper body of the Othmen creature.

XXXI

THE STORY OF DISDEMONA

Otello was in a foul mood, his captain could see, and he suspected it was going to get fouler before the night was done. He had already had a report from the guardsman who had been sent to the tavern to find the man who had accompanied the scribe to ask about his wife. He told how he had been attacked outside the tavern and left unconscious. The guardsman described how he had fought bravely to defend himself against a gang that had dropped from the rooftops and managed to snatch the mask off one of them before they overwhelmed him. He produced the cracked and broken mask as evidence.

Then Otello had inspected the dead men found in a building, with same masks. He wanted answers of his men that none could give him.

"Who were these masked men? Why could no one identify any of them? If they had already assassinated one of the Council of Ten and attacked one of his guardsmen, who had killed them?"

And over and over in his own mind, and what did his wife Disdemona have to do with it all?

The only clue they had been able to find was a tattoo on one of the dead men's arms. The mark of the Guild, the society that serviced the apothecaries of the city and traded in secret potions and rare herbs and metals, and smuggled as much as members of the thieves' quarter.

"We are going to the island of the Guild," he ordered. "Gather men and gather arms."

His men were not happy with the order. The Guild were dangerous men, possessed of charms that could protect them from ordinary weapons. They could dispense invisible clouds of poisons that could make a man fall asleep and wake up an old man. Or he might go blind on the spot. Or his manhood might turn black and fall off.

But they were more afraid of Otello's temper. Grudgingly they boarded several dark gondolas and set off across the canals. Captain Casio led in one boat and Otello in another, with Ensign Ipato at his ear.

"Is it wise to bring Captain Casio on this trip, my lord?" he whispered into his general's ear.

"Why?"

"A difficult choice, I admit," said the ensign. "But I have heard that he has contacts in the Guild. Perhaps he knows more than he is allowing."

"Do you think I should have left him behind?"

The ensign sucked in his teeth. "Also a difficult decision. I think you might watch him more carefully to discover if he is with you or not with you."

Otello said nothing.

"Tell me, my lord, did he ask you whether he should stay behind and guard your lady?"

Otello was slow to answer. "He did."

The ensign nodded. "And we are approaching a dangerous quarter that might be a trap set against us?"

"I have considered the possibility."

The ensign nodded again and said in a lower voice, "It is just a passing thought, my lord, but one that might need to be spoken – and then forgotten if you thought it of no worth – but who would gain if you were killed in such an ambush?"

"Who indeed?" asked the Moor in a bear's growl of a voice.

"It is not for me to say," said the ensign. "Forget I had ever spoken." He took a half step away and then added, "But I do have a feeling that we are suddenly pawns on a large chessboard, being played."

The Moor said nothing else and did not turn his head away from the Guild island ahead of them in the darkness, except to once or twice look across at the boat beside them with his captain in it.

The boats reached the island with difficulty as the waters seemed to be running strangely against them. They tied up silently at a partially submerged landing and the men climbed out and made their way up the few steps to assemble in the dark shadow of some building. "No noise," hissed Otello. "Captain, you will lead."

The man bowed his acknowledgment and, bent low, he led the men in single file along an alleyway, headed towards a house that had previously been identified as a haven for Guildsmen who needed to stay hidden. But tonight they would be found.

The captain reached the house and Otello could see there was a light inside, indicating somebody was still awake. The captain signalled to the men to form a half-circle around the door and be ready. He then stepped up close and rapped three times, then once, then two times on the door. There was no response from inside. Otello felt uneasy and glanced around at the buildings that surrounded them. A perfect place for crossbowmen to shoot at them.

Suddenly a small barred window in the door slid open and a man hissed something in a tongue Otello did not understand. The captain replied – a single word – and the man slammed the window shut and called out to those inside.

"Break it in!" commanded Otello. Two of his men stepped forward with axes, but Otello said, "No. Too slow," as he snatched one of the axes and jammed it under the base of the door and prised. The door rose up and lifted off its hinges, tumbling inside, the lock side still fastened to the door jamb.

The Moor led his men into the house and received a crossbow arrow directly into his chest for his troubles. The very tip of it pierced his armour and reached his chest, but no more. A little higher and it might have hit him in the neck. "Take them alive," he roared and was in the thick of it with his men, tumbling over beds and kicking in doors and wrestling men to the ground.

They rounded up six in total, including the man who had been armed with the crossbow. They sat sullenly on the floor, their arms bound behind their backs. Otello stood before them and said, "We have only come for information."

"They will die before they give up any information," the captain said. "They have sworn an oath on it."

Otello turned and glared at him. "You do not need to remind them of it," he said. "They can make up their own minds." Then he turned to them. "I do not want you to betray your guild. I just want you to tell me about the men who wear these." And he cast one of the white grinning masks to the floor in front of them. He threw a gold ducat next to it. "Consider it a business transaction."

The guildsmen all stared at the mask and Otello could see recognition in their eyes. One of the men spat on the mask though, showing there was clearly no love between the Guild and the masked assassins. Or perhaps that was just what he wanted them to believe.

"Can anyone tell me where I might find the men who wear this mask?" Otello asked.

None of the men said anything. Otello stared at them and then said to his men, "Search the house for illegal goods."

His men went back to turning over furniture and opening cupboards and came back with an array of vials and bags and several intricate small brass machines.

"What are these?" the ensign asked.

"Othmen devices," said Otello. "Used by Othmen spies."

"Or just those that trade with the Othmen perhaps," said the captain.

Otello turned to him and indicated that he should remain silent. The captain was holding one of the Othmen brass objects and he offered it to Otello. He took it and turned it over in his hands. It seemed to be a ball of intricate cogs and hidden blades.

He pressed a button on it and curved blades rose out of the sphere.

"Dangerous," he said.

"It might be poisoned," cautioned his ensign.

Otello dropped it at his feet by the prisoners and watched as one of the men pulled his legs a little away from it.

"But I suspect these vials are more dangerous," said the ensign. He knelt down beside the six captured men and said, "I have heard it said that the Guild can provide a potion that will make a woman lose her head and give her body and heart to the man who administers the potion. Is that true?"

None of the men looked up.

"I have heard it is as common as the poisons and drugs you sell to make a man lose his mind," the ensign said.

Still none of the men looked up.

"I have heard it said–" began the ensign.

"They will not talk," interrupted the captain.

Otello turned on him. "I would rather hear that from their lips than yours," he said gruffly.

"I am just telling what I know," he said.

"Again, I would rather hear what they know."

His captain bowed and stepped back. Otello stood motionless but the muscles on his neck twitched violently. He had a sour taste in his mouth as if there really were poisons in the air that were trying to infect him.

"We have learned all we will learn here tonight," he said finally.

"What of these men?" asked his captain.

"Leave them." He led his men to the doorway, not noticing the ensign slip the vials into his tunic. He paused as he stepped over the broken door and glanced back at the six men tied up on the floor, still not looking up to meet his eyes. They knew something he needed to know. He was certain of it. But if they would not tell him, he would leave a message for the Guild of the price of keeping secrets. "Burn it," he said, thinking he had learned quite a lot this night already, and strode down to their waiting boats.

XXXII

ELSEWHERE IN THE FLOATING CITY

The night was overcast with the moon only occasionally finding a hole to shine down on the world of mortal men below and what it saw may have scared it into hiding again. For along the Grand Canal in the very centre of the Floating City a tremendous beast had risen from the waters and was engaged in mighty combat with the Winter Seers.

Although taken by surprise, they had perhaps been planning how to react if such an attack occurred and they were quick to cast spells at the beast, keeping it from them. They were even fortunate enough to find the beast's weakness, in that they could momentarily transform it into mortal shape. For a spectator, approaching in a gondola, it was a captivating sight, seeing the many-limbed monster in a single flash of light suddenly appear as a man and then transform back into the form of a beast once more.

Only those close enough to the battle could have seen the features on that man though, to identify him as Othmen or Mongol, and know from where the spell had been struck that created such a foul creature. And although much of its body was underwater, it was possible to see that it had large limbs with sharpened ends, such as a crab might possess, but also had a large mouth with sharpened teeth, such as a shark might possess. Its head was indescribable though, perhaps belonging to a sea creature that lives only in the deepest pits and has yet to be pulled up by any mortal fisherman.

How long the battle had been raging one could not say, but the Seers' boatman had already been slain, with one of the sharpened limbs piercing his body. The two Seers stood upright in their perilously rocking boat, their hands clasped tightly and a halo-like white fire encircling their free hands. Whenever the beast attacked them they used the white fire to ward it off, but it had many limbs and they had only one free hand each.

They might have perished in that first battle had not the Shadow Master arrived. He steered his boat in fast like a deadly arrow, and rammed the beast from behind, leaping onto its back. It turned to attack him, leaving an opening for the Seers to abandon their defence and attack the monster again. They cast their incantation and again, for a mere instant, the beast transformed into a thrashing man. And that instant was enough. The Shadow Master plunged a blade deep between the man's shoulders and out through his heart. The thrashing man roared and slumped, caught half in his transformation, with his lower half still a beast and his upper torso that of a man. The Seers now leaned forward and touched the bare skin of the man and he shrieked and dissolved into water collapsing back into the canal.

The Shadow Master turned in the air and landed deftly in the Seers' boat, wobbling for the barest of moments before regaining his balance. He bowed low to the Seers and said he was glad to be of service to them. Then he noticed that one of the Winter Seers, the female, was wounded, with blood flowing from her side. He stepped forward to assist her to a seated position and while he was so distracted the second beast attacked.

It rose from the other side of their boat, a large and darker creature, also with multiple limbs, but with a more hideous head and larger mouth. Its limbs were more like those of an octopus and it looped one around the neck of the wounded Seer and ripped her from her partner's embrace, lifting her into the air.

The Shadow Master moved with a speed that could not be believed. He suddenly had a blade in both hands and was stabbing and cutting at the beast as it tried to take hold of the other Seer. He had cut it in many places, but in defending the male Seer he had left himself vulnerable and one large tentacle or limb snaked its way under the boat and seized him from behind. It pulled him into the water with the speed of a striking *serpent, such that if a witness had but blinked he would not have seen him disappear. The male Seer then stood up and tried to cast a spell over the beast on his own, but without his partner his power was limited.*

Now, almost leisurely, the beast wound another limb around his neck and lifted him clear of the boat too. Then it descended into the water, leaving nothing but the choppy water, a dead boatman and one witness to the battle – too stunned by the swiftness of it all to have even moved out of his seat.

"I truly thought you dead," said Vincenzo the scribe. "I hurried back here to write it anew so that you lived." The Shadow Master handed back his manuscript as he finished reading it, and said, "Perhaps you could downplay the size of the beast."

"What do you mean?" Vincenzo asked. "It was enormous and truly frightening."

"Yes, I'm sure it was. But think how future readers might take this tale," he said. "They might dismiss it as fantasy, having never seen such creatures."

"But such creatures are well recorded, and are known to be kept as pets by the Othmen. They train them to attack ships and pull them down into watery graves."

"Do they?" the Shadow Master asked. "Have you seen them?"

"Well, no. Of course not. But I have seen their pictures on charts and I have read accounts of them."

"And you've met the men who wrote those accounts?" he asked.

"No," said the scribe. "But anybody who knows me and hears me tell this story will say this can be believed for they know I told it."

"But years from now historians might not believe you. They might brand you Vincenzo the madman!"

Vincenzo bristled at that. "They would not dare."

"They can be a cruel lot, historians."

Vincenzo sulked. "I was going to write that I found you in the canal in the morning, more dead than alive, and brought you back here and nursed you back to strength. But then here you were, and you took those strange pills and salves, and the poisons are gone from your body and your eyes are clear again. Your other wounds are already healing. And your clothes are dry."

"No one would believe that either."

"You seem to have more powers than any I was going to create by writing you saved."

The Shadow Master just shrugged.

"But still I will write one thing into my history to make it become the way things happened," the scribe said.

"What is that?"

"I am going to record the words you uttered when I found you alive."

"Which were?"

"That wasn't meant to happen."

The Shadow Master almost grinned. Then he said, "Not a particularly stirring phrase though, is it? Perhaps best to make no particular mention of me."

"Then what should I say?" asked Vincenzo looking at his manuscript in abject disappointment. He was certain he was capturing the very feel of the battle he had witnessed. "I'm the only one who can tell that I saw two of the Seers slay a beast and then be slain by a second."

"I think the other Seers will know it by now, as will the council."

"How will they know it if I don't tell them?" Vincenzo asked.

In response the Shadow Master led him over to the window and pointed. There was a large gap of water where the Autumn Palazzo had stood the night before and the outer parts of the city were notably listing underwater.

The scribe blinked a few times as if taking it in and then said, "What shall we do? Our city is at risk of falling."

"We shall save it," said the Shadow Master. "It will be a mighty victory and the greatest moment in your great city's history."

"And I will write it safe!" Vincenzo proclaimed.

"Yes, you shall write it safe," the Shadow Master agreed.

"Telling it just as it should be!"

"Well," said the Shadow Master, "at least to a point."

Vincenzo picked up his pen. "I'm going to start by writing you back under the water of the canal now."

XXXIII
THE STORY OF ISABELLA

Isabella Montecchi felt a bad headache forming. She had slept by herself in a small chamber, but could still hear Captain Selvo snoring like a donkey a few chambers away. She was tired and she now thought her decision last night was a poor one. She should not be punishing the old captain for the Othmen envoy's actions. But she was in no mood to spend the next few weeks having her Palazzo dock cluttered with the ships of horny old men hoping to bed her and win her hand.

There were already four ships tying up at her palazzo dock, and if she didn't put a stop to this soon there would be half the ships of the city there within a few weeks. The thought pained her. How many nights of lying next to drugged and snoring old men could she endure? She was sure her mother would quip that it was just like marriage, but her mother would also advise her that since she had gotten herself into this mess, she should turn to herself to get out of it.

"Nerissa," she called.

Her handmaiden came in, grinning from ear to ear. "Have you seen the ships, my lady?" she asked.

Isabella frowned. "I have," she said wearily.

"Shall I schedule the captains in, one each night?"

"No," said Isabella firmly. "I want you to tell each of them that

I am preoccupied, or sick, or anything, and that they have wasted their time in coming here."

The handmaiden looked down at the floor and moved her hips a little this way and that. "Umm, we could, my lady, but..." She didn't go on.

"Yes?" Isabella asked.

"Well, we have learned that the Othmen envoy has put up a poster around the city stating that if any man is turned away by you, it will be proof that you are not a woman of your word, and not to be trusted in business either."

Isabella felt a throb in the front of her skull. This was a declaration of war. A war she would have to fight alone. "Not a woman of *my* word?" she asked. "Whose idea was it for this ridiculous wager anyway? It was his!"

"Umm – it was yours, my lady," said her handmaiden softly.

Isabella frowned again. She was right. It was her own idea.

"Well tell them... I don't know... we must be able to tell them something!"

"I could tell them that there is already a suitor with you," she suggested.

"Captain Selvo?" Isabella asked, aghast.

"Well, no, my lady. I mean, a younger more handsome man. We could tell them that you had a suitor and that no man should come calling with his ship until you had made a decision about him."

"But how am I going to conjure a young man out of the blue?" Isabella asked. "We can't invent a fictitious man to fill this role. Or are you suggesting that you might dress up as a young man and pretend to be my suitor?"

The handmaiden looked quite shocked at the idea. "No, my lady. I mean there is one young man who might fit the role well."

"Who?"

"He calls himself Giannetto," she said. "And he is young and handsome and has a ship at his disposal." She looked at her feet and blushed a little as she said this.

"And how do you know this?" Isabella asked.

"His was the first ship to dock here this morning," she said. "He has seen you in the city and says he is smitten by your beauty and wants to win your hand."

Isabella rubbed her forehead with the palm of her hand. "So I should invite him to dinner this evening?"

"Yes."

"And after tomorrow when he wakes up in bed alone and realizes he's failed also? Won't the old men just return with their ships again?"

"Not if my lady finds the young gentleman pleasing and offers him a different flagon of wine," the handmaiden suggested, looking at her mistress with a wicked grin.

"I think you will both be quite disappointed," Isabella said coolly. "But if it will buy me some time to think my way out of this quandary, go and tell the young man he should come back at dinner time and send all the other ships that arrive today away."

"Yes, my lady," her handmaiden said, and bowed low. "And I'll ask Marina to turn the old captain out of your chamber."

"Thank you," said Isabella. And then, just as her handmaiden had reached the door, she asked her, "How handsome exactly?"

XXXIV

THE STORY OF GIULIETTA

Giulietta's parents tapped lightly on her door, with a knock that a mouse would have considered timid. "I think she is still asleep," her father said. "Let's wait until she's awake."

"It's after eleven," said her mother. "It's time she was up."

Her father wrung his hands. He was considered a bold man of action as a merchant, with a cool head when it came to disasters and trouble, but the one thing that unnerved him was the threat of his youngest daughter's tantrums.

"You go in," he said. "She might not be dressed."

His wife rolled her eyes and tapped a little louder on the door and then opened it.

"I'm not up yet, what are you doing coming into my bedroom?" Signor Montecchi heard Giulietta shout at her mother. Then he heard the soft voice of his wife saying something to soothe their daughter and after a moment she called him into the room.

"Good morning," he said, peeping his head around the corner of the door. "I trust you slept well?"

"Hmmph," she said. "How would you feel if you were woken up from a sleep?"

He didn't answer but came and sat on the end of her large bed with his wife and held her hand, thinking it might present the right image in some way. "We'd like to talk to you," he said.

"Well I don't want to talk to you," she said and threw her head onto her pillow, pulling the covers up over her face.

"It's important," said her mother.

"It never is," said Giulietta.

"I think there's going to be a spectacular new dress involved," said Signor Montecchi. His wife dug him in the ribs with her rather sharp elbow and he tried not to react as Giulietta's head slowly emerged from its cocoon like a hibernating small creature looking for the spring light.

"How spectacular?" she asked.

"Very spectacular," Signor Montecchi said, and held his wife's hand tighter to avoid another dig in the ribs from her elbow.

Giulietta sat up and almost gave them a smile. "Will it have gems and velvet?" she asked.

Signor Montecchi looked at his wife, who sighed a little and said, "I imagine that it may. I was thinking pearls."

"Diamonds?" asked Giulietta hopefully.

"Pearls!" said her father.

She pouted for a moment and then asked, "It should be light blue then, to go with the pearls."

"Uh," said her father and met his wife's eyes again. Neither wanted to be the one to say it. "The dress will be white," he said softly.

"Oh no," Giulietta said. "That is not this season's fashion at all. White is so dreary, reserved for confirmations and weddings and things."

Her father and mother held each other's hands tight, waiting for the ducat to drop. But Giulietta went on, "I really don't know what you were thinking in supposing a white dress would be anything that I might want. How should I ever stand out wearing a white dress, even if it was covered in pearls?"

"Well," said her father. "It really needs to be white, you see, because this type of dress is only ever white."

She stared at him blankly and said, "That's ridiculous." She looked to her mother who was busily looking at her feet. The ducat dropped.

"You don't mean…?"

Her mother and father looked up at her meekly.

"You can't possibly mean…?"

"We do," said her mother.

"Well we do, if you're thinking what we're thinking," said her father.

"A wedding?" she asked.

And suddenly her mother and father couldn't stop talking. "You'd make such a beautiful bride," said her father.

"I think it's about time you took the possibility of us finding a good suitor for you seriously," said her mother.

"He's quite wealthy," said her father.

"His parents are very much looking forward to welcoming you into their family," said her mother.

"We are certain you'll be very happy," her father said.

"He's really the most delightful young man," said her mother.

And then Giulietta screamed. The noise of it shook some small spiders out from behind the tapestry on her bedchamber wall, the windows rattled in their frames and her father thought for a moment that a trumpet blast was being sounded just outside the door. "Why would I ever choose a husband that you picked?" she shouted. "I'm not getting married to anyone you find for me. I hate him already. I hate you too. I hate you, I hate you!" And she started kicking her feet on the bed frantically.

Signor and Signora Montecchi jumped to their feet and beat a hasty retreat out of the bedchamber, closing the door behind them. One of the serving maids had come up and was standing there with a look of concern on her face. The poor girl was new though, and didn't know any better. Signora Montecchi shooed her away.

Her husband straightened his clothes and said, "Well, I think that didn't go too badly at all."

"Much better than I'd expected," said Signora Montecchi.

"I think we can start making preparations then," said her husband.

"Yes. Although I think it wise to invite a few of her friends over first and let them gush about how handsome and rich young Signor Paris is, and she'll be in agreement with them in no time."

"A splendid idea," said her husband and strode off down the hallway, rather pleased with the way the day was turning out.

XXXV

ELSEWHERE IN THE FLOATING CITY

The Seers sat in a darkened room, with a low flame in the centre. They were acutely aware of the sets of empty seats about them and the pressing risk that another pair of seats could be made empty any day.

"Have you talked to the Council of Ten?" asked the male Summer Seer.

The female Spring Seer nodded her head. "Council of Eight," she said. "Have you not heard, Signor Candiano was slain his bed last night."

"I heard he was with a young whore and his heart gave out,' said the female Summer Seer. "That hardly makes it an assassination."

"His heart gave out because a dagger was driven into it," said the female Spring Seer. "Long after the whore had left him."

"Council of Eight, then," said the male Summer Seer.

"Which will be the Council of Seven as easily as we might become a single pair of Seers if we do not find a way to defeat these assassins and Othmen Djinn soon," the male Spring Seer said.

The chamber was quiet for a moment. Then the female Summer Seer said, "We have had a vision."

The other two Seers sat forward in their seats. "Why did not you say so?"

"It was most unclear."

"Tell us what you saw," said the female Spring Seer.

"It was a vision of four boatmen, rowing strange dark craft, making their way along the canals of the city. But the city was shrouded in mist and smoke, and there was no sign of life in it."

"Tell us about the boatmen," said the male Spring Seer.

"They all wore dark hooded garments. One carried plague in his boat. One carried famine. One carried chaos and the last carried death."

The male Spring Seer rubbed his chin and leaned in close to whisper something in his wife's ear, who mumbled something back to him.

"Do you know what these visions mean?" the Summer Seers asked them.

"As you say, it is unclear. But I do not like the sound of it."

"There was more," said the male Summer Seer.

"Yes?"

"They rowed their boats around and around the canals of the city, leaving large swirling currents behind them that slowly dragged the whole city underwater with them."

The chamber was silent for some time.

"Did you tell the council about it?" the Spring Seer asked.

"No. They would know less what to do with it than we do."

"There was one last detail," said the female Summer Seer.

"Yes?"

"The four figures all had the same face, although it was masked and half-hidden it was possible to see this."

"Would you know the man if you saw him in anywhere in the Floating City?"

"Yes. Anywhere."

"Then we have a chance. He must be found and destroyed or we will all be destroyed by him."

XXXVI

THE STORY OF DISDEMONA

"Come to bed. I am waiting for you!"

But Otello did not respond. He sat in the outer room brooding as he had been brooding since returning from the previous night's patrol.

Disdemona called to him again. "Does something ail you, dear husband?"

"I cannot sleep," he called back.

"Is there anything I can do?"

Otello spoke back in a low voice, "I would rather you had done nothing."

"Husband," she called again, but he did not answer. Then he heard her come into the room and stand by the door. "If you wish me to go back to bed I will, but not until I hear what troubles you?"

"Sleep eludes me, that is all," he said.

"It eludes me too when you are gone," she said, coming over to him and laying her hands on his shoulders.

But he shrugged her off and stood, pacing about the room like a caged animal. "Does not the presence of Captain Casio allow you to sleep more peacefully?"

"It is heartening to know he is there," she said.

"And did you not miss him when I required him to come with me on the patrol last night?"

"Of course I missed him," Disdemona said. "His company is light and easy and I always feel safe when he is here. It was a good choice to have him look over me."

Otello muttered, "But whose choice was it really?"

"I fear you are in an ugly temper," she said. "And I hope I have done nothing to contribute to it. But if I have not, it is not fair that I should be subject to it."

He did not answer, but sat down again, staring at her.

"You are poisoned with some foul temperament," she said, and then suddenly saw the mark on his chest where the crossbow bolt had struck him. "You are wounded!"

"It is nothing," he said. But she reached into her bodice and took out the kerchief with the strawberries on it that he had given her and placed it over the wound.

"From my breast to yours," she said.

He looked at her, standing close to him and his gaze softened. He placed a hand on hers and felt anew the wonder of touching her. Wanted to pick her up and take her into their bedchamber and lock the door from all the troubles of the outside world and just be there with her. Forever. If only she would say to him that she was not repelled by his dark skin. If only she would open her heart to him and say what she really felt for Casio. But she pulled her hand free and poked at his wound, the pain shaking the thoughts from his head.

"If this had gone a little deeper you might not be sitting here now," she said, admonishing him.

He pushed her gently away from him. "It is nothing," he said. "The man's aim was good, but he barely pierced my armour."

"Why didn't you tell me?" she said.

"It seems there are some things that stay secret between a man and his wife."

"I would rather you told me everything."

"If I had come home from killing a man, would you rather that I tell you all the details of it?"

"No," she said. "Please do not. I cannot bear to think that such gentle hands are also strong against other men and do them violence."

"As I would not believe that one as tender as you could ever cause a strong man such pain," he said.

"I would rather face your tender side than your cruel one."

"And I yours."

"Your words seem to have two meanings tonight," she said.

"If you find different meanings in them it is only because you are searching for them," he replied.

She put the kerchief back inside her nightdress and then crossed her arms. "Why are you in such a temper? Is it something to do with the dangers to the city?"

He did not answer her.

"I would rather know where you are at all hours of the day and night," she said.

"That would be convenient for you," he muttered.

"You are in a fouler mood than a wounded bear."

"A bear can easily be put out of its misery."

"Is there more danger to the city than you are telling me?" she asked. "There is so much talk of assassins and Othmen beasts in the canals. I would hate for something to happen to you."

"What might happen to me?" he asked. "Why would you even think it?"

"You live a dangerous life in your profession," she said. "You face danger daily. And nightly. It is often in my thoughts that one day you might not prevail."

"Is it indeed?"

"Yes, my love. My life would be barren without you."

"Barren? Explain that to me."

"No joy would grow in me anymore. No seeds of happiness would sprout. I would be barren."

"These are strange words you use."

"Metaphors," she said. "Do not worry about the words. Instead take their meaning."

"I do take their meaning," he said, moving away from her a little. "Tell me, something I have always wanted to ask you. You insist on sleeping with a candle lit. Do you fear the darkness?"

"I am discomforted by it, yes."

"So the blackness is less preferred to you than the light?"

"The darkness, my love," she said. "That darkness of not knowing what lingers just out of arm's reach. The sounds of night sometimes make my skin prickle."

He turned and gripped her wrists strongly. "And does it send a wave of revulsion through you?"

"Your choice of words is too strong."

"Disquiet, then? Discomfort? Disdain?"

"The nights without you are all of those."

He let go of her arms and let her fall back to the bed. "And if you lay abed with no candle alight, you would not know if I stood a few feet away from you, close enough to reach out and touch you." He leaned forward and put one hand around her throat.

"I would hope to feel your presence," she said.

Otello stood up. "I must return to the darkness. I have other work to do this evening."

"What troubles you, husband?" Disdemona asked again. "You are full of strange thoughts this evening. Come to bed with me and I'll chase them from you."

"No," he said, "I must spend some time alone with my strange thoughts for a while yet."

Disdemona watched him gather his things and leave, closing the door heavily behind him. The force of it seemed to suck the air out of the room and she suddenly felt giddy. She staggered over to his chair and sat in it, placing her hands on the documents he had been handling. She lifted them away as if scalded. As if she could feel his anger in them.

She sucked in a deep breath and was suddenly overwhelmed by a memory of herself as a small child. She was being led across to the Floating City by a tall dark man in a dark cloak. She closed her eyes tightly to try and recall more details. There were two of them. A small boy that she was clinging to. Someone she loved dearly. Then they were being dragged apart. She was crying and holding out her hands for the boy. It felt like they had been joined physically and the pain of separation was ripping their flesh apart.

She put a hand to her chest as if she could feel it even now. The pain of something being ripped apart inside her. A pain that had lain dormant for all these years, and that loving Otello had been a response to. A need to have that close love again. But his rejection of her now had ripped it apart anew. She gasped for breath and fell off the chair, shocked at the strength of it. Something in the world had changed to awaken this inside her. She wanted to conquer it and suppress it, as she had obviously done many years before. But instead she curled into a small ball on the floor, shivering against the chill of the stones, for she was a small child again, and the pain and fear and uncertainty overwhelmed her.

XXXVII

ELSEWHERE IN THE FLOATING CITY

The Duca of the Floating City could feel a troubling ache in his aged bones. Some days, like this, he felt it would be better to admit to the other counsellors just how ill he was, step down and spend the mornings sleeping late and then playing with his grandchildren. What a glorious life that would be.

But if he wasn't wearing the Duca's chain, he knew who would. Signor de Abbacio or Signor Hermino. They were a dangerous couple to be such close conspirators. Each on his own was probably controllable, but together they were formidable. Signor de Abbacio was as rake thin as he was pious, and possessed of the maddened stare of a zealot. Signor Hermino was large and stocky, just starting to run to fat, and although he had a jovial and clown-like manner, he was as much a zealot as his co-conspirator.

Their mantra at every council meeting was that there needed to be firmer control of the city to save it from peril. And at each new meeting there was a new peril. The Othmen Djinn that was lurking in the waters of the city. Othmen spies and assassins that were targeting the council. The threat of a trade war from the north. The threat of the Mongols to the east. The threat of their own countrymen to the west.

At each council meeting they had put forward a motion that the Duca should appoint one of them with special emergency powers to address the crisis. And at each council meeting he had managed to defeat their efforts. But he was tired. And he was sick.

Signor Tegalliano had warned him that they were planning to make a move to take control of the council and advised him to play each man off against the other, and let them devour themselves with their ambitions rather than devour the city. But it had gone beyond that point and Signor Flavius was dead. As was Signor Candiano. At each council meeting there was one less moderate to call on for support.

That their city was facing a perilous hour he did not doubt. But how to deal with it was a major point of difference.

He closed his eyes and tried to imagine he was sitting in a plain wicker chair in his garden with his youngest grandson playing at his feet. The boy liked to tell stories and would be rolling a ball or something and making up the most fanciful tales about it being a dragon. The Duca smiled and felt it hurt his face muscles a little. Had it really been so long since he had smiled?

He thought he should perhaps take a nap to restore his energies. Or have one of the Seers prescribe him some potion or other. But their abilities were limited, he knew. Like they were limited in their ability to ward off the Djinn and safeguard the council from assassins.

But as they had advised him recently, they could not be expected to keep the city afloat and protect the council members. He knitted his brows and tried to concentrate. He had a feeling there was a solution to everything lying just out of his grasp if he could only piece all the disparate parts of the problem together.

But there were so many pieces to contend with. The Guild were protesting about Otello burning down one of their buildings, which he had been engaged in to no outcome while another member of the council had been assassinated on the very streets of their city which he had been charged with keeping safe.

Signors de Abbacio and Hermino were advising that Otello should be removed from his position as general of the city – but of course they would. He was one of the few honest men who the Duca could rely upon to protect the city, even if he did it in a ham-fisted way at times. He would certainly remain loyal to the Duca though and not tolerate any move of force against him.

The Duca felt himself drifting a little. How wonderful it would be to close his eyes and never open them again, he thought. Never to have to look at the visages of the Seers or the council members again. He would miss his grandchildren though, he knew, and used that thought to pull himself back again.

He opened his eyes wide and sighed. It was too much to hope that all his troubles would go away, but perhaps one day without another crisis it was possible. That was surely something he could hope for. Surely.

XXXVIII

ELSEWHERE IN THE FLOATING CITY

The ship crept silently into the city in the pre-dawn light, emerging out of a thin mist that had shielded it from the sentries at the mouth of the lagoon. It sat low to the water and had only one sail set and moved at little more than the pace of a man swimming. Against the regulations of the city it did not fly any flags that identified its country of origin nor the status of a merchant or passenger vessel.

It made its way stealthily towards the row of ships that were already tied up on the eastern side of the city, where cargo was unloaded and loaded, and where merchants would be busily trading their wares come the light of day. No one saw the ship tie up and a small boat lowered from it to the water.

If anyone had been awake at this hour they would have seen about a dozen faces in the small boat, all peering intently into the early morning lights that shone through the gloom ahead of them, and they might even have heard the occasional whimper of a babe in arms.

The boat made its way quietly towards one of the lesser-used docks and the bedraggled passengers climbed out and made their way up the stone steps. Some wore once-fine garments, now soiled and ripped. Others wore the clothes of labourers and servants. A few days in the city and they would revert to those roles, but for now they helped each other up the steps, lifting a few bundles of possessions and children.

One man, who sat at the oars, held the boat steady until everyone had disembarked. He looked up from his task to see one man had not yet left the boat and he nudged him with his foot to urge him to get a move on. The other figure fell to the bottom of the boat. The man stood up from his position by the oars and, taking a dagger from his belt, lifted open the robes that the figure had wound tightly around his face.

One glance and he dropped the robes back and also discarded the dagger, letting it fall to the bottom of the boat with a clatter.

Turning to see that everyone else had made their way up the steps and was gone, he stepped out of the boat carefully and then put his foot to it and pushed it back away from the dock. With luck it might drift back out to sea. Or it might be found in a few hours. Either way he would have enough time to find somewhere safe with one of his relatives.

He looked around to make sure no one was about and then he too hurried up the stairs and disappeared into the Floating City.

High above them though, in a palazzo window Signora Montecchi watched the dark figures scuttling into the city and it brought back to her mind a memory of a similar night, many, many years ago now. She sighed and wrapped her shawl tighter around herself, remembering the promises that had been made then too. Then she shivered, for that time that they had long talked of, but always hoped would never arrive, had come.

XXXIX

ELSEWHERE IN THE FLOATING CITY

Vincenzo the scribe was creating the world anew. Or trying to. He had several sheets of paper spread out on his writing table and was trying to chart the city's recent history and the stories of the three Montecchi sisters but was finding it difficult to tie all the disparate strands together. If, for instance, he had the power to change one or two events, as the Shadow Master had hinted at, where should he use that power?

Could he return the slain Seers? Or would that entail also rewriting the knowledge of anybody who had known they were dead? Or should he rather write something that protected the remaining Seers, and ensured the city stayed afloat and did not sink beneath the waves? Could he write away the Djinn, or at least any further attacks from them?

And what about the assassins? Should he save the council from attack? There were too many smaller stories to deal with. Too many lives to save and change. And instead he found himself writing snatches of faint memories of the city when he had first arrived there. The way he had felt its movement under his feet when he first stood on it, such as was only ever felt by first-time arrivals, and never felt again afterwards. But he also had a memory of having stood there as a much younger child. And the more snatches of memories he wrote, the deeper they took him into this half-remembered world. There was a young girl. A dark chill winter's night. A tall man and a woman bundling the young girl away. He had felt so cold inside himself. The stars had looked like ice formations in the sky. The stranger had held his hand and then let go and was gone. The darkness enveloped him and he felt the city moving under his feet.

"It is like a puzzle half solved, isn't it?" said a voice behind him. Vincenzo jumped and spun around. The Shadow Master was standing there behind him.

"How did you get in?" Vincenzo asked. He had bolted his door particularly to avoid being caught like this.

"Better than 'who are you?'" said the Shadow Master and stepped closer to look at Vincenzo's notes.

Vincenzo swept them all together. "I am trying to make sense of it all."

"But consider that the sense might only be apparent at the very end, when everything has played out."

Vincenzo shook his head. "I need to see some sense now."

"Everything will converge," the Shadow Master said. "There will be only one story instead of a dozen or so."

"A dozen or so?" asked Vincenzo, holding up his fingers and counting. "There are the three Montecchi sisters, Disdemona, Isabella and Giulietta. There are the Seers. There is the council. There are assassins. Are you telling me there is going to be more?"

"Oh yes, much, much more."

Vincenzo let his shoulders slump. "And you seem to be the only one who knows what is going on and what is happening, or going to happen, and yet you refuse to share this with me!"

"And yet," said the Shadow Master, "you are the one that has been granted the power to write the future of your city and what is going to happen within it. So you tell me, what will you write?"

Now Vincenzo's fingers twitched just a little, as if the challenge was tempting him to pick up his quill and start writing the city's future at once. "I would write of turmoil and hardships but ultimate peace and prosperity," said Vincenzo.

"What? No chase and love interests?"

"Chasing what?" asked Vincenzo, but the Shadow Master ignored the question. "I would write our city saved," the scribe said.

"And how would you save it precisely?"

Vincenzo leaned back in his seat. "I would have the Othmen defeated. I would have our trade routes opened. I would have the assassins caught. I would have the Seers rid our waters of the Djinn."

The Shadow Master nodded his head. "All right. But what if for every intervention you created that favoured the city you had to accept some loss in return for it?"

"What type of loss?"

"Perhaps a death. Perhaps an attack. Perhaps illness."

Vincenzo nodded his head again. "This has become a game, I see, and I must therefore plan very carefully and not make too many decisions at once, until I know the impact of the losses I must sustain."

"Good logic," said the Shadow Master. "And what if for each positive outcome you engineered you found the loss you had to incur was greater?"

Vincenzo frowned now. "That's not fair," he said.

"I don't recall saying it had to be fair," the Shadow Master said.

"Then what incentive should I have for changing the future if the losses were worse?"

"What indeed?" asked the Shadow Master.

"Then perhaps I would choose not to intervene," Vincenzo said.

But the Shadow Master shook his head. "No. Your task is to write the future. That is your burden."

"You change the rules too often," said Vincenzo sulkily.

The Shadow Master said nothing for some time and then said, "Tell me about your first memory."

Vincenzo thought hard for a moment. "I was on the road, in a wagon. I was laying in the back wrapped in blankets and I had a book in my hands. I could not read the words on the page, but had a strong longing to. I was running my fingers over the marks and making up to myself what they meant, reading out some nonsense."

"Nonsense?" asked the Shadow Master.

"I suppose so," said Vincenzo. "I don't remember the story I was making up."

"Are you sure? Wasn't it something about being a mighty warrior and dispatching all the villains that attacked your family?"

Vincenzo said nothing for a long while. "Yes. I can remember it now that you say it." He stood up and then sat down. "How can you know that?"

"What if I am the warrior that you created?" the Shadow Master asked. "A little late, I admit, but here nevertheless." And he bowed.

Vincenzo closed his eyes a moment. "No. Wait. You're confusing me."

"Or is it the dreams you sometimes have that you are a character in somebody else's story?"

"Stop it!" said Vincenzo. "Stop it!"

"Am I messing with your head?"

"No. Yes. I don't even know what that means."

"Have you ever wielded a sword?" the Shadow Master asked suddenly, changing the topic.

"Not really," said Vincenzo. "Not in a fight or anything."

"Here," said the Shadow Master, and with a fluid move he was holding out one of his curved deadly blades to Vincenzo. The scribe took it by the hilt and felt the weight of it. It was incredibly light. He moved it around in his hand and saw the Shadow Master watching his face intently.

"Does that bring back any memories?" he asked him.

"No," said Vincenzo. "Should it?"

"You hold it well," the Shadow Master said.

Vincenzo passed it back to him. "I prefer to wield a quill pen," he said.

"And which do you think is more effective in creating your future?" the Shadow Master asked. "The pen or the sword?"

Vincenzo regarded him for a moment and then said, "Both together. And I have the answer to your riddle about how to write of the future and overcome larger losses."

"Yes?"

"I would write a saviour like you," he said.

XL

THE STORY OF ISABELLA

"I'm not going to know peace until I give in to your scheming, am I?" Isabella Montecchi asked her handmaiden. The other woman gave her a knowing victorious grin. An increasing line of old sea captains had besieged her entranceways each day, and her handmaiden kept reminding her that the only way to be rid of them would be to agree to let one of them court her. And she just happened to have chosen the perfect one – as she reminded her mistress many times.

Isabella had already changed her mind, having agreed to dine with the young man and then sending him away after making him wait for most of the day out in the hot sun. But he had shown up early the next day and dutifully taken his place in line behind all the other hopeful old sea dogs.

"Tell him to dress for dinner and be here early," she told her handmaiden. "And make sure all the other men hear it."

Her handmaiden bowed and hurried out of the chamber as eager as if she herself would be having a meal with the handsome young man. Isabella watched her go and wrung her hands. She had watched the young man from her window, and yes, he was handsome and yes, he seemed rather nice and well bred, but she was just not interested in a man in her life at the moment.

The accursed Othmen envoy was going to ruin her! Several of

her more reliable – and married – captains had come to see her and told her that word was going all around the ports that her ships were marked for attack by the Othmen. It was said they had put spells on them that meant they could find them in any weather and they would slaughter the crews and take all cargo, or just sink it into the ocean. There were stories that Othmen sages could conjure up storms to dispel a fleet of ships ranged against them, and could as easily have a fat merchant vessel becalmed so they could easily overtake it and plunder it. And it was said she had personally insulted the Othmen Empire and they could not let the insult go unchallenged.

As a result crewmen were deserting her employ and that meant no ships going out. And that meant no income coming in to offset her ongoing costs. She sighed. It would not just be the ruin of her, but the ruin of the city as well. Her ships were stuck at dock unmanned and a goodly amount of the city's other ships were lined up outside her window there, with their captains seeking to win her hand.

The city would soon run short of food and medicines and textiles, and would run short of civil order soon afterwards. Their city was effectively besieged without the Othmen having to send a single soldier or ship against it. And she'd heard and read enough accounts of what went on within siege cities as food shortages began to tell. The rich would still be fed, but at increasingly high prices, and black marketeers would crawl out of the gutters, enforcing their territory and prices with cut-throat villains. The poorer people would fight over food and then start eating animals and rodents. There would be a steady stream of refugees leaving the city as it grew weaker and weaker. If she could not find a way to effectively combat the accursed Othmen envoy's tactics, any enemy would find the city an easy target for conquest.

"Those damned Othmen and their arcane enchantment and their bloodlust," she cursed. "And their lackeys!" Dinner would be a good opportunity to take her mind off this battle.

She was pleasantly surprised by the young man, Giannetto Scali, when he was finally ushered into the dining room. She had again left him waiting outside while she had snacked. She wanted him hungry. And thirsty.

He had entered and bowed low and told her it was a pleasure to meet her, showing no displeasure at all at being kept waiting. She said little and bade him sit. He did so and would not touch his food until she had picked up a small pastry. And even then he ate only sparingly.

"Tell me about yourself," she said.

"There is not much to tell," he said modestly.

"Surely you have a life that you have lived, and as such you will have a story relating to it?"

"I would rather hear your own stories," he said. "There is so much to learn about you."

"Indeed," she said. "Might I ask what you know already?"

"So little," he said.

"Tell me. I'm curious."

"I had heard you were the most beautiful woman in the Floating City and certainly the most beautiful woman in any city."

The handmaiden, standing at the wall beside the door, covered her mouth with her hand and giggled a little. Isabella shot her a glance. She had heard such flattery many times and was immune to it.

"And what else have you heard?"

"It is not so important what I have heard, as what I have observed," he said. "For I first saw you in the markets some weeks ago now and was immediately smitten by the sight of you. You were far more beautiful than the stories had given you credit for. And I was filled with sorrow that you were a widow who had lost her loving husband and had to carry the burden of his business. But you seemed to bear it easily on those lovely shoulders."

And it was he who glanced down, having spoken the flatteries. Then he said, "The truth is, I have become somewhat enchanted by you and when I heard of the wager I knew I had to take part, at least to sit with you like this and be near to you."

"And of course, a chance to win my hand and my fortune?"

He waved his hand in the air as if shooing a pesky bug away. "What could be more valuable than being here with you?"

"Spending the night with me perhaps?"

Now Giannetto blushed and looked down at his meal. "I admit I have become somewhat enchanted by the idea of that too," he said softly. "And I would be a fool or a liar if I did not say so."

Isabella smiled. Just a little. Despite herself she was finding that she was slowly warming to this young man. It was hard to estimate his age without asking him, but certainly it was no more than twenty-one. Or perhaps twenty-two.

"Now tell me about yourself," she said.

He looked up and smiled, happy to be on sounder ground. "My father was a merchant in the Walled City to the west. He had three sons, of which I was the youngest. One year ago, almost to this very day, he called us to him. He had been unwell for some time and felt his last moments were approaching. He read out his will to us. My two elder brothers were to get a half each of his fortune and I was to get a letter of introduction to my father's best friend, the merchant Ansaldo, here in the Floating City."

"I know him," said Isabella. "He is a good man. But were you not disappointed to have been left out of your father's will?"

"Why should I be?" Giannetto asked. "My brothers are tied to their estates and I have been able to travel across our country and see the most wonderful sights it has to offer. Tonight being the culmination of them."

"Continue with the story," she said, reaching one hand up and playing idly with her hair.

"Well, after many adventures I finally reached the Floating City and on my first day I saw the most wondrous sight. A woman who was so perfect that if I had dreamed her I could not have created something more lovely."

She arched an eyebrow.

"I found my father's dear friend and told him of my father's death and we both wept over it. Then he said I should be his godson and he has allowed me to learn the ways of his business until I was competent enough to be trusted with my own ship of trade goods to try and make my fortune with."

"And where did you sail to?" she asked.

"Your dock," he said.

She met his eyes. "Won't your godfather be disappointed if you lose it all?"

"Why should I lose it? Is it more dangerous to be here with you than to brave an ocean storm, or a reef, or pirates, or the Othmen?"

Isabella did not answer. "I think," she said slowly, "I have had enough food and stories. It is time to go to bed."

"Lady, I am at your service," replied Giannetto.

Isabella then held up a hand and beckoned her handmaiden over. "Bring us some wine," she said. And then added, "The finest wine!"

The handmaiden's face pouted just a little in disappointment, but she bowed and walked across the room to fetch it.

XLI

ELSEWHERE IN THE FLOATING CITY

It was becoming very rare for any of the council members to be walking the streets either in the dark, or with less than half a dozen guards – and yet here was Signor Faliero loitering furtively along one of the quieter walkways of the Floating City, under the Bridge of Smiles, wondering if what he was doing was wise, or incredibly stupid. The city seemed larger from down here, or perhaps it was that he felt smaller, tucked away in a dark cranny out of the light. He spun his head slowly at every sound and felt his stomach lurch whenever another person walked into the alleyway, but so far they had all walked slowly past him.

He tasted sweat on his upper lip when he licked his lips quickly and decided the likelihood of folly was rising over the likelihood of wisdom with each passing moment, and he exhaled heavily and turned to make his way back home.

"Don't take another step," a voice suddenly hissed at him from the shadows at his side.

He froze and felt his buttocks tighten in reflex. "Don't... don't hurt me."

"Just step back to where you were," the voice hissed.

"What... what... do you want?" Signor Faliero asked.

"For you to stay where you are."

"Don't hurt me," he said in a voice full of fear.

"I'm not here to hurt you. I'm here to save you."

"What… what? I don't understand."

"You don't need to understand. You need to be quiet."

"Who are you?"

"A man who is clearly better at following instructions than you are. Be quiet!"

Signor Faliero nodded. Then he said in a much lower voice. "What are we waiting for?"

"Assassins," said the voice.

Signor Faliero gulped heavily. "I was invited here by Signor Tradonico," he said. "I trust him fully. He said he was going to reveal a conspiracy against the city to me. I still have his letter."

"Show me," hissed the voice.

Signor Faliero reached into his robes and pulled out a small envelope. He held it out and a hand stretched out from the shadow and took it. Then he saw a man step out of the darkness and hold it out to the night light. He knew this man. He had seen him somewhere before, he thought.

"I know you," he said.

The other man didn't respond. He held the letter closer to his face and then said, "This is a forgery."

"Yes, I know you," Signor Faliero said again. The man looked at him and met his eyes. "Vincenzo the scribe."

"The historian!" he replied.

"How are you involved in all this?" Signor Faliero asked him.

"That's a good question," he replied. "To which I myself have more questions than answers."

"So what are we to do now?"

"We wait," Vincenzo said.

"For what?"

"For me," said a sudden deeper voice and Signor Faliero was startled to see a dark figure in a hood and cloak descend rapidly from the rooftops above and land lightly on his feet beside them. Signor Faliero drew back in alarm and held his hands up before him. But the man didn't even pay him any attention. He said to the scribe, "There is no one out there." Then he turned to regard Signor Faliero and said, "At least nobody intending you harm." He bowed just a little, and said, "Show me the letter."

Vincenzo handed it over and the stranger held his hand up and a soft light seemed to glow from his fingers. "I would have sworn it was Signor Tradonico's hand," Signor Faliero said.

"Vincenzo is the superhero of handwriting," said the stranger, handing the letter back. "If he says it is a forgery then it is."

"The super what?" asked Signor Faliero, looking to Vincenzo for explanation. But he looked as confused.

"That's not the question," said the stranger. "The question is, why would someone trick you into turning up for a meeting that didn't exist and then not try and kill you?" He looked to both the citizens of the Floating City, but they still looked a little confused.

"Unless..." said the stranger, and then smacked his forehead with his palm, the way they did in Umbria. "Unless it was to keep us out of the way." He looked at Vincenzo and said, "Oh dear. Come. We must hurry." The stranger set off at a run, followed by the scribe, trying his best to keep up with him, and Signor Faliero further behind.

The stranger led them down several alleyways, pushing his way politely past citizens they passed, and over some footbridges until he stopped at a larger bridge, peered down into the canal from the centre and then leapt right over the railing. Signor Faliero saw the scribe run up to the spot and peer over the edge, and then continue running over the bridge.

He was panting heavily and sweating more than he thought healthy for him when he finally reached the same spot on the bridge. He looked over and saw the stranger on the small stone walkway by the canal's edge under them, leaning over a body. He rested one hand on the stone railing, thinking he was going to throw up. Perhaps from the effort, perhaps from recognizing the bloodstained body down below him. It was Signor Tradonico.

Undoubtedly also lured here by a forged letter by the assassins who perhaps knew that he had uncovered their conspiracy.

He saw the scribe now come out from an alleyway and join the stranger by the body, panting almost as much as he himself was. "Do you know him?" said the stranger, in a voice that showed no sign of being puffed.

"Yes," said Vincenzo. "It is Signor Tradonico. Of the Council of Ten."

"Council of Seven," corrected the stranger.

"Let me guess," said the scribe. "This wasn't meant to happen, no?"

Signor Faliero felt his head spinning and his heart beating heavily in his chest. He had to sit down or it would be the Council of Six in a moment. He slumped to the ground and then waved away a young man who walked past offering to help him to his feet. After recovering his breath somewhat he stood and looked over the railing, expecting to see the scribe and the stranger. But they were gone. Only the body of Signor Tradonico was there. And whatever secret about the conspiracy against the Floating City that he had uncovered hidden within it. Then he noticed the masks on the stonework below him and recognized where he was. They were at the carved weeping masks of the Bridge of Tears.

XLII

THE STORY OF GIULIETTA

Romeo Cappalletti turned to look over his shoulder and make sure that no one was following him, then knocked on the old wooden door once, then twice, then once again. He was in high spirits and didn't even turn around to make sure that nobody was lurking in the shadows behind him anywhere, as was his usual custom.

A small window in the door slid open and a hooded figure stared out at him from the darkness.

"It's me," said Romeo.

"I can see it's you," the figure said.

"Let me in."

"Why?" asked the figure.

"I have some most excellent news."

"For me or for you?"

"For me," said Romeo.

"Then why should I care?"

"Let me in and I will tell you all about it."

"Is there going to be any payment for me in this?" asked the hooded figure.

"Yes," said Romeo. "A very handsome payment too."

"How handsome?"

"As handsome as a beautiful maid is beautiful."

"So there's a maid involved," said the hooded figure.

There was a sudden splashing in the canal nearby and Romeo turned quickly to see what had caused it. He scanned the water and saw concentric circles where something had just submerged into the water. "Open up," said Romeo again, "and I will tell you all about it."

Friar Lorenzo da San Francesco drew the bolts back, and let Romeo squeeze into the dim room beyond. Romeo thought he looked more sallow than ever. "You need to get out and enjoy the light of the city more," he advised him.

"And you should keep your opinions to yourself more," the friar said. "Now what business brings you here today?"

Romeo smiled and held out his arms widely. "I am to be married."

The friar stared at him and then looked at Romeo's open embrace. Surely the boy wasn't expecting a hug for this news.

"And what is the good news?"

Romeo frowned. "You will perform the service for us."

"To the Lady Rosaline?" the friar asked cautiously. Or perhaps incredulously.

"It is not the Lady Rosaline," said Romeo. "It is another."

"What is her name?" asked the friar.

"Does it matter? Why is a name so important? What's in a name?"

"It matters to me, particularly if you are so reluctant to tell me."

"Would you perform the marriage ceremony without knowing her name?" Romeo asked.

"I think not," said the friar.

"Even if you were rewarded handsomely?"

The friar considered. Romeo knew the man's weakness for Othmen drugs.

"How handsomely, I ask again?"

"As handsome as my love is beautiful," answered Romeo.

The friar took a deep breath in. "Only if you tell me her name."

"You may not like it," cautioned Romeo.

"I would like it less not to know," he said.

"All right. It is the Lady Giulietta Montecchi."

The friar reacted as if he had been kicked in the rear by a donkey, his knees buckled a little and he was suddenly gasping for breath. "Are you... are you mad?" he asked. "Are you determined to be strung up in the city square with your testicles stuffed into your mouth? Are you determined to start a war between your two houses? Are you determined to..." But words failed him.

"We are in love," said Romeo simply.

The friar reached around for a seat and sat down heavily. "This is a drug-addled dream," he said, "and I shall awaken from it momentarily and laugh at how I believed you said you were determined to marry Lady Giulietta Montecchi and that I would perform the wedding service."

Romeo folded his arms and waited.

"Or perhaps it is just a jest that you are trying to test the health of my ageing heart with," the friar said.

"It is no jest and it is no dream," Romeo said.

"Then perhaps it will seem one in a moment." The friar turned and reached for a small pipe on the bench behind him. He lit it with a long taper from the hearth and drew in several long deep breaths. He blew out the thick sweet smoke and offered the pipe to Romeo who shook his head.

"Does your courage return as your eyes cloud over?" asked Romeo.

"Courage is a strange thing," said the friar. "It comes to us when we have no need of it and then departs when we are looking for it. It is a friend when we are using words and deserts us when we turn to actions."

"And the Othmen drugs bolster it," said Romeo.

The friar nodded. "It is true. They do. But such is the foolhardiness of this venture, that even the Othmen spices do not turn folly to fair-mindedness." He closed his eyes a moment and frowned, then he opened them with an almost sly look. "Are you

aware of the parlous state of politics in our city at the moment
and the possible turmoil that this proposed wedding will cause?"
he asked.

Romeo waved a hand in the air. "We will be wed," he said
firmly. "And if not by you then by another. For we are in love."

"Ah – love," said the friar. "Then that changes everything. I had
thought it simply a whim, simply a crazed notion. If you had said
it was love, I should never have been so reticent. Love is a motive
I never hear."

"You are mocking me," said Romeo.

"If I am to put my livelihood, my life and my testicles on the
line I think I am entitled to."

"Your testicles are in no danger I think," said Romeo.

"Unlike yours," said the friar.

"My testicles are my business," said Romeo.

"Perhaps more than your wit, since they seem to be doing all
the thinking for you."

"We will be wed," Romeo repeated.

The friar grabbed Romeo by the shoulders. "I seem to be
caught in some web of time whereby I find we are having the
same conversation over and over with a different maiden having
bewitched you each time."

"No," said Romeo. "This is very different. Enchantment
happens when we touch. It is true. You will see when we stand
here together before you."

The friar snapped his fingers at Romeo's crotch. "It is hardly
enchantment," he said.

"No, you don't understand," said Romeo. "Real enchantment."

"Of course, of course," said the friar, "The earth trembles and
the waters rise and lights fill the sky."

"Exactly," said Romeo. "Have you seen it before?"

"I have heard it before," said the friar, releasing Romeo and
pacing back and forward in the small room. "But tell me, how do
you think you will escape this alive?"

"We have thought it all through," said Romeo, sitting the friar down and putting his hands on the older man's shoulders. "We shall be wed in secret. No one will know of it but us. Then we will sneak out of the city and set ourselves up to live somewhere far away where no one will ever find us. No one will ever know us."

The friar thought on this for some time and then asked, "You are so smitten that you would leave the city of your birth?"

"She is my homeland," he said. "And I am hers."

The friar sucked in his cheeks and Romeo could see he was wavering. "There will be no danger to you, but great profit," said Romeo. "Our parents will know nothing of it. You will be an innocent in this."

"All right," he said finally. "If it is kept secret then I will agree to help you. It may be that this marriage will trigger greater things than you can ever imagine."

"Yes," said Romeo and grasped his hand in two of his and started pumping it heartily. "You have made me the happiest man in the city. And you shall be rewarded handsomely enough to spend your days in clouds of Othmen spice."

The friar nodded, smiled and then asked, "How handsomely exactly?"

XLIII

ELSEWHERE IN THE FLOATING CITY

The two sets of Seers were as close as they had come to being pleased for a very long time. It was such a simple but effective idea that they each felt ownership of it – that they should stop searching just for individuals that might have powers, but start searching for couples, bringing pairs together, for it was the joint powers they were after.

They had spent a long day matching boys and girls until they felt they had found the final pair. It was a gruelling experience for them, to be certain, having to be submerged in water, or subjected to flames and they had clearly traumatized many of the children. But, on the other hand, while there were some nasty burns, nobody had died.

The girl who sat before them was Rosa, who her parents had said was thirteen, and the boy was Mario, probably a year or two her junior.

"It is undoubtedly them," said the male Spring Seer. He had been particularly impressed with the way they had managed to create an air pocket underwater to keep the water from them. They had been fastened to each other with chains and lowered into the bath tub together. They had struggled, of course, and spluttered as the water covered them, but then they could clearly see the bubbles forming around their heads and a large bubble created for them to breathe. Rosa had even smiled back at them from underwater.

They were a little bit clumsier with the flame, but they would be able to grow their powers with the experience and knowledge that the Seers possessed. It would be a mighty combination, the potential and energy of youth with the experience of age.

"She is pretty, yes," the female Spring Seer whispered into her partner's ear.

"Pretty enough," he said in reply. "And what do you think of him?"

"A bit young to be certain," she said. "But I'm sure we'll make something grand out of him, won't we?"

"Grand indeed," said the male Spring Seer.

"You must hold hands," said the female Summer Seer and the two youngsters shyly took hold of each other's hands.

"That's it," she said. "Maintain close contact at all times. That is vital."

"At all times?" asked young Mario and looked down at his feet.

"Yes. At all times."

"But what about… well, when we're asleep?"

"You will sleep together."

Both children blushed at the thought of that.

"And what about when… well… when we need to do private things?"

"You will have no private things from each other," said the male Spring Seer.

"Not even, well… What about going to the privy?" asked the boy.

Rosa blushed so hard she almost let go of his hand.

"Even then," said the female Spring Seer. "You will stop feeling awkward about it very quickly." But it did not look like they would.

"Do you remember when we were first paired," the female Spring Seer whispered to her husband. "I fear we were just as awkward."

"But we don't have the luxury of time we had then," he replied. "We must ready them right away."

"If those random bursts of power we have seen from them are any indication," she said, "they might be ready far quicker than we allow for."

And then the female Summer Seer asked a question that had been nagging at the back of her mind for some time and had only now crept through. "Yes, but if they were so powerful why didn't they demonstrate it to us in our trials? Should we have expected more?"

She looked to her partner and then across to the other Seers.

"Are you suggesting there might be another pair out there with the gift?" the male Spring Seer asked. "What are the chances of that?"

"Slim," she said. "Extremely slim. And yet…"

"Give them a chance," said the female Spring Seer. "Wait until the transformation and then see if you don't feel as strongly about them as I do."

The female Summer Seer nodded her head. "Yes, we will know then."

The boy took a quick look at the girl to see if she knew what they were talking about, but the look on her face showed she didn't know either. She did give him a quick smile though. That made him feel a little less anxious about things.

THE STORY OF DISDEMONA

Otello felt his anger moving slowly through his blood, making his whole body rage. He had been summoned to see the council again and they had left him standing in the antechamber. Just standing there. Like a servant.

His captain was due to report to him mid-morning and of course Disdemona would now be there alone with him. He ground his teeth and felt a dull bitter taste in the back of his mouth. He would have liked to turn his head and spit, but instead he stood there, maintaining control over his body. Not showing his anger to anyone about him. The way he had not shown any anger when Disdemona told him that she did not trust his ensign and preferred to be under the care of the captain. Exactly as his ensign had predicted.

He knew, of course, that if he so wished he could pull out the small dagger concealed in the small of his back and cut the throats of the two men at the doors in front of him, and just march in, demanding the council address him.

But he just stood there. Waiting.

Eventually the door opened and some courtier or underling asked him to come forward. He pushed his way past and stepped into the council chamber. He looked around at the seven men, refusing to let his vision linger on the three empty seats. Some of them, like Signor de Abbacio and Signor Hermino stared at him with hungry disdainful looks. Signor Montecchi wouldn't even meet his eyes.

The Duca looked like he had aged several years in a few days. He greeted Otello politely and said he had to convey the council's displeasure that another councillor had been lost.

"Why play with words?" Signor de Abbacio cut in. "Signor Tradonico, our brother on the council, has been cruelly assassinated. Cut down. His blood spilled on the streets of our city. And Signor Candiano was slain in his own bed! Proof again that the Othmen are trying to kill us all, and proof that the general is unable to do anything to protect us."

Signor Hermino led several of the councillors in slapping their palms on the table to indicate their agreement. And their displeasure. Otello said nothing. He had walked into ambushes before and refused to be drawn into this one further.

"You have been charged with protecting us!" Signor de Abbacio said, pointing his finger at Otello.

The Moor turned to look at him and met his eyes. Know thy enemy, he thought.

"We put our trust in you," the signor continued. "You swore to protect us from the Othmen's enchantment and their blades, but have done neither." Then he stood up and leaned forward, his finger pointing more stridently. "I think we could be as well protected if we had asked Othmen mercenaries to do it."

Otello felt the anger in his blood rising to a boiling point. He knew just how easy it would be to reach out and crush the man's windpipe. Or push his fingers into his eyes, digging out the jelly lumps. Or drag him over the table by his hair and smash his head onto the marble floor. He ran over in his mind how easy it would be to kill all seven men here. That's how he'd like to dispatch Signor de Abbacio – with his bare hands. Then he would draw out the small stiletto hidden in his leather jerkin and step across to Signor Hermino. He'd stab him in the throat and let him bleed to death, trying to call for assistance. The man was a bully and probably a coward. Then he'd turn to de Abbacio's other supporters, Signors Monegano and Tegalliano. He'd stick them in the lungs. Let them die over several days, bleeding internally. Signors Montecchi and Faliero he'd stick in the eyes. They weren't too bad and would die quickly.

The Duca, however, he wasn't quite sure what to do with.

"Our general is entitled to defend himself from your accusations," said the Duca, in a soft voice.

Yes, he'd leave the old man be, Otello thought.

Signor de Abbacio sat back down again and said, "Of course. Of course. I was just wanting to make sure he was aware of the severity of our concerns."

Otello turned to face the Duca and bowed his head a little in acknowledgment of his authority.

"How do you defend yourself?" the Duca asked him.

Otello kept facing the Duca and said, "I would lay down my life for the council and the city. You know that."

The Duca inclined his head a little. "We do not doubt your loyalty," he said.

"We doubt your effectiveness," said Signor de Abbacio.

Still Otello did not turn his head to look at him. "I need time. I will destroy these assassins. And I will rid our waters of these demons. But I need time."

"How much time?" asked Signor de Abbacio. "Enough time for the council to be destroyed and for the last Seers to be slain so that our whole city sinks into the sea. Will you then stand before us and say that you still need just a little more time? Water is already lapping at our ankles and you ask for more time. The blood of our brothers flows in that water and you ask for more time."

"I can defeat all our enemies given a little more time," Otello said.

"I can feel the eyes of these accursed assassins on me at all times," Signor de Abbacio said. "I can feel the talons of these

beasts pressing at my entrails." He smacked his palm on the table.
"We have no more time."

Otello did not answer him. Signor de Abbacio folded his arms
and said, "We should summon a Djinn-slayer."

Now Otello turned to fully regard the man. "They are
treacherous dogs, trained by the Othmen. Better to trust a scorpion
than to trust a Djinn-slayer," he said.

"But we have lost trust in you, general," said Signor de Abbacio.

"We should summon the Djinn-slayer," said Signor de Abbacio's
lackey, Signor Hermino.

"We must vote on this," said the Duca. "It is truly a dangerous
proposition."

"Dangerous times demand dangerous actions," said Signor
de Abbacio.

The Duca looked uncomfortable, but said, "All in favour raise
your hands."

Signor de Abbacio and Signor Hermino led the vote, thrusting
their hands up high and turning to look at those members of the
council they knew would vote with them. Slowly two more hands
went up. Signor de Abbacio smiled widely.

"I believe that four votes is now a majority of the council," he
said smugly.

XLV

ELSEWHERE IN THE FLOATING CITY

The port guards saw the ship sailing listlessly towards them and alerted the commander that although it appeared to be one of the Floating City's own vessels, she flew no flags of identification. The commander called out the sea guards and three small ships were dispatched to cut the vessel off at the mouth of the lagoon.

They approached it warily. There had been stories circulating that the Othmen would try and attack the city and they were renowned for their cunning and stealth. Every suspicious ship would be stopped and checked. The sea guard themselves had no real desire to find a ship bristling with Othmen warriors, and were happy to challenge vessels from a distance to prove who they were and then board them and gruffly search them when it was apparent they were just merchantmen.

But this vessel was different. There were very few crew on board that they could see, and those they observed seemed to be moving about as if drugged.

The commander, whose job it was to oversee this work, called on his three small vessels to stay well back. He was in his fifth decade of life and had a preference to reach his sixth, which he knew would only be possible through caution in all things.

"Identify yourselves," he called to the ship, through a metal hailer that amplified his voice, making it sound gruffer than normal.

Nobody on the ship responded to his hail, and it kept coming towards them. "Ready yourselves," he said to his men, and a few of them shuffled their feet, as if that was what readying themselves entailed.

"Identify yourselves!" the commander called again to the vessel. "Or else we will be forced to take action."

A few of the sea guards looked at each other, wondering just what action the commander might order them to take. They were poorly armed and their vessel was much smaller than that bearing down on them.

The commander chewed his lip, half expecting a phalanx of Othmen archers to suddenly rise from behind the ship's rails and send a storm of barbed arrows at them. But instead a single elderly woman came to the railing and called out them, "Let us pass. Please."

The commander looked at her and frowned. "You are not showing the required flags," he called. "Where are you coming from?"

"From Kaffa," she called back.

He knew it well. It was one of the Floating City's colonies to the north east, along the waterways of the Russ. But he had heard it was being besieged by Othmen troops.

"What news from Kaffa?" he called to her.

"The city has fallen to the Othmen. We are refugees."

All his men looked at each other in alarm. The city was extremely well defended with high walls, and over the decades many armies had tried unsuccessfully to take it.

"How?" he called. "Kaffa is impregnable."

"We had thought so," she said. "But the Othmen hurled plague-ridden corpses over the city walls on their catapults. The whole city became infected. Men, women and children. The suffering was terrible."

"Othmen swine," he muttered. He was on the verge of ordering his men to allow the ship to pass, when a thought closed his throat.

"Have you plague on board?" he called.

"We are refugees. Please let us pass."

"Have you plague on board?"

"Many of us are citizens of the Floating City," she called, "and request our right for admittance into the city."

The commander chewed his lip again, coming close to drawing blood. Any citizen of the Floating City did have a right to be admitted to the city, but if the ship was carrying plague…

He called a third time. "Are you carrying plague? Answer me or we will take action." His men seemed to take a small step back from him, as if more reluctant to take this action, whatever it was, against a plague ship than against Othmen archers.

"We have sick children in need of medical care," the woman at the ship's rail called and she turned and beckoned with her hands and then two more women came up to the railing, both holding babes who the men could now hear crying with choked and gasping wheezes.

The commander stood there for some moments, as the ship bore right down on top of them, until one of his men asked, "What should we do? Should we stop them?"

"How will we stop them?" asked another.

"They have a right to enter the city," said a third.

"But we have a duty to stop them," said another.

The commander felt that whatever he said next would determine if he would reach his sixth decade still in his position or not, but words failed him. He would be criticized for whatever decision he made today, he knew.

"Burn the ship," said one man.

"Let them pass," said another.

"Make them drop anchor."

"Send them back where they came from."

If he let the ship past or turned it back he was certain the council would decide it was the wrong decision and he would receive some punishment for it.

"Quarantine," said another. "Put them in quarantine and let the council decide."

The commander turned to the last speaker to see who it was. A young man he'd had his eye on for promotion for some time. "Yes," he said aloud. "Escort the vessel to the Isle of Sorrows and keep it there under quarantine."

He looked up to see the faces of the three women at the railing of the ship, so close now he could make out the dark blemishes on their skin, like he could clearly see the look of desperation in their eyes. He had heard that the plague was transferred by touch. But others said it was enough to breathe the same air that a victim exhaled.

"And any man who comes in too close contact is going to be left on the isle with them, understand?"

The vessel's crew started moving now, hauling on lines to turn them about to escort the ship through into the lagoon. The commander gave a satisfied nod. Putting them into quarantine was as much as no decision at all, but he had learned from his many years as an official that no decision was often the best decision of all.

XLVI
THE STORY OF ISABELLA

Isabella found herself a little distracted today. She was trying to concoct a plan to send four ships to the ancient kingdoms to the south in secret. They would not even know they were sailing on her ships, so as to avoid the crews deserting her in fear of the Othmen vendetta against her. They desperately needed to bring more grain into the city, but there were so many things to consider. The likely weather patterns at this time of year, the possibility of lesser pirates and where they might be, how good a crop the kingdoms had had and what prices they would be seeking. Also which captains should she send who would be both able seamen and competent traders? And the ships, she had to balance speed against storage capacity.

And of course the risk of an Othmen attack. There were times she wondered if they really did have some enchantment that allowed them to find a ship anywhere on the ocean, whether at day or night, or it was just a bluff by the Othmen envoy. And then there was also the envoy. She still had to find a way to outwit him. She had already taken a gamble in sending a letter to a Graecian nobleman of her husband's acquaintance, gossiping about the envoy's excess and corruption, accusing him of keeping a harem of young women and living like a sultan on Othmen funds. There was a very good chance that the letter would be intercepted, or even that her husband's acquaintance would sell the information contained in it to the Othmen. The first accusations might only get them a little riled, but when she also suggested that he had turned his coat yet again, and was now working for the Floating City against the Othmen – they would want his blood.

He would undoubtedly be warned by friends and informers and decide to take his many purloined treasures and flee further to the west, taking his poisonous lies with him.

So many things to concentrate on, but today she found her thoughts kept drifting back to moments of conversation with the young captain Giannetto, from the evening before. It had really been most pleasant.

She frowned. If it had been her handmaiden who had been continually distracted in her work by thoughts of a handsome young man she would have admonished her. And if it had been one of her captains, moping distractedly over a young woman, she would have been more than a little annoyed with him. But there was nobody to chide her but herself – and she found that she could not rely on herself to do so. Every time she told herself to concentrate on the task before her, she would find her mind turned slowly to the way the young captain had smiled or something witty he had said. Or even something particularly clever she had told him.

She stood up from the desk, walked to the window and looked out over the ocean that all her wealth and her livelihood came from. For the first time in as long as she could remember since her husband had been killed, she found she did not have an overwhelming urge to take a ship and sail off over the horizon.

Then she crossed over to a looking glass and considered the woman there. The familiar face but with the soft edges of a smile to it. "Who are you?" she asked. "I'm not sure I know you." The face looked back at her, unanswering. "I'm not sure you should be trusted to doing business," she said to herself cautiously. "Not today." She was trying to decide if she liked the face she was looking at, and asked, "What do you think?"

"Um, about what?" asked her handmaiden.

Isabella spun around and saw the woman in the doorway, looking a little confused. Isabella waved her hand in the air, dismissing the question without answering it. "What is it?" she asked.

Her handmaiden, she saw, also had a smile to the edges of her mouth and she tried hard to pull her own down into a frown. "It's a message for you," she said. "From a suitor."

Isabella's face now did drop into a frown and she said, in a harsh voice, "I told you I would take no more messages from these old suitors. I have no desire to meet these unknown men."

"This one is not unknown, my lady," said the handmaiden, holding out a letter.

Isabella stood there for quite some time before walking across and taking it from her. Surely one of her own captains would not have the audacity! She took the letter, expecting the other woman to withdraw from the room, but she did not. Isabella looked at her and then looked at the letter, letting her gaze drop to the signature first. It was well written, with a distinct flourish, and read Giannetto Scali!

She glanced across at the handmaiden who had suddenly found something very interesting on the floor at her feet to be examining. She looked back to the letter. Giannetto had written that he was full of apologies for his behaviour the night before and could not understand what had happened to him, and would be filled with shame until his dying day if she did not agree to let him have supper with her again tonight, and he would have a second vessel and cargo readied by then. The rest didn't need to be written.

"I suppose he's waiting for an answer?" Isabella asked.

"Yes, my lady," said the handmaiden.

Isabella tapped the letter and threw it to the table amongst all her papers and then walked back to the looking glass. Her instincts were to say no, but she could see the woman in the glass was going to say yes, and could see the faint smile lines clearly returning to it again.

XLVII

ELSEWHERE IN THE FLOATING CITY

The Djinn circled Vincenzo slowly. He turned and tried to keep it within view, but it sank deeper into the waters and he felt the swirling currents where it swam past him. He spun and tried to find it, but could not see it. Then he felt it brush against him as if taunting him, and he turned again, and then felt the coarse touch of scales against the back of his legs.

He kicked out, vainly hoping to scare it away. He wanted to keep turning to keep it in front of him, but his limbs were as sluggish as if he was underwater. He tried to lift himself free, but felt himself sinking deeper. It was water but it wasn't. He could breathe, though it felt thick and stuffy in his mouth. The waters gripped him, but were dry.

He reached out his arms to find something to grab hold of to pull himself free, but there was nothing. He looked up and saw the buildings and bridges of the city. And he saw stars about him. As if the city was floating in the night's sky. As if the canals were not filled with water, but something darker and heavier.

And the Djinn circled in closer, the large head leaning in closer to his, as if just wanting him to know it was there. He saw the red fire in the eyes and the jaws open in a wide mocking smile.

Vincenzo tossed and turned in his thin bed, legs entangled in the blankets, trying in vain to avoid the beast that circled around inside his head.

XLVIII

ELSEWHERE IN THE FLOATING CITY

The commander of the marine guard had just enough time to feel pleased with himself for solving the problem of the plague ship when a breathless young private came running with the alarming news. An Othmen vessel had been sighted approaching the city. The commander looked at the private as if he was talking a foreign language and had him repeat it slowly. Then he began trembling and found he could hardly stand, as he called all men to stations and sent word to the city to send reinforcements.

By the time an extra fifty men had arrived and taken up positions around the outer walls of the floating fort that stood by the lagoon entrance, they could see the enemy ship. It had that Othmen cut of sharp points and menace that all knew, though few of the soldiers had actually seen.

A few old hands who had fought the Othmen already told the other men to be vigilant, for the Othmen would hurl balls of fire at them from a long distance. Or poisoned darts that they would not see until they struck them. Or they'd send naked men covered in oil, swimming unseen through the water to climb up the walls at their rear and attack them. Then the ship would bear down on them like a wraith, they said.

But the vessel was actually approaching very slowly, and was flying diplomatic flags of truce. That had to be a trick, of course.

The Othmen deceits were legend. The commander, leaning on a battlement edge to hold himself up, as if his backbone had been ripped from his body, ordered a warning shot fired over the bow of the ship as soon as it was within range. But to his consternation, the ship dropped anchor, just out of cannon range and a small boat detached itself and rowed straight towards them.

Even the launch had the cut of sharp points and danger to it. The commander looked for the young guard whose advice he had taken earlier, and asked him, almost casually, "What would you do if you were in my shoes?"

"Wait for Otello," the young man said.

"Yes, Otello," the commander answered. "That is what I would do too. We must summon him at once."

But the younger man shook his head. "He will be here as soon as he hears of the Othmen ship."

He was right, of course, and the commander turned his telescope to look towards the Floating City, expecting a vessel with the Moor on board to come rowing out to them at any moment. He swivelled back to look at the Othmen launch and then back to the city, but the only vessel he could see approaching was the Othmen one.

"Why doesn't he come?" he asked – and nobody could answer him. "The launch will be here momentarily." But then he saw, to his continued consternation, that the Othmen launch was not even making its way towards them but was heading directly for the city.

"I wonder if we should fire on it?" the commander asked, as if it were a rhetorical question.

"I wouldn't," suggested the young man. "What if it is a messenger?" He looked at the commander who seemed not to understand. "With an important message," he added.

"Or an assassin?" asked the commander.

"Or carrying a treaty?" said the young man.

The commander chewed his lip. He wanted to sit down and

have somebody tell him the ship had gone away. He would be removed from his position for letting the Othmen go past. But he might be punished worse if he killed a messenger. "It's some Othmen trick," he said. "Why else does he not surrender to our investigations, as is custom?"

"Who can understand the ways of the Othmen," the young man said. "He must be important though, to presume to just bypass us and head straight for the city."

"Important, yes," said the commander. "But it could be a hellish trick too."

"He'll be met at the docks by over a hundred guardsmen," the younger man said. "No single Othmen warrior could face that many men. He's more likely a messenger."

The commander chewed his lip for some moments and then snapped his fingers at an underling. "Quickly. Take a message to the city. We are letting a representative of the Othmen pass."

The underling looked surprised. "Letting an Othmen into the city?"

"No," the commander said sharply, as if addressing a simpleton. "We are letting him pass. The city guard will decide if he is to set foot into the city. Now go!" Then he turned his telescope back to the launch. He could now make out six large black men rowing at the oars and a single figure standing, becloaked in a dark garment, in the rear.

He then sent a strict order to all the assembled troops that none was to fire on the launch unless they were fired on first. Then he sent another order that none were to mock it or call out insults. Then a third, that men should keep their weapons ready nevertheless. He watched carefully as the launch got closer, but the figure did not even turn his head to acknowledge the existence of the marine guard with their weapons pointing at him as he came alongside them and then rowed past.

The tall figure in the rear of the launch had a dark turban wrapped around his head with only his eyes showing, and stood as aloof as a regent or prince.

"What if he's a Djinn?" the commander heard one of his men ask. "What if we've let a Djinn into the city? What will become of our families?"

The commander, having already let a plague ship into the city that morning, could only turn his telescope to the city dock where he could see a small army had assembled, and pray that his day was not going to get any worse.

As the launch approached the city, those vessels moored closest to its path lifted anchor and moved further away as either the wind or oarsmen would allow. Word of the Othmen vessel had spread through the city faster than a flood tide, and several of the council members and Seers had lodged themselves by windows in the buildings nearby to witness events. They had even decided to temporarily restore their faith in Otello as the city's delegate to meet this Othmen menace. The Moor chose only ceremonial armour and went unarmed, except for a single curved knife, hidden in a sash behind his back, and pushed his way through the ranks of the nervous guardsmen to be closest to the water's edge. The men around him whispered and shuffled like nervous horses smelling blood or fire, and he held out and arm and bellowed, "Silence. And be still. You are the protectors of the Floating City." The men paid him immediate heed, as men always did, and stood ramrod straight. All eyes were on him and he nodded his approval. Just once. Then he turned to watch the slow progress of the launch making its way towards them.

It was moving almost leisurely and Otello knew that was deliberate. The six large black men he could see at the oars would put a small sailing skiff to shame in a race, he was certain, if they chose to. Or were ordered to. These were men who had been castrated and had had their tongues ripped out, and only lived to obey orders. He wondered if he would have to kill any of them today.

Then he turned his attention to the figure in the rear of the vessel. He watched how he moved his body just slightly with the rocking of the boat, and it seemed to Otello that he was searching the crowd of soldiers to seek him out. So he took a step forward and put his hands on his hips. He knew the Othmen considered black-skinned races inferior and were dishonoured when he had defeated them in battle. And he was determined that whatever type of battle ensued today, he would dishonour this Othmen.

The launch was soon within hailing distance, but neither did the figure in the vessel call out to anyone standing on the stones of the city, nor did anyone in the city call out to the Othmen. The boat rowed right up to the stone stairs at Otello's feet and one of the black-skinned slaves turned to cast a rope and make it fast there to an iron ring. Then the figure in the rear leapt lightly out of the boat, landing on the steps like a cat. Then he strode up the stairs boldly and at the top of the steps, paused a moment and looked around at the city buildings, completely ignoring both Otello and the hundred or more guardsmen assembled there. He took a few steps to the right and then the left and Otello noticed the way the guardsmen backed away from him as he did, and knew that if the figure had chosen to walk through the city, the guards would part before him like darkness fleeing from light.

He wondered if the man were smirking under that black cloth turban mask. Otello noted he was as tall as himself and very lithe. He also noted the sword the Othmen wore at his side and the richness of his dark clothes. Jewels were stitched into the edges of them. The figure then turned and met his eyes. Otello was surprised to see emerald green eyes regarding him, for Othmen had eyes as dark as coal.

Otello knew he should step forward and introduce himself, but he chose to wait. The figure regarded him a moment longer and then lifted a hand to the black material wound tightly around his head and began unwinding it. So slowly. And the face, when it emerged, surprised. Otello heard the gasp from the ranks of men behind him, at the feat of enchantment they witnessed. The figure had long dark hair and thick red lips. Had the face the shape of an Othmen, but the colour of a Grecian. The face was haughty, but was beautiful.

She turned and looked at the men now, and saw them wither a little before her glance. Then, finally, she turned back to Otello. She regarded him carefully, and smirked. Then she stepped closer to him. He found he had to contain himself from a sudden maddened impulse to draw his dagger and lunge at her, as he saw remarkable strength and danger in the way she moved. What a piece of work this woman was, he thought.

"I am Shakri al Basak," she said in a slightly gravelled and accented voice, and with a slight bow of her head.

"I am Otello," he replied. "I stand here for the city."

She nodded. "I know you. In other times we would be enemies. But today we are not. I am the new Othmen envoy," she said. "The old one will be taken out to my ship in a cage within the hour."

XLIX

THE STORY OF DISDEMONA

The ensign had been trying to concoct an excuse to get close to Disdemona for most of the day. He'd had more success in concocting the Othmen potion that he was feeding Otello in his drink to fuel his madness and jealousy. It had been a valuable find at the island of the Guild. But Otello had been withstanding it. A lesser man would have long ago succumbed to it fully, and have been putty in his hands, unable to resist the poisonous whispers he had been feeding him.

He needed something more. He needed to ignite those fires of madness and jealousy in him, the way a barrel of oil could be ignited by as simple a thing as a candle flame. And his flame would be a simple strawberry-engraved kerchief. If only he could get his hands upon it.

But Disdemona wore it close to her breast, almost never being without it. And that would take a master of distraction and the subtle hands of a thief to procure. Fortunately he knew where to obtain both – but finding an opportune moment would be a lot harder. That was until the Othmen ship arrived. The story went around the city faster than any of the council's decrees ever had. A single ship had arrived. Six ships had arrived. An Othmen fleet had arrived. A single small boat was making its way to the city. A single Othmen was riding a Djinn into the city. A half-human half-Djinn Othmen had emerged from the waters in the harbour, demanding a truce. Declaring war. Surrendering lands the Othmen had captured from the Floating City. Seeking a trade treaty. Wishing to form an alliance against the Mongol empire. Wishing to end their conflict through hand-to-hand combat of champions.

Everybody wanted to see what the Othmen looked like. They were afraid and they were intrigued. The ensign knew it would be like the way people were drawn to the scene of a violent accident. And Disdemona would be no less likely to want to see this Othmen than any other citizen of the city. More so, most likely, since the Othmen were the part of her husband's life that she was least likely to ever understand – and if she found she needed to understand her husband more than at any other time, she would be drawn to see this Othmen as he arrived at the city.

The ensign gathered two men to him, who went by the names of the rat and toad, and they made their way to the Bridge of Sighs, where the curious and horrified would have to cross to find a safe viewing vantage in one of the houses around the harbour. Only those who had friends whose houses actually overlooked the harbour would actually have a chance of witnessing anything, he knew, and that meant more nobility would be on the streets and plazas, to visit a long-neglected friend or relative, than had been out and about in many weeks.

It would be a good day to be a pick-purse, he mused, knowing that if he did not have the two men in his employ they would be busy enough on their own. The first man, the rat, was a small thin fellow with fingers that could reach into the deepest pocket undetected, and the other, the toad, was a stout ugly fellow, handy in picking fights and ending them with a hidden blade. Both regularly sold their services and their silence.

The ensign had them assemble just in front of the bridge and he made his way up onto its arch, where he could observe the crowd and sight Disdemona. The crowd pushing their way past him was strong, but he growled at those who jostled him so that people stepped around him. The populace pushing past him were little more than sheep, he thought. People like him had a right to rule them and if not for a trick of fate, having him born to a lesser family, he knew he would have been a ruler of men. He should have been the one giving the commands that the sheep followed, not men like the Duca or Otello.

He turned his head and spat into the canal. The Moor wasn't even a believer. He was a heathen. And black skinned. Every time he touched the beautiful pale skin of Disdemona there should have been an outrage across the city. But that time would come.

He scanned the crowd for her. The city was alive today, its citizens like a garland of different-coloured flowers moving about, bringing the cold stone and brickwork to life. The people were all buzzing with talk of the Othmen. Merchants were leaving their stalls and school teachers were leaving their classes. Servants were finding excuses to leave their households and others snuck away. Strangers on the narrow streets were asking each other what they had heard or knew, and the ensign occasionally told a passing citizen that he had it on good authority that the city guard had declared they would cut off the heads of any Othmen who stepped foot on the Floating City, and they would be able to witness the deaths of many Othmen today. But only if they hurried to beat everyone else.

He scanned the crowd again and then he saw her, moving her way through the crowd with just one handmaiden beside her. He made a quick hand signal to the two men to let them know she was approaching and saw them readying themselves. The ensign wished it was himself who was going to put his hand into her bodice and grab the kerchief, but he knew he would not be able to do so without grabbing, and cruelly squeezing, her pale breast. Since she had spurned him he had dreamed many nights of violently having his way with her. But he would hang for that. Far better that she suffered at the hands of her own husband the Moor.

The ensign took his passions out on cheap whores, paying them more for their bruises. He had tried to seduce one of Disdemona's handmaidens for a time, thinking he would use her to get to her mistress, but she had rebuffed him too. He would bide his time to be avenged on her as well.

He looked to the rat and the toad and looked back to Disdemona, as if this was a chessboard before him and he was moving all the pieces around so it would play out just as he wished. First the toad would jostle her violently and then turn to apologize, while the rat would dart a hand in and steal the kerchief. The toad could then stand there with his bare hands open if she felt something. The feeling of knowing this made him grin like a lunatic. He was filled with the elation of it.

If they were as good as they claimed he would not even know the moment it happened, but he doubted it. Then she was in front of the bridge, being squeezed by the crowd, her handmaiden pushed back a little behind her. She was moving her hands about, trying to get the people to stand back from her, but the crowd would not be parting for her today.

He saw the toad move to step in front of Disdemona, and then suddenly a hooded figure blocked his path. The toad tried to push him aside, but the man did something to the toad and he disappeared beneath the crowd. Then he saw the hooded figure step across to block the rat, and he too disappeared from sight. He blinked rapidly and shook his head a little. What was happening? This was not how it should be playing out.

He now saw Disdemona move onto the bridge, with the crowd pushing her along, and the hooded figure was gone. He felt his elation turning to dread. Then he heard a squeal as someone in the crowd called out, "Murder!" And he watched the crowd part around two places where men obviously lay on the ground, dead. It would be the rat and the toad.

He was confounded. What had just happened? And before he could regain his composure, Disdemona was standing before him and was then pressed into him by the surging panicked crowd. She didn't even recognize him as she tried to turn her head and find her handmaiden. He looked down into her handsome chest, pressed against his, and felt his hands rising towards it.

The crowd pressed again, with more calling out 'Murder,' and she was pressed so tightly against him that he was bent back over the railing of the bridge. He could have bent down and placed his head between those breasts and suckled like a babe. He could have grasped them in both hands and squeezed. He could have put his arms around her and pulled her tight to him. But then the crowd had surged again and she was pushed past him, squashed into another man, and then another.

He watched her as she was jostled across the bridge and spilled out onto the other side, and then saw her reach into her bosom for that strawberry-embroidered kerchief, perhaps to press it to her mouth and stifle her distress. He saw the consternation on her face when her hand came away as empty as his own had. The look on her face may have mirrored his own, and then the crowd carried her out of sight.

L

ELSEWHERE IN THE FLOATING CITY

The Seers were preparing for a ceremony that had not been conducted for many decades. "Everything will change tonight," the female of the Spring Seers said as she sat the two youngsters down in a twin seat in the middle of a darkened chamber. "You will realize your full power over time, but it all starts this evening."

"Yes, today everything changes," said her husband.

"Will it hurt?" was all the boy Mario asked, and the Seer smiled back at him as if he was a simpleton. "Many things in life hurt," she said. "But that does not mean they are bad."

Her husband, with one hand still in hers, stood before the young girl, Rosa. He laid a hand on the side of her cheek and said, "So pretty." She drew her head back from his a little, having seen the types of looks he was giving her in many men's eyes before today.

"Patience," said the female Spring Seer, giving her husband's hand a slight squeeze. She turned to the girl and said, "Do not be afraid."

"I'm not afraid," the young girl said. The Seer nodded her head and smiled, though she was thinking that the young girl had plenty of reason to be afraid, but it would be better if she was not.

The Summer Seers stood by a small fire burning in a brass pot, into which they were casting herbs, filling the room with a sickly-smelling smoke.

"It smells," said the boy.

"Many things smell," said the female Spring Seer. "If you don't like the smell, breathe through your mouth." She smiled again. He nodded his head and did so.

"We are ready," said the male Summer Seer.

"Come," said the female Spring Seer, holding out her hand for him to come and take it. He and his wife walked across, and all four then joined hands, forming a circle around Mario and Rosa. They shut their eyes and began mumbling in a strange tongue and Mario felt a shiver run up his spine and the sudden urge to flee the room. He looked across to Rosa, and saw her eyes were wide. He wondered if she felt it too. Or was he feeling it from her, through their hands. Since they had been holding hands for such long periods they were starting to feel things from each other.

"This is wrong," he started to tell her, when suddenly the two Spring Seers let go of each other's hands and reached out to them. They grasped their heads in their gnarled old hands and squeezed. Mario felt thumbs digging into his eyes and sharp fingernails probing for his ears and digging into them. He wanted to scream, but could not. Then he felt a thumb drop into his mouth and prise it open, but he could still feel both thumbs pressing into his eyes, digging at the jelly of his eyeballs. Now there were several fingers prising his mouth open and thrusting deep inside his throat. He tried to shout out but his airway was blocked. Something long and dry was moving down his throat and deep into his chest and stomach. He felt his body shaking and felt Rosa's hand clenching his so tightly it was like they were being crushed under a heavy stone.

The pain went on and on and on and then suddenly started lifting from him. There were no more hands on his face and he opened his eyes. The lids were clammy as if stuck together, but parted and he saw he was looking at himself and Rosa sitting there. He did not understand and turned his head to see who was holding his hand. It was the female Spring Seer, staring back at him with an equal look of confusion. "What happened?" he asked in an addled old-man's voice.

Then the boy who was him, sitting in front of him, stood up. He lifted Rosa from her seat too and then stretched and smiled. "I promised you that today everything changes, did I not?" he said.

LI

THE STORY OF GIULIETTA

"You're oblivious to anything that doesn't concern you, aren't you?" said Romeo's good friend Marcuccio.

"What do you mean?" Romeo asked him. The two young men sat at an outdoor café by the Square of the Lion, drinking wine.

"Did you know that a new Othmen envoy arrived in the city today? A woman! And did you know there is going to be a ceremony to induct two new Seers?"

"I thought the Othmen kept their women tied up and masked, or something like that," said Romeo.

Marcuccio shook his head. "Obviously not all of them," he said. "They say this one dresses like a warrior and faced down Otello. He's not a man to be easily intimidated."

"He's to be my brother-in-law," said Romeo. "That will be a useful thing."

"Or not a man to upset," his friend said. "What if he thinks you are treating Giulietta like an Othmen and comes looking for you?"

"He'll never find us," said Romeo.

"Where are you going to go to?" Marcuccio asked, picking up the bottle on the table and topping up their cups.

"I'd like to tell you, but if I did, then when Otello tortured you and bit off your testicles one by one, you might tell him."

Marcuccio laughed. "How did you know that I have often

dreamt of the Moor putting my testicles in his mouth?"

Romeo laughed too.

"To the Lady Giulietta, then," said Marcuccio and raised his cup.

"To the Lady Giulietta," said Romeo.

The two men raised the cups to their lips when an angry voice behind them said, "Do you mock my cousin?"

Romeo put down his cup and turned his head. "Tebaldo Montecchi," he said. It was Giulietta's cousin. A boorish man who fancied himself a swordsman and merchant and so many other things it was laughable. "I thought the air smelled a little foul suddenly."

The other youth, his brow knotted into a single angry line, took a step closer to the two friends. "I have been looking for you," he said.

"I am flattered," said Romeo. "Do you want a loan or some advice?"

Tebaldo took another step closer and put a hand to his sword hilt. Romeo and Marcuccio's eyes followed his hand. "I think he's out of sorts today," said Marcuccio. "Perhaps we should invite him to drink with us, rather than just insult him."

"But a little wine might make him meaner," said Romeo.

Marcuccio shrugged. "Perhaps we should ask him," he said. "I hear he speaks our language."

Tebaldo pushed a chair to the floor and drew his sword. "Mock me not," he said. "I can bear your dishonours, but it is the dishonour you do my cousin that I must avenge."

"It is just a toast to her health," said Marcuccio, raising his hands in a peace offering.

"You dishonour her more than that," said Tebaldo, his sword tip wavering from his anger.

"What do you refer to?" asked Romeo cautiously.

"You attended the ball at her house in disguise. Do not deny it."

"Ah," said Romeo, smiling a little once more. "Oh that. I meant no dishonour."

"Your mere presence was a dishonour," Tebaldo spat. "You have insulted her and dishonoured our house and you must answer for it."

Romeo sighed. "He's such a boor," he said to Marcuccio. "All right. We duel. Five days hence in the gardens of antiquity."

"Now," said Tebaldo, and brought his sword down onto the table, knocking their cups and wine glasses off it. The two friends jumped to their feet. Romeo backed away quickly. "Not so fast, not so fast," he said. "You must do me the right of having time to prepare and work myself up into a state of rage equal to yours."

"I would have agreed except for the way you mock me," said Tebaldo. "You will answer for it now."

"Patience, patience," said Marcuccio. "You know the council's decree. It is a banishable offence to attack or slay another in a public place."

"Cowards," said Tebaldo and lashed out with his sword, cutting into Romeo's shirt, slashing the expensive cloth. Romeo looked shocked and fell back, tangling his feet in a chair and falling over, while Marcuccio quickly had his own blade out to parry the return stroke.

The few patrons of the café fled at the sound of metal on metal, calling for help.

"This is not your fight," growled Tebaldo.

"You seem to make it mine," Marcuccio countered. "And you might find me a more equal opponent than Romeo, who is better with words than he is with a sword."

"Then have at you," spat Tebaldo and thrust at Marcuccio, who deftly parried attack after attack.

"I am growing bored," he called to Romeo, "Do you wish to take over?"

Romeo, with his own sword in his hand, attacked Tebaldo from his flank and Romeo laughed at the look on his face. "If you apologize now we will let you walk away," he said. Tebaldo, in response, whistled loudly and Romeo saw three more young men draw swords and start walking towards them.

"I think our sport is done," said Marcuccio, holding up his sword. "Let us now talk seriously about how honour will best be restored as you will soon be cousins."

Tebaldo, his blood so hot it boiled behind his eyes, took the opportunity and thrust his blade at him. Marcuccio tried to jump back and the blade just pierced his chest. He looked down at the sudden red blossom that sprang forth on his tunic. "A scratch," he said.

Romeo now jumped between the two men, to prevent Tebaldo stabbing his friend again and Tebaldo turned his rage on Romeo, lunging at him. Romeo dodged the stroke though, and it passed under his arm, fully piercing Marcuccio. Romeo did not even notice for a moment until he heard his good friend fall to the ground behind him, tipping chairs and tables.

"Marcuccio," he called.

"I am slain," he said. "Your conflict has claimed another innocent life." Blood trickled up over his lips and he spat it to the ground in front of him. "Your blade was poisoned," he accused Tebaldo.

"It was not," he protested, the sight of the bleeding man suddenly robbing his rage.

"It was a poison that the war between your two houses has brewed. We should have been friends all, but fight to the death for nothing of any worth other than honour." He coughed and spat more blood. "I wish a curse on both your houses until the poison runs its course."

"No," said Romeo. "Do not speak so."

"I speak so and mean it," said Marcuccio. "The closeness of death makes me speak plainly."

"I did not mean to kill him," said Tebaldo, turning to his friends, who stood stock still.

"But I mean to slay you," said Romeo, truly infected by the poison that Marcuccio had died of. He slashed at Tebaldo. The other's defence lacked strength and Romeo quickly fought past his guard and stabbed him in the heart, twisting his blade fiercely before pulling it free. Marcuccio gasped and his breath bubbled as if he was underwater, drowning in his own blood.

Romeo only vaguely heard the call of citizens saying, "Murder." Barely registered the sound of the guard pushing their way through the witnesses towards him. Saw only the look on his dead friend's face and the glazed look in his eyes, as empty as his own grand plans for the future.

LII

ELSEWHERE IN THE FLOATING CITY

One more lone boat crossed to the Floating City that evening. This one from the mainland, travelling at night, when all traffic from the mainland was prohibited. There was a single oarsman and a single passenger, both dark-clad, and moving under the cover of clouds.

The oarsman was more cautious of the occasional stirrings in the water than he was of encountering any of the city guards. Men could be bribed or fought. Monsters in the water could not. He had demanded ten-fold his normal fee for the crossing and the stranger had agreed to it. Then he had demanded the payment up front and the stranger reached into a pouch at his waist, counted out the coins and flung them to him. "Half now, half when we arrive," he said in an accent that the boatman could not place and knew better than to ask. If the man had wanted to make conversation about his homeland he would be crossing to the city during the daylight, and telling the city customs officers his story.

The boatman had smuggled many men into the Floating City and many goods. And they were as silent as each other on the trip across the narrow strip of water. His oars were wrapped in cloth to dampen their sounds and the boat was painted black and sat low to the water. Before departing he made sure that any passengers were able to press themselves flat to the bottom of the boat if a vessel with a lantern came too close to them.

But those customs men were fools. They illuminated their boats and talked too much. It was fair behaviour for the bribes they took though, so the smugglers knew just where they were at any time.

Most men who were sneaking into the Floating City went to a lot of trouble to disguise themselves, wearing a mask or hiding their face, but the man he was carrying across tonight did not. He had a short sharp beard, dark eyes and he was sure his sister would describe him as handsome. His fingers were covered in some type of metal gloves, extending half down the fingers and ending in points.

The boatman only looked at them briefly while sizing the man up. He looked rich. That was the most important thing about him. So they waited for the clouds to thicken and pushed off from the shore. The boatman was looking at the man sitting in the rear of his boat as he rowed, and could have sworn the man's eyes shone like those of a cat whenever he looked straight at him, but for most of the journey he was looking about at the water around them, as if watching something there. That unsettled the boatman a little.

More so when the stranger suddenly put his hand to his lips and said, "Shhh!" The boatman stopped and turned his head to look over his shoulder. He couldn't see any lights on the water, just those of the Floating City ahead of them. Then he closed his eyes to listen. There was no sound of voices or oars. "What is it?" he asked in a low voice.

"Shhh," said the man again. Then the boatman heard it. A soft splash of something moving in the water nearby. It was too big for a fish. Then again. Closer. He felt a chill run through his veins. The boatman waited until he was certain the water was still again, and then dipped his oars into the waters once more, moving them slowly forward.

It proved rash. The water swirled around the boat as if something was swimming around and around beneath them.

"Not a word," the stranger cautioned, in the softest of voices, and then pulled out a small pouch from inside his tunic. He reached in and grabbed a handful of what looked to the boatman like silver dust, and cast it around them into the water. It sparkled, even with no moonlight, and settled on the surface of the water.

The swirling and thrashing stopped.

The two men remained completely still for some time and then the stranger nodded his head. "Go on," he whispered.

The oarsman put his oars back into the water and continued rowing. They made their way into one of the lesser canals of the city and pulled up at a dock. It sat lower in the water than usual, with only the top step free of the water.

The stranger stood to step out of the boat, but the boatman held out an arm and stopped him. "My fee," said the boatman. "You still owe me half my payment."

The stranger's hand flicked quickly and the metal gloves he wore flashed under the city's lights and the boatman fell back, gurgling as if he had fallen into the water. Drowning in the blood of his own cut throat.

He fell flat into the bottom of his boat and the stranger stepped out and put a foot to it, sending it drifting back out onto the waters. The water swirled a little ahead of it. "An offering," the man said in his native tongue, and then turned and walked into the city.

The Djinn-slayer had arrived.

LIII

THE STORY OF ISABELLA

Giannetto awoke to find his mast erect and an empty place in the bed beside him. He couldn't believe it. It had happened again. He rolled across and breathed in her scent. She had been there beside him throughout the night and he had failed to win her. He reached down and took hold of his member and began stroking it, groaning a little, trying to imagine it was her hands holding him.

A sudden cough roused him. He looked down and saw an elderly lady at the foot of the bed. The same old crone who had been waiting to pass him his clothes and lead him out of the house as before. She was trying very hard to hide a smirk. He sighed and threw a pillow over his face, wondering just how much worse his humiliation was going to get. Then he remembered the loan.

"Oh dio mio!" he said with an altogether different groan.

Back out on the chill stone streets of the Floating City, Giannetto began to ponder his predicament. He had borrowed the ship and trade goods from his uncle to woo Isabella, certain he would succeed this time. Now he had lost it. And he had no way of paying it back as he had promised.

He made his way to a wine tavern, went inside and slumped at a bench, ordering the largest pitcher of the cheapest wine they

215

had. At least he could continue his humiliation and return home as drunk as a peasant.

He had just begun his second glass, however, when a stranger sat down beside him with a small flagon of much nicer wine and said, "If you're determined to drink yourself silly at this time of the morning, you should at least do it with better wine." He poured Giannetto a cup.

"Who are you?" asked Giannetto, taking the cup nevertheless.

The man shrugged. "Call me Marco. I work for many people. My last master had to leave the city in a hurry, but had charged me with fulfilling a task before I left it too."

"These are dangerous times," said Giannetto. "Many people might well follow your lead and leave the city. Alas I cannot be one of them."

"How so?" asked the stranger.

"I have debts here to pay."

The man nodded. "Yes, we all have debts and I think it worth having them all settled before the Othmen arrive at our shores."

"You think they will come this far?"

"It is only a matter of time." He took a long drink of his wine and asked, "What is your trade?"

"I am a ship's captain. Or I was. I no longer have a ship."

"Let me guess," said Marco. "Isabella Montecchi?"

"Yes," said Giannetto. "The story is that well known?"

He shrugged. "My master was very familiar with the story. Is there any truth to it?"

Giannetto sighed. "The only truth worth knowing is that I have tried twice and failed," he said. "And I cannot try again. But I don't believe anybody loves her as much as I do."

"Why do you love her?" asked Marco.

"Ah," said Giannetto with a smile. "Who could not? She is beautiful. She is proud. She is clever. I have admired her from afar, like many others, but to spend an evening with her, dining with her I mean, you cannot imagine how wonderful she is. I feel

like a moth drawn to a flame. Like a ..." He searched around for
another metaphor.

"Like a man in love drawn to his intended?" asked the man.

Giannetto held up his cup in a toast. "Exactly," he said, and
took another deep drink.

"Are you familiar with the Othmen saying that the third time
is the charm? If you were to believe that, the third attempt would
certainly win her hand."

Giannetto looked at him and cocked his eyebrow.

"Well, not just her hand," he said in a conspiratorial voice. "If
you know what I mean?"

Giannetto held up a finger and waved it a little at the man. "I'm
beginning to like you. But I have no means to borrow a ship and
trade goods."

"Who did you borrow from last time?"

"From my uncle. But he has no more ships that he could lend
me, even if I could assure him of success. The Othmen have been
attacking his trading vessels as if they knew where they were
going to be and when."

The man tut-tutted. "Then perhaps I can introduce you to a
man who my master did business with regularly."

"Who is this man?" Giannetto asked, seizing on the possibility.

"He is a moneylender and a Son of David. A reputable man."

Giannetto sat back in his chair and thought about that. "He
would lend me the money?" he asked.

"I am sure he would if I put in a good word for you."

Giannetto nodded his head eagerly.

"There would be a condition though," Marco said.

"Yes?" asked Giannetto.

"He will ask for a rather unusual guarantee of the loan."

Giannetto took another drink and waited for him to go on.

"The condition would be that if the loan was forfeit, then you
would forfeit a pound of your flesh in return."

"A pound of flesh?" asked Giannetto, incredulously.

"Just so," said Marco.

Giannetto licked his lips. "Do you mean from my own body?"

"Of course," he said and laughed. "But consider it nothing more than an eccentric request. It is something to do with his religion. These things are not to be taken literally you know."

Giannetto lifted the cup to his lips, but then set it back down. "But what if I should again fail?"

"What if I was to give you a charm guaranteeing that you did not?"

"What type of charm?"

The man reached into his garments and brought out a thin silver chain with a star-shaped talisman on the end of it.

"It looks Othmen!" said Giannetto in surprise.

"I am not sure of its origin," the man said. "But it carries enchantment. Watch." And he held it over the half-empty cup of wine and Giannetto saw the liquid in the cup begin turning, like a small tidal pool. "My master gave it to me and charged me to give it to the most needy man I could find in the city, and your story makes me think that it is you."

The man held out the charm and Giannetto took it. He felt a slight tingling in his fingers. "Who is your master?" he asked. "He must be a truly singular and generous man."

The man smiled. "He would laugh to hear you describe him so."

Giannetto proffered his hand to Marco and they shook. "I had thought this an unlucky day," he said.

The man smiled. "You should not believe in luck. Believe rather that all things are planned out. Very carefully planned out indeed. Now here," he said, and passed a slip of paper across the table. "This is the moneylender's name and address. Tell him that Marco sent you."

Giannetto took up the sheet of paper. It was very expensive and the penmanship quite official looking. And he had a moment of doubt as to whether he might make a suitable candidate for the loan. No matter, he would beseech his uncle to make it on his behalf. As long as the condition was nothing to be taken seriously he had nothing to fear.

LIV

ELSEWHERE IN THE FLOATING CITY

It had been a long, long time since the Spring Seers had been so young and they were enjoying the pleasures that come from a young body. "They are too young for that!" the Summer Seers had said, seeing the lust in the young couple's eyes when they had left the chamber, but that was the voice of bitterness and jealousy. When you found yourself suddenly in a young body free of any of the trials of age there was nothing you were too young for.

They were left with Mario and Rosa to console. The youngsters had suddenly found themselves aged beyond imagining and without the knowledge and experience of the Seers they did not know how to hold the decrepit bodies together. Mario had wet himself and Rosa was sobbing uncontrollably, just from looking at her hands. They would keep a looking glass from her as long as was possible.

"It is nothing to be upset about," the Summer Seers lied. "It is just a temporary thing."

Neither child seemed consoled by the idea. "Your bodies have great powers," the female Summer Seer told them, coming across the chamber towards them. "You will learn how to harness them. But you must maintain the bond." Or you will die, she neglected to tell them.

She held up her husband's hand to indicate that they should

do the same, but the children were too distraught to pay them enough attention to follow her bidding. The male Summer Seer was having a great deal of trouble focusing on the fact that these were not the people he knew, falling apart before him, but were in fact children. It seemed to him that if he ever let go of his own control he might behave just like them.

The female Summer Seer sensed this in him and squeezed his hand tighter, forcing him to focus. But in return a little of his doubt filled her. It was too much like looking into some mirror of the future, she thought, or alternative reality. She drew in a breath and said, in a stern voice, "You can wallow or you can adapt. There is nothing else for it now." Neither child responded. She felt annoyed, it should have been the Spring Seers doing this, rather than cavorting and exploring each other's flesh like a pair of love-starved youths. But again, she wondered how she would respond if it were her and her husband in their bodies. It had been a long time since the flesh had held pleasures for them. Who wouldn't dream of the smooth and unblemished flesh of youth? And with a partner who knew your every whim and wish.

The Spring Seers had undoubtedly sacrificed a lot of their powers to choose the bodies of these two children, but they would regain that in time. As the two children would regain their senses and come to understand their responsibilities – in time – and then there would be three sets of Seers once more. As they would undoubtedly find another set of Seers eventually.

Still holding her husband's hand she stepped forward and pulled one shaking hand from Rosa's face and pressed it into the boy's hand. "Hold it," she commanded. Mario hung onto it for a moment, but Rosa pulled it back to cover her mouth, as great racking sobs were now escaping her. The Seer grabbed it again and pressed it once more into Mario's hand. "Hold it tighter," she told him. He looked at her, blinked and did as he was told, as Rosa tried to pull it back from him again.

She stepped closer to Rosa and raised a hand to strike her face, but could not bring herself to do it. She could easily have struck the female Spring Seer as she watched her leading her child lover out of the chamber, but she could not bring herself to strike the face of the woman in front of her. They had endured too much together.

She stepped back and said to her husband, "Let's leave them alone for a bit. They may need the solitude to recover."

He knew that was very unlikely. What they most wanted was undoubtedly comforting and some explanation they could accept. But they were not going to get that here. "Yes," he said. "I hope they find that possible."

"In time," she said to her husband, and turned to lead him out of the chamber. So many things would happen in time. She would adapt to the reality of who were children and who were not, and they would adapt to the fact they were now Seers and with that came great sacrifice and they would adapt to finding a new balance of their powers to protect the city.

"I fear we do not have that luxury of time," he said.

"I fear so many other things above that," she said, and they left the chamber without once looking back.

LV

THE STORY OF DISDEMONA

Otello returned home that evening in a troubled mood. He had been as much captivated by the Othmen envoy as he had wanted to slay her. She was terrible and she was beautiful. She was as dangerous as she was alluring. He found thoughts of her kept running through his mind. What colour was her skin around her breasts? Was it as dark as that on her face, or was it a little lighter, as he had found in some women?

He had never had any interest in Othmen women, who hid themselves under dark robes and were said to be either as bony as old camels or as plump as fattened chickens. And hairy. He had heard it said they had body hair all over and the hair on their mons was as thick as that of palm trees growing around an oasis.

But a half Othmen and half Graecian was like a dangerous mix of drugs that individually brought on a mild stupor, but taken together robbed a man of his senses. And he wondered if her legs wouldn't prove to be a strong as a dancer's and her arms as strong as a warrior's. It must be something wonderful to have congress with a woman who was as much a warrior as she was, he thought.

By the time he reached his home and dismissed his guardsmen, he found himself filled with mixed emotions. On the one hand he had been fantasizing over a woman other than his wife, but on the other hand, his wife had been more than overly familiar with the captain. For all he knew she had wed him simply because she was smitten with the idea of finding out what his body was like unclothed and pressed against her, as he had been smitten by a similar idea with the Othmen envoy.

And had she perhaps tired of the novelty of his dark skin and longed to be with a man more like her own race now? He knew her father and mother had warned her of such things, as if they knew them to be the truth. Perhaps he should have chosen a wife of darker skin, or perhaps he should have chosen a wife who he could wrap up in layers of clothing and forbid from ever being in the company of another man.

He then asked himself, if she was really being true to him, as she vowed was the case, why did he no longer find favour in her? Why did he mistrust her? He had a sharp nose for deceit, he knew, and it had saved his life on many occasions, and he felt it around him now.

He came to their bedchamber after a cup or two of wine to find her sitting up waiting for him. She sprang to her feet and came across to help him out of his clothes, but he shrugged her off. She stood back and asked him, "Have I done something to displease you?"

"I don't know. Have you?" he asked.

She lowered her head and he saw it shake a little. "My lord finds fault with me in so many ways," she said. "What has happened to the love and affection that you once showed me daily?"

He kicked off his boots and then unbuckled his ornamental armour, letting it fall to the floor. She kept her eyes down, waiting for him to answer, but he said nothing, only lifting off his shirt, then undershirt and then unfastening his breeches and stepping out of them. She glanced up at his near-naked form and then lowered her eyes again.

What was that look in them that he had seen? Fear? Loathing? Something else?

"Look at me!" he commanded. She looked up briefly and then

lowered her eyes again.

"Are you afraid of me?" he asked softly.

She nodded her head a little.

"Why is it that you proffer fear to your husband?" he demanded.

"I am afraid you no longer love me as you once did," she said and began crying. She reached into her bodice and took out a kerchief to wipe her eyes. And for a moment he felt something soften inside him and he reached out and took her hand, drawing it gently from her eyes. Then he saw the kerchief.

"Tell me," he said in a soft voice. "Where is the strawberry kerchief that I gave you?"

"It was too precious. I have locked it away for safekeeping," she said too quickly.

He held her hand tightly. "Then bring it to me now. I would see you wipe away your sadness with its softness."

"I cannot," she said. "I have misplaced the key."

"Then bring me the box you have put it in and I shall break it open with my dagger," he said.

"I cannot," she said again. "It is too precious."

"Show me," he said.

"The box is not here," she said. "I have taken it to a locksmith to have it opened."

"A locksmith?" he asked. "Which one? I shall have a man fetch it back for you."

"I don't recall his name. He was in the street of metal workers."

"How will you fetch it back if you don't remember his name?"

"I remember the shop."

He held onto her hand tightly but still she refused to look up at him. He pushed her roughly now, sick of the thin lies she had served him up for their bedtime repast. She fell onto the bed and started sobbing again.

"I want to see that kerchief on the morrow," he said. "It wounds me greatly that you do not have it, as much as it would wound me to find you had given it away."

"I would rather die than give it away," she said.

"Then we will speak no more of it tonight," he said. She climbed to her knees on the bed and wiped her tears.

"Will you come to bed now?" she asked.

"I find I am no longer tired and will sit up a little longer," he said. "There are important matters I need to think upon."

"Would you like my company?" she asked timidly.

"No," he said. "The consequences of these things are great, and are best considered on my own."

LVI
THE STORY OF GIULIETTA

"What ever happened to that pesky scribe who was meant to be writing our family history?" Signora Montecchi asked, but none of her three daughters seemed to be paying her any attention at all. It had been a long time since they had all come around for a morning together. She had a fine spread of pastries and light wines laid out for them in their garden, but they had all arrived late, leaving her waiting there on her own, and each seemed quite out of sorts.

Isabella looked at her first, and asked, "Who?"

"You know, that scribe that was charged with writing up the family history."

"Oh yes," she said. "I haven't seen him for some time. I suppose he's off busy writing somewhere."

"Disdemona?" she asked.

Her second-eldest daughter looked at her as if she hadn't heard a word. "I'm sorry," she said. She was not her usual self at all today, and she looked like she had the responsibilities of the Council of Eight – or was it Seven or Six now – upon her shoulders.

"The scribe," said her mother. "Has he been to see you?"

Disdemona looked like she was thinking about the question, and said, "No. I've not seen him. Why? Has something happened to him?"

"I simply don't know," her mother said. "He may have been murdered or run off to fight the Othmen for all I'm aware. I'm asking if any of you have seen him recently. He is, after all, charged with writing our family history." There was no point in asking Giulietta, of course, since there was nothing her daughter could have done without her knowledge.

"It was tiresome," said Isabella, "being interrupted in one's work to answer questions about aunts and uncles and what one did as a child."

"I was just thinking that he might have something more interesting to write about now," her mother said. "Certainly more interesting than stories of old aunts and uncles."

"Whatever do you mean?" asked Isabella. "What does she mean?" she asked Giulietta.

"I never know what she means," Giulietta said. "But she usually means well."

"I mean," said Signora Montecchi. "Somebody has clearly stolen my three daughters and left these poor imitations in their place." She pointed at Isabella first. "You, who have always been the most attentive daughter are acting today like you are too busy thinking about business matters, or something, and would rather not be here. And you," she said to Disdemona. "You, who are normally the most bubbly and happy of women, seem nothing but morose today. And you," she turned to Giulietta. "You are almost pleasant today!"

She stared at her daughters, but none of them answered her.

"Well?" she asked.

"What is it like being married?" Giulietta suddenly asked Disdemona.

Her sister looked at her with eyes that seemed to be holding back tears, and she said, "It can be difficult."

Her mother looked at her in surprise. "Whatever is the matter?" she asked. "Are you having troubles?"

"Then ask me," said Isabella to her youngest sister.

"But that was so long ago, you'd hardly remember," said Giulietta. "It must be many months since you even had a man in your bed."

"Giulietta!" said her mother.

Isabella, who had reddened a little, said, "It doesn't feel like that long to me."

"What are you saying?" asked Giulietta, leaning forward. "You have a lover?"

Isabella reddened further.

"Giulietta!" her mother admonished again.

"Tell me," Giulietta almost squealed. "What is he like?"

"Your imagination is running away with you," said Isabella dismissively.

"Yes. Running away," said Giulietta mischievously.

"Marriage is too complex to try and be captured by a single word," said Disdemona, as if she were a few lines behind in the conversation. "For some it is not a word, but a sentence."

"A whole story!" said Giulietta, missing her sister's meaning.

"Yes, just a story really," said Isabella, missing Giulietta's. "A fantasy to be toyed with."

Their mother watched her three daughters in consternation, and then said, "Yes. I should find that scribe and have him sit down with you and see if he can get any sense from you. I certainly can't!"

She looked at them and suddenly wanted to reach out her arms and gather them close and protect them. She knew that the time of losing them was approaching and that she would be left with only one child when it was done. And she did not even know which one it might be. The weight of the knowledge of that was almost unbearable.

"Ah, there you all are," said Signor Montecchi, coming out into the garden. He came across and stood beside them, without sitting down. Signora Montecchi smiled, hoping he'd liven the conversation up in his characteristic way, but he seemed just as distracted as their children.

He took a slow breath and then said, "I have some bad news to tell you about cousin Tebaldo."

LVII

ELSEWHERE IN THE FLOATING CITY

The Djinn rose out of the Grand Canal in broad daylight, startling dozens of citizens who were going about their daily business. They looked on in horror to see the beast that remained as hidden as a dark fear to most people, now rising high above the waters in plain sight.

The Djinn looked something like a human on its upper part, although it was larger and more muscled than any human could ever be. The arms were like giant logs, and the neck like that of a bull. The face however was that of a monster, with huge teeth and a flat nose and slit eyes like some reptile. And the head was covered in spikes that proceeded down the Djinn's back.

From the waist down, however, the monster was something else. Perhaps serpent, perhaps cloud, perhaps smoke. That part of the body seemed to move and reform hypnotically as if it lacked solid substance.

Most of the citizens were rooted to the spot in terror at the sight of the beast, wondering if they were safe enough standing away from the water. For what if the Djinn rose higher, revealing some monstrous legs that could enable it to climb out onto the city streets? What if it had a giant tongue that could lash out, like a lizard, and pluck people from where they stood? The citizens began slowly moving away from the canal's edge.

Except for one man. He strode forward and stood before the Djinn and held up his arms to it. The beast immediately turned its attention to him and roared like some mythical creature. People ducked low where

231

they stood, but the lone figure did not move. Then he reached down and drew two swords and whipped them around in the air, as if taunting the monster. He slid them back and forward along the blades of each other rapidly, creating a high-pitched wail that seemed to pain the Djinn.

It rose higher out of the water and then began moving slowly towards the lone figure. And perhaps he surprised the beast by leaping into a small dinghy by the canal's edge, slashing at the hawser as he did so, his momentum carrying him out onto the water. The Djinn seemed to laugh and it leaned forward and reached for the figure, its huge arms and hands coming slowly towards him. But as soon as it was within reach the man's twin swords flashed like he held two bolts of lightning and there were sparks where they touched the Djinn and it drew back in fright. Then the figure reached into a pouch at his waist and threw small metallic-looking barbs at the Djinn. Where each one struck there was also a spark and the Djinn roared in pain, its cry so much more terrible now. The man reached for more of the enchanted barbs, for surely only enchantment could have this effect on a creature of enchantment, when the Djinn suddenly sank beneath the waters.

The gathered crowd edged a little closer to see what had happened. Had the figure defeated the Djinn so easily? It was obvious the figure in the dinghy did not think so, because he reached into another pouch and pulled forth a handful of some powder that he cast upon the waters. Whatever it was, it had some power over the Djinn, because it brought it to the surface again, this time nearly under the dinghy, threatening to tip it over.

But the lone warrior kept his footing and balanced the dinghy as it rocked wildly and slashed again at the Djinn as it reached out for him. It howled in rage again and then all the citizens witnessed its lower half form into a large tail, like that of a serpent, that snaked under the dinghy and came up on the other side, attempting to seize the brave man. But he was ready for it. He slashed his swords both forward and backward, cutting at its hands and at the monstrous tail that was trying to encircle him.

Again the beast roared a terrible roar and sank beneath the waters.

Those on the city streets were transfixed. What would the beast do next? What would the lone warrior do? They saw him look around carefully, *as if he could see the beast below the dark waters there. And perhaps he could, because he then moved his feet in the boat, dropped one sword and took up the other in two hands, raising it above his head, just as the Djinn burst up from the waters, directly under the boat, splintering it with the force of its attack. As the very boat under his feet burst apart, he plunged his sword directly into that loathsome spiked head, piercing the skull with a flash of sparks and fire that was so bright people had to turn their heads and shield their eyes. The Djinn let out an awful moan and seemed to deflate, the huge torso withering and the snake-like trunk disappearing like mist being blown away on the wind. And for a moment it appeared to take on the shape of a man, perhaps one who had been bewitched by the Othmen to become a Djinn, or perhaps an evil necromancer who had chosen to turn himself into a Djinn. Whatever the creature's origins, this warrior's enchantment was stronger than the Djinn's, and it sank beneath the waters, dead or dying, as the man stood astride it.*

And then, most amazingly, the figure leapt onto a few planks of the boat, balancing on them without falling into the water himself. He turned to the crowd and held aloft his swords and called out to them, "I am come as your salvation!" His dark beard and black-rimmed eyes marked him as a foreigner, who would normally have been the source of great mistrust and suspicion amongst citizens of the Floating City. But this man, this Djinn-slayer, was as a hero who had stepped out of the legends of old.

He stood there in triumph and now we could see him more fully. His leather vest was set with silver charms and arcane armoured rings, and his bare muscled arms were bound by metallic bracelets, with leather thongs around his upper arms. His legs were also bound in metal and leather thongs. And, as citizens rushed to their boats to bring him to shore, he threw his head back and let forth a loud victory cry that sounded as bestial as the roar of the Djinn.

Vincenzo looked up to see what the Shadow Master thought of his account of the battle. He had been leaning over his shoulder as he wrote it, quite unsettling really, but Vincenzo had concentrated on capturing the excitement of it while it was still fresh in his mind. He was rather pleased with it, too, but the Shadow Master just frowned.

"Well," the Shadow Master said at last, "I'm not sure you have to make such a fuss about the man's muscles nor his cheap circus acrobatics."

Vincenzo stared at him and said, "But I have created something very difficult here. I have faithfully captured the battle as if I myself were wielding the swords. Surely."

"Some people are born with swords in their hands," said the Shadow Master. "Some achieve swords, and some have swords thrust at them."

"You want me to rewrite it in some way?" Vincenzo asked. "Make it different from what I saw?"

The Shadow Master didn't answer the question. "So what exactly does that feel like, to wield a pen like a sword?" he asked.

"It feels like you have just emerged from underneath my manuscript, like the Djinn rising from the waters, shattering it into pieces, and that I should drive my quill pen deep into your skull?"

The Shadow Master looked at him in surprise for a moment, and then said with a pleased smile, "Touché!"

LVIII

THE STORY OF GIULIETTA

Romeo Cappalletti was no stranger to the two rather smug-looking guards who brought him before the city magistrate. Nor was he a stranger to the magistrate. The guards seemed very pleased to have him in their grasp today. The young man had previously been charged with disturbing the peace, petty brawls and even one case brought by a jealous lover that he had bewitched the man's fiancée into falling in love with him and then spurned her. It had all made interesting theatre, but the magistrate had always dismissed such charges with an irritated look on his face.

The guards had been in the job long enough to know that while there was one set of laws for the city there were two different ways that they were applied. One was for the poor and one was for the rich. Normally Romeo and his like would get a stern lecture from the magistrate, at most, and then be sent back out onto the many streets and small plaza cafés to continue to treat the city as their playground. But murder! That was going to be something that no nobleman's family, no matter how wealthy or influential, could expect to get away with lightly.

But by the look of him, Romeo actually expected to get off the charge, carrying himself with his characteristic cockiness and bravado. Even a night in the city cells had not humbled him. The guards were going to have trouble keeping the smirks off their faces when the magistrate passed sentence on the brat.

By the look of things his family didn't think it would go so easy for him either, as his mother and father had actually bothered to come to witness the session today. He also had that drug-addled Friar Lorenzo da San Francesco with him, and it was a mystery how he'd never been dragged before the magistrate himself. Rumour had it that he both traded in and used banned Othmen potions and had secret links to the Othmen. He seemed to have a strong interest in Romeo's fate, so maybe there was something they were both involved in that might be uncovered. Then they'd have him before the magistrate too. It all had the makings of a very fine day!

Romeo, standing between the two guards, tossed his forelock over his head several times, and gave his parents a conspiratorial wink, as if they'd paid off the magistrate or something. But they just looked back at him glumly. Clearly they had their heads more grounded in reality than he did, the guards noted. And they also noted there was no apparent love between the Cappalletti seniors and Friar Lorenzo da San Francesco. Not only did they sit apart from each other, one of his guards noted the terrible scowls that Signor and Signora Cappalletti sent in his direction.

Perhaps the members of the council had other knowledge about the friar? There were stories of Othmen spies in the city, and perhaps the friar had been implicated with them? That was not impossible, with his love of Othmen spices, he would have contacts and the means. He wondered if any accusations were going to be made in court today. That would be something grand. He would take delight in arresting the man. And torturing him to get a confession. He might be the man who uncovered the plot to take over the city from the inside. He might identify the assassins and their ringleader as this degenerate friar. There was a cunning intelligence in his eyes that others who did not see criminals all day long might not notice. He might rise from being a humble guard to hero of the city. Yes, but pigs might fly too, he thought, and tried to rein in his fantasies.

"This is going to be a memorable day," said the other guard softly, through lips well practised at talking without moving.

Romeo looked to see if they were talking to him, but the other guard said, also in the same soft voice, "You'd be well advised to keep your eyes on the magistrate, boy, and also to keep a respectful tone in your voice."

"Not that it will do you much good really," said the other guard.

"I think your day has come, lad," the second guard said.

"I'll have you both dismissed for insolence and brutality," Romeo hissed back at them, also not moving his lips.

"Normally I'd apologize," said the first guard, "but I seem fresh out of apologies today. Do you have any?"

The other guard said, "Yes. I've got one tucked up inside my arse for just such an occasion as this. Let me fetch it. Oh, hang on, it's just a fart."

"Hur-hur-hur," the other guard laughed, still not moving his lips.

Romeo flicked his forelock again dramatically.

"That's a nice gesture," said the second guard. "It'll go down a treat in prison. That forelock will give them old lags something to hang onto as well, while they drill you."

"Hur-hur-hur," said the other.

"I'll have your uniforms," said Romeo.

"It wouldn't fit you," said the guard on his right.

"Hur-hur-hur."

"Silence," said the magistrate, looking up from the papers he had been reading.

"Silence," bellowed one guard at Romeo.

"Hur-hur-hur," said the other.

The magistrate, bedecked in grand red robes, and wearing the gold chain of office, also wore the customary three-faced mask, showing one side smiling, one side bitter and the front of the mask that sat over this face, shouting with rage. It was meant to be a symbol of the different judgments that could be made, and to mask any emotion the magistrate might be feeling, but the effect of the three contrasting faces was always to unsettle those the magistrate looked at. It was also a good way for the magistrate to hide his rather large nose that had long since blossomed from excessive quantities of fine red wine. The guards, who had seen him unmasked, knew the effect on his face was to make his eyes look small and close together. He was also known to suffer gout and indigestion and the guards could predict how badly either was plaguing him on any day by the harshness of his sentences. And they could see today they were giving him hell. That made them very happy.

"Romeo Cappalletti," the magistrate said. "You have been charged with wilful murder, and with armed attack in a public place. How do you plead to these charges?"

"Not guilty by necessity of self defence," said Romeo calmly.

"Explain yourself," said the magistrate.

"Tebaldo attacked us and slew my dearest friend Marcuccio before attacking me. I was merely trying to defend my own life," said Romeo and bowed. "If it please the court."

"It does not please the court," said the magistrate gruffly. "I have here a half-dozen statements that you provoked Tebaldo and then slew him in cold blood."

Romeo looked like somebody had slapped him. "What witnesses?" he asked.

The magistrate waved a handful of papers at him and Romeo knew they would have been Tebaldo's friends. He was a fool to have not sought out his own witnesses, whether they had been present or not. "They lie," said Romeo. The magistrate glared at him. "Or rather they err, because they do not understand the truth of it."

"Which you are now going to explain to me?" asked the magistrate.

"Yes," said Romeo.

"And based on your word I will then dismiss the charges?"

"Yes," said Romeo gaining a little of his confidence back.

"Your word against half a dozen witnesses?"

Romeo had a sinking feeling in his stomach. "If given time, I can procure witnesses to support my side of the story," he said, turning to look at the friar, who began to reluctantly climb to his feet to concoct some pretence to help Romeo.

"Undoubtedly," said the magistrate. "And undoubtedly I would find each and every one of them guilty of contempt of court." The friar sat back down quickly. "The council's law about fighting in public and attacking other citizens is made more important than ever due to our perilous situation. Our city is under siege and as such we need every able-bodied man, and to attack a fellow citizen could therefore be construed as an act of treason against the city!"

Romeo's mouth dropped open.

"Hur-hur-hur," said the guard.

"I can obtain witnesses," said Romeo. "I can pay repatriations. I can do penance."

"None of which will do my poor cousin any good," the magistrate said tersely. "She has lost her son and both she and the law demand justice. Romeo Cappalletti, you are banished! If you ever return to the Floating City it will be your death." And he banged the small wooden figure of a chained man that he held in his hands on the tabletop in front of him.

The guards dragged Romeo away while the magistrate turned to the next matter before him. "No," said Romeo, "I am to be wed!" He turned his head to his mother and father. His mother put her head into his father's shoulder and cried. His father would not meet his eyes.

Romeo turned his head the other way and called on the friar. "Help me!"

"Don't despair," said the friar, waving his hands at Romeo like he was casting spells in the air. "This just expedites your plans."

And while Romeo, being dragged away by the two grinning guards, did feel many things – being expedited was not one of them.

LIX

THE STORY OF ISABELLA

Isabella was not unhappy to hear that Giannetto had returned yet again, and her handmaiden had organized the evening meal for them both already. "He has another ship loaded with trade goods?" Isabella asked.

"Yes, my lady," her handmaiden assured her.

"I am starting to feel sorry for the boy," she said. "I have half a mind to refuse him and save him the loss which is surely going to ruin him." Her handmaiden frowned. "But tell him to be here at the usual time." Her handmaiden nodded her head with a smile, and hurried away.

Isabella was feeling buoyant. The extra ship could join the fleet that she was about to send to the land of Ancients for grain. With the former Othmen envoy gone so suddenly from the city the lies about the Othmen attacks on her ships were slowing. And men were being coaxed back to her employ, even if at inflated salaries. But grain would again reach the city and food shortages would be averted. And neither would she lose her fleet and palazzo to creditors. That small part of the fight to save her city that she was playing a part in, appeared to be going very well.

She spent most of the day trying to concentrate on business matters, but found her mind kept wandering. As the day wore on she found she was starting to feel as excited as a young girl going to meet her betrothed. "How absurd," she admonished herself, and several times she stood in front of the looking glass and came close to giving herself a lecture. It would be a pleasant meal with enjoyable conversation and then she would send the young man away disappointed, she told herself.

But she could see that other her, looking at her from the looking glass, was slightly upset by that idea. There were two Isabellas, she felt. One who was predisposed to turn young Giannetto away, and one who was glad to be seeing him. It was the tug of war between them that had unsettled her all day long, and she should make a firm decision about which self should win this battle, she knew.

Come the evening, she again had him wait longer than was needed, and then had her handmaiden escort him in to sit opposite her, and he again bowed low and told how she was more beautiful even than he had remembered. Was that it? she thought. Was it just the pleasure of having a handsome young man paying her endless compliments that made her agree to this once more? If so, her vanity was costing him dearly and she should learn not to pander to it.

She tried her best to put on a cold face, but his incessant optimism and good cheer made her smile. "Tonight I feel very lucky," he said.

"Do you believe in luck?" she asked.

"Everyone believes in luck," he said, "when there is a chance to win one's heart's desire. Only afterwards do we convince ourselves that if we obtained it, it was only due to our talents. If we do not obtain it, however, then that could only have been because of bad luck, or the cruel whim of fate."

"Then you certainly believe in bad luck," she said.

"Up until tonight," he said.

"My, how confident you are," she teased.

"Your presence fills me with confidence," he said.

As the handmaiden served them, Isabella could not help noticing that she fussed over Giannetto, leaning a little too close to him, and she also seemed to be wearing a rather low-cut dress tonight. And did she touch Giannetto with her breasts as she served him? Despite herself she found a small shoot of jealousy fill her when Giannetto turned and joked with the handmaiden.

"So tell me what you will do if you fail me again tonight?" she demanded, drawing his attention back to her.

"Does this meal satisfy you?" he asked.

"Yes it does," she said.

"And does our conversation satisfy you?"

She inclined her head a little and then said, "Yes, it does."

"Then I hope to complete the evening by satisfying you in other ways too."

She saw the grin on her handmaiden's face as she turned and scuttled out of the room. "You are very bold to talk of such matters."

"I meant you would be satisfied by my company," he said. "Did you presume I meant our successful voyages and explorations in the bedchamber tonight?"

Now she could not hide a smile.

"I am an elder woman," she said. "I have voyaged and explored much. Are you sure you could show me new places that I have never visited?"

"I may be younger," he said. "But I am very adventurous and I have read many maps and heard stories of far away exotic lands that I think prepare me well for any such explorations."

"What if I told you that no matter how exotic the lands you took me to, I had visited lands more exotic and wondrous?"

"Then I would ask you to take us both to them," he said. "For I am sure you would long to revisit them once more."

She fixed him with a stare. "Your confidence belies your successes to date."

"It is my successes tonight that I am confident in," he said.

Isabella found it hard to bring the meal to an end, but the evening was getting late, and the handmaiden kept interrupting them, saying, "I have prepared your chamber, my lady." And, "Is there anything else I can fetch you, my lady?" Finally she turned to her and said, "Thank you. It is time for us to retire for the evening. Just a final glass of wine before we go. Please fetch the best wine, which we have saved until last."

The handmaiden fetched the wine at once and poured both her mistress and Giannetto a cup, but Isabella said, "I need to excuse myself. Please drink yours and I will meet you in the bedchamber." He raised his cup to her and drank. "As is your wish," he said.

She left the room and went to one of her smaller rooms while Nerissa led Giannetto to her bedchamber once more, knowing he would again take off his clothes, climb into bed and wait for her. And she found herself looking forward to the sight of his naked sleeping body again.

She sighed. She would have to put an end to all this nonsense. This would be the last evening. She would find another way to rid herself of the besieging fleet that wished to bed and wed her.

After a suitable time had passed, Isabella rose and went to her bedchamber. Her handmaiden stood at the door. "Is there anything else, my lady?" she asked.

"That will be all."

"Yes, my lady." The handmaiden hurried away, as if she had somewhere very important to be.

Isabella entered the chamber and closed the door. Once more Giannetto was lying in the bed, fast asleep. She walked across to him and held her candle over his body. His member was quite erect in vain anticipation, and she felt a sudden impulse to reach out and touch it. Just to softly encircle it with her fingers and feel it move under her grasp. Instead she reached out and touched his arm. He was well muscled and she found it pleasurable to place her fingers on his skin.

She gave the softest of sighs and placed the candle on the bedside table. Then she took off her gown and slipped into bed alongside the sleeping Giannetto. She lay there a moment, and could suddenly not resist lifting herself up and leaning over him.

And then, it may have been the wine or the conversation or some other urge she was uncertain of, but she kissed him lightly on the lips.

To her surprise his eyes opened. And his arms softly encircled her, and he pulled her back towards him, kissing her this time.

She wanted to pull away. To resist his slow embrace. To demand to know how he was not asleep. But she let him kiss her and then again. "How?" was all she said, between deep warm kisses, as he ran his hands across her bare back.

"Shhh," he said, and slowly pushed her onto her back, letting his kisses work their way down her body. And then a second surprise, when she found just how very, very ready her body was for a new lover.

LX

ELSEWHERE IN THE FLOATING CITY

The Shadow Master didn't even see the hand coming until it was near his throat. He froze as it came to rest at the base of his neck, his hands already at his blades. But he didn't draw them. Anybody who could move so swiftly and so silently needed to be treated with extreme caution.

The Othmen envoy stepped fully out of the shadows and slid her hand up to his face. She squeezed the cheeks and asked, "Why does your face seem familiar to me?"

The Shadow Master turned his head away, but she kept her hand on him. "I'm sorry, signora, I don't believe we have been introduced."

"Not many people can move through these decadent streets as silently and unseen as you do," she said to him. "So I thought to myself, I should get to know this man a little better."

"This is a city where being silent and unseen is a virtue," he said, turning his head back to get a better look at her. She was as tall as him, and had a face so beautiful one longed to stare at it, like staring at the sun. But he knew that was a trap too, and moved his eyes quickly to look for her left hand. It was half hidden in a cloak.

"So I have heard," she said, drawing a little closer to him. "Which is why I find it much more interesting to observe who walks along these quiet underpasses and alleys than the main thoroughfares."

They were on a thin path by one of the canals under a bridge. "And my first thought was that a man who is being so careful not to be heard or seen must have a secret worth knowing."

The Shadow Master tried to twist his face out of her hold, but was surprised at how strong her grip was. "Everybody in this city has secrets," he said. "But what makes you think anybody is willing to share them?"

"For the right price, or the right reward, I have found there are few secrets."

"Then you haven't been in this city long enough," he said. "There are some secrets that lie within the very stones of the buildings that will not be released for any price."

"Hmm," she said, now bringing her left hand up, and running it along his forearm. Feeling his muscles or searching for weapons?

"Is that why the Othmen want to take the city apart stone by stone?" he asked.

She stepped in closer still. The Shadow Master kept his eyes moving, from her eyes to her hands. This was the moment of most danger. He tightened his fingers on his sword hilts and saw the slight grin on her face. She felt the movement in his forearm. Knew just when he would move. So he did not move. He just stood there.

"There are so many secrets," she said, leaning her face in close to his, her lips almost touching his, "about you that I'd like to know."

"Such as?" he asked.

"Aha," she mocked. "That has to remain my secret." Then she pressed her lips to his. Tightly. He tensed. The air around them seemed suddenly devoid of oxygen, replaced by something light and flammable, reading to ignite at the slightest spark. She took her time and then drew her head back from the kiss. He remained immobile. And now her confidence seemed to drop just a little.

"Who are you, man of shadows?" she asked.

"A stranger," he said.

"But are you my enemy?"

"Am I yours?"

"I don't know yet," she said. Then she pushed him back a little. He let her, and took one step backwards. But no more.

"I will be keeping an eye out for you," she said.

"And I you," he replied, knowing the shadows of this city had just become much more dangerous.

He stepped back from her slowly, not turning around until he was quite some distance away, and at a corner where he could put some cover between them. She was as likely to fire a weapon at him as she was to blow him a mocking kiss, and he did not want either.

The Othmen envoy waited until he was gone, smiled to herself and then lifted her left hand from within her cloak to examine the kerchief with embroidered strawberries on it. He would not be happy when he found it missing, she knew, and he would be quite an adversary when he decided against her. But to her surprise she was holding an old rag.

"How did he do that?" she mumbled, through gritted teeth.

LXI

THE STORY OF GIULIETTA

"It's all going to be all right," Friar Lorenzo da San Francesco said once again. But Giulietta did not believe him. She kept her head buried in her pillow and muttered something that the friar could not make out, but it sounded to him like she wanted to die.

"Listen," he said, lowering his voice. "I have a special message for you from Romeo."

Her sobbing stopped at once and she slowly lifted her head from her pillow. "You know Romeo?" she asked.

"I was going to marry you both," he said.

She now turned to consider him closely. This thin pale beggar of a friar who her parents would never have let into the house had he not said he had heard of her ailment and believed he could cure her of it. For she had taken to her bed and refused to eat and drink – except for garlic snails and truffles with sweet wine – when she had heard that Romeo was banished from the city.

Her parents had tried everything to get her to stop crying into her pillows and to tell them the cause of her misery, but whenever they came into her room, bearing threats or bribery, she simply cried louder. They were beside themselves. This was extraordinary behaviour – even for Giulietta.

They had summoned a doctor, an astrologer and were considering summoning her sisters to see if they could get any sense from her, when the thin and straggly friar arrived on their doorstep.

"How do you know our daughter?" Signor Montecchi asked him haughtily, looking over his poorly-kept robes, as if addressing a travelling charlatan who had promised to make him young and virile again.

"Through a mutual anonymous friend, who has asked me to intercede," he said and turned his head a little, listening to the wailing echoing through the palazzo from an upstairs bedroom. "But if you do not wish my services, then I shall leave you in – uh – peace."

"Not so hasty," Signora Montecchi said. "We didn't say we do not wish your services, we just need to be certain about your credentials. You understand of course."

"Of course," he said and bowed.

They regarded each other for a moment and then the friar said, "It won't take but a moment. If you would perhaps fetch her downstairs."

"She will not come," said Signora Montecchi. "We have had to escort the doctors up to her very bedchamber."

The friar frowned. "Ah," he said.

"Is that a problem?" Signora Montecchi asked.

"I can alleviate her distress, but it must be done in private."

Signor Montecchi puffed up like a defensive caged bird. "I cannot of course allow that," he said.

The friar bowed again. "As you wish. Then I shall leave you in – uh…" He turned his head again to listen to the wailing.

Signora Montecchi glared at her husband and said, "What if we found a chaperone?"

"I would rather that she did not overhear my words," said the friar, wringing his hands. "It can be delicate, you see."

"But what if she were deaf?" asked Signora Montecchi. "One of our old housemaids, Estella, is quite deaf."

The friar considered this like they were bartering over a sale of some kind and then said, "I think that will be sufficient, if that meets your husband's approval?" He turned to look at Signor Montecchi, who was about to refuse the offer as unprecedented, when the distant wail increased in volume and he considered how many more nights with no sleep he might need to endure. "All right," he said, his puffed-up chest deflating.

So the friar, accompanied by Estella, was led to Giulietta's bedchamber and after knocking and being ignored, he let himself in. She had continued to ignore him for most of his allotted short time, until he mentioned Romeo's name in a soft voice. Now he had her full attention and stood looking into the tear-soaked face of a girl much younger than he had supposed, with a fierce determined fire in her eyes. Good, he thought. She would need that.

"Tell me, does he send me his love?" she demanded.

"Uh – yes," the friar said, signalling her to keep her voice down. "He does."

"Tell me his exact words," Giulietta said.

"He sends you his love," said the friar quickly. "Now you must listen carefully. We have a plan."

"A plan!" she said and clapped her hands together. "Tell me, tell me."

"Yes, yes," said the friar, stepping closer and holding out a hand to her, taking one of her hands in his. She felt him squeeze it. Felt a tingling. Felt his closeness. Looked up into his eyes and felt as if he was mesmerizing her somehow. "You will not fear any danger," he said, "for you know that Romeo and I are only thinking of your safety and happiness." His voice had changed. Become deeper. And soothing in some way. She wanted him to keep talking. Keep promising her things.

"Yes," she said. "My safety and happiness."

"True love can overcome any adversity," he said. "And you are driven by true love, are you not?"

"Yes," she said. "We are."

"Good," he said. "Good. Then no harm will come to you."

"No harm," she said. There was some enchantment in his words, she felt. This friar had some hidden powers that he was willing to use to make her safe. To protect her. She smiled.

"We have a wonderful plan," he said. "And you shall play your part in it well, without fear and with complete trust in us."

"Yes," she said. "I will." She would do whatever he asked of her. As long as he kept holding her hand and kept talking to her in that deep sonorous voice.

"Then everything will turn out as it is meant to turn out," he said. Then he reached into his dirty robes and pulled out two small vials. "Oh," he said. He looked at them blankly a moment and pulled the cap off one and sniffed it. Then tasted it. "No. The other one." Then took another taste. He held the vial out to Giulietta, trying to move his body to block Estella from seeing what he was doing. "Definitely this one," he said, pressing it into her hands.

"What is it?" she asked. "A love potion?"

"Of sorts. It is a rare poison. It makes you appear as if dead."

Giulietta's eyes widened.

"But that is a ruse," said the friar quickly, taking up her hand again, letting his voice play with her. "You will be thought to be dead, but will be very much alive." Giulietta didn't say anything. "It lasts about a day and a night," he added. "Enough time for your parents to mourn you and then place you in the family crypt on the Isle of Mourning." He nodded his head, as if that would be enough for her to understand everything.

"I will awaken in the crypt?" she asked, and shivered.

"Yes, and Romeo will be there waiting for you to awaken." Then, as if suddenly remembering, he said, "I have a letter here to him explaining everything. If you would put your name to it for me, he will know that you know your part in this plan." He reached into his robe again and pulled out a small piece of parchment and a leaded pencil. She took it and read it over and then scribbled her name on the bottom of the parchment placing a long string of hearts after it.

The friar looked over his shoulder to see what Estella was making of all this, but she seemed to have dozed off standing there, much like a horse is able. He looked back to Giulietta and said, "Wait until midnight before taking the potion and your parents will find you as if dead in the morning."

She stared at him, feeling tears come to her eyes and she said, "Thank you!" And she pushed the small vial down between her breasts. The friar reddened at the sight of their pale roundness and had to all but tear his gaze away. He turned and bumped into Estella. She glared at him. He smiled. There was a knocking at the door, telling him his time was up.

"You're a saint," Giulietta called to him. He bowed and left her room.

After seeing the friar out of their palazzo, Giulietta's parents hurried up to find her sitting in front of her mirror, practicing how wistful she would look when Romeo found her. They looked at each other and blinked. It was amazing.

And it hadn't cost them anything!

LXII

ELSEWHERE IN THE FLOATING CITY

"I ask you again," demanded Signor de Abbacio of the Duca. "What do you plan to do?"

"I heard you the first time," said the Duca softly.

"But you didn't answer me."

"No," he said to the man, watching the way he thrust his fists onto his hips. Then the Duca turned and looked at the large map of the Floating City that was spread out on the council table before them. Signor de Abbacio had been showing the Duca the areas of the city that were now underwater. Many of the best citizens were having to wade into their homes and move to upper floors.

And more boats had arrived from Kaffa carrying plague people. They had all been relocated to the Isle of Sorrows, but attempts to keep them there were not proving effective. They snuck across at night, risking the Djinn, to hide themselves in the city. Already there had been several cases of plague reported from the poorer quarters.

"You must turn back the boats!" Signor de Abbacio said.

"Many are our citizens," the Duca said softly.

"Plague victims are nobody's citizens," Signor de Abbacio said. "The plague does not respect nationalities and neither should we."

"And yet, when they sent riches back from the city of Kaffa we were proud to call them our citizens."

"That was different," said Signor de Abbacio.

"No. It was only different because the besieging Mongols had not yet started catapulting their plague dead over the walls of the city. Trading death rather than silks and spices."

"We must turn back the boats," Signor de Abbacio said again, like it had the power of an incantation. "You are condemning our citizens to death. And that will weaken our city and leave us vulnerable to Othmen attack." He strode across and smacked his hand on the tabletop. "You are an old fool," he said. "Don't you see every time you fail to make a decision it leaves us weaker and more vulnerable to Othmen infiltration? They will not even need to invade us, they will just appear on the horizon one day and wonder where our city has gone."

The Duca smiled at the idea of that. But it seemed to enrage Signor de Abbacio. "They will find smoking ruins, a few towers sticking out of the water and corpses floating, bloated and stinking," he said.

"And they would turn and run away, I think," said the Duca, and he saw Signor de Abbacio's eyes fill with hatred for him.

"Are you telling me that this is a deliberate tactic of a man so afraid of the Othmen that he would rather see our city destroyed than face them?"

Now the Duca banged his own hand on the table. Then he held up the golden chain that was fastened around his neck, pulling on it with one hand as if choking himself. "What do you think this is?" he demanded. "A toy? It is the symbol of my rank of office, and you should respect it rather than covet it."

Signor de Abbacio did not even lower his eyes at the accusation.

"It looks like a chain," said the Duca, "but you have no idea what it really is. It is a burden that is heavier than you could ever know. It does not just confer the title of Duca of the city, but it binds one to the ancient knowledge about our city that is revealed only to the Duca!"

Signor de Abbacio looked puzzled. "What are you talking about?"

"Something I fear you will never understand. You could easily place this chain around your own neck and proclaim yourself Duca, but you could never understand the responsibility that comes with the knowledge that goes with it."

Signor de Abbacio sucked in his cheeks a moment and said, "We must turn back the boats." Turning the conversation back to something he understood and felt some power over.

"Ha," the Duca said. "Do you really think that will change anything?"

"The people are scared and they want the plague stopped. We have a responsibility to the people of the city."

"Our responsibility is to all our citizens."

"But if you fail to act you will have let plague take our city."

"And if I act it will lead to the death of our citizens."

Signor de Abbacio looked churlishly at the map of the city. "It is a simple matter of numbers," he protested. "Like adding profits and losses. If we stop the ships, those from the city of Kaffa will die, but less of the citizens of our city will die."

"Can you be so sure about that?" the Duca asked. "Have you asked the Seers if they can treat or prevent the plague? Which decision will actually be sentencing more citizens to death?"

Signor de Abbacio stared fixedly at the old man.

The Duca sighed and said, "Let me tell you a story about our city. This was at a time before you were born I think. My father, who was also Duca of the city, was dying. He was a great man who was loved and respected by everyone. Well, by most people. He had his enemies as we all do."

Signor de Abbacio did not respond to that.

"He had me when he was quite old, and I was about sixteen years old when he lay on his death bed. It was he who told me the secrets of the city, long before I became Duca myself. He was dying of the black lung disease that he had contracted from the Isle of Sorrows. He had gone to visit the people personally, to hear their grievances, one of which was the city's lack of interest in treating people there who had contracted the sickness."

Still Signor de Abbacio did not say anything.

"My father told me that he had two choices. He could put the island to the torch, cauterizing the wound to protect the Floating City from the disease. Or he could quarantine it, refusing to let anybody come or go, until the disease had run its course. And do you know what he did?"

Signor de Abbacio shook his head. "No. What did he do?"

"He told me that he hoped I was never faced with the same choice, and if I was that I would make a better choice than he did."

"What did he do?" Signor de Abbacio asked. But the Duca turned his back on him and started to leave the chamber. "What did he do?" Signor de Abbacio called after him, shouting now, as if it were vital to know as the key to his gaining the chain of office. "Tell me, what did he do?"

LXIII

THE STORY OF DISDEMONA

"Come," said the ensign to his commander, Otello, and the general followed him like he was in a trance. He led the Moor out of the barracks and down to the canal and they took a dark small boat around to the water gate at Otello's house.

Otello seemed not to be listening as he told him that he finally had proof of the captain's treachery against him. He saw the Moor looking up at his house.

"It looks so grand from the outside," Otello said. "But did you know that there are many chambers that are not safe to inhabit? There are walls that are unsound and there are some floors that are rotting. When I was appointed general of the city and given this house I thought it a palace. I, who was used to sleeping in soldiers' quarters to have my own palazzo! But only slowly did I discover it was granted to me because nobody else wanted to be responsible for the cost of restoring it. I had thought the city had accepted me. Was rewarding me." He laughed. "Like I believed that she really loved me."

The ensign said, "We must be silent. Even your servants should not know that we are here."

"I grew up in a small village of stones and tents, did you know?" Otello said, as if still not hearing him. "Life was cheap. You could as easily be killed for looking at a warrior the wrong way as you could by disease or enemy raiders. You might be killed for the price of a single copper coin." He looked at his house again and then turned and spat into the waters. "It is only in wealthy cities like this that life is considered worth so much more and to be valued accordingly."

Then he turned to the ensign. "How much would you consider your own life was worth?"

The ensign looked uncertain and scared for a moment.

"Or how much would the life of my wife be worth?"

"I could not hazard to guess," the ensign said quickly.

"Many, many hundred gold pieces, I'd wager," Otello said. "If I had carried her away as a hostage rather than won her heart, I dare say her father would have paid that sum to get her back safely again."

The ensign steered the boat up against the water gate and tied it securely. "We must be quiet, my lord," he said.

But Otello said, "And yet, in the village I grew up in, honour had an inestimable worth. You could not place a price on a man's honour and certainly no amount of gold was considered recompense for insulting a man's honour."

"Yes, my lord," said the ensign in a whisper, trying to bring his thoughts to a close.

"But in this city honour is worth nothing," Otello said. "It can be besmirched without a second thought. Perhaps that is why so many citizens like to go masked, because they are constantly losing face to even their closest friends and family."

"My lord does not deserve the way he has been treated," the ensign said. "He has been raised up by the city when they needed him and cast down now they no longer value him. The same way your captain pretends to be a loyal friend, but is wooing your wife all the while."

Otello turned and reached out a strong black arm, seizing the ensign by the neck. The man squeaked and gurgled. "You shall not put voice to these thoughts that plague me," he said. "It is bad enough to have them flying around in my head."

"I take them back," the ensign said quickly.

"If only you could," said Otello. "Once spoken, words cannot be re-caged. They are not doves to fly away over the mountains. They stay like mosquitoes, buzzing around your ears."

"My lord," said the ensign, worried he had been drugging the Moor too much and his madness was likely to be unpredictable, even dangerous to him. "You should not dwell overly on this. It only causes you pain."

"If I am not to dwell on this, then why have you brought me here?" he asked. "Would you be a better friend if you had never told me of your suspicions and left me to stand on the outside of my palazzo believing it to be sound and beautiful within?"

"That is for my lord to ultimately decide," the ensign said, starting to sweat a little with anxiety. "I am only the instrument of truth."

"Yes," said the Moor, seeming to focus a little more properly now. "The truth. It is time to know it."

"Yes, my lord," said the ensign and led the general into his own rear courtyard. They were in the garden and the ensign put a finger to his lips. The Moor just nodded. The ensign led them across to a garden house that had a white latticed wall on one side. The two men stood in the shadows inside. Disdemona was on the far side of the garden, sitting on a chair reading a book.

"How beautiful she is," said Otello. "I find it hard to believe any treachery ever filled her heart to see her like that."

The ensign put a hand on his general's to warn him to be quiet. "Such is the skill of her treachery," he said softly, "that it is not easily seen."

The two men stood silently for some time, watching Disdemona ask a handmaiden to fetch her a drink and then resume reading in solitude again. "How did you know she would be here?" Otello asked in a whisper.

"It is her habit to read in the garden at this time each day," the ensign said. "The hour when callers are most likely to come."

Otello just nodded and they waited. As a hunter in a hide might wait for his prey. As a warrior in ambush might wait for the enemy. As a doubting husband might wait for any sign of his wife's unfaithfulness.

Finally their prey, their enemy, the proof of unfaithfulness arrived. A handmaiden came to bring news to Disdemona, obviously of a caller, since she put her book down, smoothed her dress and hair. Otello felt the blood pounding in his temples at this sight of her preening herself.

Then the captain entered the garden and came and stood before her. She offered him her hand and he took it, seemingly to linger overly long with it. She patted the seat beside her but he did not sit, he dropped to one knee as if he was going to offer her a present of great worth. And with a grand flourish he reached into his breast and pulled out a white kerchief with red strawberries on it.

Otello stopped breathing. The ensign felt the air around him start to boil. Disdemona jumped to her feet and took the kerchief from him and pressed it to her bosom. As if she was pressing him there. And then she took his hands in hers and drew him close to her.

Blood filled Otello's eyes and left him blind to anything other than what he chose to see. The ensign leaned closer. "Leave the captain to me. I will kill him to avenge your honour and prove my loyalty. But Disdemona I will leave in your hands." And he watched with bitter pleasure the way the Moor's large hands opened and closed, as if they were around her thin beautiful neck already.

LXIV

ELSEWHERE IN THE FLOATING CITY

The Othmen envoy's eyes opened just a crack. The rest of her body remained completely motionless. She was suddenly wide awake and listening for the sound again. The soft hiss of a roof tile being moved. She waited. Then she heard the sound of cloth brushing wood.

Now she knew what to listen for she could almost feel the weight of a man being lowered onto a ceiling joist above her head as the wooden beam gave the slightest of creaks. Then the sound of a padded foot adding weight to the beam with infinite patience.

Very slowly she moved her own hand up under her pillow, her fingers encircling the dagger hilt there. Then she waited again. Listened to the sounds of the waters lapping against the building. Listened to a distant bird call. Listened to a nearby house creak a little like the call of some distressed night animal – as it undoubtedly settled a little lower into the water. And she heard the sound of a hatch in the ceiling cautiously sliding open.

Her breathing did not change though. Her eyes opened a little wider and she looked for the slight change in the light in the dim room made by a dark figure lowering itself from the ceiling. She waited. Then she saw it. As soft as the change made by a thin cloud crossing the moon.

And still she did not move. Did not turn. Did not cry out. She waited.

Then the figure dropped, landed lightly next to her bed and she felt the dagger suddenly against her throat. The same instant she had her own dagger up and under the chin of the figure looming over her. The figure paused and she heard him take a short and sharp intake of breath. Then she felt the sudden pressure of his chin against her dagger, moving his head closer to hers.

She felt the dagger prick the skin and then she moved her hand. Back. Let the man's face come closer. She held the dagger there, slowly retreating as he advanced on her, both knowing that just the slightest pressure would cut deeply into his throat.

But he kept moving until his lips were a whisper away from hers. A breath. A heartbeat. A blood drop. Then he said her name. Her real one. The one that no one else knew. And she leant forward herself, feeling the blade at her own neck give way just as it broke the skin there.

Then she was kissing him. Biting his lower lip until she could taste blood. She heard the sound of the daggers both falling to the bed. Heard his feet move on the floor. Heard the bed creak a little at the addition of his weight to it. Heard herself say his name.

She looked into his dark and familiar eyes and felt his hands moving firmly up her body, grasping her breasts and then moving further, up to her neck, grabbing it just as tightly.

"I have missed you," he said.

"And I you," she said. "I expected you earlier."

"I was busy," he said. "Slaying Djinn." And they both laughed. A soft and intimate laugh that wound its way around the dark corners of the room and slipped out the open hole in the roof into the chill night.

LXV

ELSEWHERE IN THE FLOATING CITY

Vincenzo drifted in and out of sleep trying to understand if he was dreaming or recalling a story he had read, or perhaps creating one in his mind. He was standing before a rank of soldiers. Maybe they were Othmen. Maybe they were something other. They had swords drawn and shields up. They wore metal helmets and were advancing on him cautiously. As if they feared him.

And he looked down into his hand and found he held a sword. Held it as casually as if it was an extension of his arm. He looked at the soldiers and knew they would cut him down easily. He looked around and saw the Shadow Master standing beside a stone column casually watching him. He wanted to call out to him, but no voice would come.

He looked back to the soldiers and tried to cast the sword from his hand, but it would not come away from his fingers.

The first soldier stepped out of the rank and slashed at him and Vincenzo threw up an arm to catch the blow. It fell upon a metal arm guard, numbing his arm. He took a step back and looked to the Shadow Master. Why wasn't he coming to help him? The soldier swung his sword again, and this time Vincenzo held up his own sword to parry it. The force of the blow almost knocked it from his grasp and he fell to the ground.

The soldier advanced on him, his comrades circling him, as if each was keen to be the one who dealt the death blow. He saw the sword descending and tried to cry out, as though if he could just find his voice it might somehow deflect it. The sword sparked loudly in front of his face, striking another sword. Vincenzo looked up and saw a dark figure step over him, spinning in close to the soldier, rolling down along the length of his sword arm, and coming up hard against his shield. The soldier tried to push the figure back, but already his sword was coming around, striking the soldier under the base of his metal helmet, almost severing the man's head from his shoulders.

Then the second and third soldiers were upon him, closing in on either side. But the figure didn't even hesitate. He stepped through them and right amongst the soldiers, forcing the remaining men to bump and clash as they tried to keep their shields up but still engage with him. He bent low and slashed at two of the men's exposed legs. One fell and he was through the gap, cutting and hacking at the soldiers from behind. They struggled to spin around, their shields too entangled to move quickly.

He was weaving amongst them now, moving so rapidly it was like they were drugged and unable to move quickly, and he was dodging their feeble blows with ease. He cut them down one after another until there were ten dead and dying men on the ground. And Vincenzo could feel the strength in the man's arm and the feeling of victory. The figure turned to look back to where the Shadow Master still stood, leaning against the pillar, and then towards Vincenzo on the ground. But he was no longer there. He was the dark figure wiping blood from his sword with the well-practiced ease that he would wipe excessive ink from his pen.

LXVI

THE STORY OF ISABELLA

There was a small part of Isabella Montecchi that wanted to be angry at her handmaiden, Nerissa, for not giving Giannetto the drugged wine as she had been instructed to. But, in truth, it was a very small part of her.

She stretched languidly on the bed and felt Giannetto wrap his arms around her naked waist and pull her close to him. She turned her head to look at his face, eyes still closed and half asleep. She saw the small twitch of his eyelashes, like butterflies preparing to take flight. She saw the colour of the three light lines in the skin around his eyes, smile lines like a delicate bird's feet. She saw his thin beard as a forest of hundreds of individual hairs. And she saw the curve of his full lips and it all made her think of the pleasure she had taken from them throughout the night.

She let her gaze drop lower over his naked body, recalling the snug feeling of completion in how it fitted so well against her own body. She admired the shape of his arms and the rise and fall of his chest, and then looked back to his face, surprised to find his eyes now open. Surprised to see how very beautiful he looked, lying there, looking at her.

"And where shall we go today?" he asked.

"Go?" she said. "Why do we not lie here a little longer?" And her hand snaked down his torso, fingertips sliding along his warm skin.

"I think I might take you to far away exotic lands," he said. "And we shall dance to enchanting music and taste strange sweet fruits and we shall think nothing of our lives and our debts in the Floating City. We shall only think of each other."

Isabella stretched her body again, this time leaning into his, feeling it respond to her closeness. "But I want to stay in bed," she said, her fingers searching for him.

"And we shall," he said. "Have you heard the stories of the Othmen's enchanted carpets that can fly?"

"A children's tale," she said.

"Perhaps," he said. "But every children's tale is born from some truth."

"Shall we adjourn to the carpet then?" she asked mischievously.

"Far better," he said, "if we journey on our enchanted bed. It will carry us over the waves like a galleon of the skies. It shall rise up and float over the clouds, and we shall look down on the foam tops of the ocean like they were small feathers. We shall drift over deserts and rivers and high mountains and we shall find a lush oasis where we shall land our bed under shady trees and rest."

"And the musicians?" she asked.

"Oh yes," he said. "They shall come across the deserts, riding on camels. Have you heard of camels?"

"I have seen drawings of them."

"And they shall also bear servants with sweet meats and wines. The servants will be wrapped fully in cloth with just their eyes showing."

"But isn't that the way the Othmen women dress?" Isabella asked.

"No, no," Giannetto said. "There are many other peoples to the lands south of here than the Othmen. The sand-dwellers dress like this, men and women both."

"Yes," said Isabella. "We shall do this then today." She clapped her hands and called for her handmaiden, Nerissa. It took a moment for her to appear, her head coming around the edge of the door cautiously. "Come!" said Isabella.

The handmaiden came into the room with her eyes cast down.

"Fetch a sheet," Isabella commanded in a harsh tone. The handmaiden looked a little confused, but did as she was ordered. "Now wrap it around yourself," Isabella said.

"My lady?"

"Do you want me to do it for her?" Giannetto asked, making as if to rise from the bed. The handmaiden looked panicked for a moment, until Isabella said, "Dress like the desert women do."

"My lady?" she asked again.

"I had better show her," Giannetto teased.

Nerissa turned away as he sat up in the bed, and quickly began wrapping the sheet about herself. Isabella pulled Giannetto back to the bed, stifling a laugh. Finally the handmaiden turned and asked, "Like this?"

"You have to cover your face," said Giannetto, "so that only your eyes show."

The handmaiden adjusted the sheet and tucked it in tighter in places. Then stood there.

"Splendid," said Giannetto.

"Yes, splendid," said Isabella. "Now fetch us exotic sweetmeats and cool drinks."

"Wine," said Giannetto. "But no cups. I shall drink it out of the crevices of your body."

The handmaiden spun around again, certain they could see the blush on her face, even though only her eyes showed.

"Hurry," said Giannetto. "We have a long journey ahead of us and are famished."

"No. Don't hurry," said Isabella. "Come back in half a candle's length. We are not at our journey's end yet. We have many clouds to soar over and many mountains to climb still." The handmaiden scuttled from the room, almost tripping over the sheet. Isabella and Giannetto burst out laughing and she slid a leg over his. "So," she said. "Shall we attempt the mountains or the waves first?"

And their day passed as he had promised it would, dozing and eating and drinking and enjoying each other until they fell asleep again, quite sated, and slept like children, bodies twisted in uncomfortable intertwined positions, but smiling and content.

Isabella awoke upon sunup the following day. Her head hurt a little from the wine, her belly was a little swollen from the fine foods and other parts of her hurt a little from equal over-indulgence. She placed a hand under her head and looked at the young man lying there beside her. She considered for a moment the big question in her heart. Was she willing to fulfil the absurd contract and be won by this handsome young man? No, she didn't think she would. Rather she had won this man, to be her husband.

She smiled and laughed a little. The movement woke him and he opened his eyes and looked around. He licked his lips, clearly feeling a little unwell too, and blinked. Then he looked to her and smiled. "I was dreaming," he said. "We had travelled far away to an exotic land in the deserts. But it wasn't a dream at all, was it?"

"No," she said.

"And look," he said. "A memento of our trip." He held up his hand and she saw the ring that she had pressed upon him in the night. In the darkness of night it had been done as play, while they were making vows about all the other enchanted journeys they would take together, but now in the bright light of day she held her breath in anticipation of how he would treat it.

"Did a gypsy woman give it to you promising it would bring you good fortune?" she asked.

"No," he said. "My true love gave it to me as a bond that we shall be wed."

She smiled and leaned in and kissed him. "Then promise me you will never take it off again."

He wrapped his arms about her. "Never," he said.

She kissed him again and then lifted her head above his. "It was a wonderful journey," she said. "But now I see we are back to our lives and our debts in the Floating City." They both smiled, but she watched the smile fall from his face like a bird struck down by an arrow in mid-flight.

"Oh gods!" he said. "The debt!"

LXVII

ELSEWHERE IN THE FLOATING CITY

It had started raining on the way back from the Isle of Sorrows, just confirming to the Duca's small retinue how ill-advised his idea to visit the island had been. He had stayed overlong as well, talking to the plague people and listening to their grievances about being kept isolated from their families on the island where they could see the Floating City, and often their family homes, but not visit them.

The bright lights and city colours that must have taunted them each evening now turned to dull grey in the rain and his physician started mumbling and grumbling again. The man was perhaps overly old for his position and the best that could be said of him was that he was quite an expert on a wide variety of ailments since he suffered from so many of them himself. He had been most reluctant to make the trip in the first place and had said repeatedly that it would be dangerous. Said the plague people might take them all hostage. Said they would have to burn all their clothes and even the boats they had travelled in when they returned to the city.

The Duca was thinking that he couldn't burn the things he had seen or heard though. The plague people were kept under constant guard. They were housed in overcrowded ramshackle buildings. There were families with children and old men and women there.

They were treated like prisoners or enemies captured in battle, he thought.

He had heard it said that plague people were sneaking into the city at nights, rowing across on any old debris they could find and then hiding with family and friends who would take them in. And why shouldn't they? The miserable have no other medicine than hope. The guards on the island denied anyone had ever escaped, of course, but the Duca doubted they even kept a head-count on who was there. They had no desire to come into close contact with the plague people and huddled in a single quarter as if besieged.

"Are we quite sure the waters are still safe?" he heard his physician ask, peering around at the dancing rain-pelted waters about them.

"The Djinn-slayer assures us they are," said the captain of the city guard. Normally General Otello would have had the duty of accompanying the Duca on a visit like this, and the Duca missed his quiet presence. The physician was intimidated by him too, and would have most likely kept his complaints to himself.

Soon they were approaching the city's edge where they had departed and the Duca looked into the rainy darkness to see a small party there waiting patiently in the rain for them. The Duca's boat docked first and the men waiting for them bent down and started fiddling with ropes and things. The Duca was eager to be in out of the rain, and stood, assisted by the captain, and just for a moment wondered why there were only three men to greet them. There should have been many more.

Then the three men lifted their heads. They wore the grinning white masks of the assassins.

"Stay down," said the captain, pushing the Duca back into the boat, drawing his sword and stepping between the Duca and the men who had now drawn daggers. He blocked the first dagger thrust and then punched the man hard in the face with the pommel of his sword. The assailant fell back and a second stepped over him. He was quicker than the first and his dagger thrust cut the captain on the arm. He cried out and dropped his sword. The Duca's eyes went wide as the assassin turned his face towards him.

But the captain caught his sword as it fell, with his left hand, and brought it up to block the next thrust that was made towards him. The move caught the attacker by surprise. The captain then swung at the man, but it was a clumsy blow and landed on his mask, cracking it.

The attacker stepped back, suddenly more interested in protecting his identity than in defending himself. But the third man was already stepping forward, weaving his dagger in the air like it was a snake, mesmerizing its prey. The captain did not look at the blade though, instead focusing on the eyes of the attacker. He waited until he saw them ready to strike and flicked his sword out in a long thrusting stroke that brought him close enough for the man to drive his dagger into his eye.

But he did not. For the captain's sword had pierced his heart. He fell to his knees with a gasp and the captain fell too, trying to pull his sword out as the first assassin slashed at him again. The dagger cut deeply into his leg and the captain cried out in pain, almost falling into the water. The assassin stood, but he was too late. The second boat had come alongside them now and guards had drawn their swords and leapt at the assassin, quickly striking him down.

The Duca looked now for the second assassin, expecting to see him make one last attack, but he could see the man scuttling off into the darkness across the cobblestones, cursing and holding his broken mask to his face. Then everything was chaos as the physician started calling murder and the other boats were alongside them and men were taking his arms to lead him to safety.

High above, in the window of a tower that was protected from the rain, the scribe Vincenzo watched the Shadow Master lower his raised arm and retract the small crossbow that had been affixed to his wrist.

"You could have got him before he reached the shadows,"

Vincenzo said, indicating the assassin who had escaped.

"Only if the Duca was in real danger," he replied.

Vincenzo was taken aback. "That looked like real danger to me," he said.

But the Shadow Master shook his head. "You'll know real danger when it comes. Time will slow down as if by enchantment, and you'll remember every detail in crystal clarity."

The scribe smiled. "I never thought I'd say it, but I'd like to experience that," he said. "Though perhaps without the danger."

The Shadow Master shook his head. "The two are as much a part of each other as... well, as..." He paused.

"Yes?" asked Vincenzo.

"It doesn't matter. Metaphors were never my strong point. You'll come up with a good one when the time comes."

LXVIII

THE STORY OF DISDEMONA

The morning sun fought its way past dark clouds on the horizon to find the rain-soaked Floating City settled a little lower in the water and the Moor Otello marching up and down by the ocean's edge, ranting and grasping at the chill empty air about him. He had left his palazzo at an early hour, unable to abide the look of Disdemona's peacefully sleeping form. The way she lay there, her hair spread across their pillow, filled him with both longing and hate.

He had felt certain that if he looked into her eyes deeply enough he would see the deceit there, but all he saw was the familiar dark eyes that he had once thought more beautiful than a precious jewel. She was beyond his understanding to be able to hide her lusts for the captain so well. He could not stay in the bedchamber with her, not knowing if the captain had lain there in that very bed with her. Had kissed her and stroked her long dark hair. Had lain his head upon that pillow beside her. Had looked into those dark eyes as he took her.

Surely he would be able to see some remnant of that in her eyes. But she was too able at hiding her deceits.

The thought of her giving her body to another man filled his guts with sickness. He found her very touch abhorrent now. He wanted to vomit the feeling of it out of him. But he felt his anger and grief and pain so great that no purging could ever rid his body of it. It infused every piece of his body. It was in his fingertips and in his stomach and behind his eyelids and running through his arms and legs. He even felt it in his bones.

And yet, and yet, the sight of her lying there so peacefully in the bed, also made him want to reach out and touch her. To hold her again. To feel that which he had always felt when he held her. That feeling of safety and security. His one safe place.

She had robbed him of even that. He turned and looked into the rising sun, and sank to his knees, tears filling his eyes. How could a man endure such pain and still live? he wondered. What torture could possibly compare to this feeling of a dark worm eating one's insides out, starting at the heart?

He leaned forward until his head touched the ground and he pressed his hands to his head, squeezing it tightly as if it might somehow rid him of the pain and turmoil that filled him. He, who had once been charged with keeping the city's peace, now a violent battleground himself.

He slowly climbed to his feet and turned to look at the Floating City that some considered the most beautiful city in the civilized world. He saw the morning sun illuminating its golden domes and tiled roofs. Saw the way the water of her canals turned to silver and yet he found it ugly. This city who had once counted on him to defend it. This city he had once felt could be his home. This city who he once felt would love him as he loved it.

This city that had also betrayed him.

He would rather rip his head from his own shoulders and cast it into the sea like a cannonball than do what he knew he needed to now do to free himself of this agony. And then Otello opened his lungs and screamed – a beast-like, grief-filled roar that echoed over the city as the dark clouds engulfed the sun again.

LXIX

ELSEWHERE IN THE FLOATING CITY

It was a battle that should never have happened. The city Seers confronting the Shadow Master and using their combined powers to try and slay him. He was lucky to escape with his life for they had control of the very elements.

It was impossible to say if they had come seeking him, or happened upon him by chance, but they were out on the city streets in the last darkness just before sunrise, when the Shadow Master was following the Djinn-slayer back to his quarters. He was moving across the wet rooftops, silently, keeping an eye on the other man as he moved from shadow to shadow, when he came upon a young boy and girl. They were just standing there on the flat-topped roof of a building, looking out to where the sun would rise.

The Shadow Master might have moved silently past them, but they turned to regard him. He stepped back into the darkness and drew his cloak about him, but something amazing happened. The young girl held out her hand and a light sprang from it, illuminating him. And by the light he noticed that the young boy and girl were holding hands.

"Is it him?" the young boy asked and the young girl closed her eyes, as if sharing her vision with another. "It is him," she said.

"We have dreamt of your coming," said the boy, taking a step closer. "We have been waiting for it." The Shadow Master did not move and the boy, leading the girl, took another step towards him. "We know why you have come to our city," he said.

"To die here," said the girl, and her eyes snapped open and fixed on the Shadow Master like weapons ready to fire. He took a quick step to the right, just as a scorching white light leapt from the girl's hands and blasted the brickwork where he had been standing.

"I am not here to harm you," the Shadow Master said. But the young girl only laughed. "You cannot harm us if you tried," she said. "Do you know who we are?"

"Yes," he said. "You are children playing with adultso toys."

That seemed to make the pair of them angry and two streaks of white light blasted out at him. He moved quickly though, rolling across the rooftop and standing behind a chimney.

"You cannot hide," said the girl. "We have seen you and now we have marked you." Then a wind began to blow around the Shadow Master, a wind that tugged at his cape and then wrapped it around him. It bound him tightly and as he struggled to free himself it lifted his very body from the rooftop and slowly turned him around in the air. There stood a very old man and woman on the far side of the rooftop, who had not been there a moment before.

"I have seen you," said the old woman, "riding the four horses of the doom of our city. You must not be allowed to live to destroy us."

"You need only look into a mirror to see the destroyers of your city," he called back. "You know in your hearts what I mean."

The old woman seemed enraged when he said this. "You dare to insult us? We are the sole protectors of this city from the evils that assail it. We keep it afloat. We keep the Othmen beasts at bay. And we destroy threats to us like you."

"Are you talking to me or those creepy children there?" he taunted them.

The elder Seers said nothing for a moment and then the Shadow Master saw the younger pair walking across to join them. The four of them, two very old and two very young, all held hands in a chain and began mumbling an incantation.

"Such poor diction," the Shadow Master called to them. But his taunts did not give them pause, they concentrated more and the winds about him increased, wrapping him tighter. He laughed though and with a sudden *twist, dropped free of his cloak, leaving it caught there above the rooftops, suddenly crushed in by the winds.*

The Shadow Master rolled again as the Seers let the wind drop and sent out another beam of glaring white light at him, this one stronger than any of the previous ones. It left a burning smell in the air and crackled as it leapt towards him. But he had moved before it hit the rooftop where he had just been standing. They sent another one after him. Then another.

The four Seers let go their hands and moved around the rooftop to encircle the Shadow Master and prevent him leaping to a new roof top.

The elder male Seer bent and placed his hands on the roof itself and it came to life under the Shadow Master's feet, trying to ensnare him and trip him as he ran. He moved quickly, but finally they had him, cornered against one of the many chimney stacks on the roof. The four Seers moved in closer, walking slowly towards him.

"Where will you run to now?" the elder lady asked him. "I see no horse to carry you away."

"Again, look in the mirror," he mocked.

She glared at him and cast a bolt of white light at him. He ducked and it shattered the chimney top apart behind him.

Then he did something most unexpected, he stood and held his arms out wide. "Do it now," he said. "If you can."

The four Seers held their hands out towards him and strong blinding light seemed to spring from each of them, converging on the point where he stood. There was a tremendous flash of light and suddenly there was nothing. The chimney, the roof covering and the Shadow Master were all gone, leaving nothing but a hole that had been erased of all colour.

None of them said anything and they all walked back to the roof's edge to watch the sun rise past the dark clouds there.

The scribe watched as the Shadow Master read the account he had witnessed. "I like the style of this," he said eventually. "And thank you for not mentioning how difficult it is to clean soot out of clothing. Nor the indignity of having to creep back and retrieve my cloak. But of course no one will ever believe it happened." He paused for a moment, as if thinking. "Although I think it would make a fine parable."

"A parable?" asked Vincenzo. "But this is what happened. This is how I have written you out of death again. Written an escape for you when it seemed you had been destroyed."

"Never underestimate the power of metaphor and parable," the Shadow Master said.

"You are impossible!" said Vincenzo. "Did I or did I not save your life by my telling of the story?"

"Do you believe that you did? Belief is important."

"Give it back," said Vincenzo. "I'm going to change the end so that you get a whipping from the Seers. Like a naughty child. With your pants pulled down. Using willow switches."

"Oh no," said the Shadow Master, holding the manuscript page high above his head, out of Vincenzo's reach. "Too late. The writing hand writes and moves on."

Vincenzo glared at him. "And besides," said the Shadow Master, "we're getting close to the end of things now. The convergence. You really need to pay attention to the disparate streams if you're going to be able to bring them all together. That's where you'll be able to save your city. Like stopping all the floating islands of your city drifting apart."

Vincenzo paused and thought about that. "That's good," he said. "I never thought of it like that, but yes, the many islands of our city are like a collection of stories in danger of drifting apart as these battles are waged."

"And you are the one to save them," the Shadow Master said. "So sharpen your pen. We have much still to do!"

LXX

THE STORY OF GIULIETTA

Giulietta had spent much of the evening deciding on what position she should be in when her parents found her and presumed she had died. Her first thought was something very dramatic to make them regret all the times that they'd been cruel to her, such as refusing to buy her a particular new gown or pair of shoes. She might dress herself in her oldest dress that was ill-fitting and then they'd feel so bad that they hadn't bought her more new clothes that they'd... She thought about that and decided it wasn't such a great idea. They'd probably rush out and buy some ghastly dress that they thought was all the style and take her to the family crypt in it and she'd awaken and Romeo would be there and the first question he'd ask her was, "Where did you get that ghastly dress?"

She then thought about dressing herself in her most exquisite gown so that she would be entombed in that. But that presented a few problems as well. If she tossed around after taking the death-like potion she might crush it. Her parents would decide it was ruined and go out and buy that ghastly dress again.

Finally she decided she would be found lying in bed in her nightdress, with her face made up as nice as could be, and her favourite dress hanging by the foot of the bed, clearly indicating that she had planned to be wearing it the next day. They'd have to dress her in it. Surely.

She had toyed with the idea of writing a note that could be found with her body, but in the end decided against it. It was far better if her death seemed mysterious rather than deliberate. She would like to have written that she had died out of love for Romeo, and the letter would become famous amongst young lovers for centuries to come, but he would then be blamed for her death and if he was caught when he snuck back into the city to fetch her it would turn out ill for him.

A pity though, she quite liked the idea of becoming a martyr for all the other young women of the world.

Finally, her mind made up, she took the vial from where she had hidden it between her breasts and unstopped it. She gave it a cautious sniff and then swallowed it in one go. It didn't taste pleasant, but certainly didn't take like near-death. Then she cast the vial out the window into the canal, blew out her candle, and gently lay down on the bed.

She had been expecting some pain, but instead found a gradual numbness creeping over her, dulling her mind until she felt she was in a dream state. She felt some awareness of the passing of time, but it was as if some incidents went slowly and others came very fast.

She was aware of the arrival of the morning and the long wait until somebody came into her chamber to rouse her. Then there was a leap forward until she was surrounded by her parents wailing and weeping over her. Her mother lay on top of her body and kissed her, as if trying to breathe some life back into her body. She cried her name over and over and even shook her as if trying to waken her and wailed when she could not. She had expected to feel sad about that, but found she did not feel anything, as if the drug had not only robbed the life from her, but had robbed her feelings as well.

She was being laid out and washed and clothed, but had no idea what dress they were putting her in. Then there was a long period of nothingness until she was aware of being surrounded by people all mumbling sadly to each other. That seemed to go on forever. Then she felt hands taking her up and lifting her into the air. She was borne aloft and felt herself floating. Felt herself drift down the stairs of the palazzo and out onto the streets where the commoners walked and traded and talked noisily like cattle. She floated like a ghost and felt the lap of water beneath her until she felt hands upon her again.

The air about was chill and she knew it was the family crypt on the island of the dead. She was aware of the smell of candles and incense and prayers and more soft mumblings and tears. Then finally she was on her own. In the dark. Feeling nothing but the expectation of waiting for her lover to come and rouse her. Never doubting for a moment that he would.

LXXI

THE STORY OF ISABELLA

Isabella had expected her betrothed to come back to her palazzo confident and assured, and to take her in his arms and perhaps even lead her back to her bedchamber once more. But when he did return, near dusk, he looked like a poor cousin of the man she had lain with the night previously. He was pale and bent over as if he carried a vast weight upon his shoulders. As if he had some perilous news that he did not wish to have to share with her.

She led him to a seat in one of the sitting rooms, gave him some wine and asked, "What has happened?" So many possibilities ran through her mind. He was married. He had a disease and had infected her. He had to go away somewhere. He had a huge debt and needed money.

But he put down the cup of wine and came to her and held her. And she knew, then, that if his solution to the problem was to hold her tightly, then it should be nothing she should fear. "What has happened?" she asked again.

"I am a murderer!" he said.

Her body stiffened a little and she asked him slowly, "Who have you murdered?"

"My godfather, Ansaldo the merchant," he said. "My tardiness has killed him."

"Tell me," she said. And he looked her in the eyes and explained how he had beseeched him to borrow money from one of the city's moneylenders to finance the third ship of trade goods he had come to her with, and how the moneylender, a Child of David, had insisted on a pound of flesh as the bond for the loan, and now the moneylender was insisting on it. "I did not return within the given time," Giannetto said. "The bond is forfeited.

"I don't understand," said Isabella. "What does a pound of flesh mean?"

"It means a pound of Ansaldo's flesh, to be cut from anywhere on his body."

Isabella pushed back from him a little. "How could you make such a bargain?" she asked.

"I was assured it was simply a traditional clause that would not be acted upon," Giannetto said.

"Who told you this? The moneylender?"

"No. The man who introduced me to him. He was a fellow named Marco who I met in an inn."

"A stout fellow with a scar under his ear here?" she asked, running a finger down the side of his face.

"Yes. That's him. Do you know him? He could clear this all up."

Isabella shook her head. "I know him," she said coldly. "He worked for the previous Othmen envoy. I feel his hand behind all this."

"I even offered up a pound of my own flesh to pay the debt, but he would not take it."

Isabella shivered and wrapped her arms about him protectively. "He should take no one's flesh," she said.

And Giannetto almost sobbed, "But he will have a pound of Ansaldo's flesh in punishment for my being spellbound by your flesh."

Isabella was silent for a moment, and then placed a hand gently on his face. "And I your flesh," she said. He leaned his head into her shoulder.

"Go back to the moneylender," she said. "Give him the ship

and goods you brought with you as payment, and I will give you another to match it to give him as well."

"He will not take them. I have begged him to accept all manner of riches. He has some evil sense of victory over my godfather that even gold and treasure will not rob him of."

Isabella looked at the pain in his eyes, and felt it in her own heart. "Offer him ten ships," she said.

He looked at her and smiled, but then shook his head. "He will not take it. Not ten-fold the loan. Not twenty-fold nor more. These were his own words."

Isabella thought for a moment and then said, "This is a cruelty beyond description. The magistrates will not allow it."

"He has it in writing," said Giannetto in dismay. "Signed by Ansaldo's own hand. And he has done this out of his love and trust in me." Then, "You see, I am his murderer."

"You are not yet a murderer," Isabella said.

But Giannetto could not be consoled. "It is only a matter of time now," he said morosely. And at that she put a hand to the back of his head and grasped his hair tightly, pulling his head closer to hers.

"Listen to me carefully," she said. "I have long since learned that nothing comes to pass until it has come to pass – and I will not see you so unmanned by something that may yet be averted." She held him and let him feel the strength in her arms, reinforcing the strength in her words.

He met her eyes and said, "I do not know what to do."

She nodded her head. "Would you slay the Son of David to save your godfather?" she asked.

"I have in truth considered it," he said. "But I would not."

"Because you are afraid to?"

"No," he said. "Because it is wrong to."

"And if it was me whose life was at risk? Would you kill to save me?"

"Only in that I would offer up my own life to save yours."

"But if you killed the moneylender your life would be forfeit and Ansaldo would live. Would it not be the same?"

"No," he said softly. "It would not. For then I truly would be a…" He paused.

"A murderer?" she asked.

"Yes," he said.

"So now you tell me that you are not in fact a murderer."

"No," he said. "I am not."

She held his head a moment longer and then pulled him closer still. And kissed him. "And I am glad to hear you say it," she said. "If it is Ansaldo's love for you that has gotten him into this perilous situation, then it is my love for you that shall get him out of it. I know a man who can help you."

"What type of man?" Giannetto asked.

"A very good man," she said.

LXXII

ELSEWHERE IN THE FLOATING CITY

"You are unreasonable, ignorant and present a danger to the city," Councillor de Abbacio shouted, slapping his hand on the council table.

The councillor sitting opposite him, Signor Tegalliano, stared back at him, so outraged by the insult that he could not get words into his mouth. "That's an outrage," he finally spluttered.

"It's an outrage that you are allowed to continue sitting on the council," said Signor de Abbacio, "when any man off the street has twice your intelligence and at least three times your backbone."

Signor Tegalliano's eyes bulged and he went red in the face. "You insult me, signor," he said.

"Well done," Signor de Abbacio retorted. "I was beginning to think that observation had escaped you."

"You go too far," said Signor Tegalliano.

"You don't go far enough," said Signor de Abbacio. "And the further from this chamber the better."

The Duca held up a hand to try and bring some type of order to the council meeting. "Please," he said. "This is all a distraction."

Then Signor Hermino, seated next to de Abbacio as ever, interjected, "I think this is important to the council. If indeed Signor Tegalliano lacks either the ability to cast a vote, or the bravery to challenge Signor de Abbacio to defend his honour when it is insulted, as he claims, then how can he claim a seat on this council? Our numbers are already dangerously reduced and we have need of stout and true citizens sitting here with us."

"Abstaining from voting has never been an issue in the past," said the Duca.

"But our city has never been so imperilled in the past," Signor Hermino said. "I suggest that any member of the council who finds himself unwilling to cast a vote, should step down from the council at once."

"You should stand down yourself," said Signor Tegalliano, spittle flying from his mouth as he shouted across the table. "You are nothing but de Abbacio's lap dog, mouthing whatever he asks of you."

"Am I being insulted or complimented?" Signor Hermino asked, turning to the Duca. The Duca just looked back at him, knowing any type of answer was unnecessary, despite Signor Hermino's look of earnest enquiry.

"Gentlemen," said the Duca, "there may be turmoil in the streets, but we must be above it."

"How can we be above it?" asked Signor de Abbacio, "when our own properties and our own families are at risk?"

"Hear, hear," said Signor Hermino.

"If this council is unable or unwilling to make the hard decisions needed to ensure the safety of our city we will see our loved ones drown or die of plague. Surely we are here to represent the voices of the citizens of the city in this."

Signor Tegalliano folded his arms and stared hard at de Abbacio. "And how will your proposal do anything at all about it? I didn't like passing the security of our city over to the Moor Otello, but I like it much less putting it in the hands of that Djinn-slayer of yours!"

"Of mine?" asked de Abbacio.

"Does he not answer to you?" asked Signor Tegalliano.

Signor de Abbacio looked wounded. "I seem to recall that a

majority of council agreed that we needed to seek the expertise of a Djinn-slayer to rid our waterways of the Othmen demons that lurked there. Have you already forgotten how Otello was helpless to stop their random attacks, as he was to stop the assassins who were killing our brothers?"

"Are you saying the Djinn-slayer has slain them too?"

"I am only saying that we have had no more attacks from the masked assassins since he came to us. Perhaps the assassins fear him more than they ever feared Otello."

"All right," said Signor Tegalliano, leaning forward in his seat. "Let's put it to the vote once more and forbid any council member to abstain."

The Duca saw de Abbacio's eyes narrow suddenly. "We have already voted," he said. "Well those of us who consider ourselves men have voted."

"Then I propose we vote once more."

"I second that," said Signor Montecchi, seated beside him.

They both watched the way the tip of de Abbacio's tongue licked his lips in quick little movements as he tried to find another way to delay the vote.

"Then we shall vote again," said the Duca, waving his hand for order before Signors de Abbacio or Hermino could say anything. "We have heard all the arguments for and against I think and don't need to have them argued once more. All those in favour of our marine guard sinking any vessels carrying plague victims, suspected or proven, that refuse to turn back out to sea, raise your hands."

Again Signors de Abbacio, Hermino and their lackey, Signor Monegario, raised their hands.

"And all those opposed?"

The Duca, and the two men either side of him, Signors Montecchi and Faliero, raised their hands. Then all eyes turned to Signor Tegalliano. The Duca knew that on many issues he would actually vote with de Abbacio, but clearly he felt this proposal was beyond that which a reasonable man could support. Another man would have let it go and continued his lobbying outside the council chamber, but de Abbacio was not other men. Why he continued to goad Tegalliano to vote, when all reason said he would now vote against de Abbacio, was beyond him. And sure enough, Signor Tegalliano slowly raised his hand.

"The proposal is defeated," said the Duca, keeping all emotion from his voice.

"In the face of defeat I withdraw the proposal," said Signor de Abbacio, "and I withdraw an insinuation that our council brother did not possess courage." He forced a smile from between clenched teeth. But his eyes were as sharp as daggers. "I hope our brother continues to exhibit such courage when the patriots who value our city's safety hear of his vote."

The Duca looked at Signor de Abbacio closely, and saw victory etched deeply there. This had all been deliberately staged. He slumped back in his chair. He did not need to call on the Seers to predict Signor Tegalliano's future. His small triumph over Signor de Abbacio would surely be as short-lived as his own life would now be, and the council would then be down to six members, three on either side, all waiting for the next assassin's dagger to fall.

LXXIII
ELSEWHERE IN THE FLOATING CITY

It was another vision. Vincenzo held his arms close to himself and shivered. Or perhaps it was a memory. Or foretelling. He could no longer be sure. They crept up on him when he was at rest or deep in thought.

This one was about Disdemona Montecchi. She was trapped inside a dark tunnel and was clawing her way along the dim stone walls, helplessly trying to find a way out. And she had been calling out to him to find her and save her. Not Otello. Not the Shadow Master. Him! As if she knew him intimately, and knew that he was the only one who could save her. And he felt he did know her. It was always the fear of Otello that had prevented him from acknowledging his strong attraction to her. And now he had to save her.

But there was something in the darkness behind her that was following her, and he was filled by a thought that he could somehow dig through the earth and find her. But he did not even know where she had been. Did not recognize it. Did not even know why he felt such an urgent need to be the one who found and saved her.

Perhaps she really was in great peril, as the Shadow Master had said. And he was the one who had to warn her. But if so, why did the vision feel to him like something that had already happened?

He cursed the Shadow Master for keeping so many secrets from him. He sometimes believed that he was bringing each of the many travails upon the city. Laying a new one down and then another. The plague ships. The refugees. The Othmen envoy. The Seers' failing powers. Even his dreams seemed the Shadow Master's doing. And this one was warning him something about Disdemona. Some way he could perhaps save her from peril.

And that made him wonder, inevitably, if the Shadow Master was really trying to help save the city, or was in fact the one most imperilling it? Or was it perhaps even himself? He rubbed his knuckles into his eyes. There was no way to know but to continue to let the story play out, and that frustrated him. There was still so much he needed to know. So many deaths he wanted to prevent.

But he had to know what he had the power to change and what he could not. And the Shadow Master was the only one who seemed to know that. Damn him! he thought. Dark saviour of the city, and bringer of ruin. When he came to write the history of this great city of his, perhaps he would write him out of it altogether!

LXXIV

THE STORY OF DISDEMONA

Otello closed his eyes as he felt Disdemona lay her hand across his chest and tried to contain himself. She was already dead, but didn't know it. "How is my lord?" she asked softly.

"Well," he finally managed to say, fighting hard to keep any emotion out of his voice.

"Would my lord like me to rub any aches and pains out of his body?" she asked, moving a little closer.

He reached up and took her searching hand softly and stilled it. "No. I would rather sleep," he said. He held her hand tightly.

"I can feel your heart galloping like a stallion. What troubles you?"

"Affairs of state," he said. "There are things that need to be done that I find I have had to steel my heart to do."

"Do you wish to tell me about them?" she asked. "A troubled shared is a trouble lessened."

"Later," he said. "I am very tired."

She moved her face closer to his, but he could not turn to face her. "Then I wish you a pleasant and deep sleep," she said.

"And I you," he said, his voice close to breaking.

He lay there a moment, taking deep breaths and then came a knocking on one of the walls. "What is that?" he asked.

She lifted her head and listened. "It is probably the sound of our house settling," she said. "It is old and makes many noises."

"Hop out of bed and see what it was," he said.

"I'm sure it is nothing."

The knocking came again.

"There it is again," he said. "Hop out of bed and see what is causing it."

Disdemona sighed in frustration, but did as he asked, stepping out of bed and walking across the room. "It seems to be coming from our cupboard," she said. And just as she reached for the door, it swung open and she saw the ensign standing there – changing looks of lust and satisfaction and anger and victory swirling across his features. "Oh!" she said, before he struck her heavily with a sand-filled bag.

She fell to the floor and called to Otello, "Help me please."

He jumped from the bed, his body suddenly trembling like a fever was upon him and said, "You are the most wicked of women and this is the weight of your falseness that now strikes you."

"No," she said, rising up from the floor. "It is not true–" But before she could say anything else, the ensign struck her again.

"Silence," he hissed. "You have brought this upon yourself."

She met his eye as she fell and knew that he was mad enough to slay her. "Help me," she said again, calling to her husband. But he then leant over her and she could see a similar blood madness in his own eyes. And with the knowledge of one close to death she understood that the ensign was responsible for the change in her husband. He had somehow infected him with his bitterness and the two men had concocted this deadly scheme together, probably debating poisons and daggers and what might be the best way to avoid being caught.

She held a hand out to her husband to tell him that she had never wronged him except to love him too unceasingly and that if he would but let her live this night she would surely find a way to not only prove her fidelity but to break this spell that had been placed upon him. But the only words she was able to mutter were a guttural cry as the ensign stepped in and bashed her about the skull, knocking her head onto the tiles brutally.

Otello stood there as if entranced, his body still shaking uncontrollably.

"It is done," the ensign said. "Now come, lift her to the bed as we agreed." But Otello could not bring himself to touch her. "Quickly," said the ensign. "Now is not the time to be unmanned."

Otello helped him lift her to the bed and then the ensign took a halberd that had hung on the wall just outside the bedchamber and started hacking at the ceiling. "Help me," he said, but Otello could no more help him than he could help Disdemona when she had pleaded for his assistance.

Eventually the ensign had brought down a full rafter from the ceiling along with other debris, and he moved the largest beam to cover Disdemona's head. Then he said, "Now go. Rouse the servants. Call to the neighbours. Tell them that your ceiling has collapsed on top of your wife and she is killed from it. Blame the sinking of the city. Blame the Othmen. Wail for all the fury you feel within you."

And Otello walked slowly from the room, finally given a task that he could easily fulfil.

LXXV

ELSEWHERE IN THE FLOATING CITY

There was a feeling amongst the crowd that something quite remarkable was going to happen tonight. A considerable crowd had emerged to watch the Seers, despite the late hour, as word spread they were standing around the canal casting a spell. Public displays by the Seers were very rare and quickly became a thing of folk legend, being embellished in the telling. They were said to be able to float above the ground and rise up into the air. They were said to be able to turn night to day. And of course they were said to have control over the elements of air and water and earth and fire. And with these they would surely not just vanquish any threats to the city, but save it from sinking.

The four Seers stood around the Grand Canal that wound its way through the Floating City in the shape of a large backwards S. The courtyard on the far side of the bridge was already underwater a few inches, yet people stood there, ankle-deep in water, to watch.

The two Summer Seers stood by the canal's wide edge on a paved embankment and the two Spring Seers stood on the ornate bridge that spanned the canal. It was perhaps fifty paces wide at this point. Citizens had fled the bridge, even if they had a need to cross it, as watching the Seers was one thing, but getting too close to them was quite another. There were stories, of course, of people having been turned to statues or simply disappearing from having been too close to them.

They took their cue from the female Spring Seer, who was cloaked and hooded like her partner to hide her sudden youthful appearance. She held her husband's hand tightly with one hand and lifted the other up above her head. All the Seers followed her lead, though it looked to the citizens watching that all four lifted an arm in unison. The citizens readied themselves, shuffling their feet a little. It was surely going to require a mighty enchantment to not just keep the city afloat, but to raise it higher from the water, and clearly the Seers would have done this earlier but had to wait for the proper alignment of the stars. This would be a memorable occasion for those few fortunate enough to witness it.

Those closest to the Seers could hear the four muttering something, and were not sure if it might be dangerous to overhear them and it would send them deaf or might even grant them the power of understanding the language of animals. They shuffled one foot forward and then one foot backwards and looked around themselves nervously. Nobody wanted to be the first to step away. They made incantations with their fingers to ward off ill fortune and remained where they stood. Then they saw a pure white light slowly envelop the two pairs of Seers like they were beacons of hope for the city. A few people shuffled a little closer.

Then something started to happen in the canal. The water started to move like rain was falling on it, although there was no rain. Some citizens stepped forward to observe it more closely. The Seers then lifted their joined hands, and they saw the water start leaping and moving like it might be boiling.

Citizens looked at each other to see if others thought it safe or dangerous to step nearer. But only a few souls ventured any closer. Now the female Spring Seer threw her head back and shouted out in some strange language. The water beneath her bubbled furiously and then rose up towards her. Several citizens took a step backwards. Then the water fell away and there loomed in front of the two Seers on the bridge a Djinn. It was enormous. As large as a nightmare.

Some citizens turned and ran at once, others took a few steps away, but stayed to watch. The Djinn's body was moving and swirling like it was made of smoke or water, but the torso was that of a large thick-set man and the head was that of a demon, with horns, large pointed ears and fangs.

The two Seers on the bridge stepped closer together and cast some enchantment at the Djinn. The citizens could see a light spring up and surround it, and it struggled to free itself. The Seers by the canal's edge cast another enchantment and a wall of water crept up to surround the Djinn too. As if the weight of it was too much to hold, the Djinn started falling back into the water. Then it suddenly shot up again, throwing out its arms as if breaking off shackles, the water and light fell from it and it rose up until it was at head level with the two young Spring Seers.

They frantically cast another enchantment at it, bright light springing from their hands, but the Djinn threw its head back and gave what sounded like a mocking laugh. The Spring Seers took a step away from the edge of the bridge, understanding in that last moment that they did not have the strength that they believed they had. Did not have the power they had felt existed somewhere in the city. Understood they had made a very big mistake.

The female Spring Seer turned her head at the last moment to look into the face of her partner, who looked more like a scared little boy than one of the city Seers, and then the Djinn's claws flashed out and pierced them both through the chest. They screamed in pain and the light around them faded. Then the Djinn pulled them towards him, dragging their bloodied bodies over the bridge's rail, and it slipped back slowly into the waters of the canal with them.

Those citizens who still remained stood transfixed, like startled animals unsure whether to take flight or not. They had just witnessed something beyond their wildest mythologizing. Then the water started bubbling again, in one patch under the bridge, and it began moving across to the canal's edge where the two remaining Seers stood. At the first cry of alarm all the citizens fled, and only one or two turned their heads to see the Seers fleeing also.

LXXVI

THE STORY OF ISABELLA

"I don't understand," said Vincenzo. "We are besieged on so many fronts, there is chaos in the streets and in the canals, and yet people find time to attend a court as if this were a normal day in the city."

"The ancients held circuses to distract from the crises on their doorsteps," the Shadow Master said. "Often pitting a man against a wild beast. I suspect today will be not be as violent, but the crowd will settle for whatever they can get to take their minds off the chaos."

Vincenzo shook his head. "But then why are we here? Shouldn't we be fighting the Djinn and the Othmen threat and saving the city in some way?"

"We are here to do precisely that," he said. "You are most likely going to witness something spectacular here today that may save the city."

"An enchantment?" asked Vincenzo.

"Watch and you will see," said the Shadow Master.

Vincenzo gave a shrug and looked around the room. The court was crowded and the people gathered there really did look like spectators about to witness one of the banned battles to the death between man and beast. The two opponents who were to fight to the death were Ansaldo the merchant and an aged bent-over Son of David. For those placing bets around the corners of the room, the sympathetic money was on Ansaldo, but the wise money was on the Son of David.

The magistrate sat in his high chair, his three-faced mask hiding what he might have thought of the case before him, though the mood of the crowd was evident in the way they hissed and spat at the Son of the David when he had entered the room. His opponent, Ansaldo the merchant, however, sat on a small stool, pale and shivering, as if he had contracted some disease in the waiting cells where he would have had thieves and thugs and the low-life of the city for company.

The magistrate called for order and asked the Son of David to explain his case. The man looked around the court first, as if certain already of his victory and then proffered a piece of paper to the magistrate. The man read it and then announced, "This is a bond between Ansaldo the merchant and you, in which he agrees to forfeit a pound of flesh if he has not repaid within the given time."

The Son of David said nothing, but just bowed in acknowledgment. The magistrate then turned to Ansaldo. "And do you admit that this is your signature and that you signed this bond."

Ansaldo spoke, in a weak voice, "I did."

The magistrate waited, as if he might somehow explain what madness drove him to agree to such outrageous terms, but he said nothing more.

"Do you require anyone to argue your case for you?" the magistrate asked the Son of David, who spoke for the first time, saying, "I think there is very little arguing needed." This brought a low chorus of hisses from the audience, who the magistrate fixed with a glare until they quietened.

"And you," the magistrate asked of Ansaldo. "Do you require anyone to argue your case?"

"My lord," said a voice from the assembled spectators and a

man stepped forward. He was also masked, in an ornate golden mask, and wore a chain around his neck such as lawyers wear. "I am here to argue his case."

Ansaldo looked up and seemed surprised to see him. His eyes searched the room and found Giannetto, who nodded his head urgently, so that when the magistrate asked him, "Is this who you wish to argue for you," he said, "Yes, my lord."

Vincenzo observed the Shadow Master smile a little at his presence. The magistrate then beckoned the man forward. His walk had a swish to it, and he held his arms out with a certain elegance, that was quickly noted.

"You are not known to me," the magistrate said.

"I am recently arrived in the city from Verona," he said, in a voice that sounded like that of a very young man. "And friends of Ansaldo have commissioned me to assist him in his case."

"It is not the custom to be masked in the court," he said. "Other than magistrates."

"I beg your forgiveness," the young man said, indicating his golden mask. "But this hides an ugly blemish on my face that causes distress to those who see it."

Vincenzo leaned close to the Shadow Master and asked, in a low voice, "Is this stranger someone you have summoned? Is he the one with the power of enchantment?"

"I did not summon him," said the Shadow Master.

"And yet you do not seem surprised to see him."

"I am not," said the Shadow Master.

"Who is he?" Vincenzo asked.

"He is not a young gentleman of Verona, as he says," the Shadow Master said in a very soft voice. Vincenzo tried to stand a little higher to get a better view of the man over the crowd.

"Is he an assassin?" he hissed in the Shadow Master's ear.

"Far from it," he said. "He is a secret weapon. Watch and listen and you will understand."

Vincenzo suspected he might not understand, but shrugged

again and watched proceedings.

The magistrate then struck the table in front of him with a small block of wood. "We will proceed then." He turned to the Son of David, and said, in rather stern words, "I fear the outcome of this case and ask if you would you consider a repayment of your loan as compensation enough."

"I would not," said the Son of David, holding his chin high.

"Would you consider your debt paid if you were offered twice the sum of the loan?" the young man then asked him.

The Son of David turned to look at the young man's golden-masked face and glared at him as if he had been offended.

"I would not!" he said.

The young man then said, "As a matter of curiosity, rather than as an actual proposal, would you accept ten times the sum of your loan as compensation?" There was a collective gasp from the court. Such a sum was a fortune that a man could buy a palace with.

"I would not," the Son of David said again, with bitterness in his voice. "Understand this, if you were to offer more ducats than this city is worth, it would not satisfy me. I would rather have what my bond says is mine."

"Then I am inclined to ask if you have other motives than reclaiming your loan?" the magistrate said.

"I am but following the laws of our city," the Son of David said, and bowed low. There were other murmurs and hisses from the audience.

"Our city?" asked the magistrate. "It seems many here in the chamber disagree with your description."

And the Son of David spun to the room and glared at the people there, then turned back to the magistrate. "I am a citizen of this city," he said. "My mother was born here and left when she married my father and then converted to our religion. She returned shortly after when I was but a baby, but instead of being welcomed back by her family, she was placed on the Isle of Sorrows because she had contracted the black lung disease. She died when the island was set aflame by the city. I was saved." Then he said it slowly so that there would be no doubt about it. "I live on the Island of the Ghetto, as is the city law concerning all Sons of David. But my mother was a citizen of this city and as such I am also entitled to citizenship. As I am entitled to be treated by the laws of the city. I have it in writing from one of your colleagues that this is my due." And he proffered another piece of paper to the magistrate.

The magistrate took it, read it and visibly chewed his lip for a moment and looked to his left and right, perhaps wishing he had colleagues to consult with. Finally he said, "That is correct."

There was an unhappy mumbling from the body of the court, which the magistrate let continue for some time before calling for silence by rapping his block of wood again.

"Is the young man going to do something soon?" Vincenzo asked.

The Shadow Master nodded his head.

"And you say it is going to be spectacular?"

"Quite spectacular."

"Has he a special power to defeat the Djinn?" Vincenzo asked.

"I don't believe so."

"He has an enchantment to stop the Othmen then?"

"He is a shapeshifter, but not an enchanter," the Shadow Master said.

Vincenzo chewed his thumb. "But he is somehow vital to saving our city?"

"Extremely vital."

Vincenzo sighed in exasperation.

"Do you have any arguments to put for Ansaldo the merchant?" the magistrate now asked the young lawyer.

"May I read the bond?" the young man asked and the magistrate passed it to him and he read it over carefully. Then he surprised everyone by saying, "It seems in order. According to this the Son of David may proceed and take the pound of flesh, and I argue that it be done here and now where we may bear witness to it."

The magistrate was as much taken aback as the members of the public were. "No," cried one man in the audience. It was Giannetto. "I am the one that Ansaldo took the loan for and I am the one that defaulted on the repayment, so I should be the one who the pound of flesh is taken from."

The magistrate let him come forward and asked the Son of David if he would consent to this offer. But he refused to accept it. "The bond says it must come from Ansaldo. I am respectful of the law and will follow it to the letter."

"To the letter then," said the masked young man. Giannetto reached out and took the young man by the arm and entreated him to argue in Ansaldo's defence more rigorously, but the young man shushed him and said, "We must abide by the law."

"This law is too strict," said Giannetto, which brought a rebuke from the magistrate not to say any more.

"Come then," said the young man, stepping forward and flouncing his cape around. "Have the guards hold Ansaldo and bear his breast for the Son of David." Then he turned to the old man and said, "Do you have a knife, or shall I have one fetched for you?"

"I have a knife," he said and brought it out of his bag.

"And do you have scales, or shall I have them fetched for you?" the young man asked.

"I have scales," the Son of David said and produced those as well.

Vincenzo squeezed the Shadow Master's arm. "Are you going to allow this?" he hissed.

"I trust the young man explicitly," he said.

"This will not go well," Vincenzo said. "He is on the side of the Son of David. The crowd will tear him apart and then they will burn down and sack the Island of the Ghetto."

"Perhaps," said the Shadow Master. "But perhaps not."

"Or is this a test for me?" he asked. "Is this going to be dependent on how I write it as to how it turns out?"

"And how would you write it to be?"

"I would write it that the people in this court abandon this folly and arm themselves to help defend the city. I would write it that the magistrate declares a state of emergency and demands every grown man be recruited to militias to take up arms. I would write it that a Djinn rose through the floor and caused every person here to regain their senses and see this for a circus farce. And I would write that you tell me who this young man is."

"That would be an interesting outcome indeed," said the Shadow Master, and then put a finger to his lips, indicating that he wanted to better hear.

"I see you have come prepared to exact your due," the young lawyer said to the Son of David. "Do you have bandages and salve to ensure that Ansaldo the merchant does not bleed to death here?"

"It says nothing of such in the bond," said the Son of David coldly.

"You are correct. It does not," said the young man. "All right then, proceed."

"No!" said Ansaldo, looking around himself desperately.

"Wait," said the magistrate. "Surely it is not right to cut up a man in the court."

"We must follow the law," said the young man.

The magistrate looked pained but had to agree.

Vincenzo leaned in close to the Shadow Master again. "You have some surprise planned, don't you? Some trick of your own. A smoke cloud. Or a fireball. Surely you're not going to let the old merchant be sacrificed in this way?"

The Shadow Master said nothing. Vincenzo stood up on tiptoes again to look at the young man closely again. "I think I know. He is actually an Othmen in disguise. You will have him unmasked and then harness the rage of the people of the city in its defence."

"A good plot twist," said the Shadow Master. "I hadn't considered that one. But a little improbable I think."

Vincenzo squeezed his fists together in frustration. "You are crueller than the Othmen!" he hissed.

"Perhaps," said the Shadow Master again, calmly. "But perhaps not."

"Then proceed," the young man said again. The Son of David, emboldened by the young man's tone, stepped forward with his knife. Ansaldo, who had been trying his best to show a brave face, started breathing heavily and then fainted, falling forward off his stool.

"Lift him up," said the young man and the guards did so. "But gently. It might be kinder for him to be insensible."

Giannetto again stepped forward and grabbed the young man's sleeve. "You cannot allow this," he said, but the young man just shushed him again.

"The law will be served and justice will be served. Mark my words on it."

Giannetto looked as if he was about to do something rash, but a guard placed his hand on his shoulder and steered him back to the body of the court.

Then the Son of David stood in front of Ansaldo and the look on his face was one of victory. A triumph over all the injustices that had been done to him and his family and his mother, and this was his moment of retribution. He placed the point of his knife against Ansaldo's breast and just before he pushed it in the young man said in a suddenly cold voice, "Take great care in what you do, for you must take neither more nor less than an exact pound."

The Son of David hesitated a moment.

"And if you shed one drop of blood in this chamber your life will be forfeit as the laws of the city decree that shedding blood here is a mortal crime."

The Son of David turned and glared at the young man.

"I have studied your bond carefully," the young lawyer said. "It is for one pound of flesh only. Anything other puts your life at risk."

The courtroom fell silent and even the magistrate waited to see what would happen. The Son of David turned back to Ansaldo, his face now wreathed in conflict. He placed the knife edge against his breast again and then drew it back. He grimaced like he was in pain and said through gritted teeth, "I suddenly feel it would be better to accept the payment offered to me earlier."

"Too late," said the young man with a flourish. "You have refused that before a court. You must take the pound of flesh."

The Son of David looked around him, like a rodent in a trap and said, "I will accept half of what was offered to me."

"No," said the young man. "You must take what is your legal due. You will not receive the smallest coin that exists."

The Son of David looked like he was going to cry and threw his knife to the ground.

"You must take your legal due or forfeit the bond," said the young man. "They are the only courses of action open to you."

The Son of David knew he was beaten and he strode across the room, grabbed the bond from the young man's hand and tore it into pieces. Then he stomped out through the jeering crowd.

"That was it?" asked Vincenzo. "That was the spectacular thing you promised?"

"It was," said the Shadow Master. "It was a great victory over the forces of chaos aligned against your city."

"Uh – how exactly?"

"It is one thing to save the city from the Othmen," the Shadow Master said. "But it will be another thing to ensure it can be saved from itself afterwards. That can only happen by strengthening confidence in the rule of law."

Vincenzo stared at the Shadow Master for some moments and then said, "I had been expecting something more – well, visually spectacular."

"It is not finished quite yet," said the Shadow Master and gestured for Vincenzo to watch Giannetto heartily shake the masked man's hand in gratitude, and then ask how he could ever repay him for his services. "Ask anything," he said. "Ansaldo and I are in your debt."

Vincenzo watched the young man place his hand upon Giannetto's chest and lean in close to him. This seemed to disconcert Giannetto a little, but the young man tilted his head this way and that and asked, "Anything?"

"Um – anything within reason."

The young man then took Giannetto's arm in his own and pulled him close. "There is something I was longing for that you might be able to give me," he said.

"I am betrothed," Giannetto said quickly. "To the Lady Isabella. I cannot."

"Such a pity," said the young man, but not letting go of his arm. Then he looked down at his hand and said, "This ring would be fine payment."

"I cannot," said Giannetto. "It was given to me by my love on condition that I never part with it."

"Would you give me one night of pleasure instead?" the young man asked.

Giannetto now looked positively pained and asked if there were any other option. "None," said the young man. "Consider it as non-negotiable as the Son of David's bond."

Giannetto looked at Ansaldo, who was being gently shaken back to his senses by his friends, who were also explaining to him what had happened. "The ring or a night with me. Choose quickly," the young man said.

"The ring then," said Giannetto, sounding utterly defeated, and perhaps wondering which of the two options would upset his betrothed the least. He prised it off his finger and gave it to the masked young man. Then he went to Ansaldo's side and when he looked back the young man was gone.

Vincenzo, who had watched the scene closely, said, "I would like to witness what happens when Giannetto tries to explain to the Lady Isabella why he is missing that ring."

"She will hand the ring back to him," the Shadow Master said.

"But how is that possible?" Vincenzo said. "The young man has it."

"Do you mean the young man who mysteriously arrived in the city and who was the same height and build as Lady Isabella and spoke with her voice, though lowered a little?" he asked. "The young man who conveniently wore a mask, and bore the poise of a noblewoman?"

Vincenzo stared at him dumbstruck. "He was Isabella Montecchi?" he asked.

The Shadow Master clearly decided that question did not need an answer. Vincenzo's mouth gaped open. "Then I would like even more to witness that scene between them."

"It ends well," said the Shadow Master.

"How do you know all these things?" Vincenzo demanded of him. "It is like you have written everything out already and all the details are just a game to you."

But again the Shadow Master decided not to reply.

LXXVII

ELSEWHERE IN THE FLOATING CITY

The Duca had a feeling that if he stood there at the window of his chamber long enough he would see the Floating City sink beneath the waters there in front of him. But he also felt that he didn't have that much time left in him. The city was dying, but so was he. He was an old man pretending to still have power, when in fact it was slipping away from him each day. This was an autumn of great discontent.

He looked out onto the streets and courtyards and buildings and canals of the city that he loved so much that he felt stronger for it than he had ever felt for his children. He loved its grandeur and he loved its areas of decay. He loved the plazas and the waterways and the stagnant backwaters. He loved each island and the buildings upon it, whether they be palazzo or shack. He loved it all and not just his own island, or the immediate vicinity of where he lived, unlike some. The city was his mistress and he thought her beautiful in all her moods and weathers. He had dedicated his life to serving the city, and knew that he had failed her. Under other circumstances it would be time to step down and spend his days writing up his history so that he had a chance to influence how he would be remembered. But that was no longer a realistic option. He knew he would have to hang onto power until it was forcibly taken from him and then throw his legacy to chance. For no legacy was as rich as honesty.

Yet his father would have been disappointed, he felt. The man who had also dedicated his life to public office and right at the end of his rule had offset all of his wise decisions with one poor decision. And that he was remembered for and that the Duca had spent much of his adult life trying to avoid replicating. And yet, here he was, standing at the window's edge, contemplating a similar decision to his father.

He turned from the window and walked across to a bird cage that held four brightly-coloured songbirds in it. There had originally been five, but one had become slowly aggressive and had started attacking the other birds. He had let it do so for far too long before finally deciding to remove it. But the damage was done. The other songbirds huddled apart from each other, as if expecting the other bird to return at any moment. Too scarred or scared to sing for him anymore.

He opened a small door in the cage and reached in his hand slowly. The birds flittered away from him. He moved his hand around gently until he was able to coax one of the birds onto his fingers. Then he drew it out of the cage slowly, talking to it in a soft cooing voice. He brought the bird close to his face and looked at it closely. It turned its head this way and that, ducking and bobbing in nervousness. Once it would have let him kiss it on the head.

He took the bird across to the window and paused just a moment before casting it out. The surprised bird fell like a stone and he leaned out the window to watch it plummet towards the city streets below before recovering and taking to the air, rising and circling and then flying out of sight. He would like to lean further out the window and watch it, but feared he might emulate its fall – without the recovery.

What should he do with the plague people? he wondered. He had hoped that resettling them on the Isle of Sorrows would provide them the safety of the city while they were treated. But they were little better than prisoners there. No wonder so many stole across to the city and into hiding. He had been brought news that plague had appeared in many quarters. In the poorer streets and in the city jails. Should he round them all up and send them off to the Isle of Sorrows as well? Or should he have them moved further away, as Signor de Abbacio advocated? Turn the boats back or sink them out at sea. Go from house to house and find anybody with plague and have them put on old boats and towed outside the mouth of the lagoon. With luck the Othmen might even capture them as slaves, Signor de Abbacio had said, and they'd then get a taste of their own medicine – or pestilence.

The Duca went back to the bird cage and put his hand in once more. Again the birds moved away from him, reluctant to let him touch them. "I am offering you your freedom," he said, but the birds still flitted and squawked at him. He enticed a second bird onto his hand and brought it slowly out of the cage. This one was mostly green, with flashes of red and yellow on its wings.

"Will you sing for me?" the Duca asked, but the bird just ducked its head at his words. He took it over to the window and cast it out too. This one took to the air at once and was gone in an instant. He felt a soft pang of envy. Then he went back to the cage again.

"Come to me," he said, moving his hand about slowly, but neither of the two remaining birds would. He had to grab one, as if it was a soft fruit he was plucking from a tree. He felt the bird struggling a little in his hands and bore it to the window quickly. He opened his hand and let it recover, before holding it out, waiting for it to make its own decision to fly away. But it just stood there, bending its head and grooming its feathers.

If he even gave an indication that he was considering taking flight like these birds, Signor de Abbacio would seize control of the council at once. He would have his Djinn-slayer installed as general of the city. He may even have Othmen advisors sitting in the empty council seats before anybody could offer the slightest protest.

And he would have access to the secrets of the city that were reserved only for the Duca. Secrets that were not even shared with the Seers. What would he do with that knowledge?

"Fly away," he said, giving his hand a shake and the bird took flight. So easily.

He went back to the cage and tried to coax the last bird to climb onto his hand. But it would not. He had to grab it too. He brought it out of the now empty cage and held it close to his face. The bird seemed scared of him. He could feel its heart beating rapidly within his closed fist. Is that what it felt like to hold a beating heart? he wondered. And would it be so easy to cast it into the air to freedom.

He wished for a moment that it was his own heavy heart that he held in his hand right now. He would like to throw it into the air and watch it take flight, lighter than the breezes and the clouds. On his death bed his father told him not only how he had torched the Isle of Sorrows, where the victims of the black lung disease had been quarantined, killing everyone there, but of the day he had decided to do it. It was something that haunted his dreams every night since, he had said.

And he told him of a woman who had come to him to beg permission to become a citizen of the city. Well, to become a citizen once more. She had renounced her citizenship to marry a Son of David and move away. She had come to him as a widow whose husband had contracted the black lung disease and now had the early signs of it herself. She also came to him as a mother, as she had a young babe with her. The son of the Son of David. And she came to him as an outcast, as her in-laws had sent her away as not a true believer.

Her name was Ruth. But he knew that, for he remembered her from when he was younger. In fact he had been quite in love with her growing up. But she had rejected him for the Son of David. And now here she was, begging him to let her return to the city of her birth, with a young child in her arms.

And he, who had strived to be a fair man most of his life, found a sudden coldness in his heart. He looked at the woman as if she was a stranger. As if her tears meant nothing to him. All he could think of was her lying with the Son of David and bearing his child.

The Duca stood there by the window, his palm open and the bird gone. He had taken her to his chamber and induced her to lie with him, and afterwards he had sent her to the Isle of Sorrows. And the next day he gave the order to purge it clean with flame. That act became his legacy and the source of his nightmares. And for his sins he contracted the black lung disease from her.

The Duca held up his hand and looked at the sores that were developing on his wrists. He would not be able to hide them soon. They would advance down his hands. They were already blossoming at his armpits, and from there would spread to his upper torso and neck. Ugly black welts that would burst yellow pus when pressed too hard.

His father's last words to him were that he should know the agony of bearing the deaths of others on his conscience, and should never be tempted to do what he had done. It was a promise he had made him swear over and over again. And after he was gone, and he was but an unfillable empty hole in his young life, he had clung onto that vow, in memory of the man who had also loved the city more than he had loved him.

The Duca closed his hands and let his cuffs fall down over the sores on his hands. Signor de Abbacio would be delighted to know the agony he had contracted, and would certainly have him sent straight to the Isle of Sorrows. In the interests of the city's wellbeing, of course. But, as he stood at the window, looking not down on his city now, but up in the air, searching for any trace of his songbirds, he was more concerned with knowing what his father might have chosen to do if he had stood beside him.

LXXVIII
THE STORY OF ISABELLA

Signora Montecchi could not even enter the crypt as the weight of seeing two of her beloved daughters in death, lying there as if still alive, was more than she felt she could bear. Disdemona's body had been borne to the family crypt on the Island of Mourning along the recently-trodden path and laid in an open coffin in a recess not far from her sister.

Signora Montecchi stood outside the crypt with her last daughter, Isabella, supporting her, crying silent tears that fell about her feet like rain, her face screwed up tightly in grief. "It is too heavy a burden to have to bury one's children," she protested, her voice coming out thinly as if she were being strangled. "Her goodness is being interred with her bones."

Isabella held onto her tightly, giving her strength, and she in turn clung to her daughter, as if it might somehow protect her from any harm. "Come and sit," Isabella told her mother eventually and the two women moved across to a small stone bench under an olive tree.

"This should be a happy day for you and your new man," Signora Montecchi said to Isabella and nodded her head towards Giannetto who was in the crypt with her husband. "We should be preparing to celebrate a wedding, not a funeral."

"There is time enough for that," said Isabella.

Her mother then lifted her hands to take her daughter by the shoulders and said, "These deaths were not natural."

"What do you mean?" Isabella asked her.

"There is foul work at play here," she said. "Assassins."

Isabella shook her head. "Why would anybody choose to assassinate young Giulietta?" she asked. She did not ask the same of Disdemona, who she knew had marked herself for attack from the moment she declared her love for the Moor. He was a foreigner. Of a different faith. He had many enemies. But she had not died from an assassin's knife. She had died from the city not honouring the general with a house of sufficient quality that it would not collapse on them.

She had many times offered to house her sister and the Moor in one of her former husband's houses in the city, but Disdemona had always refused. Otello would consider it an insult to his honour, she told her. He would rather the city make amends by offering him a better house. Pride indeed comes before a fall, she thought.

Her mother now took a large breath and seemed to compose herself a little and said, "There are so many things I never told you girls. Things I always thought you could better survive the trials of life not knowing. But perhaps I was wrong in this. Perhaps I have done you all a great disservice."

"What are you talking about?" Isabella asked her.

"Your origins," she said.

Isabella's eyes widened. As girls they had often asked their parents to tell them more about where they had come from, and always had to accept the meagre story that they were orphans whose parents were never known, or had died of a rare disease, or had been slain by the Othmen. But, they had assured them, they were all children of the Floating City. They were just like every other boy and girl in the city – though they had often felt that was not the full truth of it.

"Tell me," Isabella said.

"This is not really the time," her mother said. "We are here to mourn your dear sister. Your dear sisters. We can talk of it another time."

"No, tell me now," Isabella urged.

But her mother shook her head. "I should not have spoken," she said.

"You said this was not natural," Isabella said. "That they were assassinated. Are you saying that I am at risk of being killed too?"

Her mother looked horrified, as if that idea had never fully occurred to her – or perhaps she had never been willing to accept it. She put a hand to her mouth and then looked about her, as if somebody might be listening to them.

"Who killed them?" Isabella said.

"I do not know," her mother said. "Perhaps those who seek to bring our city down."

"The Othmen?" Isabella asked.

"I do not know. But I do know that there are forces trying to bring our city down from within."

"What do you mean?" Isabella asked her. "Who?"

"Your father knows more than I do."

"Then I shall ask him," Isabella said.

"You must not," her mother said, grasping her arm tightly. "It was long ago, and we made promises never to talk about these things."

"What things?" Isabella asked, a chill suddenly walking up her spine like an ice spider. "I must know."

But her mother looked around and suddenly startled. Isabella looked up and saw a strange man in a hooded cloak standing across the cemetery looking at them both.

"I can say no more," her mother said and stood up. Isabella looked back at the figure and saw him nod at them and then step back into the shadows and trees.

"Who was that?" she asked her mother.

"Who?" she asked. "I did not see anyone."

Isabella saw that for a thin lie. Whoever it was, he had clearly scared her mother.

"We must get back to the others," her mother said and began walking across to the other mourners.

"Wait," Isabella urged. "Are we in danger?"

Her mother stopped and turned to her, her face again a mask of grief and pain. "You have always been in danger," she said. "But things must play out as they play out. That was our agreement."

LXXIX

THE STORY OF GIULIETTA

Romeo knew enough about how contraband goods were smuggled into the Floating City to find an inn where he could find a boatman with experience of navigating the lagoon at night. Though to be truthful, finding a boatman was a lot easier than convincing one to actually take him across to the city. That required him offering up the large jewelled ring off his finger.

But he was driven enough to hand it over with only a small amount of regret. The boatman he had found fingered the jewel with grubby calloused fingers several times before deciding it was more likely genuine than not, and with a grunt led Romeo out into the darkness. The two men made their way down a dim pathway to the water's edge. There were several low sloops tied up there, each painted black and near impossible to see in the darkness. How he could tell which sloop was his, Romeo was uncertain, but the man untied one and indicated to Romeo that he should climb in. Then he pushed off silently and they glided out onto the still waters of the lagoon, the lights of the Floating City burning there ahead of him, shrouded in a mist that made them seem much further away.

Romeo gathered his dark cloak about him in the prow of the vessel. He watched the city for some time and then turned back to the boatman. "Have you heard of the death of Giulietta

Montecchi?" he asked him in a soft voice.

The boatman said nothing.

"She was a noblewoman," Romeo said. "You must know her father. He is an important man in the city."

Still the boatman said nothing. Romeo looked to the man's dark outline and suddenly wondered if he could trust him. Might he get to the middle of the lagoon and tip him into the water and then turn back? It would be a safer way to earn his fee. "What is your name?" Romeo asked him.

The boatman spat into the water behind him in reply, making more noise in doing so than the soft strokes of his padded oar in the water. Romeo fidgeted nervously with the dagger's hilt at his belt. He would be able to draw it out quickly if the man made any move against him.

"It is said she died mysteriously," said Romeo, but he knew in fact she had died of a broken heart from being separated from him. "I am a friar, coming to perform a service for the family." But having said it aloud, the long thought-out lie suddenly seemed absurd. Why would a friar be sneaking into the city at night rather than travelling across during the day when traffic was allowed?

He had concocted the story only because a dangerous man like a smuggler would surely think a friar more trustworthy than a random stranger, and would be more likely to help him. Or less likely to harm him. It didn't matter. They were nearly half way across the lagoon now. If the man did not attack him by the halfway point, he would be unlikely to attack him beyond that.

Perhaps.

"They say she was uncommonly beautiful," Romeo said.

"Quiet," hissed the boatman and Romeo more sensed than saw the boatman turn his whole body towards him. This was it, he thought and gripped the hilt of his dagger. But the boatman did not move further. And Romeo suddenly understood he had not turned towards him, but had turned to look beyond him.

"What is it?" asked Romeo at almost the same instant he heard the soft splash in the water behind them.

"Hush now," said the boatman, and he bent his back to the boat's oar with more vigour, but with no more noise. "But your prayers might be welcome now, friar," he said softly.

Romeo didn't know quite what to say for a moment and then knew it was best to say nothing. If the man believed he was truly a friar, and believed that the prayers of a friar could actually influence events, then he was welcome to believe it. He himself had lost faith in the influence of friars and their promises. He had been waiting for a letter from Friar Lorenzo da San Francesco for many days, telling him what scheme he had devised to bring him and Giulietta together, and had heard nothing. The drug-addled fool was undoubtedly still in a stupor of Othmen potions, trying to come up with some half-witted and impractical idea. And his beloved Giulietta had died while waiting for him to fulfil his promise to help them.

Romeo felt a constricting around his heart as they came closer to the city. He remembered the last time he and Giulietta had been together there. And he felt tears unexpectedly stinging his eyes, and raised a hand to wipe them away, searching for his anger again. Anger kept a man strong, he thought.

"Nearly there," the boatman whispered after some moments.

"What of the city guard?" Romeo asked.

The boatman chuckled a little. "No. We're past the worst danger now. Those fools walk around with lanterns aloft. They might as well be singing and playing drums."

The boatman rowed them right up to the island of the city where Romeo had asked to be taken, and found a set of stone stairs leading into the water. "May good fortune be with you, friar, whatever your quest," the boatman said. Then Romeo was standing once more in the city of his birth, from where he had been banished upon pain of death, and the boatman was drawing away into the darkness.

Romeo lowered his head and set off determinedly. He was on the Isle of Mourning.

LXXX

ELSEWHERE IN THE FLOATING CITY

The Djinn-slayer stood in the centre of the low darkened room and watched the way the flame in the centre danced. It did not seem to have anything to feed on. He turned his head away; it was a minor trick and not worthy of his attention. He was dressed in black leather with silver rings woven through it, and his beard was plaited into two tails, with more silver set in it. His eyes were ringed with black kohl and his long hair tied back by a dark leather headband. He looked around the room once more and then turned as a door opened. Two sets of Seers walked in and took their seats. That confused him for a moment.

The Summer Seers, garbed in gold and blue, met his gaze intently, while the other pair, the Spring Seers, kept their gaze averted. He peered closely at them and saw the shape of their hands and the outline of their bodies. It really was them! Not dead! This was not a minor trick, and he would need to concentrate all his defences.

"I am glad to see you are all well," the Djinn-slayer said, and bowed low with a flourish. "There were rumours of – well – trouble."

"There are always rumours of trouble," said the male Summer Seer.

"Of course," said the Djinn-slayer. "These are troubled times and what else should they bring but rumours of trouble?"

The female Summer Seer gave a short nod, of sorts, clearly not in the mood for small talk. "We have summoned you here to demand an explanation," she said.

"I am a servant of the city, and as such am a servant to you too," he said and bowed low again.

None of the four Seers responded. He spun around to look at the Spring Seers who sat on the other side of him. The female looked up at him quickly and then dropped her eyes again. The Djinn-slayer was feeling uneasy about this. He turned back again to the Summer Seers, letting his gaze dwell on the empty seats about them as he did so. "What would you like me to explain?" he asked.

"You were charged with ridding the city of Djinn, and yet there was an attack by a Djinn. The largest we have ever seen in the city." The female Summer Seer's eyes were full of anger. Good, he thought, emotion will make them weaker.

"I did slay a Djinn, and sent others away from the city," he said. "The Othmen have clearly sent new Djinn to our waters."

"Our waters?" the male Summer Seer asked.

The Djinn-slayer bowed low again. "I do not wish to cause offence, of course." He turned to the Spring Seers, but still they did not meet his gaze. That troubled him. There was more going on here than was apparent, he knew.

He turned back to the Summer Seers. "Let me state that again with more diplomacy. The Othmen have clearly sent new Djinn to the waters of the city. I was perhaps errant in not being able to detect them earlier."

"Do you have the ability to know when a Djinn is present?" the male Summer Seer demanded, leaning forward in his seat a little.

"Most assuredly," said the Djinn-slayer. "I can tell how close a Djinn is and also how dangerous it is."

He watched the way the two Seers squeezed each other's hand quickly, the glow around them increasing a little.

"We charge you with negligence in your work then," the female Summer Seer said. "If you had been able to warn us of this latest Djinn, then–"

"Yes?"

She did not finish the sentence. The male Seer's eyes darted quickly to the two Seers behind him and then looked away. The Djinn-slayer turned around slowly and regarded the two Seers behind him. They refused to look up at him.

"Rumour has it you were slain by this Djinn," he said, stepping across to them slowly.

"Never mind what rumours say," said the female Summer Seer. "We want you to answer to this accusation." But he did not turn back to her. He kept his eyes on the Spring Seers. Until the male lifted his head quickly and then the Djinn-slayer saw the fear in his eyes. Saw who he really was.

He spun back to the Summer Seers and said, "Yes. But I must warn you, I feel a Djinn is very near now and you are in great peril." He watched the way they looked at each other and then back at him.

"Where? In the canal outside?" asked the male Summer Seer.

"Ah," said the Djinn-slayer, "That is the thing about Djinn. Many of them are water creatures, but there are some that are land creatures too. As there are some that can change their shape."

"What do you mean?" asked the female Summer Seer, but the Djinn-slayer did not need to explain. His body had already started to grow. His chest was swelling, bursting the leather and silver rings from him, and horns were starting to emerge from his head.

All four Seers watched in horror as the Djinn-slayer transformed in front of them. His legs grew into a large snake-like tail, made of swirling cloud and smoke and he held his arms out wide, thick and muscled, as long knife-like talons grew on the ends of them. He growled a low deep rumble that filled the chamber and echoed about him.

The Summer Seers started an incantation and without even

turning his eyes from them, the Djinn-slayer swung one of his long arms behind him and disembowelled the two children in those old bodies who had been sitting there, dutifully fulfilling their roles.

The Djinn-slayer then moved towards the two Summer Seers and said, "The era of Seers is ended."

"Not yet," said a voice from his side and a silver arrow struck the Djinn in the face. He growled and spun to see a hooded man step out of the darkness.

"You!" said the Djinn-slayer.

"You!" said the female Summer Seer.

"Yes, me," said the Shadow Master and leapt onto one of the empty chairs and then flipped in the air over the clawing arm that grasped for him and landed in front of the Djinn, driving a short blade into its torso and carving at his face with another, cutting into one eye. The Djinn screamed and tried to grab him, but he was already moving and was around behind it, driving his blade into its back. The Djinn screamed again, a terrible sound like a beast in great torment and it spun to try and catch him. But again he had already moved and was now behind the chairs where the slain couple were and he raised his hand and fired another arrow from a crossbow on his wrist. The bolt struck the Djinn in the other eye and he bellowed and threw his hands to his head to protect it.

But his tail, one instant a swirl of smoke, was suddenly solid and it snaked around behind the Shadow Master and caught him, flinging him to the ground. He rolled to avoid it coming down on him, as the Djinn searched for him.

"Quickly, while it's injured," said the female Summer Seer trying to conjure up an enchantment to bind it, but the Djinn spun towards her voice and reached out one long arm. The talons struck deep into her stomach. She gave a sigh and fell forward. Her husband, still holding her hand, ducked low as the other arm sought for him.

But now the Shadow Master was on his feet again and he called to the Djinn. "You missed." The blinded creature spun back towards him, a growl of rage filling the chamber. The Shadow Master cut at the arm that reached for him and leapt over the thrashing tail. But the other arm snagged his cloak and threw him off balance.

The Djinn heard the Shadow Master strike the floor and sprang towards him.

"Now," called the Shadow Master and the Djinn faltered in its attack, its blinded face spinning back and forward, trying to hear if there was another assailant.

"Prepare to die, monster," said Vincenzo the scribe, stepping into the flickering firelight. He held a sword a little awkwardly in his hands, cutting the air in circles in front of him.

"Can that be the voice of fear I hear?" said the Djinn, tilting its head a little, blood running from its ruined eyes.

"Yes," said Vincenzo. "It is the voice of a man who is afraid and who is not familiar with wielding weapons, but it also the man who has already slain you."

"And how could that be?" asked the Djinn in its deep voice, moving quickly across to where Vincenzo stood, its arms spread out to cut him to pieces.

"For I have already written your death," Vincenzo said.

The few sentences were all the distraction that the Shadow Master had needed. He was suddenly standing behind the Djinn with a deadly curved sword raised in both hands. He brought it down with a slight grunt, and the Djinn's head fell from its body.

Vincenzo watched in horror as the headless torso and tail lashed around before finally ceasing. There was deep dark blood running across the floor from the beast's body that stank horribly.

"Oh," said Vincenzo. "I wrote that he turned back into a man."

"Maybe the next one," said the Shadow Master, who was already beside the Seers, looking at the deep wounds in the female's stomach. Her partner held her hand tightly and had his other hand pressed to her abdomen, keeping her alive. Keeping himself alive too.

"That wasn't meant to happen," the Shadow Master said.

"Is she going to die?" Vincenzo asked.

"Not quite yet," said the Shadow Master. "We cannot allow it if we are to stop the city from sinking beneath the waters."

LXXXI

THE STORY OF GIULIETTA

Romeo drew his dagger and bracing his arm drove it quickly into the place he was aiming. It went in smoothly. Then he twisted it, first to one side and then to the other. Nothing happened. He drew it out again and looked at the chain. He would need to find a weaker link. He searched up and down the chain by moonlight and found what looked like a link that was not so well sealed. He drove his dagger into the link and braced himself to twist.

He had found the Montecchi tomb easily enough, and had stood at the gates to the crypt and looked in. There were candles burning which he knew meant somebody had been in there recently. But perhaps it was just to tidy the place up, he told himself. Surely the family paid somebody to come and light candles each evening.

He had shaken the bars and found they were solid and then spied the chain holding the gates shut. A part of him had wanted to call out to Giulietta and ask her if she was in there. But it was absurd, of course, for if she was in there she would not be able to answer him, and if she was able to answer him she would not be in there. He was not thinking straight. He looked down and saw his hands were trembling. All his fears had come to this moment and they were filling his whole body with their torments.

He was afraid to open the tomb, yet he was more afraid not to. He had to know if the stories of his beloved's death were just malicious falsehoods spread by her family to lure him back to the city to avenge Tebaldo w death. As he suspected. But they presumed he would go to the Montecchi palazzo to find the truth. Who, after all, would try and break into a tomb?

"Romeo Cappalletti, that's who," he said as he twisted the chain fiercely. But it showed no more sign of breaking than the previous link had. He twisted harder, and mumbled Giulietta's name, recalling the last time they had touched, on her balcony, and how it had filled him with lightness and strength and a sense of wonderment. And the link suddenly parted. The knife cut through the metal as if it was old rope and the chain fell away and the gates opened. He did not notice though, so eager was he to step into the crypt and disprove his worst fears.

He took a step into the tomb and immediately felt the temperature drop about him, bringing goosebumps to his skin. He put away his dagger and rubbed his hands together. A chill fog formed in front of his mouth, filling the whole tomb it seemed, like a winter's fog off the canals.

He paid it no heed though for he could feel his heart suddenly beating like a war drum as he walked towards the light of the candles ahead, each a yellow glow in the mist-filled tomb. A few more steps and he could make out the figure of a young woman, dressed in white, laid out in an open coffin, as was the custom of the Floating City with the newly deceased.

"Oh no," he said, and felt the chill of the tomb enter his blood. His legs began shaking as he took another step forward. "It cannot be," he said. "It cannot be true. If she was dead I would surely know it in my heart and I know that we are going to be together. I can feel it." His words echoed about him, as if he was not alone, and that gave him some small comfort. "I can feel it," he repeated.

Two more steps and he could see her face and his legs stopped shaking. One more step and he was certain. It was Giulietta's sister Disdemona. He felt a wave of relief flow through him. "Somebody has got the story confused," he said to the dead woman in front of him. "Somebody has mistaken you for your fair sister." He stepped up close to the coffin and said, "I am sorry to find you dead like this, but it is a sorrow tempered by happiness." He looked at her face and saw it was battered as if she had died violently, even though makeup had been applied to hide the fact. "I will say a prayer over you," he said, "and then depart, sorry that I never knew you better."

He lowered his head and mumbled a few words of prayer, thinking how the poets would write an epic poem about this episode one day, telling the story of how his bravery was rewarded by discovering it was not his beloved who had died. Then he turned to leave. And he saw the other woman in the side alcove. Also surrounded by candles. He closed his eyes a moment and then reopened them. Surely he was hallucinating. How could there be another woman in the tomb? Or was this some reflection of the light playing tricks on his eyes. He looked back to Disdemona's body and then to the other. No, it was another.

"Oh surely not," he pleaded. "It is too cruel." And he tried to walk across to the alcove to look into the coffin. But his feet would not obey him. They had not strength, as if they knew already what his mind was not willing to know. "It is not her, it is not her, it is not her," he began chanting, as if saying it aloud might make it so. But in two more hesitant steps he could no longer deceive himself. It was his beloved Giulietta. His betrothed. His everything.

His head spun and he had to grasp the sides of the coffin to hold himself up. "No!" he called aloud, the sound echoing around his head like blows being struck upon him. He leaned forward to touch her, but found he could not. As if some force was keeping him away. "Giulietta, my sweet," he said. She looked so alive. So unblemished. So unlike the empty look of death on her sister's face. And then he started weeping, large wet tears that fell to the ground about his feet, pooling together and winding all around the coffin until they encircled it.

He did not even see them as he struggled to reach out and

embrace her, but then decided he knew why he could not. "It is because I am still in this earthly realm," he said. And then he drew his dagger. "So I shall join you there. We shall not be separated by a thing as meagre as death." He stepped closer and looked down at her lovely face and started weeping again. Then he thrust the blade deep into his heart, as if the force of the blow might somehow cut out the pain he felt there, and he fell onto the coffin, his tears and blood running across his beloved, moving over her body and seeking out her eyes and mouth. His last conscious act was to press his lips to hers and think how wondrous the poems would be that the poets would write of this moment.

LXXXII

THE STORY OF DISDEMONA

"Do you know who I am?" the elderly woman asked Captain Casio as he woke to find her sitting by his bed.

He nodded his head. "You are Signora Montecchi," he said. "Disdemona's mother."

"Yes. Disdemona's mother," she said. The captain's once neat small black beard looked grizzled and unkempt and his eyes were blood-filled and glazed. "They say you are dying," she said.

He pointed down to his missing leg under the bedsheets. "The knife I was struck with was poisoned. They cut off my leg, and cauterized my arm, but the infection had already spread too far."

"I am sorry to hear it," she said. "You were a good friend to my daughter."

"I was charged with looking after her," he said.

"And you have been most ill used as a result," Signora Montecchi said.

He nodded his head.

"The real poison was the ensign," she said. "He was the one who stabbed you."

"He came to me afterwards and told me it was Otello who had ordered it done. Told me many evil things about him that I could scarce believe."

She lifted her shoulders and then dropped them again. "He was

335

the one who told the Moor that you and Disdemona were familiar with each other."

The captain struggled to sit up and placed his hand over his heart. "I swear it is not true."

"I know it is not true," she said, placing a hand on his shoulder and pressing him back to the bed. "The ensign has confessed to everything. He poisoned the Moor's mind, he attacked you, and he even tried to assassinate the Duca."

The captain fumed. "If I could rise from this bed I would seek him out and slay him."

"That will be done surely enough," she told him.

"And Otello?" the captain asked. "What of him?"

"The Moor," she said, unable to say his name, "was arrested after the ensign accused him of murdering Disdemona, and claiming it was an accident. He was tortured to gain a confession, but he would not utter a single word."

"He is a very brave man," the captain said.

"Perhaps," Signora Montecchi said. "But he withstood all the tortures that could be applied to him, although they broke his bones and defaced his body. He will never be a soldier again."

"I am sad to hear it," said the captain. "He was a most gallant general."

"He killed my daughter," Signora Montecchi said softly.

"But did you not say the ensign poisoned his mind?"

"It is not enough for me to forgive him."

"Then I should not talk of him any more in your company," the captain said.

She smiled. "It is you who are the gallant one, I think."

He tried to protest, but she shushed him. "There are other things you should know," she said.

"Yes?" he asked.

"They say the torture cleared the Moor's mind for he wept for the loss of Disdemona and raged and screamed her name. But only when alone in his cell. When confronted by the torturers he remained silent. As if he wanted them to kill him in trying to wring a confession from him."

The captain looked grieved to hear this.

"It was only at their exasperation with getting his confession that they brought the ensign in for questioning and his stories started conflicting. He accused you of being in cahoots with the Moor in murdering Disdemona in the same breath he accused the Moor of murdering her because she was your lover. Then they decided to put him to torture to exact the truth."

The captain nodded his head. "Yes?"

"They say he cried like a child as the first hot irons were applied to his skin and he told them everything. And while he said it was a falsehood that you had been familiar with my daughter, he said that it was true that you loved her. Is that so?"

The captain tried to hide his eyes, looking all around the room, but eventually had to return them to her. "I do not know how best to answer you," he said.

"It is all right," she said. "There are many, many futures that only play out in our heads. No harm was done by it. My daughter chose her own path in life. The one I would have chosen for her would not have pleased her at all. I knew how it would end when she first declared she was going to wed the Moor. I would have stopped it if I could, but it was always going to end this way, no matter what I did."

The captain lay there and watched the elderly lady dab at her eyes with a small kerchief.

"Why do you tell me this?" he asked softly.

"I just sometimes like to think we might have taken a different path, and she had chosen to marry a man like you, rather than the Moor," she said. Then she stood up, pressed a hand to his shoulder and left the room as quietly as she had come.

LXXXIII

THE STORY OF ISABELLA

"Clear the room of these," the doctor said, indicating the many objects Ansaldo had brought back from his foreign travels that decorated his bedchamber. "They may have foreign contaminants on them."

"Nonsense," said Isabella. "If that were true he would have long ago succumbed to them." When she had heard how sick Ansaldo had become, she sent for the family doctor at once. He was a stout middle-aged man, who had seen the best of fifty years, but still liked to dress as if he had only seen thirty of them. He grunted and turned to examine Ansaldo. "How long has he been like this?" he asked Giannetto, as if Ansaldo might be too incapable of answering for himself.

"Since the night he was kept in the cells before his court case," Giannetto said.

"Ah yes," said the doctor, "a wondrous legal battle that was. I have heard all about it. Is the young man still in the city? I would like to engage his services on a legal matter I need some advice on."

"Perhaps I could find him," said Isabella, but Giannetto cut in quickly, "He has moved on, I am sorry to say." He pressed his hand upon Isabella's buttocks and pinched her. She opened her eyes wide, but said nothing.

"A pity," said the doctor. "I heard he was quite brilliant."

"Yes," said Isabella. "Quite brilliant!"

"But our patient?" said Giannetto.

"Of course," said the doctor, turning his attention back to Ansaldo. "Now let me see." He laid his hand on Ansaldo's forehead and then pulled his eyes open wide to look at them in more detail. "Hmmm," he said, as if reading an interesting text. "It could just be the effects of his ordeal," said the doctor.

"He has pains under his arms," said Giannetto.

Ansaldo lifted up his left arm. "Under here," he said.

"Hmmm," said the doctor again. "Open his nightshirt."

Giannetto leant forward and fiddled with the strings at the neck and then opened it wide. The doctor put his hand in and prodded around.

"Lift it off him," he said. "I cannot see well enough."

Giannetto worked at the garment, Ansaldo trying to help, until Isabella came over and deftly took hold of it and drew it over his head. Ansaldo's arms were still up, as the nightshirt was not quite free of his hands, when the doctor exclaimed in surprise and jumped back from the bed. "Everybody get back from him," he said.

"What is it?" Giannetto asked.

"Plague," said the doctor.

"Nonsense," said Isabella. And she leaned in closer to look at the dark ugly welts under Ansaldo's arms. "Oh dear."

"What is it?" asked Giannetto again.

"It is the plague," she said.

Everyone in the room now took a few steps away from the bed while the doctor fussed around in his bag for his long-beaked mask.

"What will we do?" asked Giannetto. "Have we all become infected too?"

"It is too early to know," said the doctor, fitting his mask. "But I think not. This is an early sign only. I have been told it is only infectious when these welts fill with pus and burst."

"Then why do you need your mask?" Isabella asked him.

"Just a precaution," he said.

"Is there anything you can do?" Ansaldo asked.

"There is one treatment for early-stage plague that I have read of," said the doctor.

"Then do it," said Ansaldo, sitting up in the bed a little. "Act while you can."

The doctor looked at him squarely and said, "It is drastic."

"I will pay whatever is needed," said Giannetto. "I will fetch whatever herbs are needed. I am at your service to do whatever is required to cure him."

The doctor said nothing for a long time and turned his stare between Ansaldo and Giannetto. Then he exhaled slowly.

"Yes?" asked Ansaldo.

"You must cut the infected flesh from him," said the doctor flatly.

Ansaldo's head fell back onto his pillow and Giannetto pulled Isabella to him and put his head into her shoulder. And wept.

LXXXIV
ELSEWHERE IN THE FLOATING CITY

Vincenzo paused over the blank parchment in front of him and blinked his eyes, as if he had just written a story there and now found it fading away before his eyes. He had been trying to save his city, trying to avoid writing the images that kept playing through his mind. Trying not to write that he had been standing on the streets of his beloved city, his sword red with blood and the city sinking around him. Not wishing to say he could feel it rocking and moving as it slipped slowly beneath the waters.

He was trying not to write that he was then in the water. It was thick and warm and he was struggling to rise above it. Clawing back to the surface to emerge and look around at the vast empty lagoon. As if the city had never been there. Even the tallest towers had sunk beneath the waters.

He had no desire to write that he turned to the closest shore and began swimming, the waters holding him back like they were thick with seaweed. He reached the beach ahead of him slowly, and drew himself up onto it. The wide stretch of sand was as blank as a white sheet of parchment. He began walking and looked down to see his footprints like dark words there, being written across a page.

He stopped and looked ahead of him. The Shadow Master stood there. Waiting for him. And just for the briefest of moments he was struck with a spark of clarity. Knew what the marks of his footprints would say as he strode across to him. Knew what it all meant. Knew everything. Knew who had to die and why, and knew who he could save and who he could not. Knew what things would cease to exist and what would remain. And knew his own role in it all.

And he just had to write it all to make it turn out right. Place a single word on the page and then another one. And another.

He had written five pages, knitting all the pieces together and saving his city from ruin, when the voice disturbed him. "Come," he said. "We must hurry. It is time for the final act."

LXXXV

ELSEWHERE IN THE FLOATING CITY

The boats drew into the canal's edge silently, bringing a hundred forms of death.

On a map, the Floating City looked much like a large heart, and because of the canals there were so many passages where one could penetrate that heart with deadly intent. The men in the boats were Janissaries – elite Othmen warriors who were trained from young children to withstand pain, endure privation and kill ruthlessly. One hundred of them inside the Floating City would be like a whole army.

The Othmen envoy stood at the canal's edge where the boats pulled up and the Janissaries awaited her commands. Behind her stood six men wearing the white grinning masks of the mysterious assassins.

"So, the end has come," the Othmen envoy said to the figure next to her.

"I'd rather we think of it as a new beginning," the figure said.

"About that," the Othmen envoy said, without even turning to look at him. "I may have misled you somewhat in your expectations."

"You promised I would become the new Duca," the figure hissed.

"And you shall," she said. "I think we can consider the old Duca as good as dead already. Ten of these men will seek him out and kill him. They have the maps of his palazzo that you provided and will cut their way through his guards to take him in his sleep."

"Then we can consider me the new Duca already as well," he said.

"If you wish," she said. "And in that case, our promise is fulfilled." Then, at a hand signal, the Janissaries climbed from their boats and assembled in ranks in front of the Othmen envoy. She smiled at the look of them. Their dark muscled bodies glistened with oil. Their faces showed no expressions. They stood completely still, awaiting her command.

"It will be a glorious alliance," the figure said. "The merchant might of the Floating City and the military might of the Othmen. We will conquer the known world together."

"Ah," she said. "That is where I think I might have misled you."

"What do you mean?" the figure asked.

"It is not our intention to form an alliance with the Floating City. It is our intention to sink it." As she said this her hand flashed out with a short curved blade that drove deep into the figure's chest, cracking ribs and puncturing his heart. She pulled the blade back, and he sank to his knees. He gurgled something incomprehensible and fell to the stones, his mask coming loose.

"No," he said, his words bleeding out in gasps. "No. This is not how I have dreamed it." She looked down at his face, watching the disbelief mix with the fading dreams of grandeur as he sank into the arms of death. The madness finally going out of him.

"It was a drug-addled dream," she said. "A dream that dooms you to be the shortest-reigning Duca of the Floating City." She wiped the bloodied knife on her tunic. "You should have stayed a friar, and not dreamed of a world where you could govern the destinies and beliefs of all men."

She kicked Friar Lorenzo da San Francesco's corpse and turned to the other men behind him, who included the friar's acolytes, Signors de Abbacio and Hermino, hiding behind their absurdly grinning masks. He had come to them in secret, and had dangled promises of power to turn them, making them addicted to its madness in turn. And now all their desperate dreams were bleeding away across the cold stone at their feet.

They started taking steps away from her. Away from the friar. Away from the blood. Until she called, "Stop. Nobody move." They stopped.

She looked at them carefully and then said, "Show yourself!"

None of them moved. "Is this how you killed my brother?" she asked. "Sneaking up behind him in disguise like a coward." Still, none of the figures moved.

"I know you are there," she said. "There were five of you behind your master a moment ago, and now there are six." Still nobody moved. "Archers!" she called and the front row of Janissaries raised small strong bows, each with an arrow ready and pointed at the six masked men. "Kill them all!" she said and almost as fast as thought the men fell under a torrent of arrows. Except for one. He had pulled a short sword from beneath his cloak as the archers fired and had cut the two arrows out of the air that were intended for him.

"There you are," she said, unsheathing two swords slowly, letting the sound of metal withdrawing from sheath whisper menacingly into the night around her.

The figure reached up and pulled off his mask. "Your brother?" he said. "I never saw the family resemblance. But I guess that makes me the Djinn-slayer now."

Her features moved from beautiful to hideous in anger, and she pointed one of her swords at him. "Is this a sword I see before me?" he asked.

"I will gut you and make you eat your intestines."

"Only if you say please," he said.

"Mine will be the last face you see before you die," she spat at him. "You know I am faster than you."

"Ah," he said. "I may have misled you somewhat in that."

She spat at him and then her body started growing, her arms stretching and long talons emerging from her fingers and her legs turning to a long smoky tail.

"Uh-oh," said the Shadow Master. "I didn't see that one coming."

LXXXVI

THE STORY OF GIULIETTA

Romeo felt Giulietta stirring beneath him as the life flowed out of him. He felt lights and fire dancing about them. Felt the earth beneath his feet moving like it was alive. Felt the air around him grow warmer. He saw his tears were winding their way through Giulietta's body, intermingled with his blood, chasing out the too-large dose of poison that she had taken. Felt his body slip to the floor as if now lifeless. And still he saw.

He saw Giulietta's eyes open and stare about her, amazed at the dancing lights, like a host of fireflies but larger and each that touched her filled her with warmth. She shook her head a little as if it was clouded by a dream and then put her hand to her lips, as if she had felt something there and wanted to know what it was. She took her hand away and looked at it. There was blood on it. And yet she felt no pain.

She looked about as if she was waking up in heaven and only slowly did she realize where she was – in the tomb. She should be waking up to her betrothed's embrace. But where was he? The friar had promised he would be here. She sat up and looked about. Saw her sister's dead body on the far side of the crypt and put her hand to her mouth again. How could that be? She climbed out of the coffin to go to her, but then saw Romeo collapsed on the floor beneath her coffin.

She put her hands to her head and tried to scream. Wanted to shut her eyes and block out this dream that had become a nightmare. Wanted to go back to sleep and awaken in her own bed with her mother comforting her. She opened her eyes and nothing had changed. The lights still danced about her head and she knelt down beside her beloved. Taking his head in her hands. She tilted it up and saw the eyes were vacant.

But he could see her. He tried to talk to her. Tried to lift his arms and put them around her. Tried to stand. Tried to say her name.

"Romeo," she gasped. "Romeo." Then she saw the dagger still thrust into his chest. Saw it and knew everything that had happened. She wept with a fierce resolve and said, "I am coming to join you." She pulled the dagger out, spilling blood across her white dress and then placed the point over her heart.

She leant down to kiss him and felt his hand encircle the dagger's handle alongside hers. Giving her the strength she needed to push it firmly. It pierced her body and drove deep into her heart. She gasped and fell onto her beloved, wrapping her arms around him as she lay dying. And she too saw the brightness drifting out of their bodies. Saw it entwining and circling about the chamber, saw it fill the whole tomb with the brightest and purest of white lights. Felt it spread out into the night and seep into the ground at her feet. Felt it shoot up high into the night like a comet. Felt it spread out over the island and flow into the canal, filling the water with a glow like phosphorescence. Saw how powerful their love was.

Together they saw the Djinn in the canals thrash about in their death throes, like eels being boiled alive in water. Saw the plague people look at their hands in amazement as a light spread across their bodies, reducing their welts. Felt the earth deep beneath the Floating City rise up from the bed of the lagoon to form solid columns under each of the islands of the city, holding them there in place. Saw the last of the female Seers spit blood as if a sword had been thrust through her guts, and topple forward dead, followed by her husband. And finally she saw Disdemona sit up in her coffin, gasping for breath like she had just emerged from the ocean's depths, out-swimming death.

Then Romeo and Giulietta saw the lights fading. And then they saw nothing. Together.

LXXXVII

ELSEWHERE IN THE FLOATING CITY

The Othmen envoy rose up above the Shadow Master, her hair billowing out like one hundred serpents and then she sank suddenly to the ground. She stumbled as her billowing torso started transforming back into that of a human. She looked confused.

"What is happening?" she demanded.

"Oh dear," said the Shadow Master. "There goes all the enchantment." He pointed with his sword. "What light through yon darkness breaks? Why that is the last of it. And that sound in the water, that's your cousins dying."

She held a hand to her chest as if there was pain in the transformation.

"Sorry," he said. "I know this could have come at a better time for you."

She glared at him with naked hatred and said, "I will still kill you."

"You and what army?" he asked. "Oh, silly question."

She leapt at him with her sword drawn and he stepped back and blocked her with his two swords. The Janissaries unsheathed their own weapons and moved forward, surrounding him. "Did I mention my reinforcements?" he said as he stepped back again and again, as her blade flashed at him, sparks leaping where their swords struck.

"The city does not have enough men to defeat one hundred Janissaries," she cried. "And you cannot defeat us on your own."

Instead of replying, he spun around quickly, as if warding off the men surrounding him, and a dagger flew out from his cloak as he moved, striking her in the shoulder. She dropped her sword and gasped in surprise. He stood up and said, "That's why I brought a friend." All she said in response was, "Kill him!"

The Shadow Master spun again to knock more arrows out of the air that were fired at him and then turned to chop the point off a spear that was thrust at him. He leapt in the air as another slashed at his feet and evaded a set of bolos aimed at his neck. "Now is a good time to help," he called. And one of the masked figures lying on the ground stood up shakily. He seemingly plucked the three arrows out of his body, the tips blunted by his body armour, and took off his mask. It was Vincenzo the scribe.

"Now you're in trouble," said the Shadow Master. The Othmen envoy ignored him and pulled a whip out of her belt. She cast it at him and he raised a sword to cut it, realizing as he did so that it was the wrong thing to do. The whip was woven through with strong metal threads and it wrapped around his sword tightly. He looked at the smile on her face as she looked beautiful again, smiling graciously to him. It was another weapon he seemed not prepared for. The instant distraction cost him his advantage as several other whips snapped out, catching his other sword and both arms.

"Now, this time you will die," she said, almost sounding sweet.

"Now is a good time to remember the feel of a sword in your hands," said the Shadow Master to Vincenzo. And the scribe drew his sword. He twirled it in the air once. Then again. Much faster. Then he looked up at the closest Janissaries and smiled. No longer Vincenzo the scribe. His battle memory returning. He knew how this was going to play out, as if he had written the scene in great detail already. Two Othmen warriors rushed at him, scimitars drawn. He dodged the first and cut down the second, then turned and cut the forearm clean off the first man at the wrist.

"Cue fanfare," called the Shadow Master as Vincenzo leapt at the next three men advancing on him. He ducked the first sword, came up on the attacker and hit him hard in the chin with his shoulder. He then snatched the sword from his attacker's hand and pushed the man's body at the two Janissaries who were slashing at him. As they tried to evade the body Vincenzo leapt high, jumping off the falling man's body and coming down on top of the two men. He cut one at the neck and pierced the other in the face. The three bodies fell together.

The Othmen envoy watched in disbelief as Vincenzo cut a path through her warriors towards her and she unclipped a small bronze device from her belt and cast it at his feet. He did not even see it spin like a top, and then it exploded, sending out a thick yellow gas. Vincenzo and the Janissaries who were enveloped by it all fell to the ground the instant they breathed just a trace of it, and started shaking uncontrollably.

"And now you," the Othmen envoy said, reaching for another brass device at her belt. The Shadow Master, held now by several whips and surrounded by sharp spear points, did not know what the Othmen device did, and had no particular interest in finding out. He said, "All right, play time is over." Then with a seeming ease he pulled his arms free, his twin blades cutting through the whips and knocking away the spears. He moved so fast the Othmen envoy thought she must be suddenly drugged. He cut his way through the whole Janissary force like a reaper cutting his way through a wheat field. Men fell to the left and right of her as he whirled and slashed and leapt like nothing she had ever imagined possible.

"No!" she screamed, and screamed until they were the only two left standing and he stood with his bloodied sword blades both crossed at her neck. One hundred Othmen warriors dead at his feet, and he just smiled at her as if it had all been a game to him. "Who are you?" she hissed.

"Always, who are you?" he said. "Never, how did you do that?"

She fumbled for the device in her hand, but then it fell to the ground harmlessly as her head was cut from her neck. Her headless body stood defiantly for some moments before falling, like a marionette with the strings slashed.

LXXXVIII

THE STORY OF THE SHADOW MASTER

"I can't believe you let me die!" Disdemona said, punching the Shadow Master hard on the shoulder. "You're such a bastard."

"It all worked out well in the end," the Shadow Master said. Vincenzo stood with one arm protectively around Disdemona. The three of them were in a small shaded courtyard, with Signora Montecchi. A reunion of sorts.

"He promised me that if I wrote things anew then they would turn out like that," said Vincenzo. "And I believed him. I really thought I was changing things – not that it was him doing it."

"I still don't understand how he left you here as children, and then returns to claim you as adults, and then is somehow going to do it all over again," she said. "It is against any laws of nature imaginable."

"You get used to it," Vincenzo said.

Disdemona gave him a look, and then said, "Well, no. You never really get used to it."

"How many times has he done this to you?" Signora Montecchi asked.

But the Shadow Master cut in. "You looked after her well," he said. "You certainly taught her to speak her own mind."

"As was my promise," she said to him. "To let them choose their own futures because that was how it must be."

She looked back to the young couple and then said, "I imagine these are not even your real names, are they?"

"What is in a name?" asked the Shadow Master.

"Everything and nothing," she said. "But surely you have used them enough. Stolen their memories and made them pawns in your game until you were ready to claim them again. Surely they have now paid enough for whatever penance they have due to you?"

"We all have our penance to pay," said the Shadow Master, and looked up at the distant sky.

Signora Montecchi watched him for some moments and then said, "Tell me once more about the possible future that exist around us."

The Shadow Master looked back at her and said, "You need to believe that all possible futures can exist somewhere, and if you had the power to change the course of your world to that of a new possibility, you can effectively shape your destiny. Control your future."

She nodded her head slowly as if almost grasping what he was telling her, before feeling it slip away. She shook her head. "I can only see how life has played out behind me, not before me. I will grieve for Giulietta though. She was a spoiled brat at times, but I was immensely fond of her."

"She saved the city," the Shadow Master said.

Her mother nodded. "At least I will still have one daughter when you're all gone."

"Yes," he said. "And grandchildren too before long."

She smiled. "That would be nice." She turned to Vincenzo and Disdemona. "Do you two ever plan to settle down and have children?"

They looked at each other and grinned awkwardly. "I don't know, do we?" Disdemona asked the Shadow Master.

"There are many futures that are not yet written," he said. "But also many places to go and many futures to rewrite." Disdemona and Vincenzo looked at each other and sighed.

"He is going to do it to you again, isn't he?" Signora Montecchi said. "Take you to a new place and leave you there as children again, through his enchantment or whatever it is. And you won't even remember each other until it is all ended, and then you'll have such small time together before he takes you away from each other once more."

"The bond of their love draws them together and enables greater changes to be made," the Shadow Master said. "They are my power."

"No," said Signora Montecchi. "I don't think you ever reveal your power to anyone. Nor who you really are. That will always be kept from us, won't it?"

He bowed low to her, as if she had just succeeded in cornering him in a game of chess, and he was acknowledging the move. But he did not say if she was right or wrong.

"This time I won't forget you," said Vincenzo to Disdemona.

"No more than you will forget yourself," said the Shadow Master.

"I hate working for you," said Disdemona.

"I never promised you that you wouldn't," the Shadow Master said.

They all looked at each other until Signora Montecchi asked, "So what happens next?"

"Well, if I was writing the story, your husband would become Duca and bring a new era of prosperity to the city. Your golden age would be before you, not behind you. And he would be handed the great secret of the Floating City and would choose to destroy it."

"And that secret is?" she asked.

"If I told you it wouldn't be a secret," he said.

"I will just ask my husband then," she said determinedly.

"Well, I don't suppose it really matters anymore," he said. "The great secret of the Floating City was that the Seers were the ones causing the Djinn in the canals and the bringing of plague and turmoil. They believed they were saving the city, of course, but they were inadvertently creating these things out of the people's fear."

Signora Montecchi looked at him in disbelief. "We were creating the monsters?" she asked.

"Through your fear," he said.

"A fear that the monsters and plagues and so on increased," said Vincenzo.

"Exactly," said the Shadow Master. "There is always a cost for the use of enchantment, and sometimes it can ultimately be such a great cost that it destroys those who wield it. But there are no more Seers now. No more enchantment."

"Giulietta would have been the greatest of them, wouldn't she?" said her mother.

"Yes," he said. "And the most dangerous to the city."

"So," said Vincenzo, "I was thinking we should stay on a few more days, just to make sure that everything is all right." He squeezed Disdemona's shoulder and she bent her head back and kissed him.

"Light of my life," she said.

"Light of my heart," he replied.

"I didn't say everything would be all right," said the Shadow Master. "There is still going to be hardship and wars and diseases to battle. But the people of the city will rise to the occasion. Mostly."

"Let them stay a few days," said Signora Montecchi. "This city is for lovers. They deserve some time together after the way you treat them."

"Well," he said. "Normally I'd think it an indulgence. But Vincenzo does still have some work to do here."

"I do?" he asked.

"Yes. You have to finish writing up the stories of the Montecchi sisters, and then leave them around for somebody to find and use in their own work."

Vincenzo laughed. "I think it will take me at least a fortnight," he said, and kissed Disdemona again.

The Shadow Master stood. "You can have a week." Then he bowed and was gone.

Signora Montecchi watched him go and then leaned close to Vincenzo and Disdemona and said in a soft voice, "We tend to like our stories very short here, it leaves more time for – well, other things."

A NOTE ON SOURCES

The three main storylines in the Floating City are taken from the Italian "origin stories" that Shakespeare adapted into the plays *Othello, The Merchant of Venice* and *Romeo and Juliet*, using the original names and spellings and major plot devices.

From Giraldi Cinthio's *Hecatommithi*, published in 1565 (1855 translation by JE Taylor):

> *There once lived in Venice a Moor, who was very valiant and of a handsome person; and having given proofs in war of great skill and prudence, he was highly esteemed by the Signoria of the Republic, who in rewarding deeds of valor advanced the interests of the state...*
>
> *It happened that a virtuous lady of marvelous beauty, named Disdemona, fell in love with the Moor, moved thereto by his valor; and he, vanquished by the beauty and the noble character of Disdemona, returned her love; and their affection was so mutual that, although the parents of the lady strove all they could to induce her to take another husband, she consented to marry the Moor; and they lived in such harmony and peace in Venice that no word ever passed between them that was not affectionate and kind...*

From Luigi da Porto's *Giulietta e Romeo*, 1530:

> *At the time of Bartolommeo della Scala, according to the narrative,*
> *two noble but hostile families resided in Verona – the Cappelletti*
> *and the Montecchi. Wearied with fighting and somewhat intimated*
> *by the threats of the rulers of the city, the quarrelsome factions*
> *had lately observed a kind of truce. One night Romeo Montecchi,*
> *disguised as a nymph, followed his indifferent lady to a masquerade*
> *ball given by Messer Antonio Cappelletti. When the desperate youth*
> *was finally obliged to unmask, all the guests were astonished not*
> *only at his beauty, which surpassed that of any of the ladies present,*
> *but also at his audacious entrance into his enemies' house. As soon*
> *as Giulietta, the only and supernaturally beautiful daughter of*
> *Antonio Cappelletti, caught sight of Romeo, she realised she no*
> *longer belonged to herself...*

From Ser Giovanni's *Il Pecorone* (the Dunce), written in the 14th
Century and printed in 1558:

> *There lived in Florence a merchant, called Bindo, of the Scali*
> *family, who had visited Tana and Alexandria several times and*
> *had been on all the long voyages which are made on business. This*
> *Bindo was very rich and had three fine, manly sons, and when he*
> *came close to death, he called the two eldest and made his will in*
> *their presence, bequeathing all he had in the world to these two*
> *heirs, and to the youngest he bequeathed nothing. When this will*
> *had been made, the youngest son, called Giannetto, heard of it*
> *and went to the bedside and said to him, "Father, I am amazed*
> *at what you have done — not mentioning me in the will." The*
> *father replied, "Giannetto, there is no creature living to whom I*
> *wish better fortune than to you, and therefore I do not wish you*
> *to stay here after my death, but I want you to go to Venice to your*
> *godfather, Ansaldo, who has no child and has often written asking*

me to send you to him. Moreover, I may say that he is now the richest of the Christian merchants. Therefore, I want you to go, as soon as I am dead, and to take this letter to him – then, if you know how to behave, you will become a rich man..."

...It happened early one morning that Giannetto saw a bay with a fine harbor and asked the captain what it was called; he replied, "Sir, that place belongs to a widowed lady who has ruined many gentlemen." "In what way?" said Giannetto. "Sir," he replied, "She is a fine and beautiful lady, and she has made a law: whoever arrives here must sleep with her, and if he can enjoy her, he must take her for wife and be lord of the seaport and all the surrounding country. But if he cannot enjoy her, he loses everything he has." Giannetto thought for a moment, and said; "Do everything you can and make for that harbor..."

...When Ansaldo saw that he was resolved, he began to sell all that he had in the world and to equip another ship for him: and so he did, he sold all he had and provided a fine ship with merchandise: and, because he lacked ten thousand ducats, he went to a Jew of Mestri and borrowed them on condition that if they were not repaid the next June on St John's day, the Jew might take a pound of flesh from whatever part of his body he pleased...

ABOUT THE AUTHOR

Craig Cormick is an award-winning author and science communicator who works for Australia's premier science institution, the Commonwealth Science and Industrial Research Organisation (CSIRO). He is a regular speaker at science communication conferences and has appeared on television, radio, online and in print media.

As an author he has published over a dozen works of fiction and non-fiction and over 100 short stories. His awards include an ACT Book of the Year Award and a Queensland Premier's Literary Award.

craigcormick.com • *twitter.com/CraigCormick*

Meet Elizabeth Barnabus, resourceful investigator operating in a very different England...

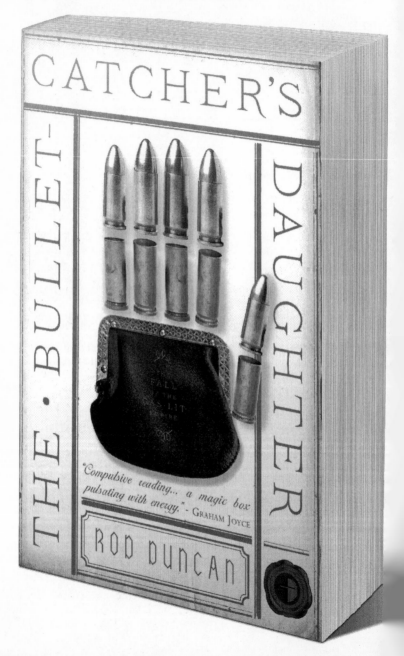

CATCHER'S

THE · BULLET-

DAUGHTER

"*Compulsive reading... a magic box pulsating with energy.*" - GRAHAM JOYCE

ROD DUNCAN

UNSEEMLY

· SCIENCE ·

"A MAGIC BOX PULSATING WITH ENERGY... COMPULSIVE READING FROM THE GET-GO."—GRAHAM JOYCE

ROD DUNCAN

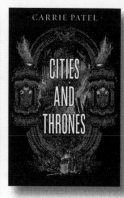

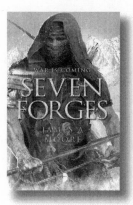

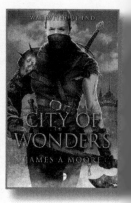

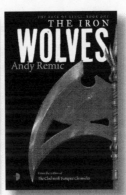

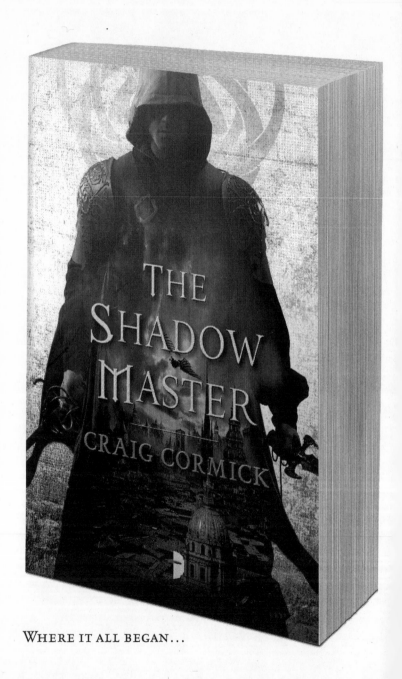

THE
SHADOW
MASTER

CRAIG CORMICK

WHERE IT ALL BEGAN...